MW00891688

Seeds of Blood

C. Chancy

This book is a work of fiction. Names, characters, place, and incidents are either products of the author's imagination or used fictitiously. Any resemblance to actual events, locales, or persons, living or dead, are entirely coincidental.

Copyright © 2017 by Christel R. Chancy

All rights reserved, including the right to reproduce this book or portions thereof in any form whatsoever.

Cover Art by Mirella Santana
www.mirellasantana.com.br
Stocks and Materials used: Depositphotos & Shutterstock.

Manufactured in the United States of America
ISBN-13: 978-1975897215
ISBN-10: 1975897218
Library of Congress Control Number: 2017913792
CreateSpace Independent Publishing Platform, North Charleston, SC

Chapter One

Monday, October 20th

"Under the right circumstances, you can kill a werewolf with a pointy stick."

Seated off to the side of the crowded briefing room to help with visual aids, Detective J. Church felt hairs on her neck shiver in a sudden breeze; the mass intake of breath from her fellow cops. She felt like sucking all the oxygen out of the room herself. If you could do that, if werewolves weren't as invulnerable as Hollywood and everyone on the dark side of the supernatural arrogantly sniffed....

Then it didn't matter if beige paint was peeling off the door-frame, some of the blue uniforms were dirt and other-stained, or the bitter scent of over-boiled coffee hung in the air. This was the prettiest room Church had ever seen.

Myrrh's going to change our world. Church smirked, just a little. *Again.*

The ancient hell-raider stood straight and tiny at the front of the room, white hair wisping out from under her shadow-shift's hood around a sober young face, chalk dusting her hands almost as white. Most of Intrepid's cops had looked askance at the wheeled green blackboard in front of the room, one of the younger patrol officers muttering about how could you learn anything from someone so out of touch they couldn't even use a laptop?

That pretty much died out as Myrrh put a few clattering strokes up. Didn't matter if she could barely reach the top of the board. The fact that the hell-raider could freehand sketch a wolf skull right in front of them, front and side views - well, Church didn't have to pretend to be amazed.

The old-fashioned Chalk and Talk. Church put one more careful stroke into her notes. *So is she doing that so we wake up and focus on Old Doesn't Mean Useless, or because this is the kind of thing Aidan can wrap his head around?*

The half-demon fire mage was one desk away, taking his own notes soberly as grizzled Detective Heath two rows from the front. Fiery red hair cast back the overhead lights as he frowned in concentration; amber eyes flicking from notebook to chalkboard and back as if he were comparing Myrrh's sketch to memories of bullet-shattered bone.

Church grimaced, determined not to throw up no matter how her stomach lurched. Technically some people would say she shouldn't be here. But it beat sitting in her apartment staring at water-warded walls on paid administrative leave while Detectives Mitchell and Roger helped the State Bureau of Investigation investigate the werewolf carnage she and the two Hunters had left around one very dead murder victim two nights ago. Besides, Captain Sherman wanted somebody keeping an eye on their two time-displaced magical crazies, and so far Aidan and Myrrh hadn't really tried to give her the slip.

Don't think about the investigation, Church told herself firmly. *Raphael testified that there was cannibalism going on, and the pack attacked us. Self-defense is legit. Poor kid.*

Poor *werewolf* kid. The fact that right now they were looking at Myrrh tap where on the skull to hit for the quickest kill made the detective both relieved and very, very nervous.

Don't think about what gunpowder and brains smell like. Nothing burnt, nothing bloody, nothing dying, Church told herself grimly. *Just bitter coffee too many hours old, dry chalk in the back of your throat, a bit of overripe banana bread somewhere in the crowd....*

Myrrh Shafat tapped the chalkboard again, a bit above and inside from the top of the spinal cord. "Lycanthropy is a mystical curse, but it must act through the physical medium of the body.

The part of the brain that controls regeneration is here. Destroy that, with whatever method you can, and the werewolf will be dying, or dead." She turned, gray eyes sweeping her startled audience. "You will note that my focus is often on lethal techniques. There are several reasons for that. First and foremost, as officers of the law well know, it is far more difficult to *restrain* a prisoner, unharmed, than to kill him. And that is when you are dealing with ordinary mortal strength. A supernatural creature, like any violent criminal on mind-altering drugs such as PCP, may not stop short of lethal force."

Oh man, do I know that already. Church shuddered, remembering a swarm of slavering wolflike bodies, a drowning pool of evil water. Not to mention the twisted bearlike *thing* she and her partner Tom Franklin had almost been sacrificed to.

Looks like ex-partner, now. Her next swipe of a pen almost tore through the paper. Church still didn't know how long Tom had been making *deals* with Steven Savonarola, but she planned to find out. Soon.

Steven should be dead.

Yeah, well, *Christophe* Savonarola had been dead, body and all. For almost twenty-five years. She'd read his damn coroner's report

Only that hadn't stopped Christophe's soul from pulling the great hellish escape with Myrrh, and now the newly-renamed Aidan Lindisfarne was taking notes on killing werewolves and trying not to set things on fire when he got stressed. Which was a lot, given he kept expecting the walls to start bleeding. Just, you know, because that was a *thing* in Hell, along with chains, humiliation, and a bunch of stuff he clammed up tighter than Fort Knox rather than talk about.

A warm breeze tickled her cheek. Church tasted the passing vapor, and sighed in relief. False alarm. Just coffee steam, not smoke.

"Second," Myrrh's hands gestured across the board, "part of

your authority as officers of the law comes from the fact that you are lawfully allowed to use lethal force not only to protect your-selves or others, but also to stop a crime in progress. Supernatural creatures have tried to place themselves above mortal law by restricting access to their more common banes, such as silver bullets, while at the same time exaggerating their strengths. They would have you believe Hollywood's portrayal of their abilities is true; that only a chosen few can fight them, and that no one should." Gray eyes raked her uniformed audience. "This is a lie. It is an *evil* lie. Any human can kill a monster." A small, wry smile. "The trick is to survive to kill it. And with luck, to survive untainted by their curses yourself."

"Vampires can bench press trucks!" someone called from the back.

Myrrh raised an unimpressed brow. "Why, so can I; and so can any mere mortal, if the truck has been properly lightened and enspelled first. The number of vampires whose demon has existed on the mortal plane long enough to develop that level of physical strength is, and has always been, very small. The average vampire is stronger than a human, yes. But if they are less than two decades old, that strength is closer to three times a mortal human's. Which means it is not unlike dealing with an evil chimpanzee."

Church tried to cough rather than laugh. The image of a long-fanged, red-eyed, bloodsucking chimp....

Was still pretty damn scary, honestly. But a survivable scary.

That's what she's trying to teach us. Whoof.

"Third." Myrrh took a long breath, patient as waves eating the shore. "I am, as many would call it, a Hunter. Specifically, I am a hell-raider." She met each startled gaze, one by one. "I am not a cop. I am not *law enforcement*. I am called when there is danger - immediate, life-threatening danger - to those mortals less fortunate, and less lethal, than myself. When there is an innocent chained to a blood-smeared altar, or a child with fangs at her throat - I do not stop. I do not hesitate. I do not *negotiate*." That wry smile ghosted across her face once more. "If you have seen the entirety of the Nightsong video, you have seen Nuria Cruz' reaction to learning one such as I yet lives. I assure you, that was not rehearsed."

And that was another ow, as far as Church was concerned. Coral had posted that vid online, sneaky, snarky gorgon that she was; gaining record numbers of views before someone had complained to the site's censors to shut it down. *Hate speech* and *fomenting violence against minorities* were two of the complaints Church knew of. Never mind that Myrrh had been attacked first, and she and Aidan had only defended themselves.

Very effectively defended themselves. Against vampires. Church smiled sourly. *Which is why those fanged bastards want it down.*

Good luck with that. Xanthippe Coral had made plenty of accounts on different websites just to play whack-a-mole with would-be PC censor types, and other people had copied the original to post it themselves. Myrrh's blazing sword was all over the internet; a fiery ancient genie out of a bottle.

Or twenty-one years of bottled-up rage all cutting loose, Church thought grimly. *There's a lot of angry people out there.*

On the one hand, Church couldn't blame them one bit. She'd seen up close and personal what the darker side of the supernatural could do. On the other... Xanthippe Coral was an awesome movie buddy, and Raphael had fought down werewolf instincts and common sense to help save her life. Not to mention Myrrh and Aidan were as supernatural as any vampire... or demon.

Hate and death help build a Demongate. And we've got one set and ready to go off right in downtown.

They'd done a quick and shaky patch job on whatever kept all Hell from breaking loose. But Myrrh hadn't marked out all the foundation spots on this side of reality yet, and there was only so much one person praying could do to crack the ritual deaths of who knew how many people. Father Gray O'Malley and Father Ricci were organizing prayer groups, and Detective Eagleman had apparently seen enough when Steven's demons possessed the captain to ask Old Man Conseen to scatter corn pollen and who-knew-what over various crime sites. It ought to make Church feel like they had things under control, and yet....

Less than two weeks to Halloween. I've got a bad feeling about this.

"But back to werewolves, and more specifically their banes." Myrrh picked up chalk again. "If you do wish to take a werewolf alive, then first and foremost, you must know how to avoid infection. Many methods have been tried over the millennia; I will tell you one I *know* works, most of the time."

Church stared at the quick sketch of a shot glass, with a brief list of drink proportions. "...You're kidding."

"Two-thirds Jägermeister, one-third Goldschläger - it is effect-ively a Starry Night with blessed salt dusting," Myrrh shrugged. "Some like to add a twist of lime, but it is not necessary."

Not going to facepalm, Church thought, stunned. *Just not.*

"It works on the same principle as a gin and tonic for malaria," Myrrh addressed dropped jaws across the room. "Jägermeister has well over fifty herbal components that promote healing and health in the hunt; Goldschläger has gold, which serves as a sacrifice and medium to carry the celestial power drawn by the blessed salt. Taken once a week - every phase of the moon - it drops your risk of infection from a bite from fifty-fifty to closer to one in ten."

"Wait," one of the younger patrolmen waved a hand. "You can get bitten and not turn?"

"It does happen, yes," Myrrh nodded. "I suppose you've been lied to about that, as well." She turned back to the board, sketching an odd cone. "The second part of a Hunter's precautions against infection is far less pleasant."

Uh-oh.

"This is St. Hubert's Key." Myrrh tapped the board. "Blessed is better, but... essentially, you heat the iron of it red-hot, and cauterize the bite."

Church swallowed, all too able to imagine the scent of seared flesh.

"Applied within two hours, it also cuts the risk of infection near in half. Together, the Hunter's tonic and St. Hubert's Key slash the odds from one in two, to near one in a hundred," Myrrh said plainly. "The Key also reduces the risk of rabies, so it was often used when man or hound were bitten by what seemed a wolf, whether magic was suspected or not. Over the centuries it has saved many lives."

Heath straightened in his chair, pen tapping paper. "If these things work... how come Father O'Malley never said anything?"

Pain crinkled the corners of gray eyes. "That, you will have to ask him. I can only tell you what I know from *my* dealings with the Church. Which considers me a heretic."

Church tensed. O'Malley'd kept a lot of cops in one piece. This wasn't going to be good.

"As a priest, Father O'Malley must answer to his ecclesiastical superiors," Myrrh said, very precisely. "I will spare you a lecture on liberation theology; you should look it up for yourselves. But it has been a grave problem for the Church's interactions with Hunters, these past several decades. Yes, werewolves are ill with sin; as is every mortal life in the world. And in part, because of that illness, the human soul should not be held accountable for all of the demon wolf's actions. But werewolves are also carriers of a demonic contagion, and our Christian duty to minister to the sick does *not* demand that we set aside all measures to protect ourselves." She paused. "There are apparently those in the Church who believe otherwise. I will note only that they tend to live within the Diocese of Rome itself, or similarly well-guarded environs, and so rarely risk meeting fangs in an alley."

O'Malley has to answer to Rome. Church gripped her pen tight, shaken. *And the higher-ups-*

Obviously had their heads where they couldn't see the light of day. Why was she even surprised?

"I do think, if you were to ask him to bless salt and iron, he would be glad to provide," Myrrh said quietly. "He is a good man. But he is bound by his oaths. As are we all, or who would trust us in defense of the law, and the innocent?"

Church breathed out, relieved. The tension in the room had gone down. Because O'Malley *was* one of the good guys.

But he's been holding out on us. Like he did with me and Savonarola. Going to have to remember that.

"Once you have taken what measures you can against infection...." Myrrh eyed the board. "Forget Hollywood. *Any* weapon can hurt a werewolf. One that is well-fed and under the full moon will simply regenerate from most ordinary weapons... until you hit them with enough damage to overwhelm the curse." A wry smile. "A few ounces of C-4 will, generally, suffice."

Church tried not to bury her face in her hands. *Ooooh boy.*

"Silver is the most effective metal against many creatures, because it easily conducts celestial energy." Myrrh pointed to the four-by-two grid she'd sketched on the board. *Celestial, terrestrial, infernal* and *fay* labeled the columns across, *blocked by* and *enhanced by* labeling two rows under each. "As lycanthropy is usually a curse born of demonic origin, that energy is diametrically opposed to the werewolf's cursed attributes." Her finger shifted down and left, where iron blocked fay and infernal. "I know this seems counterintuitive. Iron is a stable stellar creation, eternally opposed to the infernal, which makes meteoric iron the best weapon known against demonkind. Based merely on that, one might think werewolves should be as vulnerable to steel as silver. Unfortunately, while lycanthropy is a demonic curse, it is mediated through a human body. The iron in mortal blood is sufficient to block any external effects of steel. If you do encounter a shape-shifting wolf that is harmed by iron instead of silver, you have a problem. It is most likely either a fay creature, a spellcaster, or a true demonic. All of which require different countermeasures *if* you plan to take them alive. Yes?"

The young cop she'd called on looked like he wanted to be anywhere else. "...Demons aren't real."

"If the Demongate opens you will have very visible proof otherwise," Myrrh shrugged. "Otherwise, I refer you to Father O'Malley, the Bible, the Torah, the Mahabharata, and quite a few other religious and secular texts. I have provided a list."

A hearty snort from the right edge of the room. "You didn't say the Koran."

Church stifled a sigh. That'd be Officer Glover, who had a chip on his shoulder at the best of times-

"I did not." Shadows fell across gray eyes. "Any faith who names its deity the *Father of Lies* will by definition have great difficulty in dealing with demonic influence. Islamic folklore has some helpful information on dealing with djinn and ifrits. The texts, however, are... less than benign."

Church's shoulders stiffened at the sudden ice in Myrrh's tone, the aghast silence from her fellow officers making her wish she could sink through the floor. *And this would be why Father's glad there's no mosque in Intrepid.*

What Myrrh would do if there were, Church wasn't sure she wanted to find out. She'd only had an hour or so yesterday to poke the internet about whatever grudge Myrrh had from Alexandria, but the quick look was more than enough to make her queasy.

Myrrh was a Christian in Egypt; an Egypt that was Christian for four hundred years. *Then Mohammed's followers came through like Attila the Hun. Murder, looting, raping, slavery....*

Church didn't know how much of that Myrrh had seen first-hand. She was kind of afraid to ask. Given that Myrrh could actually die and *come back-*

Yeah. Definitely afraid to ask.

"But as we are on the subject of banes, I am glad you brought that up," Myrrh smiled.

...That is not a nice smile.

"There are four banes most commonly used in lands under

Mohammedan control," the hell-raider went on. "Decapitation, defenestration, stoning to death, and fire. Most particularly fire. Naphtha and its various relations are well-spread through those deserts, and with fireproof weavings from Afghanistan available through trade, fire has been part of Muslim tactics since that faith began." Gray eyes looked into memory. "One of the most common ways to clear a nest of heretics - werewolves, vampires, Magians, or Christians - was to call upon the *naffatun*. Those warriors were provided with gear woven of *hajar al-fatila*, what we call asbestos; then doused in naphtha, and set afire to fight."

A chill shivered through Church's shoulders, crawling up her spine. That was... Myrrh didn't even look upset. Just coldly, rationally angry. Like the graying mother of a cold-case murder victim Church had talked to once, when the bastard had finally been caught twenty years later.

That's someone who would carve a perp's heart out with a spoon, if it would do any good. She just knows it won't. Yet.

"It is, of course, effective," Myrrh went on, calm as a crackling fire. "And given that faith holds that those who slay and are slain in destroying Allah's enemies are transported straight to heaven, there is no reason *not* to burn an entire village down to slay one vampire. After all, the victims will be sent to their reward, and the *ummah* preserved. One life means nothing, in the eyes of Islam; the idea that the individual soul has value, and should be saved... is a weakness of their enemies, and one Muslims are enjoined to exploit whenever they may." She shrugged. "I prefer not to work with Muslim Hunters. They leave a horrible mess."

Church found her mouth open, and shut it before her tongue dried out. If there'd been one hint of snarl in Myrrh's tone, one trace of disgust, the barest hint that this was personal rather than professional....

Facts. Just facts. At least for her. Oh man, I have to look this stuff up, if she's really right....

Well. If Myrrh was, it wasn't just the demons that Church was scared of.

"Though to be honest, I avoid Hunters in those lands unless there is dire need," Myrrh stated. "They have a problem respecting vows of chastity. And it is disheartening to the spirit to kill a man you worked beside to slay monsters, simply because you are an infidel woman and thus considered rightfully his prostitute and his slave. If he can catch you."

There was a kind of buzzing in Church's ears. She had to lean her chin on her hand, the end of her pen cap digging into skin, and just breathe. Each word was crisp and clear; settling into place with all the implacable force of Judge Hang 'Em High MacRory handing down a verdict. Just like in the church kitchen, when Myrrh had calmly and matter-of-factly explained that the world didn't *work* the way Church had always thought it had to.

Glover straightened in his chair, smiling like he had a royal flush. "Young lady, Islam was one of the first religions to give equal rights to women...."

Church couldn't blame him for trailing off. She'd seen *vampires* flinch from that look.

"Rights," Myrrh said, deadpan. "*'And when they are disobedient, warn them, then send them away, and if they continue, beat them'* One might note that is the holy instruction to a man for his several wives. There is no such *right* for a wife against her husband."

Glover stiffened, and waved it off. "That's a misreading of the English translation, lady. It really just means *chastise-*"

"I am quite willing to debate the translation of *waidriboohunna* with you. In English or Arabic. Later," Myrrh stated. "For now, our discussion is banes. And adopting the methods used in Islamic territories against the supernatural would be both hazardous to our health, and damaging to the soul. For our faiths hold that each individual soul is precious, and all effort should be made to save a life. As officers of the law, you would no more burn an apartment building to the ground to kill the vampire in its basement than you would allow a suicidal man to jump. It is *wrong*." She smiled again, just as chilling as the last. "And so, if you honor your oaths and the lives of your fellow citizens, you should thank whatever deity you cherish that this land is not held under sharia law."

Church took a deep breath, because the rational people in the room were in shock and she didn't want to give the irrational ones a chance to react. "What's that got to do with fighting monsters?"

"Besides the fact that these days they tend to use napalm, rather than simple naphtha or flamethrowers? Oh, a great deal. One of the more specific defenses against many supernatural creatures, that does not kill innocent civilians, is the sound of church bells, and voices raised in prayer," Myrrh stated. "*Make a joyful noise unto the Lord* is sound mystic defense, as well as an expression of faith. This is found not only in Christianity and Judaism, but in Buddhism, the many paths of the Hindu beliefs, and every faith native to the soil of this continent." Myrrh paused, deliberately, gaze fixed on Glover's. "In lands Islam controls, this is forbidden."

Wait. What?

"Consecrated wine is another vessel of faith, and so a weapon against darkness," Myrrh went on. "In lands Islam controls, this is also forbidden."

Well, yes, everyone knows what-

"One of the foremost weapons against the darkness is reason, logic, and the use of skilled tactics," Myrrh stated. "The faith of Mohammed teaches that logic does not exist - that water only runs downward, and fire only burns, because their Allah wills it so. Did he will something else tomorrow, the world would be otherwise. Which means nothing is predictable, no one can plan the future, and if demons attack there is nothing you can do about it, because all is according to Allah's will." She paused. "That faith also bans chess, holding its practice, and the will to plan and strategize it teaches, as damning as the touch of swine's blood."

Church blinked, hearing the stunned whispers across the room. *Seriously?*

"And of course, the most basic weapon against monsters *is* a weapon," Myrrh said dryly. "In lands Islam controls, weapons are only allowed *to Muslims.* An infidel who dares to carry even a knife puts not only himself, but his entire community at risk of fire and the sword - for those are the terms of the Pact of Umar." Gray eyes were colder than blizzard winds. "I can do this all day, Officer Glover. And I will, if I must. But Captain Sherman has asked me to speak of methods to fight the supernatural, not aid it. In *very* brief terms, Officer, the faith preached and practiced by Mohammed and his followers strips humans of the most effective ways to save their lives from evil... and *deliberately* strips as many as it can from those who are *not Muslim.* For we unbelievers are all bound for hellfire, as an honest imam will tell you; *companions of the fire, to dwell therein forever.*" She shrugged. "It is, however, very difficult to find an honest imam, given the Koran sanctifies *taqiyya*, the holy lie to unbelievers to advance the faith of Islam and the advantage of Muslims over infidels."

Church eyed her fellow officers, wondering which of them would break first.

Myrrh turned back to the board. "Silver and hawthorn may currently be controlled substances, but there are other banes. For example, I noticed a flyer for meditation on the Diamond Sutra on our walk through town the other day. Those who follow Buddhism or the Hindu traditions are often troubled by the rakshasas, who are said to be slain by brass - an alloy of copper and zinc. This is true, but some of the older translations refer not to brass as those of the West know it today, but to the five-metal compound called *panchaloha*, which when properly made also contains meteoric iron, or ordinary iron and lead if that cannot be found, with sometimes zinc and tin in the place of lead-"

"You can't say that!"

Called it, Church sighed. *Oh boy....*

Myrrh glanced back at where Officer Glover had shoved his chair back to stand, her face the picture of surprise.

It's not, though, Church realized; and wanted to rub her eyes, because if this was what Father O'Malley called the Sight, and not something regular cops could see, they really were screwed. *She knows exactly why he's pissed off. She's setting him up.*

"I know lead has an ill reputation these days, much of it well-deserved," Myrrh said innocently. "Yet it is a component of that sacred alloy, and leaving out that fact would do none of us any good."

Definitely setting him up.

And apparently someone had given Glover enough brains to survive on the street after all, because brown eyes narrowed at that guileless face, and a dark hand slammed onto his desk.

Myrrh was silent. Waiting.

"This is going up on the department site. We're all going to have the press hold our feet to the fire for this. Half of what you've got up there is hate speech, and *everything* you just said." Glover flicked his gaze across his fellow cops, a challenge; then glared at Myrrh. "You need to start picking your words, or you're going to get locked up. If you're lucky they might find the key in twenty years. Or maybe you'll just get dumped in the rubber room where you belong. We could all get arrested just letting you talk, you dumb-"

Fire crackled between Aidan's hands.

Church tried not to facepalm. *Yeah, I saw that coming.*

Myrrh sighed. "Aidan...."

"What was that? I was feeling like a persecuted minority over here." Aidan's tone was all mischief, but amber eyes glittered like spears. "You know, one of those demons these guys say don't exist."

"Frustrating," Myrrh allowed, fury lightened from her gaze by silent laughter. "But Officer Glover is not wholly wrong."

Yanking his gaze away from vanishing flames, the patrolman shrugged out his shoulders, jaunty as the street. Church tried not to wince.

Myrrh seemed not to notice. "From what research I have had time to do since we returned to Intrepid-"

"You mean you cornered Father Ricci with coffee and a notepad," Aidan grinned.

"Well, yes," Myrrh admitted. Looked back at Glover, and shrugged. "It is quite possible I will be charged with... many things. So perhaps you might do me the grace of riddling this conundrum, Officer." She pointed to yet another sketch on the board, breaking down magic into sorcery, enchantment, wizardry, and magery. "Ignore the legal consequences. Given I am an enchantress, whose magic is worked by words expressing the truths of the universe, why on Earth would I weaken myself by lying?"

"Not to mention, she's kind of hoping someone does charge her," Aidan informed the room at large. "Since this is still America, and slander's only slander if it's not true - legal discovery on that would be *awesome*." He stretched his arms over his head, languid as a rousing lion. "After all, when it comes to bells and consecrated wine and all, she could demonstrate. In open court. For TV cameras, even."

Sometimes I have no trouble at all believing that guy came out of Hell. Taking out her phone, Church tossed a sudden idea into a quick internet search. After all, if Myrrh was right, meteoric iron was about the nastiest thing to a demon out there. And steel was just modified iron. So maybe there was a chance she could find-

Well, I'll be damned. Church stared at a line of listings. *Thank goodness for space geeks*.

No, no; that bit would get her in trouble, that other piece wasn't nearly sturdy enough for anything she could think of....

Hello. That might work.

The price on the wrench made her wince, but-

Unbidden, Sword Aariel's golden eyes burned in her mind; a demonic fire-lion on two legs, ready to pounce and devour.

Right. Church shivered, feeling those flames burn at her soul. *What's the price of one moderately lawful detective's soul, next to*

a few scraps of green paper?

Still steep. And it was almost two weeks until Halloween. Surely Myrrh could get the Demongate shut down by then.

Unless she gets herself arrested.

Church thought over the past forty-eight hours, sighed, and placed her bid.

"You two are serious?" Glover scowled. "Are you nuts? You think anyone's going to let you show off banes in open court?"

"Officer Glover." Myrrh's brow quirked up, a silent *bring it*. "The problem is not the use of banes, but the full and frank discussion of banes, and where and why they are needed. Which is, truly, a free speech issue. If the court can be kept focused on that - yes, I think we can win." A chuckle. "Though I would prefer not to be arrested for the next two weeks. It would be very inconvenient for our efforts toward cleansing the city of the Demongate."

That didn't raise half the buzz of whispers Church expected. Maybe because those who could believe it were in shock.

But either her fellow detectives were made of sterner stuff, or they'd just had enough coffee and sleep to deal with the idea. She saw nods, even if some of them came with hands tearing out a little aggravated hair.

"Inconvenient!" Detective Heath leaned back to give Myrrh a look askance. "O'Malley said you were... *out*, for twenty-five years. Can you even afford a lawyer?"

"Oh, yes." Myrrh leaned a dusty hand on the side of the chalkboard. "It's not the first time I have had to deal with being greatly out of time and place. I have measures to safeguard an unexpected return on each continent. Though I hope to avoid ever ending up in Antarctica." For a moment, she looked positively green. "No way off that frozen hell save by air or water. That would not be my idea of a good time." She took a breath, as if she would shut that thought away by sheer willpower. "So. Now to vampires.... What is it?"

Captain Sherman was staring at her own phone as if it'd

sprouted fangs. "Taber Howe's in the building. And he brought *files*." A brown brow rose as she skimmed down the text, before she looked Church dead in the eye. "One of them's for you."

Taber Howe. Church sucked air past her teeth. Steven Savonarola's favorite lawyer. The guy whose firm also played defense for vampire mistress Nuria Cruz, and who knew how many other creeps on both sides of the supernatural line. The guy she'd last seen fleeing Myrrh's ringing words with his suit-tail between his legs, dropping papers meant to serve Aidan with various legal whammies for interfering with the deceased Christophe Savonarola's grave and identity.

Which, given Steven was the guy who'd murdered his older brother in the first place, kind of redefined chutzpah. And how.

Taber Howe's here with paperwork. Church grimaced. *Oh, this can't be good.*

~*~*~*~*~

Perched in his borrowed chair near Church's paper-littered desk, Aidan stared at Howe. Howe stared back.

Heh. The old "break them by staring" trick. Aidan gave the sweating lawyer a lazy blink. *You want to see who can out-patience who? I can wait all day. I can wait all year.*

...Bad fire-mage. Deliberately terrifying people is kind of on the dark side. Even if he is Steven's lawyer.

Still, Aidan didn't exactly feel like stopping. Not when it gave Myrrh time to run her own quick check of Howe's files, fingers hovering over neat manila as she whispered under her breath.

"Cursed be he that perverteth the judgment of the stranger, fatherless, and widow...."

Or maybe it was a bit over her breath. Howe was definitely sweating.

Aidan smirked at him. "Is it hot in here, or is it just me?"

Church was giving the lawyer her own hairy eyeball. "Don't

incinerate him, he might be a witness."

The way Howe's eyes bugged, the lawyer just might be, at that. From what Church said about how people thought reality worked, most people had never met a mage. They were used to slow ritual spells and enchanted items, the kind a wizard or sorcerer could put together. Maybe the kind of like-to-like poppet magic some enchanters called up with models of the real-world bit they were trying to change. Fast magic, like Myrrh's chants or his own fire-calling, were not something the average person had ever seen. Yet the lawyer was sweating.

And we know Steven could do water-magery. On top of enchantment by way of woodcarvings, and *sorcery calling up demons.*

How Steven had pulled off learning three different kinds of magic in the course of a human lifetime was worrying Myrrh. It was worrying her a lot. Aidan didn't have all the details of why, yet - but if Myrrh said that Demongate had appeared in Hell way too fast, he believed her. If Steven could work more magic than the average spellcasting bad guy, and *faster-*

Then it doesn't look good for the good guys. Even if he is dead.

After all, for someone with demonic blood, death was only a temporary condition. Aidan should know. "You going ahead with that stupid lawsuit?"

"The legal situation has not changed simply because my client is deceased," Howe gritted out. "I will see you brought before a judge for vandalism of a grave, interfering with a body, and attempting to assume Christophe Savonarola's identity by means mystic and otherwise."

Weird, Aidan thought. He wasn't even flinching at his old name anymore. *Guess when an enchantress helps someone rename themselves, it takes.*

It probably hadn't hurt that Myrrh had called him nothing but Aidan for two decades in Hell. Well, that and the occasional, "pest". Usually while she was making sure he got water to drink, the closest thing to clean food to eat, and a few winks' sleep some-where some vaster demon wouldn't inhale him in one swift gulp.

Ah, Hell. Where everything is trying to kill you, down to water that wants to drown you for drinking it and cliffs that shake you off for climbing them.

He kind of missed it. Say one thing about constant torture and fear for his soul, it kept him focused. Facing down someone who might be trying to do the right thing, by Howe's own lights, and wasn't a clear and present physical danger?

I don't know what to do with that anymore. I just... don't.

Well, he'd better start figuring it out. Church had been a life-saver for the both of them, but she had more than enough trouble of her own.

Just - talk to the man. Try. Aidan cleared his throat. "Mr. Howe. None of those charges are going to stick, and you know it. For two of them, I've got one hell of an alibi."

Aha, there was the twitch again. And from the way Church and Myrrh were *not* looking at Howe, they'd caught it too.

"As for that last one," Aidan kept going, "Any sane judge is going to look at what you bring in and toss you out on your face. I don't think I've ever *claimed* to be Christophe Savonarola."

Technicality, there. He hadn't claimed to be, because he *had been* Christophe.

But then, technicalities mattered to the law. And to magic.

"I'm the wrong age, and no matter what you said two nights back based on either somebody letting stuff slip they shouldn't, or *illicitly gained police reports-*"

Howe had enough nerve left to bristle. Heh.

"If you take my prints," Aidan waggled his fingers, "pretty sure they won't match up with the coroner's report. So if you're saying I'm taking anyone's identity - well, how?"

At least they wouldn't match *now*. Some people thought finger-prints were a gift from God, your own mark in the world forever, and if that was true... well. The first night he'd come back, he just might have had the prints that ought to be on a dead body. Brrr.

But when Steven had burned down the county courthouse, he'd burned the legal name change documents linking Aidan and Christophe as one person.

And nearly burned me out in the process....

Lucky him, Myrrh and Church had been on top of things. Myrrh had dragged him back from the brink, and Church had slapped him back to life with her recognition of him as *Lindisfarne*.

If someone with the Sight sees who you really are, they can name it.

Myrrh had power. But Church was a cop of *here* and *now*. Intrepid's police force had named him Aidan Lindisfarne, and Aidan was pretty damn sure if Church ran his prints *now*, they'd come back tied to nobody else.

Because this isn't the body that died. It's a construct.

Not real. A magical creation, like Myrrh weaving her own body out of her jade-set skull and dawn's first light. Though according to Myrrh it was real flesh and bone. Just - not what he'd been born with.

Gives us both an edge on werewolves, because we *don't need to worry about getting bitten. Our souls aren't linked to this flesh, so the curse can't use it to latch on to us.*

On the one hand, that was one heck of a relief. He had enough problems setting off fires when he got stressed out, he didn't need turning furry on top of that. On the other....

Hell. The cops have to be so scared.

Which made him want to have a *talk* with Father O'Malley, because if the priest had known about Myrrh's Hunt drink to tamp down the risk of infection, and hadn't told the cops...

Aidan had tasted Church's fear, when the detective had opened up on Raphael's corpse-eating pack. And he couldn't blame her one bit. Church was a good person, solid and determined to do what was right, soul glowing warm through shrouding flesh. Yet she'd felt she had no choice but to shoot to kill.

If we hadn't been there, she would have died. A pack in a feeding frenzy wouldn't leave anyone alive.

Or so Myrrh had told him. Aidan hadn't seen that for himself, yet.

Hope I never do. Aidan leaned back in his chair, comparing the muddier glow of Howe's soul to Church's clearer light. *So is that because of working for Steven, or just from being a lawyer?*

Well, no, that wasn't fair. He'd been in pre-law himself. He'd just gotten out, once he'd figured out the ethical grays and maybes you had to accept to defend a client you knew damn well was guilty wasn't good for his peace of mind. Architecture, things that had to be put together in a solid world, a definite yes or no on what a beam could support and stay intact, and which shortcuts would wreck it completely - that'd been much safer.

Until it wasn't.

Though that hadn't had anything to do with the coursework. More ice and knives of glass and *betrayal-*

"Aidan." Myrrh's voice reached through black fog; shoved memories of a graveyard crypt back and away. "Aidan. It's all right. You're here. You're breathing."

The chair arm was hot under his hand, gray plastic covered in tiny bubbles. Oops.

Howe was not just sweating, but pale. Damn. He hadn't meant to scare the guy.

...Well. Not *that* much.

Myrrh left the file to Church, stepping to Aidan's side to look him in the eye, gray calm as a cloud-shrouded sky. "Are you here?"

"I think so," Aidan managed. "Sorry. That wasn't...."

"You have nothing to be sorry for," Myrrh said quietly. "Coming back to life is never easy." She tilted her head, regarding Howe with ancient stillness. "If you press this suit, I will see that Aidan is defended. You will lose, and both of us will be most annoyed. We have a great deal to do, and a very short time in which to do it."

Pale brows drew down. "If we succeed in our tasks, we may deal with your suit in due course. If, however, we fail due to your delays...." She sighed, and shook her head. "Then it is most unlikely any of us will be alive to contest your claim."

"*Miss* Shafat."

Aidan sat up, disgruntled. In two words, Howe had managed to fit in doubts of Myrrh's marital status, name, and sanity. He ought to take *notes*.

Howe was ramrod-straight. "Attempting to intimidate the plaintiff in a case-"

"Howe, if she was trying to intimidate you, you wouldn't be standing here." Church thumbed the folder, then turned her full attention to the lawyer. "You saw the Nightsong video. What we're after is scarier than vampires. I saw it." The detective shivered. "Just part of it. One demon. And it's in my nightmares."

Aidan grimaced. Yeah; the hellhound he'd met decades back had been terrifying enough. The malursine had taunted them, laughing as it lusted after pain and death. Definitely worth nightmares.

Church's voice sank, so low Aidan wasn't sure the detective could hear herself. "Still can't believe he just walked away."

Wait. Aidan blinked, stunned. *She was scared of Aariel?*

He had to bury his face in his hands, because *duh*. Sword Aariel, armsman and enforcer for Demon Lord Yaldabaoth, was the kind of scary most souls only saw *once*.

Have a guy beat how to survive into you for years, you kind of forget that most people don't live long enough to get scared.

Unbidden, he felt the warmth of Aariel's claws stroking his hair.

I don't know if he loved Mom. I don't know if he could. But he respected *her. He was* proud *Mom snuck me out of Hell's power.*

A demon had respected Phoebe Savonarola more than her own husband. If that didn't say everything about the mess that was his family, Aidan didn't know what did.

"Demons." Howe's tone was dismissive, but his complexion still hadn't gained any color. "Detective. You're on administrative leave for several reasons already...."

"Oh, don't even try it," Church said tiredly. "The captain, Father O'Malley, and half the fire department will be in testifying what they saw so quick, your papers won't have the chance to cool down from the printer. You worked for Savonarola, Howe. Right about now every law enforcement officer in this city is starting to find out what that meant."

"Mr. Savonarola was one of my clients, true," Howe said stiffly. "However, if he were the type of man you insinuate, Detective, he would never have ensured that this information would be available in the event of his untimely demise."

"Sure he would have," Aidan muttered, eyeing the thick stack of papers. "Nobody does revenge like a ticked off," *demon-blood*, "sorcerer." He glanced up as the lawyer raised an indignant finger. "Don't start with the whole slander thing again. He was a sorcerer, we saw it, and what he summoned tried to kill all of us." Aidan waved at the file. "And if I know Steven - and believe me, I know him better than I ever wanted to - if this is his last request, I'd check under my car to see if the brake lines are still in one piece. Steven *breaks* his toys when he's done with them, Howe."

A swift inhalation. "Is that a threat, Mr. Lindisfarne?"

"A warning," Aidan shot back, suddenly tired down to his bones. "Be careful. Please? Steven's killed enough people already."

Dark eyes narrowed. "Mr. Savonarola is deceased."

"A, don't think anyone's found the body, and B, that doesn't slow Nuria Cruz down," Church noted. "I'd check your house for gas leaks, too. We don't want anybody dying in Intrepid for the next few weeks. This mess is big enough as it is." She flicked her hand toward the man, obviously fed up. "You don't want to prejudice a possible investigation, right? So let me read in peace."

"Charming as ever, Detective." Shoulders very straight, Howe walked out the door.

Eagleman leaned back in his chair, black brows up and interested. "Hey, could you take a look at ours, Shafat? You know, just in case."

"I would be glad to." Myrrh headed for his desk. "Church's file was clean, so hopefully yours will be as well...."

"Clean, huh?" Aidan ran fingers through his mane of hair, watching Church open her folder with the wary air of someone approaching an angry dire raccoon in a trap. "Doesn't make sense."

"You don't need magic to do a lot of damage," Church said dryly. "Isn't that the point Myrrh's trying to pound through people's heads?" She shuddered. "Napalm, for the love of-"

Aidan had to grin at how fast Church bit that off. "Deep breaths. You'll get used to it."

"Did you?" Blue eyes almost cut him, challenging. "Ever?"

"No." Aidan tried to keep a shudder from crawling up his spine. "No, you never really get used to... down there. It eats at you. All the time. Even if they mess with your head so you forget you were ever human, even if you can't remember what dawn tasted like, you always know something's... horribly wrong."

Church was silent a moment too long. "So... what does dawn taste like?"

Aidan froze, wide-eyed. Because how could anyone not know, it was warmth and cinnamon and a kitten rub against his cheek-

Dawn is... light. To most people. Not food.

"Okay, I'm going to just say this once," Church sighed, after the silence made it clear he was stuck for words. "You and Myrrh are *very weird*. I can live with that, because even if you dragged me into fire, chaos, and mayhem, you had the decency to drag me - and Tom - out of it in one piece. I don't know what Tom got himself mixed up in, but he's been a good cop, and a decent partner. He's alive. I owe you for that."

"You don't owe us," Aidan started.

Church lifted a hand.

No fool, he shut up.

"I owe you," the detective repeated. "So I can put up with a little weird. I'm just going to say that when most people talk about a taste of dawn, they mean coffee. I know you remember coffee."

"...Yeah."

"You just got back from... a very bad place," Church went on. "Give yourself time. Get used to the world being normal. It'll work out."

Nice words. But Church didn't sound any more convinced than he was.

The world's not normal. I'm not. Normal people don't put their hands on a quarried stone, and hear the mountain grumping about being taken for a walk. Normal people can't set the dishtowels on fire just by losing their temper. Normal people aren't....

Heh. That was probably most of Church's problem, right there. "Aariel kind of surprised me, on the lawn that night," Aidan admitted. "I just - by the time I knew he was moving, it was way too late to run. I didn't expect-" *To be left alive. To be petted like a cub. To be told - Yaldabaoth's not my father. Aariel is.*

Good lord, did Aariel actually think he was *cute?*

Church gave him one more sidelong look, then gave in and opened the file. And sighed. "Oh great, I'm going to need an accountant." She groaned. "And a dustpan."

Aidan took the implicit invitation, and leaned close enough to get a good look at the stylized sunrise logo. "Suntrust. Isn't that-?"

"The bank you two *sort of* blew up? Yes," Church drew out the word, eyeing Myrrh as the hell-raider finished murmuring over Eagleman's folder and headed back their way. "You know, the arson investigator's still tearing his hair out about just what happened there. I'm going to take a wild guess, and say he's hoping the lab comes back with some known explosive he can tie onto the both of you. Or maybe just you, Myrrh. Since it was your box that went up."

"Then he hopes in vain." Stopping beside Aidan's chair, Myrrh smiled wryly. "There have been times I have indeed been forced to use blood for rune-tracings, but that blood was always mine. I guarantee that which was on my vault, was not. The bank exploded due to vampiric entrapments. That is not something I am capable of."

Aidan had to stifle a snicker. Vampiric entrapments, no. Explosion? Oh boy, he'd bet Myrrh had a half-dozen ways to manage those.

Church squinted at her. "You know damn well that bank didn't."

Which had every detective in hearing range craning their ears this way, even if they never glanced Church's direction.

"Ah, but if the arson investigator wishes to implicate me in the blast, he must first propose to the court that vampires and a simple blessing are an explosive combination." Myrrh stood relaxed, glancing over the Suntrust papers. "Which would neatly poke a hole in their claim to be revived humans. At which point, the fact that they are demons could enter the courts as admissible evidence, and those surviving Hunters imprisoned or locked in insane asylums would have new grounds for appeals." A quiet breath. "And it might clear the names of some of the dead, which would be great comfort to their survivors."

Church stared at her. "...You thought that out less than twelve hours after you broke out of Hell."

"Hmm, no," Myrrh admitted. "At the time, I knew only that vampires were involved, and there would be an opportunity to meddle in their affairs most strikingly. That it might have other benefits, I only considered later."

Aidan nodded, turning the scenario over in his head. "It'd probably take a few more cases, but it'd set precedent. Could work."

Church looked between the two of them, and slugged down more coffee. "Thought you weren't a lawyer."

"I'm not, thank God," Aidan allowed. "I just grew up in it. And...."

He couldn't say it. He tried, but the words froze in his mouth. So long in darkness trapped with endless scrolls, hunting through them with Aariel and other lesser demons for flaws, loopholes; anything that gave one dark power an advantage over another.

Loopholes that snared human lives in their coils. How... how could I...?

It would have been easy to say Aariel had forced him to, just as the Sword had forced a lost soul to learn to fight, or suffer torments worse than death. Easy. And a lie.

I had to learn. Had to. Steven kept summoning me, trying to use me. If I couldn't find a way to break loose he'd have had me burning innocent people....

And the people in those contracts, those souls caught in binding words and demonic loopholes, weren't innocent.

Doesn't make it right.

Which was Hell all over. All the choices you had were bad.

Not choosing's still a choice.

It didn't help. Icy stone walls rose around him, mortared by ever-flowing red lava that crusted and cracked with every breath. The looming weight of shelves upon shelves pressed down, stacked with papers and fine black leather and clay tablets older than most history; old enough he tasted their crumbling surface like blood and muck choking his throat-

Blindly, Aidan grabbed for his throat. Too close, too tight, he couldn't breathe-!

Soft. Warm. Just a little prickly.

Hair. Braided hair, holding a slight weight of sharp stone.

Myrrh's hair.

He closed fingers on braided white, and breathed.

Myrrh's here. Myrrh's alive. I'm not in Yaldabaoth's court. I'm not in Hell.

Maybe if he told himself that enough, he'd believe it.

"...Aidan?" Church's hand flattened file documents, as if that might keep out fiery oxygen if his stress lashed out at stray paperwork. Who knew; on Earth, that might work. "You need more coffee?"

Maybe less, Aidan thought wryly. *Or maybe just something to burn. Should have picked up some votive candles when I was at the church.*

Although that he felt bad about. Living on Earth again meant, well, *living*. Doing responsible human stuff, like finding an apartment and a job. Not sleeping in church pews and letting Myrrh's old stash carry him on the books as some kind of odd apprentice.

Though given what was after both of them, sleeping in church pews was actually something he could let slide. Consecrated ground. Staying in a hotel might be hard on innocent bystanders.

And... Myrrh was regarding him, that well of calm like cool water over his fevered soul. "It's never easy, coming back," the hell-raider said quietly. "It helps to be busy with a needed task." She turned to Church. "What do you plan to do? You are, technically, on leave."

"Yeah," Church drew out in one frustrated sigh. "But what's in here... and everybody's already up to their ears trying to sort out the courthouse mess, who knows how many cases that's going to tie up, and...." The detective's eyes narrowed. "And if I don't do anything about this, what are *you* planning to do?"

"At the moment? Little," Myrrh said frankly. "If Steven left this trap for you, and you mean to ignore it, our time is better spent battling the fires we already know exist; sealing the Demongate from this side, and teaching you and your fellow officers all the lore I can before someone does try to arrest me." Shadows shifted with her shrug. "The odds are likely someone will try."

"And what if someone does?" Church's tone was better suited to sneaking up on a ticking bomb. "You said you can't do that trick with the cuffs if someone's got a legal right to hold you."

"That trick, no," Myrrh agreed, an amused light in gray eyes.

Church gave a half-strangled growl of pure frustration. "Right. Of course. Why do I even ask? Of *course* you've got more tricks up that damn shape-shifty sleeve of yours...."

Not going to laugh. Nope.

Though that itself made Aidan want to grab his head in his hands and hold on tight. Angry, scared, trying not to giggle on the floor- there was something *wrong* with him.

Half-demon. Plenty of wrong right there.

Which made him angry all over again, at himself; yes, Sword Aariel was evil and Yaldabaoth's brother and a loyal demon who'd probably try to bring about Hell on Earth, but-

But Aariel'd had them right where he could have slaughtered them all. And walked away, because killing them would have been *wrong....*

"Aidan." Myrrh's hand gripped the back of his; light, but firm. "Be in the moment."

Right. Breathe in, and out. And stop waiting for the screams on the wind. "Maybe I need some air," Aidan managed.

Church shifted her hand on the file, not quite crumpling the edge of old paper. "And maybe I need to go spring a trap."

Aidan blinked. "Say what?"

Chapter Two

"It's simple," Church said innocently, letting her car rock forward just one more inch before she turned off the ignition. "I can't get mixed up in what might be a new case in our department. But everybody's busy trying to pull files out of the courthouse ashes and werewolves out of the woodwork, so why tie up another cop chasing down what might just be a tiny bit of identity theft?"

Leaning out the opened door until the earth stopped heaving, Myrrh gave her best attempt at a glare.

"After all, we are talking about Savonarola," the detective went on, undaunted, as Myrrh lurched out of the car. Aidan followed out the back, carefully avoiding brushing his fingers across the painted metal of the door. "I wouldn't put it past him to fake up a whole slew of account numbers and other paperwork to get us all chasing our tails while he keeps his eye on the wrecking the world prize."

Myrrh stood fast as the world wobbled, tasting exhaust and asphalt in the back of her throat. At least the remnants of ash from the explosion were an honest bitterness.

I wonder where Halo has taken himself.

The unwilling street seer had probably scurried for safer environs; he'd done his best to rattle Aidan's nerve nights ago, and failed. He likely wouldn't cross their paths again unless he had more hateful foretellings to unleash.

Which means not seeing him is good news. I think.

"Why is Steven after that, anyway?" Church leaned against the car as Myrrh collected herself. "Half human, right? What makes him think he'd make out any better than the vampires would, if real demons take over?"

"Because he's stronger than they are," Aidan said flatly.

"Right, pull the other one...."

"*I'm* stronger than they are. And I grew up thinking I was pure human. Steven grew up spellcasting. I'd bet dollars to donuts he knows a dozen ways to take a vamp down just twitching the right finger." Aidan crossed his arms, and gave the cop an up-and-down look. "So before we go rattling any FBI cages, you tell us why Steven thought you'd jump at the chance to take this Agent Cushman down."

Church winced. "Um. I didn't want to bring it up, you kind of almost lost it just trying to tell us about you-"

Best to cut quick and clean. "Christophe was not the only sacrificial victim," Myrrh stated. "I have spoken with Father O'Malley. He said Intrepid's detectives have long believed you had a serial killer on your hands, fixated on Halloween...." *Oh.* "Yet what casework I have seen makes no mention of the FBI."

"Doesn't make sense." Aidan scowled. "They're so proud of their behavioral profiling, you'd think they'd jump at... oh." The fire mage shook out his shoulders, as if seeking something to fight. "But they didn't. Did they."

"Told us for years we were grasping at straws." Church's fingers clenched into fists; slowly, consciously relaxed, before she jammed them in her coat pockets. "We all thought they were just too caught up in high-profile stuff to worry about months-old bodies found in the woods. They weren't kids, they weren't pretty girls; half of them were migrants, the rest pretty much lone tourists and people down on their luck." She drew a snarling breath. "Well. Most of them weren't kids. Megan O'Connor was an exception."

Ah. That would be enough for any caring soul to feel personally offended. Myrrh nodded once, feeling earth finally firm again under her feet. "So now you wonder if it was not merely bureaucratic incompetence, but if agents are... compromised."

"It'd explain a lot."

"So would possession," Myrrh noted, looking over the parking lot for anything that hinted of the uncanny. "A spell of distraction at a critical moment. An illusion cast over your request, to encourage the mind to skip over crucial details. Even the more mundane subversion of an analyst, secretary, or janitor; anyone who might have access to records the FBI sought. There are reasons many Hunters prefer to meet face to face, or to communicate by coded letters if they cannot. Defenses can be woven into paper and ink so one can be reasonably sure they will not be altered." She paused, considering that. "Although one of the more common means to create invisible messages can leave one open to manipulation by succubi and incubi; I shall have to remember to explain, so the men on your force are not tempted to experiment."

"Just the men?" Church gave her a look askance. "Great. You're not going to just have the PC police coming down on you for religion, you'll get the feminists swarming."

Myrrh blinked, completely confused. "But why in the worlds would-? Detective. No woman has the... necessary equipment, to be so linked to materials that...." Oh dear. How to put this politely? Not that it was possible to be polite on this subject, but she would make the attempt. "Unless a creature be so formed as to require girding his loins for the battle, it is... *impossible* to create what is used for that ink."

Church stared at her.

Nonplussed, Myrrh stared back.

Church slapped a hand over her own eyes. "Oh god, I *so* did not need to know that."

"I would have preferred not to say it," Myrrh muttered, face hot. "It is much more properly addressed by a godparent."

Church peeked through wary fingers. "...I thought fairies were dangerous."

"Of course they are," Myrrh replied, even more puzzled. "What do fairies have to do with proper religious instruction on," she had to clear her throat, "such matters of the body?"

Church groaned again. "*Please* tell me you've heard about fairy godmothers."

"That is rare, but it does happen," Myrrh allowed. "Usually where fay and human worlds overlap, and the powers of one decide to lend their aid to the heirs of another, to reduce the casualty count. So a young fay might be suckled at a human breast, or a human babe have one of those Others as a godparent to teach them of that world beyond the ninth wave. But there is always a human godparent to teach a mortal child the proper ways to safeguard their souls. Just as one of the Good Neighbors would always ensure *their* child was taught the ways of magic and chaos...." She trailed off, as Church shook her head, and glanced at Aidan. "No?"

"Hollywood kind of leaves out human godparents," Aidan informed her. "And I don't think movies ever got into the suckling thing. Unless it's lady vamps feeding the poor orphan kid."

The hell-raider pictured a living child trying to nurse at a mummified undead breast, and felt her stomach twist, too incredulous to even work up an indignant fury. "That would be impossible."

"I know that and you know that, but how many people can see what vampires really look like?" Aidan grimaced. "And the ones that can - how many of them are going to risk saying it?"

"You two still serious about the whole 'vampires are really withered possessed corpses' thing?" Church put in.

"Yes."

"Ooookay," Church sighed. Glanced at the front of the bank, where sheets of plywood covered shattered windows, though someone had at least replaced the main door. "If someone could cover bog mummy skin - yeah, I could see how messing with paperwork could be easy. Though if it's that easy, how can anybody trust anything?" She checked her watch. "Told him to be here in a few more minutes. You really can't take car rides, can you?"

Myrrh sighed, torn between annoyance and gratitude. "I appreciate your care in allowing me time to recover." That was one part of ancient eras she would not miss; these days travelling long distances could be a matter of mere painful hours, rather than helpless days sick on seaboard. "I am not as sick if I can drive myself." She wasn't certain if the reason was physical or mystical. One article Father Ricci had run across on the internet hypothesized that

motion sickness was a function of whether or not the brain considered one sense dominant, sight or the perception of motion; and
given her senses were beyond the purely physical, she had no
doubt the matter would be even more muddled for her.

"No," Church said shortly.

"No?" Aidan blinked at her, kitten-innocent.

Myrrh tried to stifle a snicker. Aidan hadn't taken the ride well
either; though it seemed Church's rental had less steel in it than her
ordinary car.

"Oh god, not the eyes," Church muttered. "No. Nobody drives
my car but me."

"That's not your car," Aidan pointed out. And blinked again,
grinning.

Church muttered something under her breath; Myrrh had no
doubt Aidan heard more than she did of, *"Hardened cop, must
resist kitty-eyes...."*

Myrrh let them tease each other, focusing on the lingering
shreds of magic and power left at the scene. Not too much of a
sense of death; surprising. Had she been a sorcerer of ill intent and
powerful connections, a bank vault would have been a perfect
place to sacrifice a life to the Demongate. Even for a Hunter who
worked outside the law, getting in to cleanse it would be a difficult
night's work - and only possible if the Hunter also had the skills of
a thief, to have enough time to work without being arrested mid-
prayer. And a thief's skills combined with a prayerful faith were a
very rare thing, indeed.

Though not impossible. Myrrh half-closed her eyes, wondering
if their presence in the parking lot made the security guard
nervous. *I shall have to ask Father O'Malley if the Friends of St.
Nicholas have current recruits.*

Still, it didn't seem as if Steven had tainted this place. Which...
was not surprising, now that she had time to think. After all, if he
was half as skilled a sorcerer as he'd seemed, he would have
deduced a Hunter kept supplies in this vault. Why draw attention to

himself before his plans were complete?

We should check other banks in town, though. Just in case.

"I'm surprised the bank is still open." Myrrh watched a salt-and-pepper-haired man in a complicated hiker's vest walk out the door, a hitch in his stride as he saw them before he kept on toward a fancy black BMW. "One would think it would be accounted a crime scene."

"The safety deposit boxes, yes," Church allowed. "The rest of the bank, not so much. Cruz has a lot of pull in this town."

Which explained far too much, yet not nearly enough. "Thirty years ago, I would have been certain she was using bloodslaves, directly or as cats' paws, to work in the living world," Myrrh mused. "Take down your suspects, douse them in holy water, have them drink consecrated wine, or even grab a hank of their hair to burn in holy oil later. At best, you would have broken the link between the vampire and the corrupted soul. At the very least, you would have identified the problem." She *hmph*ed. "These days, the leader of a coven may have simply bought her influence. It is most annoying."

"Kidnapping, assault, unlawful restraint," Church sighed. "You do remember I'm a cop, right?"

Myrrh gave her a sidelong glance, amused.

"Wouldn't dare forget it," Aidan said practically. "But you notice she said *years ago*. Which makes this all hypotheticals, and not something you need to worry about. Besides. Kidnapping's a Fed problem anyway." He shaded his eyes against the noon sun. "Is that him?"

"Should be." Church watched a gray sedan turn into the bank parking lot. "Agent Joey Cushman. Don't call him Joey unless you want to tick him off." She glanced at Myrrh. "Do me a favor? No talking about kidnapping bloodslaves?"

"I will endeavor to avoid it," Myrrh said virtuously, eyes drawn by the sedan's odd headlights. Who on earth had thought it was a good idea to have merely an outline of light around the main bright lights? And why on earth would anyone have it on in broad daylight?

"Good," Church sighed. Then twitched. "Avoid the talking, or avoid the doing?"

Myrrh grinned.

"Aaarrrgh." The detective pasted on a polite smile as the agent stepped out of his car. "Special Agent Cushman. Glad you could make it."

"Let's get this over with," the tall agent groused, gun an obvious companion in his shoulder holster; a second just as obvious a weight at his ankle for any who knew to look. "Officially I'm on my lunch break. Our office doesn't want anything to do with the IPD until you figure out who's arresting whom in your department." Hazel eyes narrowed. "And we definitely don't want anything to do with someone *on leave*."

"And yet, here you are," Aidan observed. "Funny, that."

Myrrh hid a frown. What was most certainly *not* funny was the twitch in Aidan's fingers, as if her friend's hands wished to wrap burning flame around a lying throat.

Like a cat watching a cobra, Myrrh thought, feeling the intensity of Aidan's gaze like a candleflame touching her palm. *Most times he is better at hiding the predator within. What does he see, that I do not?*

She took a half-step sideways, so Aidan might be steadied by the warmth of her presence. If he sensed something outside her ken, it was likely not a peril of magic, but the spirit. If so, she was on her guard. In the meantime - throttling a potential suspect would *not* help Church's investigation.

"Wait," Myrrh murmured, too soft for human ears. "Watch, and wait."

The agent scowled at all of them impartially. "We ought to be able to clear this up. I don't even have an account with this bank. Who *are* you, anyway?"

"Special Agent Cushman, bounty hunter Myrrh Shafat,"

Church began.

Politely, Myrrh inclined her head.

"And Aidan Lindisfarne, religious refugee and possible witness to a whole bunch of things you're going to wish you never heard of," Church stated. "I hope we can clear this up, Agent. I really hope we can. The guy who handed me this," she waved a plain manila folder, which Myrrh knew held copies of the originals, "may have been lying."

From the pinched look on Cushman's face, he wanted nothing more than to declare them all liars and wash his hands of the mess.

But he can't, Myrrh mused. *She's hooked his curiosity. He says he has no account here, Church implies he does. Even if he is not lying, for his own sanity, he has to know which of us have the truth.*

If any of them did. Like Church, she believed Steven would do nothing that would not profit him, even in death. And what greater profit to evil than two honest servants of justice at each other's throats?

Yet I cannot ignore a demon's appetite for spite. Or a human's. It would suit Steven's fancy just as well to turn Church loose on someone who truly is *guilty.*

Cushman's mouth twitched. "If you think whatever you have might be evidence, why bring two civilians along?"

"Maybe she just wants to lull you into a false sense of security," Aidan said guilelessly. Amber eyes burned. "Or maybe it's got nothing to do with you, you idiot. Church saved our butts the other night, and something's *after her*. We're planning to return the favor."

Which was the truth, Myrrh acknowledged. Though they might have found a more diplomatic way to phrase the situation.

Then again, this way Agent Cushman will be focused on Aidan as one who fights bluntly, in the open, Myrrh considered. *Meaning he will miss a fire-mage's subtler ambushes completely.*

It was a tactic they'd used many times before, even when Aidan had been too wary to admit he trusted her. Most denizens of

Hell were inclined to view a fire spirit as the threat over a purely human soul. Meaning while they tried to swat a bobbing ball of flames, she had the perfect shot at their spine.

Well. Those that actually had spines.

It also meant that as Aidan focused on defending himself and pricking sore egos, she could choose what level of force was needed. And if they had by some rare chance stumbled on a creature that was only frightened, and angry, and had no malice against them personally - her incantations could be far less lethal than demonic fire.

If Cushman was involved in Steven's schemes, yet not of his own will, they would need that.

The agent scowled, disdaining them all. "Something? What kind of something?"

"Take your pick." Church shuddered. "Vampires, werewolves, things that look like an evil weasel made out of rabid greenbriar and hate - I lost count after about the fifth ugly with claws and teeth." She waved toward the bank door. "So! Shall we?"

A small smile touched Cushman's face as he headed for the new door. "Relax, Detective. Vampires and werewolves don't keep banker's hours."

"You might want to touch base with the arson investigation," Church observed, following a polite distance behind. "Esmeralda blew up when it was broad daylight outside. So she got in some-how, without tripping any alarms. And so far as I know, until someone figures out how, nobody's locked that back door yet."

That earned them all a wary look. Good.

Myrrh let her eyebrows bounce at the agent, amused. The poor man had no idea what he was walking into. The last time they'd entered this lobby it had been significantly less smoke-stained....

Hmm; they've cleaned up the glass, at least.

New tellers' windows were in place, even if the wood around them could have stood a bit more careful touching-up. The carpet was mostly clean, and the indoor ficus had had its shredded leaves trimmed off. The windowed offices for managers and higher-status bank employees looked almost normal, if you couldn't pick out that lingering sense of slaughtered demon. Only the door to the safety deposit boxes was still a pierced wreck, crime scene tape obviously keeping it off-limits.

Ed the security guard looked significantly grayer than the last time they'd been there. And silk-scarved bank manager Mrs. Gillingham didn't hesitate. "Call the police!"

"I am the police," Church said dryly. She pointed at Agent Cushman. "And he's the FBI. I think between us we can handle whatever the problem is. Agent? Mind showing her your badge?"

"That's... not necessary, Agent, we know you here." Gillingham swallowed, staring at Myrrh as if she'd slithered out of the most noisome swamp known to mortal man, with all the shuddering, crawling hordes of inhuman flesh-eaters on her heels. "Just - whatever you're doing, keep her *away* from me."

The agent frowned, obviously torn between glaring at Church and interrogating Myrrh on just what she'd done to the poor vampire-fodder of a woman. Then steeled indignant shoulders at what the manager had implied. "What do you mean, ma'am? I've never been in this bank before."

"Hmm." Church flicked her thumb across the folder tab. "Seems there's a bit of confusion about that after all, isn't there, Agent?"

Something wary moved in hazel eyes. "Let's see what you have. Since you think someone made sure my name was here."

"Your name?" Gillingham jumped in, deliberately cutting Church off. "Agent, you were in last week. We were just about to contact you, given your box was...." She shivered, and stared at Myrrh again. "How did you do that?"

Myrrh shrugged. "Given your lifestyle choice, I doubt you would believe me if I told you. Perhaps you could ask your security consultant? He might know, if his coven leader has dared to trust him with the knowledge of what Powers are anathema to vampire blood."

"You- this-" Cushman's gaze pinballed between Myrrh, Church's rueful sigh, and Aidan's not-stifled-enough giggle. "What box? I don't have a safety deposit box in this bank!"

"Well, you don't exactly have one *now*, no," Gillingham admitted. "Everything in the vault was-" She flung up her hands. "We can show you what's left."

"What's left?" Church echoed in dismay. "Damn it, Myrrh!"

"Objection. Hearsay." Aidan whistled. "I can tell you exactly what she did in that vault, Detective, and there wasn't an ounce of explosives involved. Zip. Zilch." Amber blinked at the manager. "Then again, who knows what a vampire security guy might have put in, and not told anybody about, right?"

"You have a vampire running-" Agent Cushman cut words off with a snap of teeth, eyeing patterned silk with a squint of calculation. "Let's see this box. And I want to know when I was *supposedly* here."

"Oh, that's going to be a mess." Aidan eyed the rainbow-shimmery disk in its warped plastic case. If that was a CD, no one was going to be playing it without some serious surgery to glue the cracks back together. If anyone could. "Sorry, Church."

"You never know, computer guys can do incredible stuff with broken tech." The detective folded her arms. "Still say you don't have an account here?"

"Whoever opened this, it wasn't me," Cushman bit out, eyeing the account numbers and box ID as if they'd personally offended him. "Where is that woman with the security footage?" He turned on Myrrh. "And what has her about to get a restraining order? Don't say you know nothing. I *know* that look on a guilty suspect. And she's no felon; you have no legal right to drag her in. Meaning you threatened her some other way."

The hell-raider gazed calmly back. "I merely mentioned that upper management might find her social contacts less than secure for their customers, given a vampiric coven with access to personal items tends to take shameless advantage of the fact to gain more... dietary associates, shall we say?"

"They use leverage to get more people to feed on," Church translated. "Yeah. I know. I just didn't think...." She waved a hand around the bank at large. "Well. Damn."

Aidan watched the agent's carefully neutral face, wondering what was going through his head. If this had been Hell, he might have known; human souls had a hard time hiding thoughts in what was left of their minds. Granted, most of that was a chorus of unending pain, wailing and gnashing of teeth, but it was clear to see. Here on earth, muscle and bone got in the way. It was kind of annoying-

Oh. Bad thought. Very bad.

Aidan gripped the sleeves of his trenchcoat, deliberately not looking at pictures in his head of obsidian carving off skin and flesh to the bloody skull beneath. *You're right here, right now. Daylight. Earth. Nobody's carving anybody up.*

He took a breath, trying to push away bad memories. The air had a taint of something flowery trying to cover ash; no help there. But there was Myrrh's clean scent, like storm and shadows; the fresh soap, sunblock, and gun oil that was Detective Church, and some kind of spicy cologne from Cushman that would probably make a werewolf sneeze before it bit him. Damn it, how could he help Myrrh figure out what was up with this guy if he couldn't even focus?

At least the fig tree made it. Even if they had to trim it. That's something.

Though that didn't surprise him. He might not know what nasty things that go boom had been in the vampires' wards, but he knew Myrrh. If there was any way she could funnel power toward killing the demonic and leaving everything else alone, she would have used it.

"If you can read this, you're too close." Heh. I've got to get her to teach me that one.

Odds were it wouldn't work for him, even if the Father thought demons *were* still angels at the core. Aidan could fry a vampire, one on one, but use his own power to make one go up like a candle just by a brush of celestial energy? Not a chance.

Church shrugged, getting up from the ash-stained table. "Your labs or mine?"

Cushman stared at the disk in its warped sleeve. "The state labs."

"Oh?" Church said, almost neutrally.

"Don't be more annoying than you already are, Detective. I know this looks bad." The agent's teeth brushed his lower lip, before he thinned his mouth into an expressionless line. "I can testify until I'm blue in the face that I've never walked into this building before, yet if the security cameras show someone who looks like me, a jury would believe the video. Not that the situation looks good for you, either, given you were on the scene when Mr. Savonarola's house went up in flames. Along with-" He stopped. Shuddered.

Aidan raised a curious brow. Glanced at Myrrh, who shrugged, equally clueless.

"You two. It's kind of cute." Church shook her head at them both, smile a little pinched around the eyes. "Remember Coral? There are people with cameras everywhere these days. Someone caught Aariel on vid." She turned back to Cushman. "That was what set the fire. Not us. Believe me, there's nothing we could have possibly pulled off that would have done... that."

Aidan almost spoke up. Didn't, when Myrrh's toes tapped his ankle. Because, well, he hadn't gone all out on Earth, he didn't know....

But he had a sinking suspicion he *could* have done that. If he hadn't been half-drowned and near frozen to death.

Everything in this world is so fragile.

"Breathe," Myrrh murmured, too low for human ears to catch. "It's unlikely he'll return unless the Demongate opens."

That's what I'm afraid of.

He didn't know what to feel around Aariel. He didn't know what to think. Demons lied. He *knew* that.

But Aariel had taught him how to stay alive, and arranged events so he'd cross paths with Myrrh. The one power in Hell Aariel knew was merciful enough to protect a half-demon spirit, and powerful enough to keep him in one piece.

And - he knows about hell-raiders. He knew Myrrh had a way out. And if she could....

Aariel might, just might, have arranged his chance to get out of Hell.

God, he didn't know what to do about that.

"It's too soon to do anything about your father," Myrrh murmured. "Breathe. Be. Get used to the living world again. Then, and only then, should you try to determine what you feel about someone so... complicated."

Probably good advice.

A knock, and Gillingham opened the door, laptop in hand. Peering in before she made a move, as if she suspected they'd have Cushman spread-eagled on the table with knives out. Which made him really, really *ticked-*

On the table, a stray deposit slip started smoking.

Church started, and growled. "Aidan. If you set my evidence on fire *I will be very ticked off.*"

Aidan had to huff a laugh, even as Gillingham paled and Cushman swallowed hard. Because that growl felt - okay. Good to hear. Annoyance not prettied up with manners or posturing; just plain old, *we're supposed to be working together, don't screw things up.*

"You - I didn't see any amulets," Cushman said warily. "What did you do?"

Still don't know if he's evil or not. Does it matter? Let's rattle some cages. "Got stressed," Aidan said plainly. "You can download Myrrh's lecture from the department website?" Which was a totally weird idea, being able to have your own videos out there for anyone to grab and see. But it'd help. Or get them arrested. Or both.

"There's a link from the department website," Church corrected him. "We can't risk getting the whole thing slammed by a hacker, so Coral's actually set up the hosting... and you guys have no idea what I'm talking about, do you?"

"You got *stressed?*" Cushman's voice wasn't level anymore. "What is this, some kind of - pyromaniac magic I've never heard of?"

"Hey! Sex has nothing to do with it," Aidan said indignantly. *Unless you count how I inherited it... moving on.* "I don't get it yet myself. Myrrh says I'm a fire mage. So," he had to shrug, "you're not the only guy who's going to need alibis. I'm just going to need 'em for the rest of my life, when fires go up."

Gillingham's hands were shaking so much, she looked ready to drop the laptop. Church glanced between them, and sighed, guiding the manager over to the table before she could hurt herself. "Relax, he's just a big kitty with mean shiny teeth. He wouldn't hurt a fly. Unless the fly asked for it."

"Much more harmless than I am," Myrrh agreed, voice light. "Since so far as I am concerned, you are already *asking for it.*"

"What I do with my life is my business," the manager said through clenched teeth.

"And what I do to protect those in danger after your death is mine," Myrrh replied. "Since I cannot take you to confession or expose you to holy artifacts without being charged with assault, kidnapping, and a host of other crimes, I am forced to resort to more extreme measures to ensure your body will not be corrupted. So if your... bedmate... has proposed eternal life as an option, keep in mind that I have already written your name and pertinent details in letters, to reach hands who will not be constrained by law.

Within three days of your physical death, your body will be removed from its grave, staked, and decapitated." Gray eyes regarded the bank manager, unblinking. "It is the only way, to ensure the seed of the demon does not rise in your corpse."

Aidan nodded; that really was the only way, though cremation might work for some breeds of demon. Not so much some of the Asian ones, they could reform from ashes sometimes if you didn't scatter them on running water....

The room was silent. Why?

"Did... you just...?" Cushman managed.

"Oh? Tell me, what did I just do?" There was an edge in Myrrh's voice, honed sharp as diamond. "At that point in time, Mrs. Gillingham, you will be *dead*. Your soul gone, to wherever it may find harbor. Hopefully in Purgatory. What will remain is your body, with the blood-seed of a vampire within it, feeding on death-energies before it rises with a mockery of your memories. It is," she finished thoughtfully, "a common way for many earth-bound demonic creatures to spread. And some not so demonic; though blood-born terrestrial and fay entities may come into the world innocent, or with ancestral memories they *know* are not theirs. They are, sometimes, capable of repentance, and salvation."

As vampires are not, her silence shouted.

"Mohammedan customs do have that to recommend them," Myrrh mused. "The body is buried the day of death, with only a shroud over it - it does make it easy to access for a Hunter bent on preventing further mayhem."

Aidan breathed in, and reached out to knock knuckles against her black-wrapped shoulder, somehow feeling much better. *Nope, I am not the scariest thing in the room. Cool.* "Ease up a little. She'll find out eventually, right?"

Okay, that was evil, he admitted, as the manager shuddered. *Just - it'd be nice to save somebody. Even if they are an idiot.*

"Did you-" Cushman shook his head, as if he had a hard time believing his ears. "Did you just confess, in front of a detective and a federal agent, to being a *Hunter?*"

"I don't recall having said anything of the sort here, Agent," Myrrh said calmly. "But while I may not yet understand what *viral on the internet* means, as well be hung for a sheep as a lamb. Our local constabulary is horribly undereducated in their means and options for dealing with supernatural felons. This cannot stand." She arched her brows at Cushman. "If you wish to come to the lectures, I'm certain Captain Sherman and her officers would make room."

Cushman narrowed his eyes. "If I came to your lecture, Ms. Shafat, it would probably be to arrest you."

"Miss Shafat." Myrrh's icy smile was back, though more a shadow of dark amusement than the knife she'd pulled on Glover. "And I suggest you mention my name to your superiors, first."

"We need a little more info before we know who's arresting whom," Church stepped in. "Is that the security footage?"

Gillingham swallowed, punching buttons on the weirdly skinny excuse for a computer. "I make a habit of remembering deposit boxes rented by government workers. You never know when you might be hit with a subpoena."

She thinks it really was him, Aidan thought, as the video opened on-screen. *Not looking good for you, Agent.*

A suited man walked up to the tellers' windows on-screen, and things looked much, much worse.

Cushman's lips went thinner, until Aidan thought they might crack and bleed, watching all too clear images of himself speaking with the teller in the camellia-flowered dress, meeting the manager with yet another silk scarf - sapphire and silver-patterned, this time - and finally heading toward the vault door. "That's not me."

"Wish I could believe you," Church said, matter of fact. "If it's not, though... proving that is going to be tricky."

The agent grimaced, hearing truth in her words and not liking it one bit. Took a breath, and whipped out his cell phone. "I'm going to call the county."

"Oh?" Church gave him a skeptical look.

"They can send a deputy. The deputy can take this," he nodded toward the half-melted disk case, "and a copy of *that*," he glared at paused video, "and we'll have chain of custody that won't involve either of us."

"Chain of custody?" Gillingham laughed nervously. "But... it wasn't... I saw you, Agent Cushman! We had a nice discussion about local property rates."

The way Cushman twitched, he was the kind of guy who *would* talk property to a pretty woman. "It wasn't me," he repeated. "And when I find out who it was...."

"I hear Taber Howe takes magical identity theft cases," Aidan offered.

The glare he got should have set him on fire. Seriously, who was the demon here?

"You two." Church pointed toward the front of the bank. "Shoo. Stop teasing the straight crowd." She sighed. "And if you're going to do anything else spooky, how about figuring out how Esmeralda got in here without setting off the alarms?"

"Actually...." Myrrh glanced at Gillingham. "Ed had coffee. Do you have a breakroom?"

"Well, yes," Gillingham stammered. "What does that have to do with anything?"

"Does it have a refrigerator?"

"Ye- no. Well, yes, now." The manager's fingers fumbled against each other. "It went out a few days ago. We had to get a new one delivered."

Aidan blinked, seeing where this was going. "I'm going to guess you're the one who took delivery."

"Well, of course; it's a matter of security for me to check what comes into the bank...." Gillingham's voice died.

Aidan looked at Church, and shrugged. "Big, lightproof box, delivered inside another box. All she'd have to do would be whammy the first person who opened it. Right?"

"Ugh." Church kneaded her forehead with her fingertips. "How do you stop something like that?"

"Well," Myrrh's voice was very dry, "the first line of defense is to ensure thresholds are as strong as possible. Difficult, due to the nature of a business, open to all honest citizens; but not impossible. The second, is to ensure no one charged with security is in a vampire's thrall."

Aidan wasn't sure if Gillingham would melt down or snarl and draw a knife. "You are going down for *harassment-*"

He didn't think, just *moved*, taking Church to the floor as the first shattering reached through the walls. Myrrh he knew was already flat; the agent and manager could look after their damn selves.

Shattering wood. The windows. Fire?

He didn't feel any fire. But there was a twitch of something wrong in the air. And screams.

"Get off me!"

Never argue with a mad lady cop with a gun. Aidan rolled aside and up to his feet, sparks cascading from his fingers before he could rein them in. Spared a glance for Cushman and Gillingham - the agent had had the sense to hit the ground, the manager was still twitching - and ran for the door.

After all, Myrrh was already through it.

Light vanished from her hands as Myrrh stood in the lobby, an island of sunlit stillness amid tellers still screaming behind the counter and the poor security guard calling the cops in a voice two octaves above normal. Gray narrowed, and she was a dark blur, leaping through shattered plywood-

Aidan had to stop, soul recoiling from the angular white-and-brown tangle on the floor. That - that looked too familiar....

Bones. Human bones.

From the ghosts of pain clinging to them, their owner hadn't died a natural death.

Bullet holes in the skull were a big clue, Aidan thought wryly, heading for splintered plywood; one hand ready to surge with fire or dive into his coat for a knife, whatever worked. "Myrrh?"

Myrrh shook her head. "Gone. I couldn't even be sure which vehicle carried our suspect. If any did; though most creatures with ill intent who can fly and carry a skeleton have difficulties with daylight."

"What, no dragons?" Aidan teased, trying to get those shoulders to loosen up. Whoever that poor guy had been, he'd been dead a while. No sense getting worked up until they had a target. "Why the hell would anyone throw old bones at us?"

"Most Western dragons do not fly well, when they wake out of the earth; and most Eastern dragons have better manners." Myrrh ducked through shattered wood to step back inside. "And, I do not know. Yet."

Plywood shards crunched as Church and Cushman joined them. Cushman glanced about, wide-eyed. Church... sighed.

"I swear, I didn't do it," Aidan said swiftly.

"Of course you didn't," the detective said wryly. "That would make this too *easy.*"

Cushman looked from tangled remains shot through with splinters, to shattered plywood now leaking sunlight and a cool October breeze into the lobby. "How is that even possible?"

"Bone can be quite resilient, when touched by the proper magics," Myrrh observed. "I remember one time in the Gobi-"

Church choked. Dropped to her knees by the bones, trying not to disturb any of them. "No way."

"What?" Aidan asked swiftly.

Church held her hand over that shattered skull, as if measuring holes against memory. "I know who this is."

Chapter Three

"Wow. Repeat business." Medical examiner Nick Haley laid out yet another long bone on his steel table, eyeing the head of the joint before deliberately setting it down on the opposite side of the growing skeleton. "Think the cemetery will refund part of the coffin cost?"

"So that is Eddie Colbeck?" Church pounced.

Behind her, Cushman made a noise that had the worst qualities of teeth grinding and a frustrated growl. Myrrh restrained the urge to tisk. The agent was obviously not having a good day.

Cushman gave her a dark look, evidently not approving of her or her flame-haired companion lounging back against the doorway. "He's been dead for ten years!"

"Twelve," Haley corrected, calling up dental x-rays on a monitor off to the side of the tables, plastic over the keyboard to prevent unpleasant infections of the biohazard type. "Yep, that's him. Was pretty sure just by the double-tap, but the teeth are clear. One of the first cases I ever worked," he mused. "Anyone get stuck with the rap? Officially, I mean."

Ah. There went Cushman's teeth again. Myrrh nodded. "Someone means your agency to be angry, Agent. It'd be good to deny them the satisfaction."

"Nobody officially," Church sighed. "Like you don't know who it was unofficially."

"Switch O'Connor," Cushman ground out.

O'Connor? Myrrh raised a brow.

"Any relation to Megan?" Aidan said grimly.

"Her uncle," Church obliged. "Which is why I don't get why this is turning up now. The last thing we need is to go chasing after Switch again, when we know whatever evidence we'll get from this is contaminated as heck...." She trailed off, and cast a sharp blue glance at both of them. "Distraction?"

"Almost certainly," Myrrh agreed. "After all, you did imply they are enemies, did you not?"

"If Switch had one shred of evidence himself, he'd have gone after Steven first," Church said flatly. Twitched. "Oh no. Tell me you're not thinking what I think you're thinking."

"He may be a target," Myrrh stated. "We should, at the very least, inform him someone of the supernatural has taken an interest in his alleged dealings with the dead."

"...I told you not to tell me that...."

Cushman was looking between them as if he wanted to arrest everyone in the room on general principles. "You intend to warn a hitman someone has it out for him. Enough to dig up one of his victims."

"Yes?" Aidan blinked, obviously confused. "Hitman. Kills people he's paid to kill. Right? Because if he did anything else outside the law, you guys would have arrested him for that already."

Cushman's mouth opened; closed again, as he shook his head. "...There is something *wrong* with you."

"Oh, there's plenty wrong with me," Aidan muttered.

"No, there is not," Myrrh stated. Oh, but she wished she might shake it into him by main force. "Where we both were, the Commandments were broken on an hourly basis, and honor was rare and fleeting as a sunset. A man who merely kills for money? Why should we deny him our protection? He is human, and his soul is worth saving. Just as anyone's in this room would be."

A ghost of a smile appeared on her friend's face. "And at least we know he can shoot?"

"It is a valid consideration," Myrrh winked. "After all, those who move through the shadows must be prepared to deal with... what else moves through shadows. Law-abiding citizens being most inclined to wash their hands of the matter, and let the monsters eat them."

"You're working with these two?" Cushman hissed at Church,

obviously believing it quiet enough not to be overheard.

"They kept me from being eaten by werewolves. Kind of makes me biased in their favor," Church allowed. "But seriously. Bad enough you're trying to teach everyone how to stomp on things that go bump, augh, crash in the night. Now you want to mix up with *organized crime?*"

Myrrh glanced at the pepper-haired medical examiner. "Mr. Haley. Which would you prefer? Meeting the man who laid this poor gentleman on your table, or dealing with all new corpses?"

"Honestly? I'd kind of prefer neither," Haley shrugged. "But then, I just deal with the bodies. It's your guys' job to try and make sure they don't end up here."

"An honest answer," Myrrh allowed. "Though I did note, attached inside your morgue drawers...."

Haley shuddered. "Gives me the willies, even though I know the guy who set up the charges. Damn it, there used to be a time you could count on the dead to *stay dead*."

That chilled her. "Then the list of murders must be far longer than anyone suspects," Myrrh said, half to herself. "Twenty-five years ago, coroners in this city all knew of the risks of the unquiet dead, and were supplied by various folk of faith," mostly O'Malley, though Old Man Conseen had ever been quick to descend on Cherokee dead, "with such things as holy oil to daub the deceased upon reception, so to keep unclean spirits from roosting in an untenanted corpse."

The medical examiner whipped around to stare at her, eyes wider than she'd seen yet. "Twenty-five years- you knew that old geezer Perry?"

"I did know Matthew Perry," Myrrh allowed. "What has become of him?"

"He's...." Haley made a circling motion by his temple with one gloved finger. "I mean, everybody knows now vamps are fragile, you can't disturb the body before they rise."

I will not break something. Most especially not an innocent man's fingers.

Still, there was a roaring in her ears, as if a horde of night-demons screeched on the wind. "Again, thank you for your honesty," Myrrh said with scrupulous civility. "For your information, vampiric spirits are far from fragile."

"Ah, Myrrh, maybe not," Church started.

"Medical examiner. Dead bodies," Aidan said bluntly. "Guy deserves to know."

Indeed. "So long as the head and heart remain mostly intact, even if the organs have been removed and then replaced, a vampire will still rise," Myrrh stated. "The only ways to prevent that involve decapitation, impalement, and if possible exposure to both sanctified objects and sunlight." A half-torn wrapper on the desk caught her eye, and she almost smiled. "Wrapping the corpse in a net will no more slow a vampire down to count knots than it would any being bound in a tight grave. Scattering seeds or grain in the grave, or in its path to dissuade it, only halt the demon long enough to drain those bits of life energy. So if you have been keeping those roasted sunflower seeds for an emergency, I must regretfully inform you, you are out of luck. Sprouted alfalfa in your salad would give you a much better chance."

She was beginning to get used to stunned silences. That seemed sad.

"You can stop a vampire with a salad bar?" Church snorted with helpless laughter. "Oh, I have *got* to try that."

"It won't stop them, only distract them," Myrrh warned. "Older vampires are not so easily turned aside from the pulse of living blood." She approached the metal table, close enough to check once more the sense of power she'd detected in helpless bones scattered rudely over the bank lobby. "I do not think a vampire is to blame for this, though."

"Daylight," Cushman muttered.

"Lifestyle choices," Church said dryly. "What are you looking for?"

"Something that feels like graveyards." Aidan wasn't coming any closer to the bones; not that she could blame him, given how much the steel table would hurt. "And... trees? Weird."

"Hmm." Myrrh rubbed at her brow, considering the evidence. "Unfortunately, that does not narrow the number of potential culprits nearly enough."

"Seriously?" Church planted a fist on her hip, one wry glance away from shaking her head. "Graveyards and trees aren't specific enough?"

"Wouldn't be, would they?" Aidan ventured. "Forests and graveyards - those are both places humans run up against powers they can't control."

"And so they spawn, and attract, creatures inimical to mortals," Myrrh agreed. "From the dryads and oreads of Mycenae, to the wodewose of Europe and leshiye of Slavic forests, to the raven-mockers of the Blue Ridges; to the ages past when Azaq the hard-wood tree, king of mountain plants and stones, battled Ninurta in ancient Sumeria in the form of a serpent. Death and forests are entwined, and populated with a host of predators on the unwary. Most of whom are quite skilled in illusions, making it even harder to identify what is trying to kill you." She shrugged. "And those are the older tales. Last I knew, storytellers in these hills still kept alive accounts of the blacksmith of Dalry slaying the white snake of Mote Hill, that devoured the living and grave-laid dead alike."

"A corpse-eating snake." Cushman looked as if his world had been upended, and he clung to sanity by one bent guardrail.

"It is one of the likely culprits, given we have many of Scottish descent in Intrepid," Myrrh noted. "One reason people emigrate is to *flee* monsters. Many creatures find that insulting, and will follow if they can...."

Aidan said nothing at her silence. Only took a step nearer, to touch questioning fingers to her shoulder.

It was unlikely. So unlikely. But something about the bones worried her. "I will need to speak with every holder of lore and leader of faith in the city. Especially those who have immigrated here. This - I cannot be certain. But there is a touch to the aura that feels... not quite like the creatures I last encountered, when I sought evil in Intrepid years before."

"Every one?" Church crossed her arms, as if she weren't sure whether to provide phone numbers or handcuffs. "How do I know you're not going to burn out the local Buddhists?" Her lips pursed, as if she'd tasted spoiled milk. "Not to mention the local Wiccans. Or the *Satanists*."

Myrrh raised startled brows. "Detective. I may have *disagreements* with those who follow the paths of Mahayana, Theravada, or Vajrayana, but those who seek the Four Noble Truths are often good and saintly people in their own right. India is interesting. Or it was several centuries ago...." She shook her head. "It's a slim chance, but they, like many other faiths, have legends of Things that lurk in groves and graveyards. And while the members of a faith often know the best banes for those that hunt them, they are often also its first targets. They should be warned." She shifted her shoulders, willing to admit to distaste. "Wiccans I have dealt with before. We often argue about what defines *harm*, but I do not break pentagrams merely because their owners believe I burned their ancestors at the stake. Though they do sputter when I inform them their holy witch-sign honors the Virgin Mary. And if I can be polite to atheists, I can certainly be so with Satanists. The latter, at the least, should have some concept of what they risk their immortal souls for. And some of them do repent." She grinned. "Especially if you've hauled their spirit out of barbed red-hot chains. There's nothing like *consequences* to make a soul more willing to admit the value of Purgatory."

"Centuries ago?" Haley was looking at her like she'd started clicking on a Geiger counter.

"You can be polite to *Satanists*?" Church muttered.

"Consequences?" Cushman said in disbelief.

Aidan cleared his throat. "What kind of monsters?"

"Yes," Myrrh stated to Haley, "yes, if I must," to the detective, "and yes again," to the agent, "and, like other fay-kin I've mentioned, the kind that make me think it's possible you are innocent, Agent Cushman. But you will have a *very* hard time proving it." She pointed to hapless bones. "Mr. Haley, I suggest you look for two things. Tool marks or teeth marks that indicate the consump-tion of the body after death... and tree roots."

"Tree roots," the medical examiner muttered. "Okay...."

"Tree roots." Agent Cushman dragged a hand across his face, as if today were a nightmare he could simply wipe away. *"Why?"*

Myrrh drew another breath, and shuddered, determined to make sure Detective Church kept some of her spent brass on hand. "Because whether there are tool or teeth marks, or roots, will tell us *how* it prefers to consume its prey. Living, buried, exhumed, or... cooked." She swept them with her gaze. "And with that, we might know what it *is*."

"What it is." Church kept both hands on the wheel as they passed through the trickier parts of downtown. "You say it's fay."

"The aura on the bones seems fay, yes. But it was too faint to identify. The problem is that *fay* is a general term," Myrrh stated, very deliberately. "They are creatures which are Other, sometimes harmful to man, sometimes helpful, and always dangerous."

Like a certain demon-slayer Church could mention. "So if they're fay or demons, does iron work on them, too?"

"It does," Myrrh agreed without nodding, gaze fixed on their passing surroundings as if she could hold off motion sickness by pure will. "The problem is that it may not do enough damage, swiftly enough. Almost every fay has a specific lethal bane, if you can identify it. Redcaps are vulnerable to their own teeth, and elves to church bells, while rakshasas tend to be more vulnerable to panchaloha and brass because of their associations with divine idols. But like werewolves, do enough damage in any fashion, and you will kill them." Shoulders shifted, shadow lapping against her seatbelt. "Part of the difficulty is that *fay* can also refer to those born of mixed human and Other heritage, or even ordinary mortals driven mad by contact with creatures not of this world. Which confuses things considerably for any trying to determine if a halfling is truly the culprit of evil, or just unfortunate enough to be nearby."

Like Aidan. Who was currently borrowing her phone in the backseat, discussing interfaith dialogue with Father Ricci. Or whatever the Church of Our Lady called it when they gave other spiritual leaders a heads-up that there was something nasty in town.

Still not sure she's not going to burn Vajra Hall down, Church thought, driving by the red awning-decked storefront that served as the temple's front door, right by Swamp Fox Books. She'd have to ask the local priest how he felt about sharing the same building with a bookstore that specialized in military history and tactics.

Then again, given Myrrh's own tendencies toward smitation, he might feel just fine.

"Priest Sakai?" Aidan glanced out the window, careful to touch just the plastic of the door handle. "Okay, yeah, we see it. Looks fine to me, not that I'd really know... c'mon, Father, I'm serious. I haven't been - up here, with eyes that could see that, that long. All I know is it looks light."

Good enough, Church thought, and kept driving.

"And... it looks farther away," Aidan observed. "I thought we were stopping?"

"Not until I get a chance to talk to Father O'Malley about who his favorite heretic likes to cast out with fire and sword," Church stated, watching the next light to be sure it'd stay green 'til they got there. Or, well, green-ish. "Father Ricci's going to call around the temples, covens, what have you? Fine. The O'Connors might be in trouble *now*. They've already lost one kid to Steven, I'm not going to let it be two."

"Switch has kids too?" Aidan blinked, not nearly as surprised as most people seemed to be, when it came to hitmen and families.

Then again, half-demon, Church reflected, scooting through a yellow light. *Even something as scary as Aariel has a kid.* "No, the guy's been single as long as I've known about him. His younger brother had two kids. Dennis O'Connor," she filled them in. "Firefighter, and an all-around decent guy. His wife Maeve's a school-teacher. Also a good person... most of the time."

"You'd better just call them, Father, looks like we're going to see a hitman first." Aidan closed her phone. "Oh?"

Yep. Wary fire-mage, there. "I haven't dealt with them much, I could be misreading it," Church admitted, easing back on the engine a little as they ramped up into the thicker traffic crossing the river. "But the times I was there - they're both scared to death something will happen to Dorothy. They get... clingy. Teenagers hate that. Even if there is a good reason."

"Fear can be dangerous," Myrrh observed quietly. "But sometimes, it has good cause, and preserves one's life."

"Yeah," Church sighed, low as the rattle of wheels over the Little Avon River. Aidan was trying to watch the bridge from every direction at once; all that steel couldn't be helping his nerves. "Which is why I'd *really* like to know why Agent Cushman doesn't scare you. You've been gone twenty-five years. What makes you think any of his superiors who knew you are even alive?"

"It would not matter if they are not. I am on file, with the U.S. Marshals and other agencies," Myrrh said gravely. "The government and I have had an agreement for a very long time. They leave me alone, I leave them alone. In return, they have someone they can call upon when the demonic hits the fan."

Oh, Church wanted to hit something. Too bad this was another tricky part of town, pulling away from the bridge into the smaller avenues that would eventually lead to the western outskirts where the O'Connors lived. "The *federal government* knows about demons."

"Certain departments keep the knowledge, yes," Myrrh agreed. "The Secret Service is in the Treasury Department for more reasons than defeating counterfeiting. A nation's coinage is touched by everyone; it must be kept free of demonic taint as much as possible. Or other taints," she allowed. "The fay habit of leaving leaves in place of fifty-dollar bills has ruined many poor and honest cashiers' lives."

Must. Resist. Urge. To pound head on steering wheel. "Am I ever going to have a conversation with you that doesn't veer right into the Twilight Zone?"

Aidan's grin flashed in her rearview.

Cut that off right from the start. "If you start humming the theme, *I will hurt you.*"

"Aww."

"I would very much enjoy having a conversation that does not revolve around the darker aspects of the world, Detective," Myrrh said gravely.

Church flicked her eyes away from the street just long enough to catch the pallor of the hell-raider's face, and tried not to wince. That civility, when she knew Myrrh wanted nothing more than to hang her head out the window and try not to disgrace herself, had to be *costing* her.

"But we have no time. No time," her passenger breathed. "I know not how deep the rot runs. How many have been corrupted, beyond a mere bank manager and all those innocents she has let fall into a vampiric coven's power. Odds are I *will* be arrested, sooner or later. If that chances when the balance falls toward the infernal side, and the Demongate opens...." She took a shallow breath. "You and yours must know everything I can tell you. If I am prevented from striking at the darkness, someone must."

"You could back off," Church pointed out, easing into a turn. "Play it safe. Lie low, while we get everything purified and slam it shut."

"Lady's got a point," Aidan put in. "We could try that. How

long would it take?"

"There's no way of telling," Myrrh said grimly. "Years ago, I could have been certain that quiet good works and a few determined purifications would suffice to put it down. But this Demongate was raised in less than a *year*. They are never built so fast." Breath hissed between her teeth. "We have vampires running downtown clubs, werewolves feeding on human flesh, and fay flinging murdered bones. Evil is not merely stalking the shadows, it's parading down Main Street with a brass band."

Something about the way Myrrh'd said *and fay* made a shiver scrabble down Church's spine. "Um. Forget what I said. Twilight Zone. Gimme."

"Detective...."

"You think there's something worse than fay," Aidan said bluntly. "Spill."

The hell-raider rubbed under the side of her jaw, where a pressure point might help a regular carsick mortal hang on. "The fay - those *other people* - are shapeshifters. Illusionists. Masters of taking any form but their own, and able to convince the most sensible souls into harmful actions with honeyed words. But. So far as I have known them, most fay cannot take *specific* human forms."

"You said it felt like fairies," Church protested. Because damn it, the expert changing her mind was *not fair*.

"I said it felt like the fay. There are many breeds of fay. From weak skirls of fairy wind, to the Queen of Elfland herself, who has been mistaken for a god." Myrrh sighed. "If Agent Cushman is telling the truth, if that was *not* himself under a coercive spell on that video... then it was a creature that could mimic not only his form, but the surface of his thoughts well enough to fool Gillingham into thinking they were indeed the same person."

"You think we've got a Fairy Lord loose in Intrepid," Aidan breathed. "Oh, hell."

"The hell's a Fairy Lord?" Church asked warily.

Myrrh sighed, and tried to straighten her shoulders.

"Just breathe," Aidan advised. "I got this one."

He watched Church just glance at white-lettered street signs, taking a few odd lefts and rights through the spread of Intrepid's western suburbs instead of sticking to the main roads. Giving him time to pull his thoughts together. Decent of her. *Where the heck do I start?*

Well. Maybe where Aariel had started with him. Might get some of the *oh bleep* factor through.

"Hell is... a lot of different places. And layers. Some of 'em are darker than others. Some... less dark, more scare the wits out of you. They'll still eat you, but there's a little less backstabbing." Aidan ran fingers under his shoulderbelt to check his knives were still there. "You see all kinds of people, and all kinds of things. Aariel - gave me a list of things that if I saw them, I should run. Or hide. Do not roll dice, do not argue, do not try to fight. Just get the hell clear, any way I could. Because they'd *swat* me, easy as Yaldabaoth would."

Church's hands clenched on the wheel. "You telling me some fairies are demon lords?"

"No. I'm telling you that sometimes they sit down with each other for tea," Aidan said dryly. "Or blood. Or the tears of their enemies. *Fairies are not nice.*"

"Aidan."

Gentleness. He needed it. "Some of 'em on earth are okay," he allowed. "If you don't cross them. Accidentally or otherwise. But the Fay Lords? You ask the Irish, they'll tell you fairies are the angels who got thrown out of Heaven but weren't bad enough for the other place; the Queen of Elfland dragged True Thomas through blood up to his knees, and pointed out *exactly* where Hell is. Over in Egypt there's guys like Shezmu; maybe a god, maybe a demon, lord of wild parties, wine, and dismembering gods to cook and eat them. Heck, ask souls from the Saravasti about rakshasas, and they'll tell you about asuras; heavenly creatures who got thrown out and decided to go to war with the devas, who are pretty much the good guys, most of the time." Aidan said practically. "So... yeah. Fay Lords may not be demons, but they can be just as nasty."

"Fortunately, an asura's easiest gates open at the base of Mount Meru, and there are usually devas and sages aplenty to rattle their skulls," Myrrh observed. "I might equal a sage. I cannot equal a deva." She rubbed a fingertip over the top of the window glass. "For the others... I can face a Fay Lord, or any otherworldly creature of Egypt or its surrounding lands. My lore for those areas is deep, and my enchantments well-practiced. It may be tricky; it will definitely be dangerous. But we can stand against a Fay Lord, with help."

"Great," Church muttered; coming to a full and legal stop at one of the neighborhood signs, eyeing a few stray teenagers with backpacks until they got themselves out of the road. "So, assuming we've got one...?"

"It'll be hard to track if werewolves have been eating corpses," Aidan reflected. "Their auras taste a little like wind and blood, or sometimes summer bonfires... right, not going to help." *Argh. Think.* "They act classy, but they like to drink. A lot. And party *hard.* Look for the guy who can drink the whole bar under the table and never blink." Hmm, what else. "Most of the really powerful ones are associated with water. Rivers, the ocean, you name it. If one goes under, don't follow it. They can breathe water. Humans - not to mention fire spirits - are going to be in *really big trouble.*"

"Scuba gear," Church muttered, with the air of a detective making a mental note. "That's going to bite."

Aidan sighed. "I hate to say this, Church, but - a lot of them have wind powers? And what is in a scuba tank?"

"...Okay, now I hate you."

"The big problem is they're really good at fooling your

senses." He had to stop right there, because this was Earth, and oh man.... Aidan shuddered. "And this is why Aariel said *run*, because believe me. Anything that can pull that off in Hell, where everything *including your senses* is spirit? That is bad, bad news, of the epic kind. Usually only someone like Yaldabaoth can work that kind of weird. Even *Aariel* can't weave mind-tricks that good." And when Yaldabaoth had... his hand reached under his coat, feeling for braided hair.

"Okay, what is with that?" the detective grumped. "I can see it's Myrrh's, but...." A swift inhalation. "Wait. Wait, you *came out of Hell* wearing that...."

"It is part of my spirit, freely given to one who is my friend," Myrrh said quietly. "And as it is a substance of spirit, yet not linked to Aidan's own soul through his mind, it is one thing illusion can never touch."

"Like I said," Aidan managed. "Yaldabaoth can spin illusions in Hell, too. I needed... I needed something *real*." He leaned back against the seat. "Really wish I could give you a better idea what we're up against. Didn't see many fay in Hell; not that I knew were fay. Though I saw an asura for sure, once."

"Asura." Church scowled, turning back onto one of the more-traveled roads, passing an auditorium-sized tan building that had a small green sign marking it as the local polling place. "That's the Indian version, right?"

"Kinda. Sorta. Close enough?" Aidan shrugged. "He had ten heads, ten arms, and a ruby in his navel. Skirt kind of thing in crimson silk - Aariel called it a *dhoti* - and enough gold anklets to weigh down an elephant. His hair was all braided up into a top-knot, and when he moved... it was like lightning flashing."

"...Sounds kind of hard to miss," Church said at last.

"Yeah, but that was in Hell," Aidan said soberly. "Things look different down there. Vampire demons are a mummy twisted into a mosquito. Aariel... well, he didn't change much, but how much was fire and how much was lion shifted around a lot. Heck, I was a ball of marsh gas. The only thing I ever ran into down there that looks the same up here...."

Taking a deep breath of the breeze, Myrrh smiled. "Well, I am a mortal soul. Appearances can be deceiving." She sobered. "And deception is the strongest power of the fay. The Western term is *glamour*. Though it has many names. Eagleman might know it from the Cherokees' tales of spells, and twists in reality. Creations of magic that are but mist and moonlight, yet real enough to touch while they exist. An ordinary illusion of a horse may seem to brush bushes aside, but if you look, they have not been bent, and there are no hoofprints. A glamour leaves both."

"Not just that," Aidan added. "Scent. Taste. Touch. Even down to where you feel you are in the world. If a strong fay grabs onto you and drags you into the water, you might drown right there - *even though the water's not real.*"

Church flinched.

"Indeed." Myrrh frowned. "I can see through fay glamours. But that has its own perils."

"Of course it does," Church muttered. Slowed down a little while a mailtruck pulled off to the side of the road, waiting for a chrome-laden black pickup to pass going the other direction before she pulled around it. "So how does a cop fight these things?"

"Get away from them," Aidan said firmly. "That's what Aariel always told me. You have to be close for them to whammy you. If they don't have a grip on you - they can layer whatever glamour they like on themselves, but they can't trap you in your own head." He shuddered. "And if you can't run far enough, run for a crowd. Glamour's not easy, and it has to fool *everyone* looking at it, or it goes poof. The more eyes you have on it, the harder they have to work to keep it up. I think... ten or so people?"

"Ten or so demons who are not minor, or humans strong in faith, would do," Myrrh agreed. "More for minds less skilled in meditation." A deliberate breath. "I agree on the range. Fay Lords have been slain by arrows, in the past."

"Arrows, huh?" Church glanced at both of them. "What's their opinion on cold lead?"

"I should like to find out," Myrrh mused. "One reason churches oft need new roofs, is that desperate Hunters have stolen the lead for their bullets."

"Fire works if you can get it in somewhere tender," Aidan added.

"Somewhere? Be specific," Church grumbled. "What kind of somewhere?"

"Um... wish I could?" Aidan shrugged. "They like to shapeshift to fight. But get a whole lot of flame inside whatever they are, they're going to have a really bad day."

"Lead and flamethrowers." Church was definitely not happy. "You don't need cops, you need the National Guard. And a few bazookas."

"That is the usual way humans have dealt with Fay Lords in the past," Myrrh agreed.

Church choked. "What, seriously?"

"Seriously," Aidan said flatly. "You've got to hit them with a mountain to get them to pay attention. That, or-" He sat up, banging against the strap. "Church? Fay - they're all about power. Fire, water, night, day; the works. That's the kind of thing they have power over, and that's what they have power to block. If you ever get in deep with a fairy, grab for something that's *not either*. Like... a shadow."

Church sighed. "Aidan. People can't grab shadows."

"No, but we can move them, with bright enough light," Myrrh noted. "And there are other liminal objects we can use. You know the myths of Cú Chulainn, the geasa that bound him, and ultimately slew him. The fay in other lands are similar. Aidan mentioned the asura; they, too, are vulnerable to such things. Indra, it is said, was bound by oath not to harm the asura Vritra with stone, wood, or steel; not to assault him with anything dry or wet; not to strike by day or night."

Church snorted. "Oh, I see where this is going."

"Ah, but this is a land of the Celts. Of course you do," Myrrh grinned. "Indra drowned him with seafoam, at twilight."

Church chewed that over through the next light, turning onto yet another side street that wove through the neat-trimmed grass frontyards of small family houses. "If anyone says I should wear a fishnet dress and stomp around with one leg over a mule and the other on the ground, I vote we throw him at the fairy first." A *hmph*. "You realize I'm getting you two to write all this down later. No matter how many notes I've got to wade through, it's better than being the referee with you two supernatural shuttle-cocks flying back and forth. How long have you two been partners?"

"Uh." That took Aidan aback, more than *half-demon* ever could. Partners? Partners meant you trusted somebody. You didn't trust *anybody* in Hell. Rule of survival.

But Myrrh didn't follow the rules. She'd been... well. Down there of her own choice, if not her own will. She knew exactly why she was in Hell, exactly what she planned to do to get out, and outside of that....

Faith. She had faith. Like wandering through a dark cave, and finally catching a breath of green-touched air. Just - scarier.

Yeah, well, most people lost in a cave don't know the sun can scorch them dead.

He didn't know what to say. He didn't want to hurt Myrrh, he never wanted to hurt her, but *partners* and *trust* made raw nerves scream. He didn't think Church meant to hurt him, hurt them, but-

"That is not a fair question, Detective." Myrrh's fingers pressed under her ear again, as she swallowed dryly. "Aidan was ever aware that by foul mischance or deliberate plot he might fall back into Steven's power. How could he dare to trust me when he could not trust himself? We have been comrades; we have shared dangers. It is enough."

"Let's hope so." Church glanced along the side of the road;

checking house numbers, Aidan realized. "Here we are."

Trimmed lawn, browning with autumn. Brick planters full of something like marigolds, and mulched with bright autumn leaves, catching the afternoon sun. The gray car in the driveway - Aidan had no clue how old it was, new models all looked weird to him, but polished scratches in the paint around the driver's side door hinted a few years, at least.

"Good, they must be back from school." Church pulled in beside the family car. "Now *behave*. They're not cops. They're a family who've had a terrible loss, and one detective showing up on their doorstep is going to wreck their day enough already. Be gentle. We can tell them trouble might come looking for them, but they're not the target. Switch is. They're on people's evil lists because of what Switch does, and Maeve *hates* it. Dennis...." She whistled. "I don't know about Dennis. He won't talk to his brother outside of a Christmas mass, from what I've heard. But Switch knows what happens here. And Maeve knows that, and knows if we come here it's because we want Switch to know about it, and this is going to be one big mess."

Myrrh launched herself out the passenger door and stood a moment, breathing. "We will try not to frighten them."

Church flicked a glance at both of them, but didn't push it.

Just as well, Aidan thought. *I'm going to try. I really am. But I don't know what scares people. Not anymore.*

Not when it took everything he had to turn his back on a planter full of autumn-dying flowers. Because... God. The places in Hell he'd hung out were *full* of life. Nasty, snarling, toothy life; always aggressive, almost always venomous, but alive. If something was dying in Hell... it wasn't anything as innocent as fall frosts. It was a demon draining things dry. Or a trap.

Just because I don't feel anything malevolent over there, doesn't mean there is something there.

Which was when the paranoid hairs on the back of his neck reminded him about fay, and glamours, and *augh*.

"I am so glad I'm the one with the gun," Church muttered. "Myrrh, grab him." The detective gave him an oddly sympathetic look. "Take it easy, okay? This is a firefighter's family. They're not going to take random sparks in stride."

Aidan spread empty hands; *right, right, we get it.*

Church sighed, heading around the car toward the front door. "Why did I volunteer for this again?"

"Because you are a good and decent soul, and someone has to," Myrrh observed. "And with us along, the odds are better than average you will get to shoot what annoys you."

The detective sputtered. "That's- you-!"

"I know." Myrrh heaved a sigh. "I am a terrible sinner, teasing an honest officer of the law. Perhaps I will learn better. In a few more centuries."

"Or not," Aidan murmured under his breath. "Universe would be too dull if you behaved."

...Yeah. A there-and-gone smile, like a flash of sun through clouds. That was definitely worth it.

Church hit the black-metal doorbell by the front door, listening for the chime.

Footsteps inside, Aidan noted, half-closing his eyes to listen harder. *Quick, light. Stopping for a second....*

There was a tiny round lens set in the door, about eye height. For a moment, it darkened.

Hah. Someone's got enough sense to check the spyhole before she opens the door.

Aariel would have stabbed through the panels, to teach an incautious student that such casual thoughts of security were woefully unprepared. Ow.

"Who's there?"

Aidan blinked, putting together *quick and light* with *young aura.* A kid?

"Detective Church." Church lifted her ID to the spyhole. "Dorothy? I need to talk to your parents. It's about an old case.

And a new one."

"It's *Dorren*," came the sullen snap.

No it's not. Aidan straightened, curious. *But... it could be? Weird. Have to ask Myrrh about that, later.*

"Hang on," grumped through the door. "*Mom!*"

The suited redhead who opened the door blinked at them, blue eyes shadowed with worry. "Detective Church." Her gaze flicked past to the two improbable people behind her. "And who are you?"

A quick glance told him Myrrh had smoothed her shadow-shift into a regular jeans and coat combo, fine for a light autumn day. She still had sandals, though.

"Myrrh Shafat," Myrrh nodded. "My companion and I are assisting the detective with... research into methods of self-defense. She asked our opinion on what might be beneficial in your case. May we come in?"

Behind the door, Aidan heard a breath sucked in, before light feet scampered.

Somebody didn't like that. Wonder why? Aidan nodded to the lady of the house, wishing he had a hat to take off. "Aidan Lindisfarne. Nice to meet you, Mrs. O'Connor."

"In our case?" Maeve's breath quickened. "Is this about Megan?"

"Not exactly," Church admitted. "Mind if we discuss this inside? It's complicated."

"If it's not about Megan, then why are you... oh." Her voice went flat, unwelcoming. "Of course." She stepped out of the way, eyes creased and angry. "Please come in."

Church went first. Aidan let Myrrh follow, a little hesitant to step over that very unfriendly lintel. Aariel had been clear a demon couldn't enter a household without an invitation. He'd also been clear that a strong enough demon just smashed the house into toothpicks, at which point the threshold became kind of moot.

And I got into Steven's house all right. Then again, he wanted us there.

The lintel chilled him, a gust of winter wind. But he was still in one piece.

This place feels... lost.

It wasn't anything Aidan could put a finger on. It looked like a regular house; tile floor, a bunch of tied rag rugs scattered around in calm and cheerful blues, whites, and sparkles of other bright colors. A small dining room table with homework splayed out at what had to be Dorothy's place, and warm cinnamon wafting around the corner from the kitchen. Buns, he'd bet his coat on it, and they smelled melt-in-your-mouth wonderful.

But there's an empty spot at the table. And it hurts.

Right across from Dorothy's schoolbooks. Not a scrap of paper or vase of flowers encroached upon it. One empty chair, forlorn as a cave strewn with bones.

Her parents are making her face... that. Every day.

All of a sudden, he wanted to hit something.

Come to think, where is the kid?

A flicker of motion caught his eye; Myrrh's white hair, glimmering in a mirror set like a framed photo atop a low bookshelf by the end of the table.

That is a really weird place to put a mirror.

It wasn't the only one. There was a compact open at Dorothy's place, glinting light over her textbooks. Someone's old car door mirror, resting by a tank full of guppies like a trophy from a successful kill. A little wood jewelry-box with a mirrored inside lid, right over the cold fireplace full of half-burned wood.

Huh. Subtle, but if you know what you're looking at, you can always catch a glimpse of everything here - oh. Oh, somebody's smart. Or paranoid. Or both.

Myrrh's gaze flickered over the various bits of shiny, and she nodded. Gave him a look, but stayed silent, waiting for Church to take the lead-

"We don't have anything to do with my brother-in-law. You know that," Maeve cut the detective off. "Whatever he's done, whatever trouble he's brought down on his own head, it's none of our business. You're wasting your time."

"Then I'll waste it." Church leveled a serious look at the woman. "Mrs. O'Connor. I know you don't like it, but everyone who's anyone on the wrong side of the street knows Jim O'Connor takes family seriously. Now, most of them take that as a warning to back off and leave you alone-"

"Oh god!" Maeve slumped into a wooden chair, covering her face with her hands. "What has that monster done now?"

Speaking as one of the monsters, Aidan had to step in and say hey. "Ma'am, believe it or not, for once the guy looks innocent."

The look she cast him was withering. Or, well, it was probably meant to be. Given he'd run into actual withering looks wielded by various famine-demons these past few years, it was more moderately annoyed.

Not to mention a gorgon. Whee, that was fun.... Bad fire-mage. People don't like that kind of getting stoned.

"Mr. Lindisfarne's telling the truth, Mrs. O'Connor," Church said calmly. Practiced calm, almost hiding the aura of *argh, civilians.* "This isn't something Jim-"

"Switch," Maeve bit out. "He runs with that crowd, he can have that name. He's Switch. Not Dennis' brother."

That caught Myrrh's attention. Aidan noted that, and her deliberate silence, and knew those names were important. *Someone she met before? Twenty-five years. They would've been just... kids. Oh.*

Heh. And another kid was trying to soft-step her way up behind them, never knowing *Myrrh* could probably hear her every move, much less Aidan.

Points for trying? Can't blame the kid for wanting to find out about her uncle, even if he is on the wrong side of the law. Maybe especially if he is.

"Someone wants to drag the police department and the FBI into looking at a case associated with your- with Switch O'Connor,"

Church persisted. "Whoever it was, was definitely supernatural. They might not be afraid of Switch's reputation. I'm coming here as a courtesy, Ma'am, to let you know you might want to lock your doors after dark-"

Maeve's eyes widened; she drew in a breath.

Argh, the kid's going to get herself caught. Sighing, he turned-

Holy shit what the fu-

He'd blinked. Thankfully.

It was the only thing Aidan was thankful for, as the whole world froze and *burned*.

Don't kill the kid, don't fry the house, don't stab anyone! She's a kid, she's scared, not her fault-

Myrrh's hands on his shoulders, pulling him out and away from the table. "Eyes closed! Keep them closed! Church, *corral* that girl!"

Don't hurt her, Aidan wanted to say; but holding back the fire took everything, and he was *not* going to burn a young, inventive kid who'd horribly underestimated what she'd just picked a fight with. *She's smart, she knew something was wrong... what'd she see in the mirrors?*

He wasn't sure he wanted to know.

More steel, don't-!

Water splashed over him.

At least the kitchen sink is large enough, Myrrh thought grimly, swiping a blue-and-white checked dishtowel so Aidan could lean on the steel edge of the basin without getting burned. More.

Iron filings. Myrrh bit back useless curses, shoving away the tongue of her birth for words denizens of this house might understand. "Then the man of God said, "Where did it fall?" And when he showed him the place, he cut off a stick and threw it in there, and made the iron float."

Water sparkled as she scooped it over Aidan's face and throat, diamond-white power drawing iron from seared skin to flow away with it. Her friend's fingers clenched on patterned cloth, white-knuckled; heat brushed against her skin.

But nothing is on fire. He knows who hurt him. And - he is in control. Even in great pain. "It will stop," Myrrh murmured, heart proud. "I promise, it will soon ease."

"What did you just do?" Maeve's voice rose, she was moving-

Cloth thumped on muscle, as Church stood between mother and daughter. "Something very brave, and very, very stupid," the detective stated. "Dorren. I'm not sure what you think's going on here, but Aidan's one of the good guys. He saved my life."

"So?" The young woman's voice shook; Myrrh felt fear pour off her, and knew Aidan must taste it like tar. "I'm supposed to believe the cops are the good guys? You can't even find who killed Megan!"

"Dorothy!"

"It's what you say! You and Dad both! And Uncle Jim is trying to find him, he's *trying*, and you won't even let him call me-"

"Both of you, shut up, *right now*," Church growled. "Or I'm going to bring all of you in for *assault*." A heavy foot stomped. "Myrrh! Do we need an ambulance?"

"No," Aidan managed, barely opening his eyes; face blistered, lips puffy with reaction to lethal metal. "Oh *man* that hurts." He bent his head again, so Myrrh could splash him thoroughly. "Think you got it. Oooow...." He coughed. "How long did you say it takes to stop being sensitive to that stuff, again?"

"I honestly cannot say," Myrrh admitted. "Many of my comrades had more than a trace of supernatural heritage, but yours is the most extreme." There simply weren't any half-demon hell-raiders. "It's possible you never will. Though the effects should lessen with time."

"Man, I hope so." Aidan leaned on her shoulder, turning toward the white-faced teenager. "That? Good call. Except you didn't have a backup plan. Like *running*."

No idiot, the redheaded teenager backed up, almost into Church. Maeve stood nerveless to one side, swallowing her gorge as she looked at a human face, blistered by mere iron.

"See, most things you can hit with iron, you need to stab them to take them out," Aidan went on. "Hit a fay or a demon with iron filings, it's like spraying a rapist with mace. You'll hurt them. *And then they're going to be mad*." He swiped a little water off. "Also, aim better for the eyes next time. The throat hurts, like someone stuck a brand to your skin. But unless you're willing to pick up a blade and go for the carotid, it's not fatal." A blistered smile. "Trust me, there's nothing like cold iron in the eyes to give a demon a *really bad day*. In the mouth's no fun either. Plus, if it turns out you're wrong... well, even a vamp's not immune to fine scratchy stuff straight in the blinkers." He coughed, and wiped away blood. "Neither are ordinary muggers. Guess those are still a problem."

Church sighed.

"A fay or a-" Maeve's throat worked; she grabbed blindly for a chair. "What are you?"

"Not a fairy," Aidan smirked.

Myrrh poked him in the shoulder, careful to avoid healing skin. "Aidan is a true friend and ally. I would take his advice seriously-"

"Vicious, smart, and fast," Aidan mused, almost twinkling at Dorren. "Isn't she cute?"

"-But not the frivolity," Myrrh said wryly. Not that she thought he was trying to flirt; they hadn't changed the age of consent in twenty-five years, and Aidan hadn't been back on the mortal plane long enough for a body to search after more options than mere survival. But her friend had to get used to humanity all over again, and most humans were less than sympathetic to the demonic reaction of, *aww, it tried to kill me when it didn't stand a chance, how sweet*.

"Frivolity?" Aidan rubbed a hand across his face; hissed, and let it fall again. "Who's trying to be funny? She saw a threat and went for it. Like a kitten trying to pounce Mama Lion's tail."

A red flush spread over Dorren's face, almost hiding her freckles. "I'm not- you-!"

"Oops." Aidan sighed. "Right. Guess my handle on 'that's so precious' is kind of skewed...." He blinked at the detective. "You didn't think she was cute?"

Church clapped a hand to her face. "Can I just pretend I don't know you?"

"I don't understand," Maeve stammered, reaching out for her daughter. "What happened, we ought to call a hospital... Dorothy, what did you *do?*"

The teenager shifted her balance, just enough to stay out of her mother's grasp. "I hit him with iron filings."

Ah. The defiance of one who'd been speaking to deaf ears. Worse, of one still called child who'd proven herself more right than her parents. This was going to be a mess.

"Next time, aim better," Aidan said practically, voice weary. "Might want to add in a bunch of powdered rust, too. That'll stick more on things used to sucking in energy and blood."

Myrrh tapped his shoulder. "I think we've shocked the lady enough," she murmured. "Give her a moment to breathe." She cleared her throat, and raised her voice to address the youngster. "Iron is not a bane of werewolves. Nor of vampires; the corpse protects them against most contact. How did you know to use it?"

Dorren almost spoke, gaze flickering around the room; then mulishly closed her mouth.

"The mirrors," Church realized. "You saw something in... damn, that's *smart*. Not that assaulting someone with a police officer is ever smart, but-"

The teen's fists clenched. "I didn't think he was real!"

"Not this again," Maeve said faintly. "Dorothy-"

"You didn't see it! You *never* see it! But - in the mirror - he stepped into the house and he wasn't there! Just, I...." She sniffled, and dragged in a breath to hold back tears.

"As it happens, she is correct." Myrrh focused on Maeve. "For a heartbeat, Aidan would not have appeared as himself in the mirror; for your threshold is hostile, and he is still uncertain of his safety among his fellow men." She glanced at Dorren. "You did not think Aidan was real. Have you seen other illusions? And how did you know iron might break one?"

Dorren's gaze flicked to her mother. Maeve bridled.

Which was apparently all a rebellious teen needed. "Uncle Jim got me a university library card. Maybe they stripped vampire slayer movies off the shelves, but they didn't go after musty old books in the basement. I know a *lot*."

And yet, not enough. "Keightley, or Evans-Wentz?" Myrrh hazarded. "I hope you did not wholly rely on Briggs. Her interpretations are a bit... generous in imputing human motives to those who are fay."

Dorren gaped. "You - but - nobody reads those anymore...."

Myrrh smiled. "I do. More than you know, do. And soon others will, as well."

"You two can compare assigned readings later," Church stated. "And you'd better add those to the bane lecture list. With notes." The detective set her shoulders, and met Maeve's disbelieving gaze. "Ma'am, someone supernatural dug up one of Switch's old bodies. We don't know why, we don't yet know who. But I can give you solid proof something wants us rattling Switch's cage. Which means if people here think they've been seeing things that aren't there, I want to know about it. Because they darn well *could have been there*, with magic."

"I... didn't see most of them here." Dorren pointed out the back of the house, paling. "They were - they mostly show up when I'm walking in the woods...."

"Out in the woods," Church sighed, resigned. "What was that you were saying, about forest fairies and illusions?"

"There are times I hate being right," Myrrh admitted. "Mrs.

O'Connor. Would you happen to have a cold iron knife?"

~*~*~*~*~

Church regarded the little egg-pan in her hand, and tried not to groan.

"At least she had something?" Aidan's gaze swept the woods, from frost-brittle brambles and fallen leaves up to the thinnest gold-leaved branches, and back. His face looked a lot better even these few minutes later; Church had to pinch herself, recalling red blisters cracking Aidan's skin in a half-dozen places. "From what I've seen, stainless steel is in, most places."

Dorren was in the middle of the three of them, clinging closer to Myrrh than Church would have expected. Then again, book fiends tended to stick together. "I don't get it," Dorren muttered. "You're not human, but a cop thinks you're one of the good guys?"

"Define human," Aidan quipped back. "Ask Church to show you the graveyard we pulled her butt out of a couple days back. There's plenty scarier things out there than I am." He jerked his thumb at Myrrh. "Like her. She *is* human."

"Humans with access to accurate lore are the most frightening creatures on the planet," Myrrh agreed, voice quiet. "Keep your voice down, and watch your step. I smell... burnt turmeric."

"...Damn," Aidan breathed.

Church sniffed, picking up the faintest traces of something that reminded her of an Indian restaurant. Out in the woods? Uh-oh.

"So... somebody had Indian takeout?" Dorren's eyes jumped to Church, wide and scared. "I mean, we've had homeless guys camp out here before...."

"Possible. Turmeric would not be in Western books of fay lore," Myrrh said quietly. "Not under that name. *Indian saffron*; that would be what you would have read. It does not have the curative power of true saffron, but it can still be used to ward off ghosts and unquiet spirits."

"Yeah, and I was thinking we wanted unquiet spirits warded off...." Church trailed off, putting the pieces together.

Myrrh thinks we're hunting fairies. Who eat people. And what's every spooky story out there agree on what makes ghosts? Really bloody death.

And Dorren had looked *shifty-*

Ha. Of course she did. Not in the books, sure. Smart kid like Dorren? Odds she didn't *search for "Indian saffron" when it popped up?*

Church gripped the pan in her off hand, and wondered if her gun had enough iron to make any difference. "You think we might have a kill site." She glanced at the hapless teenager they'd dragged with them; the girl who'd evidently tried to drive off evil, the way she'd slapped Aidan with iron-water. Meaning she might have just made it *mad.* "Kid. I think you should go home."

"If fay are in these woods, she would never make it there in one piece," Myrrh stated, very quietly. "Thresholds provide some measure of protection, if creatures are not invited in. There are none here."

Dorren shivered, and shoved her hands in her vest pockets, obviously feeling at whatever she'd stuck in there before they left. "You think... what I'm seeing is real. Why?"

Church grimaced. The way she'd glanced back toward where her clinging, desperate mother was on the phone to the firehouse, Dorren didn't mean anything as simple as, *why do you believe me?*

Why is this happening to us? Why now? We lost my sister - why is more darkness crashing down on our heads? What did we ever do?

Right. Like it was ever what someone *did* that landed vicious bastards, supernatural or otherwise, at their door.

...And they really ought to send Dorren back. Church hadn't come this way during the investigation, but she'd seen enough of mossy granite and leaf-rattling trees to have a grim sense of familiarity. "Tell me you haven't been coming out here."

"It's where they *found* my *sister*." Green eyes sparked defiance. "Why shouldn't I come out here?"

Outside of the fact that if Maeve had any clue her surviving daughter was haunting the crime scene, she'd have every reason to freak out? Hah. "Body dump site," Church said tersely to her two slayers of all things evil or irredeemably cranky. "Corpse-eaters or tree-hugger monsters?"

"And there were in Israel eight hundred thousand valiant men who drew the sword," Myrrh murmured, light coalescing in her grip. "And the men of Judah were five hundred thousand...."

Dorren was staring. Church didn't take the time, gun drawn and pointed down until she had a target. Hell, down might even be the right *direction*.

"Don't hear anything," Aidan murmured, almost too low to pick out. "Don't smell anything but... leaves. Wood. Old blood."

Great. Just great. "Okay," Church breathed, flicking her glance to Dorren. "Which way from here?"

The girl started forward; Myrrh caught her by the arm, shook her head *no*. "We are armed. Stay between us."

Which, Church was sadly not surprised, made the teenager bridle with incipient, "nobody tells *me* what to do!"

Only the average not-parental stranger didn't grip a glowing shaft of sunlight in pale hands, casting a grim light over Myrrh's steady stare. Dorren fumed, but swallowed, and gestured around the next maple.

Okay. Here we go-

Church skidded on leaf litter, staring at odd, spread-out holes in the dirt where a ravaged body had once lain. The last time she'd seen something like this, Tom had gone berserk on a nest of green-briar, wielding spade and shovel to dig up what'd turned out to be twenty pounds of mahogany-skinned tubers woven in, around, and through a chain-link fence.

Holes, dry and ragged. Like someone had... yanked something

up by the roots?

"Where are the trees?" Dorren whispered, creeping around the maple with Aidan and Myrrh flanking her. Her sneakers scuffed; Church's nose twitched at the hint of musty leaves. "There were a bunch of little trees here, who would- this isn't right!"

"Little trees?" Gray eyes narrowed, as Myrrh advanced on torn ground as if it were mined.

Might well be, Church thought sourly. *What the hell does a forest fay do?*

Not that this was any place to ask, not if something might be stalking them-

Limbs groaned above her head. The detective grimaced. *Whatever we're looking for, we'd better find it quick. I don't want to be out here if a storm comes up.*

Though it hadn't looked like a storm, earlier....

Light. Light where there should be none. Wind whispered of it. Earth groaned of it.

Caution, blood-memories whispered. *Sky-light. Iron-smell. The foreign jewel in the lotus.*

Dangerous. And deadly. More deadly, whispered seed-memory, than even the taint of iron or seared scent of old fire.

Too dangerous for a seedling. Retreat. Choose another prey.

But growing took so much more than sun and old flesh, and it was hungry. And there were footsteps that were not deadly.

Stealthily, it reached through soil and air. Just a little closer....

Think I'm going to go nuts, Aidan huffed a breath of leaves, leaves, and more leaves. And old blood. *Do I not see anything, or do I just* think *I don't see anything?*

He didn't like feeling blind. He hadn't been this unsure of what he saw since the last time Aariel had broken him out of Yaldbaoth's illusions, and he *did not like it.*

I'm not all the way blind, he reminded himself. *I can see the lights. Myrrh's moonlight; Church, a scattering of stars. Dorren... she's not bright, not focused; moon on misty water, she's not a bad kid....*

Moon-and-stars; human lives here. Sleepy green-and-brown; trees and insects and mice scampering through leaf-duff getting ready for winter. A warm dark red, like banked coals, seeping through the ground for more fuel-

Dorren squeaked.

There and there and - oh hell, how many of them are there-?

Aidan snarled, sparks arcing from a slash of his hand to sear roots dragging him under. The problem with forests was they were *flammable.*

Fight now, put the fire out later....

Light sang and chopped; a green limb cracked with a scream, red sap oozing thinner than blood. Church was shoving an egg-pan into the gaping maw of a knot with snapping teeth, trying to get the best angle to fire at a humanoid shape writhing out of bark and wood. Dorren-

She can't scream.

Bark-twigged fingers had her by the throat, as something that was and wasn't part of a maple smirked at them with nut-ivory teeth. And trilled, a language of purred r's and what sounded like a lot of lips and teeth playing with the air.

I feel like I should know that. Why?

Myrrh blinked, and *hmph*ed. "It's hard," she stabbed a thick root, "to threaten your opponents with your hostage," a foot stomp-ed a reaching branch, causing it to recoil, "if they can't understand a word you're saying, child of the dark forests!"

"I understand *hostage*," Church snarled. "Cover me!"

That, Aidan could do; wreathing flames around her to knock

back reaching branches, searing roots before they snared her steps.

But the fay only shifted Dorren closer to it - to her? - embracing the girl like a courtesan would an unwilling young man. "Tell the singer." The voice was breathy, leaves in the wind. "Tell her, put away the light."

"Is that all?" Myrrh wondered, light never dimming in her hands, as she shifted the blade from right to left. "Detective. *Heartwood.*"

Church's aura flared, stars coalescing into one bright point as bullets took wood straight in the throat. The fay *screamed*, flinging Dorren straight at fire-

Damp it!

Aidan grabbed her through dying flames, taking the strike of a heavy limb on his shoulder rather than her head. Oh damn, that *hurt.*

Gunfire. A singing light. He wrapped fire around them both and waited for the screaming to stop.

Church was breathing hard, changing out a clip as Myrrh stabbed light through a thicker pile of splinters. "Oh man. Oh, not fun. Oh, what the hell was that...."

"A forest fay. What sort, I am uncertain. I am not familiar with that tongue." Myrrh glanced over charred and shattered trees. "From the looks of the ground, there should have been more rooted here."

"...Of course there were," Church groaned. "I need to put out an APB on *walking trees?*"

Myrrh let the blade of light fade, walking over to crouch beside them under Aidan's still-sizzling shield of flames. "Dorren. You are alive." She smiled. "And you were right."

Dorren blinked, face smeared with ashes. "...Wow."

"Wow?" Aidan muttered, eyeing how Dorren... *brightened* as she got to her feet, fear and fury unfolding into terrified wonder. Though better that than paralyzed terror. "Whatever books you're into, kid, let me at them."

Church cleared her throat. "Guys. People. Unknown beings I sometimes wish I'd never met." She swept a hand across the newly-seared clearing, toward crackles in leaf duff. "Can we save the demon-slaying lessons for when the forest's not *on fire?*"

"Oops," Aidan said sheepishly.

"Aw, man." Dorren's shoulders drooped, watching spreading flames. "Dad's going to *kill* me...."

"Fire! The outsider asura-blood has fire!"

It whipped through leaves in the wind; rustled through brambles; crept and crawled through roots and burrows. Flame - flame was the *enemy*, to those born of branch and blood. It might sear away rival grasses so seeds might sprout, or feed succulent ashes back to the earth, but for saplings barely tall enough to tear up roots and walk? It was disaster. Destruction. *Death.*

"Swarm the fire-blood! Mob it, trample it to dusty death-!"

"Go ahead," older limbs creaked. *"As we feed on the bloodied earth, he feeds on fire. Look."*

The outsider's aura was stronger, pulsing with each indrawn breath of heat. Even as crackling stilled, overwhelmed by wailing sirens and booted men dragging out hoses, the outsider stood hale and whole as if he'd never been brushed by iron. Add that to the gun-wielding cop, the terrible bright she-sage, the sheer numbers of mortals arriving....

Leaves stilled, and roots shuffled away.

"Church." On the other end of the line, Captain Sherman heaved a heartfelt sigh. "What is going on?"

Watching Aidan wave his hands at the firemen, describing how flames had gone *poof, don't worry, we're good*, the detective winced. "Well... on the bright side, we found out part of what Steven was using the body dump sites for?"

"There are reports of wildfire. And *gunfire*. Behind the O'Connor house."

"At the secondary crime scene," Church clarified. "And yes. Yes, we had to start shooting. And - other things."

Something thumped on the captain's desk. Sounded like tired feet. "I told you to stick with them to *cut down* on the fires."

"Would it help if I said the trees started it?"

"Trees."

"Myrrh says forest fay, she's not sure what kind," Church filled in. "First thing it said wasn't English. Or anything else she knew."

"*Trees*, Church."

"Tree demons," Church clarified. "Or fairies. Really, really nasty fairies. Myrrh thinks they've been... planting seeds, where blood soaked into the ground. To sprout more of their kind. We need to get out herbs and iron for this, she says."

"Herbs and iron." The captain sounded like she was one cup of coffee away from homicide. "Can't we just bring out the chain-saws?"

"Hey, why not?" Church perked up. "We can call the linemen, the Forest Service; see if they've noticed a lot of disturbed ground in weird places where trees used to be-"

Another heartfelt sigh.

"Captain." Church squared her shoulders, trying to be serious. It wasn't easy. After all, *chainsaws*. She wanted one already. "I know what it sounds like. But... when it comes to monsters, I can shiver in a corner and get eaten, or I can jump in and figure out how to get these things to seriously reconsider the merits of a vegetarian diet. We can do this."

"We have a Demongate supposedly primed and ready to go off if there's enough hate and blood spilled around town," Sherman pointed out. "Do you know what kind of panic we're going to have if people think their trees are going to kill them?"

"Not nearly as much panic as we will if we don't tell them," Church stated flatly. "Myrrh's right, Captain. Get the word out. Get people to stop thinking of things that go bump in the night, and start thinking about the ugliest muggers ever. We can fight these things, Captain. We just *did*."

Chapter Four

"You are a very dedicated scholar of all things creepy," Aidan told Dorren cheerfully, flipping through yet another bit of copy-and-pasted text printed off the internet; on a *dishtowel monster*, of all things. "I wonder if this one's flammable?"

Holding another notebook full of scribbles as Myrrh sorted a bookshelf into good, bad, and indifferent, the kid gave him a hairy eyeball. "Do you set *everything* on fire?"

"Only if it tries to eat me." He turned to a note on holy water, and gave her a look right back. "Snatching this out of the baptismal font is *not a good idea*. This isn't chemistry; it's not like you can lift things that go boom out of the high school lab and no one will care so long as the blast's big enough. Intent matters. Just ask the Fathers for some."

"In front of my *mom?*"

Teenagers. "Death or embarrassment. You pick," Aidan stated. "Holy water's kind of hit or miss on fay anyway-"

"What was it saying?" Dorren rubbed at the red scrape bark-skinned hands had left on her throat. "It grabbed me to get to you - what did it say?"

"Wish I knew," Aidan shrugged. "If we did, we might know what it was. And then we could track it down."

"You don't know." Dorren's voice shook with fury, and no little fear.

From under her hood, Myrrh gave the girl a look of bemused surprise. "Young lady, hundreds of languages I've never heard have lived and died in the course of my lifetime. The fay can pass down knowledge lost to mortal man millennia ago. It sounded vaguely familiar, but too many tongues do." A white brow arched. "Did you know it, Aidan?"

"No," Aidan reflected. "Does that help? I mean, it wasn't

human, so I probably wouldn't... that makes no sense...."

"It makes a great deal," Myrrh informed him. "Human sin is, in a way, a universal means of communication. There are very few sane souls in Hell who cannot understand exactly what is being said."

"Yeah, right; like anybody sane could be in Hell," Dorren muttered, poking through another folder.

Aidan narrowed his eyes, trying to figure out if that shift of gray through her aura was disbelief in Hell, or in sanity... or maybe the despair of thinking she was already in hell, and no one would drag her out of it.

The same kind of hell my mother was. I don't know if she knew about Steven, but I know him. He'd have dropped hints, and smirks; never anything like proof, but enough for her to dread every time she turned around....

No, not the same kind of hell. Evil had reached in and snatched Dorren's sister; it hadn't been raised under the same damn roof.

But she's still hurt. And a kid. And I wish someone had had the chance to tell me this, so.... "You're doing the right thing. You know that, right?" Aidan said firmly. "Figuring out how to hold these things off. Making sure they won't take *you*."

Dorren jumped, wide-eyed.

Bingo. "It's okay to be alive," Aidan went on. "And we're doing our best to make sure you stay that way. That's why we're going through this stuff with you. So Myrrh can tell you what should work, and what won't, and look at what you've got so maybe we can figure out what the heck that leafy thing *was*."

"Well, that and Detective Church thinks we might terrify some of her contacts," Myrrh mused. Gray eyes widened, innocent as a kitten about to pounce a butterfly. "Do *you* think we'd terrify them?"

~*~*~*~*~

Hacker was never hard to find. Just go down to the quieter docks on the Little Avon River, and follow the smell of cheap cigarettes.

Waning sunset flashed off the hooks in the old fisherman's hat, and Church waved her bag. "I brought a foot-long."

Hacker blew a puff of smoke, and gave her late-lunch offering a jaundiced glare. "Better not be beer-battered cod."

Church stomped up to his runabout, enjoying the solid feel of the dock under her feet. No strangling roots here, thank goodness to whatever watched over crazy cops. "For the guy who hauls in more trout than the limit, every time? Not a chance, old-timer. Meatball, all the way."

By this time they had it down to a routine. No questions, no chit-chat. She tore one half in half to tuck into, he took the rest. The water made a man hungry, Hacker would say. And the old fisherman hadn't gained a pound in the five years she'd been running into him.

He still finished all of his sub before she'd taken the last bite of her own. "So."

"We're looking at body dump sites again," Church obliged. Wasn't like people wouldn't figure that out on their own. "For a couple of different reasons. One of which I can tell you about... though I'm not sure it applies to you. Exactly."

Hacker drew in more smoke, cigarette tip glowing orange. "Don't know why any of it would, Detective."

"Says the guy whose nets get a very high bones to fish ratio."

His smirk acknowledged the hit. "I find what the river gives me. So... word on the water has it Judge Savonarola's kid wasn't such a keystone of the town after all."

"More like gravestone," Church agreed. "Two sites we've checked so far, some kind of f...."

Hacker shot her a glance.

The detective eyed his wary wrinkles, and the too-still river, and rephrased what she'd been about to say. "Something that might be the *Good Neighbors* planted seeds in the killing ground. Don't know if they could do that in the river, unless they deal with seaweed, but thought I'd ask if you'd seen anything weird."

"Weird like the Jones boys trying to float weed with lobster pots, or uktena-weird?"

"Uk- wait. The weird... serpent thing Eagleman mutters about his great-uncle seeing, way back?" Church said cautiously. An old Cherokee legend, from what she understood; a huge water-snake with antlers and jeweled diamond spots, invulnerable unless you hit it in something like the seventh spot on the neck. Which, speaking as someone who'd spent considerable time on the range, meant pretty near invulnerable unless you got lucky enough to sneak up on it and count. And then hit it when it wasn't moving.

Legends are real. And this one's local. Better keep an eye out. I don't want "died from supernaturally bad breath" on my headstone.

Which made her feel like thumping her head against a nice handy piling, because this was a *legend*. Like King Arthur. And she was trying to figure out how to survive it.

Myrrh would put Arthur in a headlock and thwack him for playing around with maidens while Guinevere near got burned at the stake, Church reflected. *And Aidan would be right in there helping, like Merlin with an attitude-*

Wait. Hadn't Merlin been half-demon?

"It is. Which is why the poor bastard was his great-uncle instead of Grandpa," Hacker *hmph*ed. "Those things don't let you walk away alive. Not for long." He shrugged. "Water's been quiet, Detective. Maybe... a little too quiet."

Church tried not to shiver. "Shafat thinks we're after something tied to forests and graveyards."

"Little lady's probably not wrong," the fisherman reflected. "River's a graveyard for a lot of things, Detective."

Oh, that wasn't creepy. "You never said anything about uktena before."

"You didn't ask."

Right, because nobody sane asks about.... Church tried not to mentally slap herself. *Hunters. Demons. We're out of sane territory.* "So... you know about uktena. And things."

"Some," Hacker shrugged. "A bit. Most don't. Spend enough time risking your damn fool neck on the water, though... let's just say, I've seen more out here than I'll ever talk about."

"Well, if you know anything about man-eating tree things stalking people, could you clue me in?" Church said wryly. "And if you know anybody else I could talk to?"

Hacker raised a peppered brow. "Thought you talked plenty to the lady with the tombstones."

"She said she doesn't like being taken for granite," Church quipped.

Hacker raised both eyebrows.

"I'm trying," the detective admitted. "She doesn't want to show up at the station, and even emails are a little iffy. She's old enough to get a lot of respect from her relatives, but she blew her cover in front of a room full of cops and about half her community is panicking right now. I can't blame them. Some of them have kids. If any of them got outed at school... it'd be a nightmare."

Which made her feel like thumping her head again. Coral and her relatives knew things, 'cause they were gorgons. She'd known the woman for years and never caught on about the snakes. What else had she missed?

"Hmm. Well, you know Old Man Conseen. Comes to things around the river... can't give you names, nobody wants that spread around, but if you say you're after things with an iron hook, some-one might talk. And if you really get desperate, try that funny shaved-head guy in the red-and-orange robes, sometime," Hacker mused. "Loves to fish, never baits his hook. Weird." He burped. "Water's pretty at night, Detective. Nice and peaceful, away from all this demon bull. Sure I can't give you a ride over the river?"

"Pass," Church said, as she'd said dozens of times before,

standing up to brush crumbs off her pants. Stopped, and gave the man one look askance, fingers trying not to twitch for the bag of iron filings Dorren had made her take before the kid would let them leave. "You're not some kind of weird river fay trying to get me out on the water to eat my liver, are you?"

Hacker grinned, all stained teeth. "Not a ghost of a chance."

"You don't think the library's haunted, do you?"

Myrrh exercised true Christian patience and mercy, and did *not* drag the girl through the university library's sliding glass doors by her ear. It was far too tempting, given what she'd found in the young fool's notes. The child was lucky she'd been focused on surviving the bus to campus in one piece. "If it is not, it is not for lack of your trying. Mother Mary, what were you *thinking*, attempting Mycenaean necromancy-!"

Bringing up the rear so Dorren couldn't run away, Aidan gave them both a bemused shrug. "Give her points for taste, at least it wasn't Aztec."

"Ewww!" Dorren shuddered all over, apparently not caring if that earned her bleary looks from sleepless college students currently hogging the ground floor computers. "Do you know what they did to talk to spirits? With the drugs, the barbs, and the *tongue*...."

Amber eyes were shadowed. "Oh, believe you me, I know."

Myrrh hid a sigh, and checked yet another item on her mental list of tortures Aidan had suffered. Twenty-four years in Hell; the tally of wounds she would have to help heal, or see the man crippled in his fight against evil, threatened to only grow. Though stingray spines, at least, were not usually weapons in the hands of mortal enemies.

Don't let the youngster distract you. "I was born in a time and place where speaking with the dead, while ominous, was not a crime," Myrrh said sternly, heading for the information desk. "You, young lady, are at least nominally of Father O'Malley's church. You owe the Fathers a *very good explanation*. And an hour of your time, at the least, so they may inform you of everything that could have gone wrong when you called on Powers that have no reason to regard a Christian favorably." She cast a scowl at the girl. "Fish blood? Really? Thank the Virgin you did *not* summon your sister's spirit, with such poor energy for a hungry soul to feed on."

Behind the desk, a blond librarian's eyebrows had gone straight up.

"Mr. Truhaft." Dorren tried to smile with confidence, even as one hand twiddled a loop of dark rosary beads through her fingers. "Um. I brought you some... researchers?"

"Rather hands-on research, indeed." Myrrh inclined her head to the scholar. "We are investigating sightings near places of interest to the local constabulary. Miss O'Connor has been generous enough to point us in your direction for where she has obtained some reference material."

Blond brows lowered a hair. "You want to read *Huckleberry Finn?*"

"They sure do!" Dorren's smile was even less steady. "Read a banned book week should be every week, right?"

Out of the corner of her eye, Myrrh saw a few heads swivel their direction. Either Carly Truhaft and his fellow librarians had begun to draw attention to their books, or there really was something amiss in reading *Huckleberry Finn*.

At the moment, I would give fifty-fifty odds either way. "Aidan?"

Her friend's scan of the first floor never faltered. "Place has changed a lot since the last time I was in here. Color printers? Huh." He glanced at Truhaft. "Is Special Collections still buried in the back left?"

"You're not looking for Special Collections." The librarian

came out from behind the counter with a bit more care than just dodging the corner would account for. "Just a subset of Reference. This way."

Wise, Myrrh nodded, following. Hide the books away, and they'd be too easy to tamper with - or disappear. Put them into a public section of Reference most students would avoid, and they would be secure as a suitcase of evidence planted in the midst of Church's desk.

"Are you looking for any specific commentary?" Truhaft inquired.

"Mostly just looking," Aidan said truthfully. "I ended up in a bad place a while back. Would have been nice to have some... references."

"You do have that look," the librarian said quietly. "Some of our staff is familiar with it. Especially those who have to oversee exam week hours."

Aidan seemed to frizz, heat shimmering around him like fur on a startled cat. "Oh man. I didn't even *think* about that."

Nor had she. And she should have, Myrrh knew; college exams had students staying up past midnight, panicked and locked into the tunnel vision of their next do-or-die test. The perfect prey for far too many creatures. "How many aides have you lost, these past two decades?"

"Lost?" Dorren squeaked.

"I couldn't really say." Truhaft gave the teenager a worried look. "A lot less after your uncle gave us advice on dealing with... unregistered library users."

Librarians with teeth, then. And likely holy water stashed behind the counter in a spray bottle. Myrrh hadn't had time to give Jim O'Connor a thorough Hunter's education when the then-teenager had helped her rescue his brother from a drowning-spirit on the Little Avon, but she'd pointed him O'Malley's way and hoped for the best.

Church declares him a hitman, Myrrh thought. *Somehow, I*

doubt the best happened.

How much of that could she lay at Steven's door, and all those who'd worked to protect murdering creatures from humankind? How much was just the man himself? If he'd executed those poor bones in the morgue - that *had* been a human, before death.

Yet he gave Dorren tools to protect herself. Not the act of one lost to all hope. I have to see him.

But first she had to see what Dorren had been working with, when the girl had tried to poke spirits beyond her ken; so she could determine if it was Dorren's information or her understanding that were lacking. And either way, fix the problem before one stubborn, desperate teenager opened a portal for a ravening ogre or split part of her own energies off into a spirit-animal to inflict harm and pain. Though given the stacks of Japanese lore printed and clipped on Dorren's shelves, the youngster might skip right past relatively harmless Western manifestations to the lethal *ikiryou*.

"Now remember these books are reference, and can't be taken out of the library," Truhaft waved a finger as they rounded the corner into a set of shelves stacked haphazardly with everything from cracked leather bindings to modern glossy paperbacks. "The good news is that means they're always here, and won't be listed on your library card."

Myrrh traded a frown with Aidan. "Why would that be good news?" Though if vampires had gone after student aides, it was likely they'd tried for librarians as well. Demons knew human knowledge was the best defense against evil. But usually they tried to simply destroy it. Why would they go after library cards?

"Um - the Feds can check your checkout list?" Dorren put in, scowling. "That's what my uncle says. Patriot Act stuff. People get *caught* that way."

"The Feds can *what?*" Aidan hissed.

Myrrh felt inclined to snarl along with him. Never mind Hunters, simple citizens had the right to read and think what they pleased; for the privacy of a man's conscience was the only way to be certain any soul came to belief freely and with full heart. Who in the world thought they had a right to tamper with....

Of course. "It occurs to me," Myrrh observed, "we now have an excellent reason why someone might impersonate Agent Cushman."

"Or why he might be in here, if he's honest, trying to find bad guys," Aidan pointed out. "Or maybe just low-level corrupt."

"Or those," Myrrh agreed. Though she'd prefer impersonation. There'd been enough trust wrecked these past years already.

"Agent Joey Cushman?" Truhaft looked between them as if he hoped they were joking. "He has made requests of this library in the past. Not that we know what he was looking for. I don't think he's ever been in this section. At least, not with assistance."

Though all of them knew it'd be easy enough for anyone to saunter into this part of the stacks without assistance. The staff couldn't watch every minute of the day.

"Thought he didn't like being called Joey," Aidan mused.

"Ah." The librarian looked a bit abashed. "He doesn't. Forget I mentioned it."

"So how'd you know that?" Aidan persisted.

"Sir, we are *librarians.*" Truhaft winked at Myrrh. "Research. It's what we do."

"Indeed," Myrrh nodded. "And now we must do a bit of our own. I am quite interested to know what is here, so a donation might most effectively bolster the archive's breadth and usefulness."

From that tiny cough behind her, Aidan was trying to stifle a chortle.

Why yes, I am *amenable to using bribery,* Myrrh thought, amused. *After all, it might save lives.*

From Truhaft's sidelong glance, he read between the lines as easily as he indexed shelves. But like any good librarian, he wasn't averse to the possibility of more books for interested readers. "Let me know if you need any help."

Dorren watched him go, and breathed a sigh of relief. Caught Myrrh's raised brow, and eeped.

Good. The youngster needs some caution. "First, let us see what they have on more harmless supernatural entities, and the ways to *ask* wandering spirits if they wish to freely venture information," Myrrh stated. "If you still intend to dabble in necromancy, let us make certain you can contact entities that will not try to eat you, possess you, or rip out your soul to leave an unblinking body behind."

Dorren pointed a finger at her, wordless; turned to Aidan with a wave of helpless hands.

"You want to keep out of trouble, stick with your parents," Aidan advised. "Way we see it, trouble already has your number. Better learn how to handle it."

"But," Dorren cleared her throat. "You said I'd get in trouble with the Church...."

"Father O'Malley knows I am a heretic, and therefore dangerous to any believing soul. My congregation baptized with fire," Myrrh said bluntly. "You may assume we were not strict followers of other laws in Deuteronomy, as well. Being a *ba'al ob*, a *yidde'oni*, or a *doresh el ha-metim* was not unknown among us. Of the three, I suggest learning the ways of the yidde'oni. It is far safer for mind and spirit to ask questions of ghosts rather than to try to command them, or starve yourself in a graveyard until a wandering spirit possesses you."

"Gurk."

"Seriously, what did you think you were messing with?" There was no laughter in Aidan's tone. "Magic's not *safe*. You saw that with the filings. It's not card tricks and bunnies out of hats. It's playing with the voltage from a whole nuclear power plant. If you've got the right equipment and never turn your back on it, you're good. Slip? You're *toast*."

"You come from a lineage well acquainted with danger," Myrrh observed. "You can master this, if you so choose. But you *must* learn caution. And how to determine which creatures are a true threat, and which only odd, harmless as a blacksnake passing through the leaves." She gave the girl a considering smile. "With luck, we may be able to see one of those here on campus, when we meet Church again."

Aidan raised surprised brows. Dorren looked beyond dubious. "But you said you were going to look at...."

"Yes," Myrrh said firmly. "We are." She half-closed her eyes, knowing any teenager would bristle at that mark of adult tolerance. "You've haunted one crime scene, and you'd balk at another? Tsk."

"Did you have to bring the kid?" Church hissed, crouched behind an azalea bush that still had a few rattling dry leaves.

"You want to argue about it?" Aidan crouched right along with her, holding Dorren back with a gentle grip on her shoulder when the young lady wanted to bolt - forward or back, he wasn't sure. "Look, if someone had told me what I was up against years back, maybe I wouldn't have met a hellhound the hard way. Or if I had," because Steven had been determined, damn him, "maybe I'd have had a *chance*."

Myrrh ignored them all, eyes hooded as she knelt, one hand above dry root holes half-covered by leaf litter that'd drifted under the computer lab balcony. Testing earth and air with her own arcane senses, Aidan knew, to determine the best way to approach cleansing the body dump site.

Hope she has better luck than I'm having, Aidan thought. Right now all he felt was living ground, a comfy trace of odd paper ash, the electric-bee buzz of computers inside, and a roaring fury in his ears that Steven had blatantly dumped a sacrificed body right under the noses of innocent college kids.

Mind, his half-brother had picked an *excellent* spot. Computer lab parking lot less than fifty yards away, yet screened from view by tall oaks and leather-tearing greenbriar vines that the university never hacked at, specifically to give the balcony privacy and keep damn fool frat boys from trying out their jungle-gym skills to get into the computer lab the hard way. No regular person would get to the bare earth under the balcony without taking a header over the guardrail, first.

Throw in a few fool-the-nose tricks, a little more of the incense that seemed to linger in the air - yeah. Aidan could see a body lying here for weeks, before the scavengers got too busy to ignore.

"Right here?" Dorren was trembling under his hand. "He just - the guy who killed Megan - he left a body right *here?* Where people could-" Her words choked off.

"We don't know it was the same guy," Church said quietly. "Between you and me, I damn well hope it was. Otherwise we've got two evil sorcerers running around Intrepid and that makes me *twitchy.*"

Dorren opened her mouth... and closed it again, fear clearing into determination. "R-right. That'd be bad."

Kid has guts, Aidan decided, impressed. *She wants the bad guys taken down just as much as we do. Not just for her sister. Because this is evil, and someone's got to stop it.*

Which, he guessed, was exactly why Myrrh was dragging her deeper into this. Dorren was *going* to keep poking the supernatural, one way or another. They could let her flounder and go after everything, which would get the kid killed - or they could show her enough of the ropes so maybe she'd leave things too big for her alone.

Which, granted, would probably *also* get her killed. Eventually. Hunters racked up a lot of enemies.

Maybe in the past, Aidan thought. *Now - Coral's out to the cops. A bunch of supernaturals are. Maybe Dorren can get enough help from the good guys to stay ahead of the bad guys. Maybe.*

And there were worse fates than death. A lot worse.

Myrrh relaxed, glancing up to check where the edge of the balcony was before she stood and brushed off her knees. "Much better than I thought. Traces of incense, burned rice paper...." She tilted her head back, peeking under the balcony again at a white gleam of taped-up paper. "And a copy of the Amitabha Sutra. On very odd paper. It seems as if-" Myrrh touched it, and blinked. "Someone glued rock powder together?"

"Marble and hooves," Aidan muttered, peering at it himself. "Who makes paper out of that?"

"Marble?" Church took a look, then ducked back out from under. "Waterproof paper. Good idea."

"Waterproof-?" Dorren's eyes gleamed. "Talismans that'll work in the rain!"

"I've got it for a case notebook that can stand getting soaked by water demons, but - yeah," Church agreed. Frowned at Myrrh's intent look. "Now what?"

"Interesting," the hell-raider mused. "And yes. Waterproof talismans would be very useful." She held a finger above the sutra again. "As someone has put it to good use here, inking words that will last to be kind to hungry ghosts. It seems we have a friend on campus."

Church pointed at the holes, eyes flicking around the greenery. "Along with the walking trees?"

"There were roots feeding here, before the joss paper was burned. Some of the ash has blown into the hollows." Myrrh eyed them again, grave. "Whatever they were, they are not here now."

Church's breath hissed. "So why do I feel like I'm being watched?"

Aidan frowned, reaching outward with his senses. *There's* something *out there. I just don't know what-*

A familiar scent hit his nose. Aidan bared his teeth, and lifted a hand, ready to call fire. "Werewolf."

Church's hands were close to her gun. "Coming this way?"

"Not sure." He swung his head back and forth, trying to pin

down that waft of wind. "I think... it's moving away."

Church heaved a breath, giving him a resigned smirk. "With our luck? It's going to class."

Dorren sat down in a muted crackle of leaves, arms wrapped around herself like a life-vest. "There's... werewolves on campus. They could be in the library. They could be anywhere-!"

Myrrh poked her. "Hush. They were here before you knew of them. This changes nothing. Save that I will give you the non-alcoholic recipe for a Hunter's tonic. It is a bit trickier to make, but you obviously need it."

"You're going to...." Dorren let go, lifting the palms of her hands to sunlight as if she'd never seen them before. "It doesn't go away. The monsters - they're never going to be over."

Aidan huddled on himself, wishing he could lie to the kid. He knew what she felt. He'd felt it himself, hunted by a beast only Hell would call a hound. The world had turned dark that day, and the chill still gripped his bones.

"No," Myrrh said gently. "That knowledge has driven Hunters mad, before. There will always be more monsters. Always. For true monsters are birthed of human evil... and we are all fallen. All sinners. You can no more root out the last evil than you can command the tides." She rested her hand on dark hair. "But that does not mean we stop fighting. There is good in this world, and people who deserve our protection. And... there can be wonder, as well." She put a finger to her lips, and pointed toward stirred earth.

Aidan squinted, trying to sense anything out of the ordinary as a dust devil drifted over root holes. Red clay lifted and fell in the tiny wind, as if the breeze had hair-fine fingers-

Oh.

It wasn't pretty. A wispy, translucent nest of beetle grubs, tiny mandibles chewing at blood-tainted earth. But he couldn't feel any harm in them.

"Sin-eaters," Myrrh murmured, hand near Dorren's mouth in case she squeaked. "They don't usually have more formal names.

That might limit them; and believe me, limiting those little ones is the last thing any sane Hunter wishes. They are," she hesitated, "much like maggots, devouring taint in the world as mundane beasts clean away dead flesh."

Wind died, and the nest was gone.

"It will take them some time, but so long as this place suffers no further harm, they will cleanse it." Myrrh breathed a sigh of relief. "Our friendly Buddhist's offering was well-taken; it ensured they would find this spot."

"A friendly Buddhist," Dorren repeated blankly. Blinked, eyes seeming to clear. "You mean - there's help?"

"Whoa, slow down." Church held up a cautioning hand. "I checked out one of your anime. Buddhist doesn't always mean *human*. Right? So just because someone - or *something* - wanted to help this spot, doesn't mean they want to help us. Demongate. Hell on Earth can't be good for a lot of things. Even things that don't like people. Except maybe for dinner."

"...Oh."

The world can fix itself, with a little help. Aidan let out a voiceless whistle. Aariel's lessons hadn't included anything on that.

'Course not. Demon. He's not supposed to fix the world. Or let it get fixed-

Ice started from the nape of his neck and shivered down. "Um. If sin-eaters can fix body dump sites... how bad does it have to be, how fast, to build a Demongate?"

"Very bad." Myrrh chafed shadow-clad arms. "It takes concentrated malice, power, and long-lasting intent. I suspect yours was one of the first deaths used to anchor the foundations. What we saw on the Wailing Plains - that would have been the first Hellish manifestation, as the level of power finally breached the walls between worlds."

"...Huh."

"Don't *huh* me, Lindisfarne," Church scowled. "That's an *I'm thinking about something creepy* look, and whatever it is, I'd better know about it."

"It's just... Fay Lords are powerful, and man do some of them have malice, but - you think this really took most of the time we were off Earth to build the real framework?" He shrugged, sheepish. "The way Aariel talked about those guys, they just don't have the attention span. Isn't that half why they give up the teind every seven years? Even if Steven did have one of 'em over a barrel somehow, they'd find some way to break any deal after a decade, max. That long with a human, they're just *bored*."

Church was tense, poised between disbelief and outrage. Dorren caught her lip between her teeth, looking from him to the holes. "So something out there doesn't get bored. And that's what's stalking my family?"

"Minions of it, more likely," Myrrh agreed. "Still, that should allow us to narrow down-"

Warmth moved into range above them; Aidan held a finger to his lips for silence.

Good, Dorren's not arguing.

Careless feet stomped the balcony above; Aidan caught glimpses of a dark hooded jacket and a scruffy blond mustache as the intruder took a cursory turn around the inside of the railing. Obviously looking for trouble... and missing them entirely.

Church lifted a brow in wry amusement.

There's something... not a scent, but dark....

And that same grumpy *snarl* in his soul he'd felt around Cushman. Though with this guy it was less *pounce* and more *screw pouncing, just shred him already.*

Myrrh caught him by the sleeve. *Wait*, gray eyes said.

Right. Whoever, whatever he was, the guy hadn't done anything. Yet.

A *hmph* of breath above. Scruffy Mustache gripped the railing, lifted a leg-

Church's breath hitched, blue eyes dancing, as the idiot dropped down, just a little brush and his assumptions between his mustache and three heavily-armed professional troublemakers.

Aidan had to bite down his own giggle. Officially, Church was on leave. But if trouble walked right into her hands... well, between the three of them, they ought to be able to manage a citizen's arrest.

And I think we're going to have to, Aidan thought, as Mustache took another furtive look around and pulled a stained backpack off his shoulders. *I kind of doubt that red's cherry juice.*

"Hey!" Lighter, faster footsteps. "You jerk! Carrying raw steak around campus, ugh, that's bad enough - but you left *smears* on the keyboard!" A dark-haired young Asian guy gripped the balcony and glared down at Mustache.

Aidan breathed out, feeling less raw with that pale shimmer of soul above. If Mustache was clinging mud, the Asian student glimmered like water in a hidden creek.

He's focused. Bright as rice paper and incense- oh. Hee. This could be fun.

Because dark eyes *hadn't* skipped over them the way Mustache's had. The younger student had seen them... and from that quick blink, *recognized* them. Given how good Myrrh was at dodging reporters, Aidan could only think of one way that could happen.

So why was a Buddhist computer guy interested in the Nightsong vid?

Mustache puffed himself up to snarl, one hand reaching into his pack-

"And you better have a permit for that knife, Piers!" the younger student forged on.

Oh, he definitely did that on purpose, Aidan thought gleefully.

Church cleared her throat. "Detective Church, IPD. Put the pack down. Slowly."

Piers jumped, jaw dropping as his head jerked their way. Aidan kept himself between Myrrh and trouble, just like she was keeping Dorren behind her. Idiots like that would see *small* first, and *enchantress* only after she'd seriously messed them up. And Mustache hadn't done anything to deserve a hospital. Yet.

Something must have clicked in Piers' head, because he went a little gray. "You're not the campus cops!"

"I don't have to be," Church said dryly. "Law may say you can wave a sword around in home rituals, but if you've got it out in public, athames have to be the legal knife limit. So. Do you have a permit, or are we going to go see the locals?"

"Eric Chang." Church dusted her hands off as campus cops cuffed the protesting sorcerer-wannabe to wait for transport, smiling as she remembered the Asian computer geek's hidden slump of relief. "We should save that kid's contact info. In case he wants to get into the academy later."

After all, whatever else he was up to, Chang had brass.

"This is the limit, Piers. Maybe we're just aides, but enough is enough. You? Are out *of the computer lab!"*

"Huh." Church had to shake her head. "You know, I never would have thought *computer tech* when you said sorcerer."

"Nor I," Myrrh agreed. "Training to deal with a computer takes quite a bit of time. Most magic-users, especially sorcerers, are unwilling to devote that time to anything beyond their study of rituals and powers."

What?

"Ricci's computer didn't take much to start poking at it," Aidan pointed out. As if that surprised him, and why-?

Twenty-five years, Church remembered. "Uh, guys? Computers have changed a lot. We have them in the squad cars. Heck, the phone is a little computer. Annoying little one, sometimes...."

Wait a minute.

"Steven had computers in his workshop. A sorcerer wouldn't have stuff in there he wasn't using, right?" Church glanced between them, feeling the wide eyes of the student manning the desk behind them. "Saw a bumper sticker once, something about a computer letting you commit the mistakes of a thousand men in one day."

Myrrh's frown deepened. "A single sorcerer's glyph holds enough information to be difficult to store as an image...." She trailed off, gray eyes narrowed and intent.

"But Dorren had shelves full of scanned stuff," Aidan observed.

"And visual stuff's gotten a hell of a lot better just the past few years," Church sighed, thinking of computer-animated movies that tricked the mind into thinking it was all real, no magic involved. "So if he just called in help when he had some new tools - we could be right back to fay after all. Damn."

"It is possible," Myrrh allowed. "Though given gremlins, computers and the fay are an unlikely mix-" She caught herself. "Were, at least. I will need to do some research."

Ouch. For a moment Church considered how much catching up she might have to do, if she'd been dumped into homicide cases two decades in the future.

A lot on the tech; not so much on investigation. People don't change.

Meaning this probably wasn't the first time Myrrh'd seen low-grade crazy. Church gave the hell-raider a sidelong glance. "Demon-summoners, crazy wanna-bes, maybe-good guys tacking up sutras - how the hell do we tell them apart? I'm not going to even ask what Piers could have gotten with hot sauce for his sacrifice."

"Nothing he could control," Myrrh said clinically. "Possibly nothing at all. But the intent would have done the site more harm." Her fingers toyed with shadow in the form of a light blue sleeve. "As to how to tell benevolent magic-use from *maleficia*... I will have to take some time composing notes. It is far from simple."

"Of course it's not." Church glanced at the other half of her supernaturally inclined help. "So... what do you think Chang was doing there?"

Because she'd seen the way Aidan relaxed, noting the geek up there. Given Aidan's nerves were usually taut as piano wires... that was either an unexpected bonus, or really, really bad.

"Just passing through?" Aidan said innocently.

Church squinted at him, unimpressed.

"He could have been somebody who tried to fix the site," the fire-mage admitted. "Maybe. But that'd be tampering with a crime scene, right?"

Okay, Aidan had a point. "If he is, we could use more help."

"If he is, he's likely done as much as he can already," Myrrh said frankly. "Father O'Malley, Father Ricci, those they have contacted - they are willing to step forward, and face any legal challenge for praying a site will be purified. Chang did not. I would not put a young man in mortal danger he has not sought." Her brows went up. "And he is keeping a watch on this site. I would rather leave him alone, unnoticed, so we may focus our efforts on places that are not so guarded."

"Not to mention, Dorren comes here a lot," Aidan put in. "You *know* she's a target. You want to drag a Good Samaritan off her turf?"

"Rrrrgh." Church rubbed at her headache. Because damn it, Aidan was so right on target, it felt like he'd slipped a stiletto through her ribs.

Kid's had enough grief in her life already. The whole family has. If somebody's on campus who'll keep an eye on her, that's a good thing. But I'm a cop. I'm not out here to just bodyguard one kid. I'm supposed to protect everybody in Intrepid....

I'm a cop. I'm supposed to uphold the law. Chang hasn't done anything *wrong. Sure, I could use his help; we all could. Doesn't change that I'm a cop, Chang's not, and he's got every right to lay low and hope trouble doesn't find him. Hassling him would be* wrong.

She still wanted to talk to him. Heck, she wished the whole force could talk to him, and anybody else who knew something about the monsters that actually *worked*. But between the monsters and the lawyers she'd run into so far, Church would bet a month's salary that anyone who *did* know something covered it under the most innocent look they could plaster on.

Unless they couldn't. Like Dorren couldn't, because things were actively hunting her....

And she's trying to Hunt them right back. She doesn't have a choice. Chang does.

"How do you do it?" Church waved a hand Myrrh's way, trying to sum up the whole demonic mess they were in. "How do you pick what's the best thing for everybody?"

"By *not* picking what is best for everyone." Myrrh straightened, looking her square in the eye. "I am a skilled enchantress. I am not omniscient. I can only do what I know will be best for those about me, based on my knowledge of lore and magic. Within those limits... the Hippocratic Oath sums up a great deal of wisdom. *First, do no harm.*"

Which shed an interesting light on how the hell-raider must have met one exhausted half-demon's spirit. Aidan'd said she'd found him passed out, and kept watch over him so nothing ate him before they could talk. It'd sounded way too good to be true; after all, Hell....

First do no harm. He wasn't eating anybody, so she just... waited. And watched.

Still. "So how's that sort with what you're telling Dorren?"

"She was already walking into harm." Myrrh shook her head. "I am glad she took the bus home. It bears enough steel to dissuade most of our suspects from an assault."

Most. Great. "If we're up against some kind of fay," Church pointed out.

"If, indeed," Myrrh agreed. "We can only act on what we know, Detective. And remain open to the evidence, in case we stumble on something which we did not even guess."

Behind her, Church heard a deliberate cough.

Turning, Church eyed the head of the campus cops. Who was eyeing her right back, with the kind of look Church usually saved for stray defense attorneys. "Detective, if you're done here...."

Take the insanity elsewhere, Church filled in. *Some gratitude.* "We're done. Thanks." *Damn it, if I say anything I'll look more crazy, but - yeah.* "You might want to handle Piers' little notebook with gloves. Just in case."

The look she got said campus security wanted to handle her with gloves. Or maybe a straitjacket.

Sad thing was, Church thought as they headed out to the parking lot, she was finding it hard to care.

Almost get eaten by one demon-bear, suddenly you don't worry about how funny you look to civilians.

At least it didn't look like they were up against malurisines. This time. "Okay, we're two for two on dump sites and root holes." Church jingled keys, unlocking the rental. "Think you guys can narrow the suspect list any?"

"We can give it a shot," Aidan nodded, strapping into the back. "Maybe over dinner?"

Ooo, that was too good to pass up. "Why Lindisfarne." Sliding behind the wheel, Church fluttered her eyelashes. "Is that an invitation?"

"What - no - hey! I was just talking about food, you workaholic Sam Spade-!"

As they pulled out of the driveway, Myrrh was still laughing.

Chapter Five

Tuesday, Oct 21st

The rustling in the leaves, Stimson knew, was nothing so innocent as wind.

He parked on the roadside near a crooked oak, not bothering to lock the doors. If a human meant to steal his transport, it would only be prey for what lurked in the woods about them. And if something not human chose to make the attempt....

Mere mortal locks would do little good.

What an uncivilized place.

But uncivilized also meant no cameras, meaning a rakshasa could flex light and maya, shedding the guise of a nondescript balding accountant the police were certainly *not* looking for-

Stretch claws on backward hands, the faintest hint of tiger stripes shimmering in the sunlight-

And compact himself again, reclaiming his more comfortable disguise as Steven Savonarola's British butler.

Manners, after all. So long as he acted as Steven's agent, even if his master was temporarily indisposed, his form mattered.

Temporarily. Stimson allowed himself one thin smirk. *I almost pity the local constabulary. They truly do not grasp that for some creatures, mere mortal death means very little.*

Though given the unexpected return of his employer's elder brother, to say nothing of the hell-raider, that might change. But there was little any of Steven's minions could do about that... yet.

A wine totebag over each shoulder, Stimson advanced toward the darkness gaping under the gray granite of the hillside. The Power lairing here was great, but not stupid. Any would-be heroes who would seek to defeat him would be forced to enter the under-world, where night, roots, and the drowning power of lightless rivers would all be ranged against mere human souls.

Of course, that same dark fury could be hurled against Stimson himself. If the Power he implored tired of the game, and sought to strike before the Demongate was complete.

Stimson bared his teeth, just for a moment. It wouldn't do to show a challenge where that Power could see.

It's not good to keep a Lord waiting.

Glass clinking, Stimson advanced into darkness.

"If you were at the last lecture you may have noticed the advisory note enclosed with the handouts, suggesting you seek spiritual counseling after you hear what I am about to say in this one." Myrrh straightened her shoulders, sweeping a serious gaze across the room. There were different people present than last time. Some she suspected were reporters, while another was far too young by modern standards. But so long as Dorren chose not to draw attention to herself - the girl had earned her right to know the dangers. And given Dorren's past experiments, she needed an education on how very badly things could have gone wrong. "I am quite in earnest. Today was meant to cover the basics of benign supernatural creatures. But of necessity it will also be about sorcerers and sorcery, and the lore will be difficult to hear. In part because it is often entwined with religious practice, and even at the best of times such discussions are *tricky*. Also, note that I am accounted a heretic by the faith of Rome, so you must take my statements under advisement."

"A heretic how?" Worn fingers tapped on a desk. "And why's it matter?"

Heath, interested if wary. And it was a fair question. "In many ways," Myrrh said honestly. "It matters, because I ascribe to beliefs that make it not a sin for me to use the methods I teach against evil. For you, it may be different. I come from that group of traditions that these days you label Gnostic. Among my brothers and sisters...."

Missing, all of them. Or fled to Heaven when their burdens grew too much to bear.

Without the imminent threat of violence, it was all she could do not to keen her loss. She was one against the Demongate, she was *alone-*

I am a follower of Christ. I am never alone.

Faith. And truth. Aidan was here. Church was, even if the detective might not grasp the full terror of what was to come. All Captain Sherman's people were here, risking their livelihoods and reputations on the faith that her knowledge might save lives.

"Among my small congregation, we baptized with fire," Myrrh said quietly. "And we proved our faith in a manner which you today might call suicidal, for it killed most of us." She smiled. "Just, not always permanently."

A snort at the side of the room caught her ear, and Myrrh narrowed her eyes. Drat; she'd hoped the youngster would avoid reporters' eyes. "Young lady." If she had to, she'd use Dorren; no need to spread a true name on the internet for all to hear. And it might make the youngster listen. "I believe I did say this lecture was closed to any under eighteen."

"My uncle said you were going to talk about sorcery." The girl's jaw set, mule-stubborn. "If this is what happened to Megan, I want to know!"

Myrrh noted various pens scribbling down that name, and made a note to set detectives on the hapless reporters later. Dorren was still a minor, and there was no good reason to badger her for details on a murder. Though they would, given what she meant to cover of the truth.

"No, you don't," Aidan put in from his own desk. "I wish I didn't know." He leaned back. "Shouldn't you be in school?"

"I'm still suspended," Dorren muttered. "Stupid PC principal...."

Myrrh sighed. At least if this got out, she'd only be charged with abuse of a minor, not contributing to delinquency. Ah well. "If you have your uncle's iron nerves, then I will not evict you. You are as much in danger as any here. But you will not like what you are about to hear."

Glover tapped his pencil on his desk, giving her a look a little less angry and a little more wary than the last time. Evidently word of what had happened in the graveyard with Ginger was starting to get around. "What, you got it in for sorcerers, too?"

"Not all of them," Myrrh said clinically. "The sorcery you have been allowed to see is, for the most part, not harmful. It calls on minor powers, usually not of ill intent toward humankind, and it is paid for with benign things those powers crave. A pail of milk, a heartfelt tear; chants and incantations, sacrifices of incense and fruits. That sort of sorcery, while it may not always be safe, is not my first concern. It is... much like jaywalking."

That drew snickers. Good. Very soon, there would be no laughter.

"First, I will tell you of minor creatures that less harmful sorcerers invoke. They range from truly harmless, like echoes, to those not usually harmful, so long as their requirements are met. Hungry ghosts and lesser fay can often be called upon for information or for relief from lesser curses and disease, so long as they are paid. If not - the consequences can be dire." Myrrh stood straight before the watching crowd, unflinching. "Then I will tell you of sorcery you have not been allowed to name. Of powers drawn out with blood and lives, and worse. Sorcery that calls to demons, and the darkest of fay and elemental powers, and etched a Demongate on Intrepid in screaming murder."

Ah. Now she had their attention.

"I suspect," Myrrh added, very quietly, "you will regret having eaten breakfast."

~*~*~*~*~

Oh, this was a mistake....

Splashing her face with cold water from the fountain - the bathrooms were kind of *occupied* right now - Church took a deep breath, and commanded her heaving stomach to quit that already. She hadn't lost it when a malursine melted people with acid, she wasn't about to lose it now.

"Let me at that," a ragged voice groaned behind her.

Church stepped away, letting the captain get her fill of cool, clear, non-bile-flavored water. "I think... next time Myrrh puts in an advisory, we ought to talk to her first." *Deep breaths.* Deep *breaths.* "I feel like we took an FBI profiler into a high school gym and told him to have at it. With *slides.*"

Sherman wiped droplets across her face, and croaked a laugh. "Guess we shouldn't have let her have the colored chalk."

"Haaa. No." Church shuddered, remembering how Myrrh had drifted her fingers across each bright stick of color, and *whispered.*

"*Medu-netjer.* Write the vision; make it plain upon the tables, so he may run that readeth it...."

Colored dust had swirled into the air, following Myrrh's fingers to sketch sigils on the chalkboard that wriggled in ways Church didn't want to look at too closely.

...And then she'd stifled a snicker, because you could tell who'd seen Myrrh do something impossible just by looking around the room. Reporters were especially prone to dropping their jaws whenever Myrrh twitched flowing colored chalks into a new, more ghastly creature.

Magic. The lady is magic.

Church shuddered all over again, remembering what had come next.

I wish I didn't. I really, really wish I didn't.

Days ago in a graveyard, Ginger had horrified her by painting blood-runes to summon a demon. Now she was horrified all over again... because the way Myrrh laid it out, he wasn't alone. He was a *type*, to the hell-raider; like any serial killer to a profiler.

She's seen it so often, she can rattle it off in her sleep.

An upstroke of Myrrh's fingers cleared the board, before she sketched the rough form of a human body, facing out, in plain white chalk. "Sorcery works by using other entities as an intermediary to perform most of the magic. Sometimes those entities are invoked; sometimes they are created by the sorcerer himself. Usually himself," she'd added, glancing at Glover before he could even think about objecting. "For reasons which will become clear, the usual substances involved in a dark creation are most easily obtained by an unscrupulous man." She looked Dorren right in the eye. "When I come to methods of sacrifice, please leave the room."

The teenager stiffened. "I'm not going to-"

"The officers in your sister's case will speak to you again, I am sure," Myrrh stated. "You are by law a minor, and I have no intention of searing your soul with things that *may not have happened* to her. I will speak to the detectives, and then I will be able to give you details, if you still need them. For now - when I say so, you will leave this room, or I will ask Aidan to carry you out."

Aidan dusted off his hands, giving the youngster an understanding look. "Trust me, I'm not staying in here one second more than Myrrh needs me. I've seen this. Up close and personal. It was painful. And the guy who did it to me, didn't expect me to live through it. I don't need the bullet points."

Which should have been our first clue, Church thought now, grabbing another splash of water out from under her captain's hand. *The guy who admits he's* half-demon *didn't want to hear this.*

In her own defense, she'd read Christophe Savonarola's autopsy report. She knew just enough of what Steven had done to his own brother to get why Aidan wouldn't want to risk the flashbacks from Hell.

Oh man. I had no idea.

Church leaned her head back to stretch muscles drawn taut by rage and horror. *Keep it together. Think it through.*

Myrrh had done just that, keeping matters as clear-cut as she could. Starting with the least terrifying basics.

"First, like all magic, sorcery requires energy." Myrrh had drawn a set of linked circles: sorcerer, summoned, and sacrifice. "In some cases, that can be provided by the sorcerer himself. In others, by small gifts to the entity in question. Food, special waters, other items the creature cannot obtain itself. But for darker or more powerful entities... that is not enough."

Aidan had flinched.

"You do not have to do this, my friend."

"Yeah, I do." Aidan stood, trenchcoat flaring as he stepped to the chalkboard. "Last thing we need is for some jackass to drag this out as a distraction at a bad time." He scanned the room, amber eyes burning. Flicked open one hand, fire blazing in his palm before he snapped fingers closed to snuff it. "See, *I'm* one of those entities. My father is a demon. And there were plenty of times I was summoned."

Church could have heard a pin drop. Dorren wasn't the only one chalk-white.

"I'm not joking. I am not screwing with you," Aidan said flatly. "Can't give you details on the sorcerer; ongoing investigation. But my father is an *actual* demon. Fallen angel, bound in Hell, the works. He has powers over fire. So do I. Though I didn't find out about that until after I'd died, and my soul got dragged out of this world." He shrugged. "Give him credit for family loyalty, he taught me how to protect myself then. And left enough clues around I finally figured out how to fight a summoning. So if you know any wanna-bes, tell them not to try it. *I will end you.*"

Church clenched fingers on her pen, bands of fire searing her soul-

Myrrh cleared her throat, stepping into the room's flinch. "That is the typical reaction of any intelligent being to an unfriendly summons," she said mildly. "And with good cause. A powerful sorcerer can enslave the actions *and the will* of a summoned entity.

In short, officers - some of your ancestors were enslaved. Aidan *has been* a slave, forced to wreak harm on innocents, if only by granting a sorcerer access to information he never would have had, otherwise." She scanned the room. "I have heard that the Dark Night was heralded by fiery dragons in Times Square. Those are an excellent example of controlled sorcerous summons. If you encounter a supernatural who has never been human, who is yet attacking humans *in plain view*, the odds are good it is being coerced. Elemental spirits generally do not *care* about humans, one way or another. If a balefire is burning a city down, *you must find the summoner*."

Police work. Church grabbed that thought like a lifeline, fire fading. *Got it.*

"Sad thing is, one of the best ways to find them is by looking for the bodies," Aidan said raggedly. "And... there's a reason for that."

Myrrh touched his shoulder.

Aidan leaned into it, and looked Dorren in the eye. "See, a sacrifice isn't just energy from the person who gets... murdered. Not for a demon. It's all the energy the sorcerer can wrap up and give *with* it. Anything in the air, floating around from all the lives the victim touched. Love. Hate. Grief. Anger; demons *love* anger. Most of all, they love the kind of vicious *snarl* in a soul born out of hate and suspicion. The kind of stuff that sets riots off, and burns whole cities down to get one bastard everybody *knows* has to be guilty. Because he's *there*." By his sides, fingers curled into white-knuckled fists. "Your sister. She was...."

Myrrh's hand closed on his shoulder; *enough*. "Your sister was killed because she was young, and pretty, and a child," the hell-raider said quietly. "Because her slayer wished to draw off the hate and fury of those touched by her death, to feed his minions what they needed to build the Demongate. Your sister was a *blameless innocent*. The perfect victim to shock a whole community into horror, and the burning need for vengeance." Myrrh stood straight as a drawn sword. "*That,* is why she died."

With a strangled wail, Dorren burst into tears.

Aidan shuddered, trenchcoat shimmering from black to ash-gray in spots before it steadied again. Swiped the back of his hand at his eyes, and squared his shoulders.

Marched over, plucked Dorren up like a weeping pillow, and carried the sobbing kid out.

"Wise man," Myrrh said into the silence. "Now we come to the truly unpleasant parts of sorcery."

Church choked. *You mean it gets worse?*

Yes. Yes it did.

"Generally speaking, malevolent sorcerers come in two types," Myrrh stated. "Organized, who have a central belief system and arrange their spells and rituals within its confines. And disorganized, who cobble together shreds of power they think might work from any scrap of lore. Each of these may in turn come in two types; solitary, or one of a group.

"Solitary organized casters of any magic, but especially of maleficent sorcery, are the most difficult to catch and identify." Myrrh tapped that one of four squares she'd chalked on the board, just beside the human diagram of likely ritual wounds and disfigurements. One of the reporters lost it right then, when red slashed across a chalk body to show arteries a sorcerer took care to *avoid*, if they wished death to be slow. "For much the same reasons as organized serial killers. They identify potential sacrifices long before they cast a spell, prepare thoroughly, and have thought through how they will dispose of the victim with none the wiser. If it is an animal and they have skills in butchery, the fuel for their summons may be disposed of to an unsuspecting community, spreading magical contamination to more unwitting victims. Which is one reason many faiths have rules about who is to butcher beasts, how, and in what fashion." A long breath. "Such methods of disposal are not unknown of when the victim is human, as well."

Then she'd *really* opened the nightmare gates.

Out in the hall with cool, sane water, Church pressed the heels of her hands against her cheekbones. As if that would let her push away the images. *Oh, god.*

Disorganized solitary was more or less your around the bend odd guy with a penchant for making cats - and people - disappear. Disorganized group fit Rajas Feniger's little graveyard bunch of would-be demon cultists. *Organized* group sorcerers included the Kali-worshipers Myrrh called Thuggees.

"And yes, that is where we get our word for *thug*," Myrrh had observed, illustrating a mass grave discovered by British authorities in the 1830s, where a caravan of over a hundred had perished on a riverbank. "A rather tamed word, these days, considering what they did to travelers who trusted them with their strangling scarves...."

That led to usual methods of ritual sacrifice, which pretty much ran the gamut of every nasty thing Church had ever imagined one human being might do to another, and a couple of things she wished she'd never known existed.

"Blood Eagle." Sherman wiped the back of her mouth with her hand.

"Oh yeah," Church breathed, trying not to picture Myrrh's simple sketch of a victim's lungs yanked out from under their ribs, left to dry until the poor soul either smothered or died of shock. "Am I a bad person for enjoying the *thunk* our intrepid reporter Matt Dayson's head made off his desk when he keeled over?"

"Let's be evil people together." Sherman tried to smirk. Given how pale her face was, it didn't wash. "I'm not sure I want to know how she knows how long you have to get the poor bastard to a hospital. If you can."

"No," Church agreed, grim images of Myrrh in the back of an ambulance swarming to mind. "No, not thinking about that. No."

"It's funny." Sherman rubbed a hand over her forehead. "You'd think how people torture each other would be the worst part."

"Yeah. Yeah, you would," Church laughed, not quite hysterical. Because that *hadn't* been the worst part.

After all, summoning demons - or dark fay, rakshasas, tainted elementals, what have you - was at least calling on evil that already existed in the world. Those sorcerers that *created* entities to do their dirty work....

Create a name, create a pattern for what you want it to do, set it to suck out energy from the people it's attacking to keep it going, and breathe life into it by.... Church couldn't hold back a shiver. "I'm never going to look at porn movies as *just guys having fun* again."

Not after Myrrh had coldly, calmly, laid out exactly what one sorcerer had done to throw a court case in his favor. It had involved the ritual sexual abuse of his partner and fluids Church didn't want to think hard about, all soaked into paper inked with the pattern for an entity to make one particular judge to rule in favor of the accused, no matter the evidence. All so the man could get off for a DUI, where the other driver had still been in the hospital.

"The result," Myrrh had stated, "was that same unprotected judge also threw out cases for everything from unpaid parking tickets to two child molesters and one attempted murderer. It would have been more, but because of the tulpa's attacks both the judge and many public defenders had to call for continuances. They were too ill to go on. I'm not certain how long the tulpa would have continued to exist had we not tracked it down and slain it, that sorcerer was not the most thorough, but even a few days more would have been *unacceptable*."

"Haaa," Church breathed now, massaging her temples. "At least I know now why Aidan looked like I'd called him an axe murderer, instead of just a sorcerer."

"Oh yeah." Sherman blinked, as if forcing dark images back. "All that in Shafat's head... think she'd see a counselor?"

"I think she'd drive a shrink around the bend." Church

shivered. "Father O'Malley's got notebooks dealing with her. They go back *centuries*."

"Cen-" The word caught in the captain's throat.

"According to O'Malley," Church sighed, feeling time like lead weights on her shoulders, "Myrrh's old enough to have been in the Library of Alexandria. In Egypt. Before it was burned."

"....Uh." Sherman blinked again, as if water had dripped out of her eyebrows somewhere painful. "When was that?"

"Oh, somewhere over twelve centuries ago," Church said dryly. "She's *still* holding a grudge."

"Twelve...." Sherman whistled. "You're saying she's-?"

"Older than pretty much anything else loose in Intrepid? Yep." Outside Coral, and that was Coral's business, as far as Church was concerned. *Gorgon* was enough for cops to swallow without panicking, even if Xanthippe had specifically given Sherman both an apology and a vial of de-petrifying gem water. *And* a long list of mundane things a gorgon was just as vulnerable to as any human being. Her people liked laying low for good reasons.

"Damn." But Sherman brightened, like weight had lifted off her own shoulders. "Maybe we ought to ask her for tips. Anyone who's chased that kind of evil for centuries, and she's still got that much together...."

"Yeah," Church agreed, recalling how Myrrh had finished off her lecture, taking the time to make sure anyone who'd fainted was awake again, and anyone who'd lost it otherwise had a moment to wipe their mouths before she summed up.

"It is critical to remember that not all sorcery is evil, and not all magic is sorcery," Myrrh had stated, once everyone had their eyes back in focus. The chalkboard behind her was mercifully blank, back to plain white-on-green headings of *Sorcery, Magecraft, Wizardry, Enchantment*. "Sorcery is most easily perverted to ill purposes, because it relies on the persuasion, coercion, or creation of other beings to do your will. But a benign sorcerer - and there are some, though they tend to call themselves cunning men or women - will use what they know to form alliances with helpful or neutral entities, and to block or destroy evil ones."

Which had made Church pause to think hard. If Steven had been one of the movers and shakers behind getting the term *sorcery* out there for all magic... things were going to be a lot harder for the average Joe on the street to figure out than they already were. Ow.

"Magecraft, the work of the elements and cycles of the world, is rare. It is almost always innate, manifests first by instinct, and is often an indication of ancestral contact with other powerful creatures. It is also most easily seen as benign or evil at the time of its casting, because one can directly observe the effects," Myrrh had noted. "Those of you who have seen Aidan summon flames know his magic is just as dangerous - and life-preserving - as any fire." She'd paused. "It is the fastest means of magic, which is one reason mages are often targets, and rarely survive to learn to defend themselves. In my experience, most mages do prefer simply to defend themselves. Magecraft draws directly on the caster's inner energies. Too long invoked, it can kill."

Might have to thump people's heads about that, Church scribbled down. *People aren't used to the idea of a fire that can put itself out.*

"Wizardry is more subtle, and harder to identify in intent unless one is well-versed in the symbols being employed." Myrrh had shaped a glyph of a swooping line attached to a cross. "An invocation of Saturn in European astrological traditions may be sad and malefic, whereas in India it is associated with a long life of great note. And in both, it depends a great deal on the person or entity the wizard is attempting to affect. A person for whom Saturn is weak might be strengthened, and the intent benign; for whom it is strong, more might be overwhelming, and cause illness. Saturn is often associated with the bones, so leukemia is one sickness under its rule; and it takes knowledge of both the practitioner and the practice to know if someone was only trying to help."

Church wasn't the only one blinking at that one. Good night. *We've got to get her to write this all down!*

"Finally, you are likely wondering how I do this." Myrrh swept fingers across the board, streaking it with rainbow above the headings. "I use enchantment."

Heh. Heh heh heh, Church chuckled, watching reporters frizz, obviously determined to figure out how to do that themselves. Or at least get a lead on who'd be next in Vegas.

"This is one of the most difficult practices to master, but also most easily invoked swiftly, by words or actions," Myrrh stated. "That is critical, when one is engaged hand to hand with the supernatural. Enchantment depends on invoking the truths one knows of the universe, in order to leverage the universe into behaving as one needs it to. In short - I tell the universe what I know of it, and what I need. And most of the time, it complies."

Church felt the room tense.

"Most enchanters you will ever meet are not capable of large effects," Myrrh said gently. "Many are faith healers. Some create luck charms, or talismans for good or ill luck, or even poppets for defense or attack. *All* magic can be used for good or ill. The practice of magic is a craft. It is a work of knowledge, and all of human knowledge has seeds of the bitter and the sweet. It is, in short, a *technology*."

Say what?

"I must admit, I detest the words *paranormal* and *super-natural*," Myrrh sighed, rubbing at the back of her neck. "Those words imply magic, and monsters, and all that spring from both, are outside the realms of normal human experience. They are *not*."

Church hadn't been the only one trying not to drop her jaw. What the heck?

"Every person in this room has a soul." Myrrh scanned the crowd, gray eyes sober. "Every person here, is present in more than the physical world you see and hear. Magic is part of existence. Like steel, or fire, or air itself. Some creatures use it innately, as our own bodies use iron in our blood. Some study and control it - as a chemist would iron compounds in the lab, or a surgeon wield steel blades to open a body and save a life. Magic, yes, is energy. The *practice* of magic is technology, as much as any computer scientist laying out circuits, or a house-builder hammering nails."

Church sat up at that, making a note to go back over the Savonarola house once the fire department cleared it. If magic was tech - Steven had had all kinds of tech in his workroom, not just computers. And he'd been using way more power than Myrrh thought any sorcerer his age could, and more *kinds* of power.

Scanned glyphs. Dorren getting info all over the internet. Was Steven doing the same thing? And can we track it? That guy was organized, no two ways about it. If we knew what kind of folklore he was looking at, we might have a place to start digging for what those killer trees are.

Any way you slice it, there's something we don't know. Something I didn't see, 'cause I didn't even know I should be looking.

"Like any technology, even with the best of intentions, mistakes happen," Myrrh had finished. "And that, is when we will be called. The difficulty is not just to sort ill magic from benign. It is very, very possible for a user of magic to have had the best will in the world, yet because of a factor they did not know, do harm instead."

Makes medical malpractice look tame, Church had thought, as shaken listeners started breaking up and taking off. Aidan, of course, had been long gone - well, as far as the reporters knew. From the angry text messages on Church's cell, he'd thrown Dorren into a cab home first. Then she guessed he'd ducked into a quiet corner and waited for Myrrh to get through the gruesome spots. After all, one of the intrepid reporters might need somebody looming at them to back off, if they still saw tiny archaic lady instead of an enchantress and hell-raider who could knock them silly with both hands tied behind her back.

Here and now the captain finally moved away from the water fountain, thumping her head back against the wall as if she bore it a personal grudge. "Hell of a lecture-"

Church stifled a snicker.

"Don't start," Sherman warned. "How long will we be able to keep it up on a webpage, linked to the department or not? Maybe especially if it is. Mayor Green hasn't raised a fuss yet...."

"But we all know who he liked as guest of honor for all those speeches about how open and welcoming Intrepid was to poor, misunderstood monster types," Church finished. "I know. So, given Coral's had more than luck on her side keeping her video up, I asked." She grinned. "She said it won't be a problem, and the department site's about to get a lot harder to hack."

Sherman raised a skeptical brow.

"Apparently there aren't a lot of gorgons, but a bunch of them are in high tech industries," Church obliged. "I guess they don't call it Silicon Valley for nothing."

Sherman facepalmed.

Church took the chance for a breath, glancing around at other cops and stray nosy types still getting over Myrrh's shock to their system. Wouldn't be bad for them to hear this, either. "Believe it or not, they're hoping Myrrh pulls this off. She's got a rep in the shadows. A scary rep, because if a hell-raider shows up it's time for sane supernatural types to find cover while other things try to kill her. And... well, seems Coral's people are just as worried about demon invasions as the rest of us."

Yep, that had ears perking her direction.

"But they're... medusas." The captain wriggled her fingers as if to prove she could. "All they have to do is take a good look. Without a veil."

"For someone who's alive, yeah," Church allowed. "Vampires...." She shivered. "I asked. I don't know how it works, I plan to corner Myrrh later if we make it past Halloween, but for a gorgon to stone something it *has to be alive*. Comes to undead,

Coral's in just as deep trouble as any of us." Which was why Coral carried banes, legal or not. Ouch.

"And?" Sherman pressed.

"And, they can get killed just as dead as the rest of us by an angry mob, too," Church admitted. "Coral says every gorgon remembers Perseus, and the last thing they want is to get on the bad side of every human on the planet. They live here." *Should I say it? Well, it is in the myth, right?* "Besides. We're related. Don't ask me how, I don't think Coral's relatives let themselves get poked by geneticists, but she says the only thing that makes a marriage sticky is making sure the lights *never* come on in the bedroom."

That got snickers. Good.

Only she was missing one particular fiery not-evil snicker, and given stray reporters roaming the halls that might not be good. "Anyone seen Aidan?"

"Speak up," Captain Sherman said when Heath and Eagleman glanced at each other. "Myrrh seems to have her head on straight but I'm worried about our firebug. I'm sure all of us have thought about setting Howe on fire, but he came a little too close to *doing* it. By accident."

"The Wolfe Hotel, over on Hilliard," Eagleman volunteered.

That wasn't one of the sites Myrrh had marked for Demongate shattering by way of heavy-duty benediction. "I thought they were halfway through tearing that down," Church objected.

"Exactly," the Cherokee cop shrugged. "Where else can a guy burn a few things and not get in trouble?"

~*~*~*~*~

The most warming thing about fire, Aidan thought, was it didn't judge you. It just... burned.

He fingered a flat piece of torn shingles as they blazed. The clear shimmer in the air of rising gases, the fine line of blue as heat and air and fuel combined, the licking brushstrokes of darker blue and yellow; living sapphires and topaz, devouring the wind.

Well. A small piece of the wind. He just wanted a little fire. Enough to pour out the thinnest, skimmed-off edges of pain and rage, draining fury before it really hurt someone.

I don't even know who I want to hurt.

He let that burst of pain go, focusing on twisting flames around like kitten-yarn, tasting the level of heat he needed to burn everything clear and clean; tar, composites, who knew what. He didn't want a trace of ash left.

"Bless the Lord, oh my soul...."

Myrrh's prayers were a soft murmur in a dozen languages, drifting on the wind from where she sat on a construction stool. Not pushy, no ragged edges of painful light to catch on the dark spots in his soul. Just a tired soul seeking comfort, soothing rough waves of anger and loss in her own spirit.

Just a rhythm. Just words. Aidan closed his eyes, almost feeling his mother's rosary beads glide between his fingers. There'd been a comfort in the melody of it for a boy, even if a young man had had his doubts. After all, that was the thing about faith - there wasn't any *proof.* Just words, and the stillness of night around his heart.

Heh. Isn't that why Myrrh says she's no saint? She doesn't have to believe. She knows.

But she did believe. Even after everything she'd seen. Everything she'd stopped; everything she hadn't been able to stop in time. Myrrh believed in a good world. A fallen world, where all of them lived sinning and sinned against, yet still a place people could fight to be good, love each other, and stand against evil. To death, and beyond.

Not sure I believe in God. But I definitely believe in Myrrh.

...Heh. Phoebe Savonarola might have patted her son's head, and told him that was just fine. That was what saints were *for*; interceding with God when a mere mortal's heart was too wounded to approach that light.

Sometimes it's okay if you can't believe, she'd told him, after one spectacular bit of teenage mayhem left the principal breathing down his neck about damages, and the rest of his fellow students wading through a sodden mess of soda and broken balloons swamping Home Ec. *Sometimes it's enough just to hope. And try.*

Well. *Try* was what he was working on. If only in the line of "try not to burn things down you don't really, really mean to."

Besides. The concentration it took to separate out each last element in the shingles, to burn *cleanly*, just letting bits of slate and pebble fall, soaked up worry about everything else. Especially the little fibrous bits of underlayer. Those were *really hard.*

Wait. Am I burning fiberglass?

...Cool.

"You sure it's safe to be breathing that stuff, man?"

Aidan blinked, focusing on Detective Eagleman's cousin Lee, demolition foreman and apparently not unsympathetic to guys who just needed to *break* something. "I'm good. I'm not breathing the smoke. Maybe a little of the steam."

"Fire mages are highly resistant to the perils of their element." The hardhat glowed yellow against Myrrh's hair, a dandelion in a snowdrift. "We have both encountered poisonous gases before, Mr Eagleman. I have various warnings set to alert me should the air turn perilous, and Aidan's instincts were trained by the most lethal lava vents you might imagine. He knows well how to burn even dire poison to harmless smoke." She lifted her head, giving the Cherokee man a warm smile. "I thank you for your concern. Your men are lucky to have you."

"A little less junk headed for the landfill's fine with me." Lee scratched a work-gloved finger under the band of his hardhat. "But how the hell... seriously, lady. I've seen people use a charm or two for luck on the job. Keeping your footing on the girders. Or your head with the heights. Nothing like *that.*"

"I would be most surprised if you had," Myrrh said frankly.

"Magical ability is innate; as the build of a runner, or the eyes for a jeweler. The difficulty for those born with more power than most is to survive long enough to learn to defend ourselves."

"Defend yourselves?" Lee looked uneasily at flames devouring another thick slab of shingles. "From what?"

Aidan tried not to grimace. *Great, the vampires have really pulled this "we're so harmless and misunderstood" trick on everybody-*

Myrrh raised pale brows. Nodded. "You are familiar with raven mockers?"

From Lee's start, whatever he had expected her to say, that wasn't it. "That's right; those guys come from around here," Aidan said, half to himself. "Mom told me stories, about the fire and rushing wind...."

Which made him want to shiver all over again, remembering how *like* that he'd been, just days ago. Not that he'd ever gone after someone's heart to eat. He hoped. Go after a heart for a quick kill, yes he *had* done that. There were plenty of nasties in Hell, and none of them believed in a fair fight.

Neither do I. Fair fight means I could lose.

"They prey on the sick and weary, and an untrained child tapping into magic will often make themselves ill." Myrrh shrugged. "There are as many creatures to prey on young magicians as there are lands and tongues to call them in. I was fortunate; I was raised by folk who knew what I might be capable of, and taught to be dangerous - very quickly."

Which made Aidan want to grab her and drag her off to some quiet corner until he could get the whole story, drat it. Who'd taught the kid she must have been centuries ago to be dangerous, instead of protecting her themselves?

Someone who wanted to make sure she had a shot at staying alive, Aidan told himself reluctantly. *Like we're doing for Dorren. Like... Aariel did.*

Which tied him in knots all over again, because he wanted to believe Aariel had left him on Earth because of some faint echo of love, he *wanted* to-

But Sword Aariel was Demon Lord Yaldabaoth's loyal guardsman.

If I'm here, he wants me here. For something that'll benefit my... uncle. So what's the plan? Because like hell am I opening any Demongate.

Not a chance. He was going to help Myrrh stomp it. Aariel had to know that. More to the point, *Yaldabaoth* had to know that.

Three options. First, he doesn't think Myrrh will get the Demongate closed in time. Second, he does, but thinks we might die doing it. Yaldabaoth would love to have her down for the count permanently. Third... there's something I don't know about.

Frankly, he was betting on door number three. Aariel was incredibly good at keeping cards close to his chest. "And fairies make everything messy," Aidan muttered.

"Fairies?" Lee twitched. "What, like out of the storybooks?"

"I wish," Aidan admitted. "Try something that tried to eat a little girl." Though Dorren would probably object to the *little* part. "Long story short, if the woods look spooky, don't go in there without a flamethrower." He grinned, thinking of the look on Church's face. "Or a bunch of chainsaws. Vrrrum!"

"A woodchipper would not be amiss," Myrrh reflected. "Although no sane forest fay will stand still long enough to be fed down a chute. Still, it would help in the cleanup."

Lee pushed back his hardhat long enough to give them both an incredulous look. Tugged the brim down, and sighed. "Cousin Fox says you two are for real, but - is this something that's going to show up on my worksite?"

"If you find trees where there aren't supposed to be trees, start hacking," Aidan advised. "Other than that... probably not?"

Lee nodded. "You telling my cousin the rest of the details?"

"I am," Myrrh said gravely.

"Then I'm getting back to work," the foreman stated. "Fox

brings home more than enough from his cases. Some things... I don't want to know." He waved at Aidan. "Feel free to branch out a little. Though if you've got a way to leave the nails in one piece - never know when some scrap will come in handy."

Yeah. And more than just the nails, Aidan thought. "Myrrh. Brass works on some fay, right?" He pointed at plastic snakes of damaged electrical wires. "How about copper?"

"It may." Myrrh eyed them. "Though that is more of an Occidental vulnerability than one common to any fay of European lore. Still... my lore on how folk of this continent handled creatures when they had only copper and stone is far from complete. It could indeed be useful."

Aidan grinned, yanking wires from the bin to melt off bright colors. "So... I know about fairies, but... mostly Grimm's stuff. Not so much things native right *here*. How can they get around? It looked like they need to root like trees."

"That is common among young forest fay," Myrrh agreed. "Older creatures are more mobile; though many, like the nymphs of Greece, take one forest or mountain under their guardianship. Still, mountains may shake, and forests be destroyed; a fay does not have to die simply because its favored earth is no more. They can move about. They usually do not, but they can." She hesitated. "Though I am *very* surprised to find walking trees in Intrepid. The Smokies have forest spirits of their own; from the water-cougars of the deep pools to the nunnehi under the mountain balds. They cannot be taking this intrusion lightly."

The *other people*, his mother had called them; maybe kin to the good neighbors of Orkney lore, maybe not. Folk the Cherokee thought of as immortal, and whispered about encountering to this day. "No," Aidan muttered, dousing a flame to fish out warm copper, "bet they're not...." *Wait. Wait a minute.*

Myrrh raised an eyebrow, curious.

Aidan held up a hand; *wait*. Because he had two things tangled up in his head at the moment, and he had to get them sorted, first.

The hell-raider inclined her head, patient as moonlight.

God, he was so glad for that. He had enough jangling around in his nerves with fire and people and *being solid all the time*, no way to just blip out of a tangible grasp, it made him want to start running and never stop. But Myrrh knew how to *not talk*. It helped.

"The walking trees you know about shouldn't be here without other things - other *people* - getting cranky," Aidan stated, feeling out the idea. "So... either there's some reason they're not, or... they're not something you know about."

"Either is possible," Myrrh affirmed. "I am well-versed in the lore of monsters. But I hardly know *everything*." She granted him a rueful smile. "Or, possibly, we are dealing with creatures I do know, working in concert with a sorcerer who has no qualms about sacrificing human lives to conceal them from natives who should take offense."

"Oh, just that," Aidan rolled his eyes. "Terrific."

"Did you think this would be easy? Twenty-five years...." Myrrh rubbed her arms, as if chilled now that he'd damped his flames. "It is hard to grasp that any could stray from sanity so long, and so widely, as to leave us so... shorthanded."

"Target-rich environment," Aidan muttered. "Us?" Not that he was upset, exactly, just - who did Myrrh think *we* were?

"Those of us who seek out evil, and destroy it, so that which is good may flourish," the hell-raider stated. "In part because other-wise that which is evil would come hunting us in our beds, with a midnight snack on their minds."

Okay, that he couldn't argue with. Although.... "You know I wouldn't leave you in the lurch on this." He had to pat down the prickling hairs on the back of his neck. "Even if there is a Fay Lord."

"I know, because you are a very good man." Myrrh's eyes were gray as storms, rain in the midst of thirsty drought. "I also know that neither of us wishes to fight evil head-on and in a fair fight, if there is a better way. You spoke of the nunnehi?"

"Well, it's just... Coral's helping us out, right?" Though he didn't know if that was because the gorgon enjoyed talking to someone who didn't mangle Ancient Greek, or if she just loved watching over-arrogant bloodsuckers get their heads handed to them. "There's got to be other locals. They can't be happy about a Demongate, either. Think we could talk to them?"

Her grin lit her face, bright as that darn hardhat. "Now that, could very well be-"

"Hey!" Lee's voice carried across the yard. "You can't go in there!"

For a moment Aidan and Myrrh side-stepped each other, before he rolled his eyes and let her get in front of him. *Idiot. You've got the distance weapons, unless she needs to pull out a verse. Otherwise, let her have a clear space for the sword.*

Wait. Those looked like microphones. And cameras. "Should we run for it?"

"Running might distract other members of Lee's crew. This is dangerous work. They could be harmed," Myrrh said solemnly. "We should simply walk very fast."

"You could just, you know, maybe make them look the other way?" Aidan suggested, voice low.

"I could; and if I thought them truly hazardous to life or limb, I would," Myrrh murmured. "But we face creatures who deal in illusions. How will those reading the news know how to deal with fairies, if we bend minds as well?"

She had a point. Damn it. "I know you. There's no way you want to be on TV."

"I do not." Myrrh faded behind a plastic-tarped pile of rubble with him; nodding to one of Lee's crew as they passed, with a jerk of her head back toward the news van at the demolition site entrance. From the sardonic looks and one salute they got back, the guys weren't any happier to see cameras than they were. "But those with ill intent have already put their messages out to the world. Someone has to counter them." She took a breath. "And I have no kin to be hostages to fortune, should I state something vampires and their coteries decide they don't like."

Seventeen centuries. "I guess you'd stop tracking your kids down after the first thousand years."

"I have never had children." Myrrh walked on, matter of fact, as if he'd asked about the weather. "There were few willing to offer for an enchantress of my strength. Men disliked the idea I would be able to out-cast them if I so chose. Though some did offer after I converted, convinced they would - hmm, how is it people say these days, *straighten me out?*" She shook her head, as if at old memories of folly. "Wandering the desert as a hermit is far preferable."

Aidan blinked, feeling as if he'd asked someone for a score between one and ten and got back *blue*. "You'd rather wander a scorpion-infested desert than have kids?"

"I have helped raise them from time to time, but my profession and calling require a wandering life," Myrrh shrugged. "What I want, had I ever wished the sacrament of marriage, is irrelevant. I am a construct; of human magic, not of demonic or fay origin. This body is not capable of creating life. To so abuse that sacred gift would be a grave disservice to myself, and to any man." She cast him an amused look. "But you, my friend, are no more sterile than your birth father, and it behooves you to be circumspect if you go a-courting, for it is likely your children will be fire-callers from the very cradle."

He almost walked into a low-hanging beam.

Myrrh is- Myrrh's not- Geh?

"Are you well?"

"No," Aidan choked out, as they worked their way around the edge of the site, hopefully away from the reporters now haranguing Lee with much gesticulation. "That's... that's not something you just say to a guy!"

"Your pardon," Myrrh nodded. "I should have left that to Father O'Malley. It would be easier for a man to seek council about marriage from another man. I think? I'm never certain of these matters."

"That's not what I-"

"Though based on those I have rescued from Faerie and other realms, I would suggest waiting at least a month before you think of courting anyone," Myrrh advised. "It takes time to re-accustom oneself to this world after so long where the senses are *other*. It would be poorly done by you both if you did not have an accurate impression of the lady."

...I give up, Aidan thought, still stunned. *This is- I'm not- no. Not going to think about this right now.*

Later. With Father O'Malley. And a big cup of coffee. Possibly spiked. Alcohol burned well, right?

Worry about it later. After we get a few more sites purified.

Maybe later he'd have a clearer head about why this was *throwing* him so much. Outside of, his mom had always wistfully hoped for grandkids, and she hadn't gotten any....

Hell. I don't even know that, Aidan realized. *I mean, there wasn't anybody but Steven home when we got there, and I think Church would have mentioned if he had a wife-*

Living wife, anyway. With his brother's habits, and what he knew about sorcerers bent on raising demons, any woman Steven took to bed would have been... fodder.

I should ask Church. I don't want to, but she'd know.

And maybe the detective would have a clue why Myrrh had brought up... argh. He'd brought it up. Maybe not gracefully, there was a big difference between scampering off into the desert to avoid a guy planning to deprogram you from what a traditional Egyptian must have thought was a weirdo gods-denying cult, and not wanting to have kids at all. Right?

It's just, outside of that thing about olive oil, she never talks about family, I didn't think- ow. They must not have been happy with her. At all.

Given that was the same family that'd made sure Myrrh had

been trained as an enchantress in the first place, which implied they not just knew about magic but were a pretty dab hand at it themselves... oh boy.

Talk to Father O'Malley. Definitely.

After they got past the damn- *darn* reporters.

Aidan took another look toward the open gate where Lee was making rude gestures at the interlopers, but not distracting them nearly as much as he probably would have liked. *I know Myrrh's not going to hide us with magic. I get it. But I really don't want to deal with those guys.*

They could sneak out right here, under the web of orange construction plastic shutting out casual passersby, as long as people didn't look right this way. If the shadows were just a little darker, so people ducking under the membrane wouldn't scatter enough shifting orange light to catch the eye....

Was it darker here?

Screw it. Worst they'll get is a shot of sane people trying to get away from microphones. Aidan ducked and tugged up the plastic wall, willing to crawl on cold ground if that was what it took.

From that sense of warmth and light, Myrrh was right behind him.

Out!

Aidan flexed fingers as they stood, as if he'd been holding onto something too tightly. Damn nerves.

"This way, you damn wandering-loose idiots."

Aidan grinned at fuming blue eyes. "Nice to see you too, Detective."

"How did those guys not- never mind, don't want to know." Church crooked a finger to beckon them across the next sidewalk, where her rental was precariously parked in the one spot no one else had dared take this close to flying demolition debris. "Would you mention it before you go off to wreak havoc and destruction sometimes?"

"But we were wreaking neither havoc nor destruction." Myrrh

plucked the hardhat off her head. "Excuse me, Detective, I must return these."

"Oh no you don't." Church swiped the hat from Myrrh's hand, then eyed Aidan until he handed his own over. "I'll go tell Eagleman's cousin you're off his site. You stay here. I got a call from the Father about a location before I tore out after you two. He's got permission from the property owner to go zap it one, and I want us all in on it. Just in case we have more walking trees."

Chapter Six

"Well, at least that one went well," Father Ricci sighed, gripping hot coffee like a lifeline.

"Storage locker," Church grumped, indulging in the heat herself. It might hold back some of the nightmares. How many people had put their stuff in that rented garage since? "How the hell did you know about that one? It's not a listed crime scene."

She and the rest of the detectives were of two minds about that. On the one hand, good, knowing about kill scenes got them closer to making sure the Demongate stayed slammed like a good old-fashioned bank vault door.

Called three banks already. Better get to calling the others, soon.

On the other hand... the locker was a crime scene. A very, very contaminated crime scene, that who knew how many people had walked through without a clue, in relation to a suspect now presumed dead. And not even undead, like the vampire mistress still filing harassment and probably wrongful death suits when she got the chance. Truly dead dead. The prosecutor's office would throw them out on their ears for wasting time, with all the half-burned cases left after the courthouse fire.

At least I can make a note. In case we live through this and someone wants to legally fry Steven's butt anyway.

Someone besides the guy who owned the locker, at least. The poor rental guy had been all but foaming at the mouth after Myrrh found ant-sized holes drilled in the floor so body fluids could leak down to feed supernatural roots.

Very long roots. Church shivered, and wondered if she could get the coffee any hotter. *If those things have a root spread like regular forests, we're looking for twenty-foot walking trees. Terrific.* "So who called you about that one, anyway?"

"No one called me," Father Ricci said firmly. "Someone did call Father O'Malley."

"Someone you don't think I'd approve of, or you'd tell me right out," Church said flatly. Ran down a mental list of people she'd crossed paths with lately, and people they might know- "Switch? Switch O'Connor called?"

Father Ricci grimaced.

And O'Malley's not in the kitchen. "Giving spiritual counsel, my ass," Church snarled, rising. "When I get my hands on-"

"He is. To Aidan," Father Ricci said sternly. "You can swear at the hitman - who is, by the way, still a confessing Catholic - when the two of them get finished. Besides, Myrrh's got him first."

Myrrh sat in the rearmost pew, beside a tall redhead with ice-blue eyes. "It's been a very long time, Jim O'Connor."

"...I didn't think it could be you." The man who'd been a desperate teenager twenty-five years ago, dragging his brother from a Wailer's drowning embrace, looked cold and cruel as ever a demon had wished to be. "Where have you been?"

"In Hell," Myrrh answered the hurt under the ice, the tattered edges of a blackened soul. "Where Steven Savonarola's machinations sent me. I am sorry I could not break free sooner."

Fingers drummed on the back of the pew ahead, callused with the marks of a well-used gun. "Anyone else, I'd swear that was a lie."

Myrrh shrugged. The man had every right to doubt. He'd been through enough terror and rage to break a man, or turn them to burn their lives out Hunting; and then faced a world that condemned Hunters as murderers. "I am glad to have met your niece. Dorren is bright, and determined. I hope we have given her enough information to be cautious, as well."

"Dorothy," Switch said coldly. "She was always Dorothy,

before-" He swallowed, jaw set. "Megan's dead because of me."

"Megan is dead because of Steven, and no one else." Myrrh matched his chill. His heart was too sore for kindness. If she wished to give him a chance to draw toward light again, she had to start where he was standing.

"He meant to get to me."

"And would you let him succeed?" Myrrh raised a deliberately arrogant brow. "How powerful you will make him, even in the pit. How cruel, to wrest you from those living souls who still need you. Your niece is in grave danger. She has a touch of the Sight, as Church does, and the fay will target those likely to see them *first*."

His voice was too low to be a snarl. "So why aren't you there?"

"Because your niece has only seen them," Myrrh replied. "Detective Church has shot them. I do think they will prefer to pursue her over the child. I have left what protections around your brother's house I could. But there are limits to what I can do when her mother desperately wants me off her property for disrupting her view of the fairness of the world; that evil only targets those who deserve it, and therefore she can blame *herself* for her daughter's death, and so control the universe."

Fingers clenched on polished wood. "That's not who she blames."

"I imagine she is willing to blame anyone who stands still long enough. Including her own surviving daughter," Myrrh observed. "The mothers of the lost are often not rational. Nevertheless, you are Dorren's uncle. No matter what Maeve may call you, or whether or not she bans you from her demesne, you have the right of kin to protect your niece. Your actions, not mine, are more likely to make her a defended target, instead of a helpless one." She let her lips bend in the slightest smile. "The library card was a good idea. Lenses of sight would be a better one. I wager you are still in contact with Master Glass, or his apprentice. I would very much appreciate their number."

"What makes you think I'm-"

"From Church's files, some of your suspected kills were sniped. After the Wailer, I know you would not wish to be fooled by a glamour into striking the wrong target."

That earned her a narrowed look. As well it should.

"You know Dorren is in danger," Myrrh stated. "You know something of the nature of the threat. You can pursue your hatred and vendetta against the world, or you can take responsibility for one you care for." She paused. "And if you wish to face creatures who deal in illusions and clouded minds, that will have to start with your own responsibility for the lives you have taken."

The smirk on his face would never melt those icy eyes. "That's rich, coming from a thief of souls."

"Indeed it is," Myrrh allowed. "But I steal souls to give those locked in torment another chance at redemption. You steal the hopes, the dreams of ensouled lives. To shatter dreams is to invite despair, and to allow that deadly sin to destroy other lives. It is harmful to the soul."

"Most people I've killed? Believe me, the world's a better place with them gone." Switch leaned back in the pew, eyes creased like a lazy man-eating tiger.

"I did not say it was harmful to their souls," Myrrh said sternly. "The man I knew risked his life to save his brother. What has become of him? If we are still alive on All Saint's Day, I intend to ask why you walk this path."

Switch laughed, low and sardonic; only gradually trailing off as she remained silent. "You're serious."

"As death," Myrrh replied quietly. "Dark sorcery has been etched on Intrepid with human lives. I have no doubt at least one of those deaths came at your hands. Steven is very skilled at manipulating others into acts advantageous to him."

"Is?" Switch coiled, a rattlesnake ready to strike. "He's alive?"

"I have reason to believe his physical body has perished," Myrrh answered, very deliberately. "Yet I also know that his heritage is such that dire fate is only likely to slow him down.

Momentarily."

"Heritage?" He stood, trying to loom over her. "He was no vamp. Dead people *stay* dead."

"He was no vampire, indeed," Myrrh agreed, unfazed. Once a soul had been loomed at by Sword Aariel, mere humans somehow failed to impress the nerves. "Demons, however, are quite another matter. And for that you need not take my word, but Father O'Malley's." She drew in a breath, oddly amused. "Though that may have to wait. He's currently counseling a rather shaken soul."

Aidan slugged his coffee, and wished the caffeine were doing any good whatsoever. "Are you telling me Myrrh is a *nun?*"

Father O'Malley tutted at him, waving an instructing finger. "Now, now, my boy; you should know that as a heretic to both Catholic and Orthodox alike, she can be no such thing. I doubt she could even qualify as a lay sister. And I know too well she's made no vows of obedience." The elderly priest paused, so Aidan could catch his breath. "What she is, is a devout and sincere believer, born in the very earliest days of the faith. And what is the teaching on what lies between man and woman, as stated by the apostles themselves?"

Eep. He used to know that one. "It is better to marry than to burn?"

"That too," Father O'Malley agreed. "But marriage is two souls becoming one flesh, to go forth, be fruitful, and multiply. To do otherwise, especially in the youngest era of the Church, is nothing other than unsanctified lust, and thus mortal sin."

Sin? Myrrh? "But she's-"

"Barren," Father O'Malley said quietly. "Barren, she would say, as the dry bone and dust she draws into mortal form with the dawn. She cannot bear life, and knows it, and so she cannot enter that sacrament. It would be a sin before God, and a dreadful wrong to any man who loved her."

His eyes were prickling, Aidan knew. It *hurt*. "It's not fair."

"Shafat has never asked that life be fair, young man. Though I think I know why she told you so bluntly," the priest mused.

Aidan tried to laugh. "She's lousy with people?"

"Oh, that too," Father O'Malley chuckled. "Were she born in this century, I'd call the lass a geek, for all she dwells in ancient books rather than electrons. But mostly... she was all you had to cling to, for a very long time. And you needed her, as a man needs shelter from the blazing desert sun. But when that blistering peril retreats, to stay in the shade and avoid traveling to other, more healing oases, is a needless hesitation. She is as a barren rock in the desert. She wishes you to find a place you can grow, and live your life, and be well."

Aidan had to shake his head. "She couldn't have waited until after we know if we'll live through Halloween?"

"Myrrh has always believed in beginning as you mean to go on," O'Malley said plainly. "Or as I believe my younger congregants put it...." He reached out, and patted a very confused fire mage on the shoulder. "You, young man, have been friendzoned."

Aidan buried his head in his hands. "...I don't want to think about this."

"Likely wise," the priest reflected. "I'll own it's been some time since last we were speaking, but I suspect Myrrh would have been much subtler twenty-five years ago."

Aidan blinked. Tried to think that through. "The skull and dawn. Usually, she's just down in Hell a day or so...."

"At times longer, if her remains ended up somewhere difficult for light to reach," Father O'Malley agreed. "If that woman has a terror of anything on this earth, it would be the abyss of the sea."

Aidan shivered. It was all too easy to picture Myrrh drowning in lightless depths, sinking deeper and deeper, until light showered in a fountain and only ancient bone still drifted down....

Oh God.

"Though from records I have, it seems the skull of a hell-raider tends to find the light again, sooner or later, by what seems odd coincidence," the priest mused. "I'd say that heretic or not, there are those who have mercy on poor souls bound in Hell."

Thank God. Possibly quite literally. Although- "She was down there *twenty-five years!*" Aidan hissed.

"And when she rose, she brought one soul back to the living world, to breathe again," O'Malley told him firmly. "That woman has saved lives in this world, and souls to pass to the next, but never has she been able to bring one back to save his own life. Don't you dare tell her it was not worth it."

"But it hurt her," Aidan whispered. As if *hurt* could wrap up everything in Hell in one neat package; the pain, the lost hopes, the lies....

"And it's when we are hurt, that we need our friends the most," the priest said plainly. "Be her friend, youngster. The two of you are both injured to the soul. Let her lean on you, and lean on Church; there are so few people in this world Myrrh knows she can trust." He paused. "A little praying wouldn't hurt."

"I don't know about that," Aidan admitted. "You should have seen what happened with those barbweasels. I'm still not sure how I pulled that off. Though, never been so glad to see rats in my life-"

Heavy wood boomed. "FBI! James O'Connor, stay where you are!"

Chapter Seven

Wednesday, Oct 22nd

"There's something wrong with my life," Church announced to the shell-shocked detectives also grabbing coffee, "when I want to scream at the FBI for taking away a hitman before I can have a friendly conversation with him."

"Friendly," Heath nodded knowingly.

"Okay, mostly friendly. In terms of nobody shooting at each other," Church admitted. "Like it or not, his family's being targeted, and we can't be on top of them twenty-four seven. If he's willing to shoot monsters to keep them off his niece...." She sighed. "I hate to agree with Myrrh on this, but at least we know the guy's a good shot."

Kirsten Carlyle waved a mug. "She did say she wasn't a cop."

Church eyed her fellow detective, wondering yet again why it was easier to go out for milkshakes with a gorgon than another woman in the same hard-as-nails job. Granted, up until this past week she hadn't known Coral was a gorgon. Just a sculptor and memorial-carver with the same dark sense of humor cops never used on civilians.

Well, could be 'cause Kirsten doesn't like milkshakes. Or the fact I like people to use my last name.

Seriously, was it so hard for Kirsten to wrap her mind around the fact that *Jezebel* was not what Church wanted to be called? Especially when one of her best allies against the bloodsuckers was a priest.

Granted, she'd hated her first name a lot longer than that. She still wasn't going to change it. Her parents hadn't given her much, but they'd given her *stubborn*.

"Definitely not a cop," Church agreed. She didn't hate Kirsten.

They just didn't click. But if she could think about being polite to a hired assassin, she'd better be civil with her own people. "I'm not sure what we'll do when I'm back on duty. Maybe she'll work something out with the captain." *If we're still alive.*

And... here was the chance to ask, while she still had her nerve. "Anyone know what's up with Tom? Unofficially."

That earned her a half-dozen speaking glances. If she could just figure out what they were saying.

Heath shrugged, taking it for granted that as senior detective he'd better give her the news. "It's not looking good. Somebody's looking at his accounts, and...."

Church tried not to slump. "Maybe I'd better not know."

"Looks like Annabel had problems none of us knew about," Heath forged on. "Serious problems." He made a circling motion near one temple. "The kind of help you need for seeing things doesn't come cheap. Even less cheap if you're keeping your wife off the books so no one bounces you to a desk."

For a moment Church felt crushing pity. Then blinding rage. "That *bastard*. That... that... damn you, Savonarola, if you make it back here I am going *to rip out your spine and make you eat it!*"

"Ah...." Kirsten stepped back, pale. "You don't mean-"

"Oh, the hell I don't," Church gritted out. "What'd Aidan tell us happened before he got murdered? *He was seeing things.* Only they were really there." She breathed out, wishing she had Aidan's talent for slamming out rage as fire. "You have any idea what psychiatric meds do to someone who's *not* crazy?"

One of her fellow detectives made a choked noise. Church felt like throwing up herself.

"Shafat says fairies," Heath barely stumbled on the word, "make solid illusions. Like holograms you can touch. How can we be sure what we see is what's there?"

Kirsten looked even more glum. "How can we keep the lawyers from jumping on this in every case, saying we can't be *sure* we saw the defendant?"

Ow. This was a bunch of disheartened cops, that was for sure.

"Well, these lectures are for us," Church said practically. "Let's ask her."

"How to see what is really there." Myrrh looked over worried and interested cops, intrigued. "I should have expected you would ask the difficult ones."

"You do it all the time," Church waved her pen, blue eyes sober and tense. "I've seen you."

"Yes, but what I do is unlikely to work for any of you, unless you are the successful survivor of a near-death experience," Myrrh answered frankly. "I do not mean what some magical workers have attempted; to have their heart stopped, and then started again. Such a walk near Death will provide some measure of the Sight, if a person carries the potential for it to awaken, but it is reckless, dangerous, and often fatal. Aidan and I see what is truly there because we see as much with our *spirits* as with eyes of flesh and blood. Our souls were severed from our bodies, unhoused from bone and blood, and only returned to life by skilled magic and the grace of God." She swept the room with her gaze. "In short, we died. Very thoroughly. I would *not* advise you to try it."

Thump.

Myrrh deliberately did not laugh. She recognized the reporter that had passed out yesterday. Matt Dayson had dropped his notebook, and looked more than a bit gray around the mouth, but he was still here after her lecture on maleficent magic. Which meant he at least had guts.

Let's hope he has sense, as well. Or this will be the death of him.

"Part of the difficulty is there are several... levels, to perceptual reality," Myrrh said thoughtfully. "And several frequencies of energy involved. Someone skilled at sensing demonic auras may completely miss one of the fay underfoot; someone who works the elements might walk by a true saint without noticing more than the scent of clean air. Methods humans employ to expand their perception of reality tend to favor one mode of magical energy over another. Which is one reason tampering with demonic magic is never a good idea. It colors your perceptions of the world, damping out brighter energies, and driving souls to despair."

Stop. Not helping.

Well, at least she could start with what would *not* help. "Avoid psychedelic substances," Myrrh advised. "Mescal, LSD, ayahuasca - stripping your vision of your mind's natural defenses, without skilled spiritual protection, is asking for the worst trip of your life. Under certain circumstances, applied by skilled individuals working in a belief system that you share, then yes, such visions can give insight into spiritual imbalance, and sometimes healing. They will never bestow permanent Sight of that which is real."

Think. Calm yourself, as if you were searching for the right verse. "Do any of you meditate?"

Shifting looks; shuffling feet under desks. The reporter gave a tentative wave.

"Mr. Dayson," Myrrh nodded. "If I may ask, are your reasons for meditation spiritual, religious, for health, or other? *None of my business* is a perfectly legitimate reply."

"Just to... clear the noise out?" Dayson offered. "You know. After the day. My job's kind of... noisy."

"I can imagine," Myrrh said wryly. "Half of learning how to see what *is* there, is clearing out what is *not* there. Meditation is one of the safest, most sure ways to train your mind. It is neither easy, nor fast. But this is one reason most cultures support those who pray, and calm the rushing sea of their minds into stillness. Meditation, coupled with faith, is the most certain way to see truly... and survive the experience."

Yes. This is what they need to know.

"The most crucial thing to remember is that creatures who are normally unseen, *do not want* to be seen," Myrrh stated. "Many such creatures are harmless to mortals... *unless* they are seen. If they are, and realize it, they are outraged. Much as you would be if some uncouth stranger walked into your bathroom while you were showering, and stole your soap."

Frozen blinks. As if they weren't certain she was serious. Well, Church was, given how she lounged back in her chair with a shrugged *go on*. But the rest of them... hmm. "Genesis, chapter nine?" Myrrh tried.

More blank looks. Aside from Aidan, who huddled on himself like he wanted to sink through the floor.

Church snorted. "Okay. I give. I give! I'm letting O'Malley hand me a black book sometime. There's something *deeply disturbing* about the half-demon knowing the Bible better than the rest of us."

"I'd quote that line about the Devil and scripture, but I'd be lying," Aidan said ruefully. "What can I say? Mom started me on Genesis before I could talk. Good for her." He glanced at Myrrh. "Noah and the vineyard, right? Noah passed out naked in his tent, Ham looked..."

"While Shem and Japheth took a garment, and walked backward to cover their father without looking upon that which was not theirs to see," Myrrh nodded. "They were blessed, and Ham accursed. For in that elder time - and many of the things which wish not to be seen are *very old* - to be naked was a shame upon the person who viewed it. Not the one unclothed. Since to many creatures of power, to be shamed is to be lawful prey... *don't do that*."

"Lawful prey?" Dayson almost squeaked.

"By their laws. Not ours. And if you see them, Mr. Dayson, you have agreed to abide by their laws. Unless you have the luck and intelligence to also bring along overwhelming firepower." Myrrh cleared her throat. "Unless there is obvious and ongoing harm, if you see a creature others do not, do your best not to escalate the situation. Use politeness and civility, as you would with an ordinary citizen behaving in a manner you find odd enough to attract attention." She paused. "Of course, if someone is being eaten, all bets are off."

So. Now to the mechanics of what they seek.

"There are preparations and objects which allow seeing through illusions and glamours," Myrrh stated. "I would not say they will hold against *everything*. The strongest demonic and fay powers have been known to fool even them, for a time." She paused. "Bear in mind, I can only give firsthand testimony for a few methods. For others, I have had to observe various companions over the years. They simply make no difference to what I, personally, see."

"But they work?" Church said, intent.

"Well enough that I trust companions at my back using them." Myrrh turned to the chalkboard again. "If you have the chance to talk to Hunters in a peaceful situation, you will find they are very, *very* conservative in their methods. As am I. We use what works, and rarely experiment. Experiments, when dealing with the supernatural, all too often end up with innocents dead. So. These two methods are very, *very* old."

Green and blue chalk to sketch the painted outline of a kohl-adorned eye. White chalk in the ragged outline of a lump of glassy stone with a hole pierced through it.

"You may have heard of the fay ointment of sight." Myrrh stepped back. "That will work, when acquired from a friendly fay; but usually it is acquired accidentally, which leads to one of those Good Neighbors tracking the accidental seer down with malice aforethought. Which results in blindness, or death." She gestured to the board. "The priestly kohl of ancient Egypt is an entirely human recipe, and so does not provoke the outrage of a theft. I will write the ingredients and manner of preparation down later. I can do it in my sleep, and I have. So I would prefer to write it, so someone can look over my shoulder and point out any steps hazardous to a less experienced practitioner before they are posted up on the Web."

"Hazardous?" Church asked warily.

"One of the steps involves grinding material that contains lead," Myrrh answered. "The amount is small. In the past I've managed by finding a place with a good breeze. These days I suspect you would want a lab with a fume hood."

The detective blinked at her. "...You mean, *regular* kind of hazardous. Not magic."

Myrrh tried not to snicker. "Detective, for me magic is a regular hazard. But yes. A purely physical danger. Although the steps of proper melding and empowerment can bring some magical hazard, as well."

"So what's that other thing?" Dayson peered at the board.

"In Egypt it is called an *aggri*," Myrrh replied. "In Britain, adder's stone; in the Highlands, druid's glass. The Russians have their own names they call to the *Kurinyi* who protect their flocks. It is a stone that natural actions of the world have worn a hole through; such concentrated terrestrial energy tends to cancel out false images created by other powers. Look through the lens of air, and most deceptive magic will be revealed."

Church raised an eyebrow. "So what's the catch?"

Myrrh held up a finger at a time. "First, they are not common, though the coasts are a good place to look. Second, they are *not* created by human hands; or indeed, by any hands. The hole must be cut by natural water. It is sometimes possible to negotiate with elementals to find them, or encourage their creation. But terrestrial energy must be untouched by any other magic, if it is to serve its purpose. Third...." At this Myrrh had to smile. "You've had to restrain suspects before. I'm sure you can imagine all the ways holding up a large rock in front of your eye can go wrong."

That won her a huff of a laugh. Good.

"There are ways to create lenses that cut through spells, but they are complicated," Myrrh went on. "They are also usually focused on one type of energy at a time. But carrying several sets of lenses can be much more practical than a rock, so I will look into my contacts and see what I can find." She had to pause, wrestling down sorrow and hurt. "I'm told many of those I know are imprisoned, or dead. Of those who do survive - well. Most of them are used to working on small batches, for those they trust. Obtaining supplies for more than a few people will not be easy."

Dayson sat up straight, gaze intent. "You mean they're used to working for Hunters."

Ah. Now I see why he is here, Myrrh thought. Not that she could allow it to matter. The truth would persuade him, or not. "They work for those defending themselves and others against supernatural creatures who would prey on humankind. You call many of them Hunters, yes. But for many who do not consider themselves human, we are simply a very angry human posse, searching for outlaws. Many creatures of magic see that as quite reasonable. Some, in fact, will ask for our help, against creatures more deadly and dire than themselves. As I intend to ask any friendly denizens of Intrepid for help against what we face." She smiled. "Let me tell you of some of those other folk...."

Chapter Eight

"Absolutely not."

He may not be supernatural, Aidan deliberately leaned back in his plush visitor's chair in Howe's leather-library office, *but he's sure not harmless.*

"The Intrepid Police Department has no evidence to link Steven Savonarola to any crime, and so no basis for a warrant to request access to any property, tangible or otherwise, of which my firm is executor." Howe linked his fingers together before him, staring at Church as if she were the only other person in the room. "We have more than enough difficulties with the estate already. Certain items mentioned in the will have gone missing. And you were the last person in the house before its untimely destruction, Detective."

Beside Aidan, Myrrh kept her face perfectly straight. But he knew that twitch of lips.

Yep. Howe's hoping if he ignores us, maybe we'll go away.

From Church's glare, she didn't appreciate the insinuation. But she wasn't about to rise to the bait. "I'm letting you know we're looking for your client's esoteric research as a courtesy, Mr. Howe. We could get the Feds in on this."

"Ah yes." Howe's fingers unwove, laying flat on the desk. "I hear they have their own problems. Something about a disk that might implicate Agent Cushman in... shall we say, less than proper monetary entanglements?"

Church *focused*, aura knife-sharp. "Who told you anything about-"

"I have my sources," the attorney cut her off. "You can see yourself out, Detective." His eyes didn't flicker past her. "And take those with you."

"Interesting," Aidan murmured, as all three of them got out

Howe's fancy office door to the lobby.

"The fingerprint check, and now information on a disk nobody outside NCBI should be talking about?" Church said sourly. "He's got sources, all right. Wish I knew if he bribed them with cash or blood-"

Myrrh cleared her throat.

Aidan heard Church's teeth click, as Dayson came through the law office's front door. "Make that *both*."

The reporter eyed her right back; looked past a cranky detective right at Aidan. "Mr. Lindisfarne. How *interesting* to find you here."

Aidan gave him a kitten's wide-eyed blink. "Really? I thought I was kind of boring. Just a concerned citizen helping the IPD with inquiries. Dime a dozen."

"I rather find it interesting you are here, Mr. Dayson," Myrrh stepped in, smooth as if they'd planned it. "Gathering background information on Nuria Cruz, perhaps?"

"If I were, I wouldn't tell you," Dayson said bluntly. "Though given the Nightsong is a public corporation, the fact that they keep trying to file charges against you while this firm and others appear to be dragging their feet is... interesting."

Say what?

Myrrh's eyes narrowed, adding that to whatever pile of stray facts she kept about the current crazy state of the world. "What sort of charges?"

"I intend to investigate that more thoroughly before we have a chat, Ms. Shafat," Dayson smirked. "Wouldn't want to get hit with a libel case. Everything I publish about you is going to be unvarnished fact."

"Why, thank you," Myrrh inclined her head. "That is most professional of you."

Ooo, burn, Aidan thought, almost smirking.

Dayson scowled, then smoothed it into professional calm. "I hear Howe's filed charges on impersonation and grave tampering."

Aidan felt his heart thump his ribs, and hoped no fire flickered in his eyes. "Well, luck with that. Things we're looking at... didn't get as formal as a grave, right, Detective?"

"That's about right." Church gave Dayson a considering look, like she was wondering just what it'd take to twist one annoying spiral-bound notebook somewhere painful.

"So you don't have anything to do with the case of Christophe Savonarola?"

Son of a bitch. No wonder Howe had hoped they'd vanish. One thing to file charges and get an unwelcome mage slapped down quietly. Have Dayson put two and two together, that Steven's brother had been a sorcerous sacrifice and not some crazy Hunter's kill? It'd be hard for even the most scrupulous lawyer not to doubt his client's innocence.

I would so love to see that.

But getting his murder officially solved wasn't important; not next to making sure Steven's plan was *stopped.* So Aidan shrugged. "Do I look fifty-odd years old?"

"No." Wry humor creased the reporter's eyes. "You don't look dead, either."

"Because he's not. Now," Church said dryly. "What part of *on-going investigation* don't you get, Dayson? If we've got evidence, you'll hear about it at the trial." She waved a hand, heading for the door as if she meant to stomp a poor reporter's heart into broken dust. "Let's go."

"That's got to be some investigation," Dayson mused. "How's Detective Franklin doing?"

Aidan was suddenly glad he was the fire-mage. For Dayson's sake. The reporter probably didn't deserve to be a smoldering heap of ashes. Probably.

Church slammed the outer door open, shoulders tense as iron chains. "We've got to lose that guy before we hit the next body site... what?"

"Nothing," Aidan said virtuously, yanking his gaze away from the rental's wheels and his best estimates of how fast Church could make the poor car take a corner.

"Nothing at all," Myrrh agreed. "Although perhaps you might undertake to dodge him through a mall parking lot, instead of on the main road? Simply for the sake of my poor, fragile nerves."

"What did I do in a past life...." Heading for the car, Church frowned. "The DA may be downing shots when it comes to what to charge you two with, but civil suits? Mental anguish, pain and suffering - Nuria ought to have the pair of you tied up in court from here to breakfast. So why are the lawyers dragging their feet?"

Myrrh shrugged, approaching the passenger's side. "I've no idea."

Church unlocked the doors. "Seriously."

"I am quite serious." Myrrh glanced back at Howe's offices. "Perhaps Cruz and her coterie are aware that their usual mis-direction and mind control might backfire, if I am in the same courtroom."

"Or, y'know, could be the lawyers in town see they've got options." Aidan made sure he only touched the plastic of the door handle as he opened it. "With vampires out of the shadows and nobody who could stop them? Sure, take their cases, better that than getting your blood drained in the middle of the night. But if the creepy blood-drinkers suddenly turn up flammable...." He let out a slow breath. "Howe's not evil. Sticking his fingers in his ears and hoping this all blows over, I bet. But not evil. Sure, he's going to go after me 'cause of Steven. But when it comes to Cruz - yeah, I could see him dragging his feet."

Church grimaced. "Dayson's never going to believe you didn't enchant your way out of this."

"Dayson can believe whatever he likes." Myrrh sat down, steeling herself for the drive. "If tradition, history, and fact are not enough to persuade a man to truth, nothing is."

"Just hope that doesn't bite you later." Church got in, mulling something as they buckled up. "You know, maybe we need to tackle the Demongate another way. We need more information on the walking trees. *Different* info. And slamming shut the sites in Intrepid proper's a mess, right? So... how about we try one out on the edge of this disaster?"

"On the edge?" Myrrh looked a little pale.

"You mean, we're taking a long drive." Aidan winced. If Myrrh's map of potential dump sites was accurate... there was really only one place far enough for what Church had in mind.

An hour and a half boxed up in steel. Each way. Augh.

Locking the driver's door, Church flipped open her phone. "Hey, Eagleman. Need to borrow you for a couple hours."

"Oh, my stomach," Aidan heard over the line. *"What nightmare have you dug up now?"*

Church grinned. "Well, if we're all very lucky, it hasn't dug itself up. Yet."

"What do you mean, this old guy won't talk to Myrrh?"

Fingers in the sandy soil behind the Enchanted Waters Casino while Church did a slow walk around the old body dump site, Myrrh kept half an eye on the sparks glinting in her friend's hair. But said nothing. Aidan needed to learn to moderate his fire and his temper, yes; but so long as both were under control, there was no sense in interfering. He had good reasons to be angry.

Eagleman, for his part, showed a refreshing lack of fear. "He's a crotchety old... traditionalist," the detective grumbled, unwilling to step off the asphalt of the employee parking lot. Which showed a fair measure of self-preservation. "One of the elders responsible for getting us recognized as a tribe again, instead of a bunch of not-whites still trying to lay low after the Trail. Assimilating meant giving up the old ways, and, well...."

"And I am a known and believing Christian, so Conseen

wishes nothing to do with me," Myrrh stated plainly. "He never has, even when he was not so... traditional."

Behind them was likely one reason the medicine man had turned cranky on the modern world. When last she'd seen this place, the ground had only recently been broken; a bare, sparse place of wooden cabins and slot machines, with a blackjack table and roulette wheel still so new they squeaked. Now? Lower parts of the resort still mimicked a mountain cabin-mansion; structures all wood and warm browns, surrounded with trees, roofs echoing the flow of the waterfall near the main drive. The hotel itself was over twenty stories of glass and steel, modern as a satellite dish, and had to grate on Conseen's tribal attitudes like straw-laced wool.

Dusting off her hands, Myrrh gave Aidan a rueful shrug. "In truth, the man shows good sense. He is not the most powerful of practitioners, and I tend to attract unwelcome attention. And sometimes bullets."

That earned her Eagleman's frown. Myrrh held up placating hands. "I did not say he was not skilled, and effective. Against creatures native to these hills, his remedies are far more specific than mine."

Turning over one of the weather-dark pennies scattered in gravel washed off the lot, Church nodded. "You mean like... any doc can hit things with an antibiotic, but a guy who knows what bacteria munched you can give you what's *specifically* going to slaughter it."

"Precisely." Myrrh breathed in, trying to tease out any hints of root and branch that were not honest greenery. "Odd. Aidan?"

Her friend stalked over, still bristled in her defense. Stopped on sand and gravel, head tilted as if to catch a mouse's squeak. "That's... weird."

Eagleman swallowed. Church's hand hovered near her gun.

"Not a bad weird," Aidan said hastily. He grabbed a rattling-dry stalk of pokeweed. "This is one of the spots. I can feel it. But all the plants seem *normal*."

"No root-holes," Church agreed. Frowned, and stirred a penny with a toe. "Employee parking lot. Casinos don't pay that well. How come this change is still here?"

"Mess with luck-pennies?" Eagleman shifted his shoulders, a little red highlighting tan cheeks. "That's... not a good idea."

Myrrh raised a brow, curious. "Luck-coins are usually silver. Or tossed into water." For various reasons, the washing away of malign influence being one of them. There was a trout stream nearby on the grounds; it'd been a draw to customers even decades ago, and the billboards Church had passed marked it as a key point of interest. "What grants luck to copper here?"

"...Um." Eagleman was looking anywhere else.

"Something that doesn't want to get talked about," Aidan guessed.

The detective wouldn't look at him, either. "You said it, not me."

"Okay," Church sighed. "So I grab a book on Cherokee folk-lore, we can figure it out from there. I hear they've got the *good* ones in the gift shop. Important thing is, the walking trees *weren't here*. So... why?"

"A very good question." Myrrh frowned, scanning the ground again in case there was anything she'd overlooked. "I see no signs of destructive magic. It's possible there is something I have miss-ed, but given I can clearly sense where the blood-magic remains... I suspect whoever or whatever plants the seeds avoided this site."

"Because of the locals?" Church perked up, evidently hoping it could be that easy.

"It's possible," Myrrh allowed. "Or it could be the distance. If the seed-planter is on foot, this site may have been too far to easily travel. Or it could not like copper. Or invocations of good luck." She shrugged. "The timing itself might have been critical. This is not a fresh site. It's possible for life-feeders to plant their young or feed themselves on old graveyards, but it takes the lives lost on a

battlefield for the aura to linger more than a few years. Hmm. I
wonder if the age correlates to the number of seedlings?"

"Storage locker was... what, five years ago?" Aidan flipped
through a notebook he'd obviously lifted from Church's pocket.
"Place where Ginger got dumped was about that old, but I didn't
see root-holes. Then again, the way the pack tore up the place and
Myrrh slammed it with a Psalm, we could have missed a whole
forest. Megan was just two years. And this one's... huh. Looks like
three and a half, not one of the Halloween sites." His teeth grabbed
his lip, chewing absently down once before he started. "Ow. So...
if these things are some kind of fay, the energy might not be that
easy to sort out from regular plants. Are we really missing the trees
here, or just the holes?"

Church and Eagleman traded glances; Church's long-suffering,
Eagleman's as incredulous as if some poor benighted fool had
replaced the station coffee with decaf. "Okay," Church muttered.
"I say we burn the whole forest down. No offense."

Myrrh couldn't help it. She giggled.

Church's mouth worked; she clapped a palm to her forehead.
"...This is why Hunters are so damn *cranky*, isn't it."

"I don't know about Hunters," Aidan said practically. "But
when something tries to eat you? *Kill it with fire* is a good call."

"Says the walking matchbox," Church grumbled. "*Myrrh*
doesn't light things on fire."

"Ah, but I can afford to be more patient, Detective." Myrrh
inclined her head graciously. "I am a bit harder to kill than the
average Hunter."

From the wary glance Eagleman cast her, he was wondering
how much harder.

"A bullet will kill me as surely as any cop," the hell-raider said
quietly. "If you would think on the lectures, you would know that.
After all, what is the counter to celestial magic?"

Eagleman's eyes widened. He did *not* say *lead*.

Wise man. Who knows what is listening?

"I had another thought." Church didn't look happy about it. "What if this place hasn't been planted *yet?*"

"Are you kidding?" Eagleman glanced around, as if rabid dandelions might pop out and gnaw him with leafy teeth. "Savonarola's *dead.*"

Aidan flinched.

"Hopefully," Church agreed. "But somebody's feeding Howe *interesting* rumors to stir the pot." She folded her arms, looking over sandy ground as if she'd scan it grain by grain.

"Under other circumstances, yes, a stakeout might be wise," Myrrh observed. "But given how old this site is, and how little time there is before Halloween, I would prefer to cleanse it and move on. At the very least, we might reduce the area in which the Demongate can open."

Eagleman shifted on his feet. "This is tribal land."

"And if Conseen were willing to speak to me, I might take his opinion on what the tribe would accept under consideration," Myrrh said dryly. "Detective, you are correct; a cleansing by one in tune with this land would be more effective, with less power." And would certainly be easier on her; without the earth's own help, all the magic needed to scour out evil influences would have to focus through her own spirit. "As one who has seen her own home-land overrun by an alien faith, you have my sympathy. But either Conseen has not or *cannot* cleanse this area of the blood taint. I was near to violently ill to get here. If I use enough power to render this site no longer part of the Demongate, I will be... very sick, for the rest of today. I do *not* wish to come back." She gave him a frank look. "I will cleanse the site, that is all. Just enough to render it safe until the tribe can take their own measures for purity. I will leave nothing of myself behind. No claim of another path; no outrage, to territory that is not of the Church. I merely mean to pray."

From that quirk of Aidan's lips, he knew there was no *mere* about it.

"Casino parking lot," Church said practically. "C'mon, there's no way this is sacred ground."

"Okay, okay," Eagleman sighed. "I'm going to get an earful about this from all the grannies... just - do your thing."

Myrrh breathed deep, settling into stillness. She'd been considering the best verse for some time. They needed not only to cleanse this place, but make it inimical to the creatures stalking Dorren at evil's whim....

"Lord, how they are increased that trouble me! Many are they that rise up against me...."

Opening the back door, Father Ricci's eyes bugged. "Good Lord-!"

Hauling in one limp, miserable hell-raider like a sack of nauseated feathers, Aidan gave Father Ricci a glare that should have scorched his hair off. "Don't say it. Me and the Lord aren't on speaking terms right now."

"...Not his fault...."

"No talking," Aidan ordered. "Tell me you've got ginger ale around here. And crackers. Plain, dry, salty crackers."

Myrrh winced, eyes scrunched shut as she batted a hand against the back of his shoulder. "No food...!"

"All right. All *right*." Aidan took a quick glance around the kitchen; freed one hand long enough to drag a stool over to the sink, so she could rest her face against the cool steel rim. And lean over. Just in case. "But you're getting fluids. Or a hospital. You pick."

"Urgh."

"What *happened?*" Ricci said pointedly.

"Long car ride plus cleansing psalm plus all the ride back," Aidan said shortly, shaking out one hand where he'd come too close to brushing the sink. "You know, Church thought Myrrh and cars was kind of funny. I don't think she's laughing now."

He sure wasn't. The ride back would have been bad enough if he'd just been boxed in the car's steel cage. Myrrh had been desperately, violently ill, almost every twenty minutes. The last few times she'd had nothing left but water and bile, and his whole spine was one tight coil of panic.

You can die from dehydration. Hard and painful.

Ricci watched Myrrh swipe water across her forehead, hands shaking. "I know we were looking up motion sickness, but - have you seen a doctor for this?"

Aidan snorted. *Yeah, right.*

"Mortal medicine would do little good." Myrrh sipped water from her palm, slow and careful. "It is an illness of spirit as much as body, Father. Ask Father O'Malley, if you truly wish to delve into the substance of heresy."

The priest straightened his shoulders, eyes dark with compassion. "I'm asking you, Myrrh. As a friend."

"She *died*," Aidan said harshly. Couldn't the guy take a hint? "It leaves a mark."

"Simply put, yes," Myrrh agreed. Another sip. "Death is not lightly escaped by those of mortal blood. Whom Samael has covered with his wings, never fully leave that shadow. All of my brothers and sisters bear similar burdens." She closed her eyes, face still pale. "I drowned within the substance of a water demon. Motion as of unclean waves... does not sit well. At all." One slow breath in. One out. "These days, at least, we have airplanes. I've crossed the Atlantic without them. It was unpleasant."

Like calling lava milk "a little spicy". Snagging a cup and ice, Aidan had to shake his head. Myrrh might be averse to lying, but someone who changed the universe with her words knew how much you could do just picking the right ones.

"Salvation belongeth unto the Lord; thy blessing is upon thy people. Selah."

The end of one short psalm, and the world had *shifted*. As if clinging shadows had been pried free from sand and asphalt, leaving behind a wash of autumn sun.

We hammered loose part of the Demongate. I can feel it.

There was just *so much more* left.

Not going to cry. Not going to scream.

Though from what Myrrh had said over cheese and oranges, screaming at the Heavens was a perfectly legitimate way to pray when you were thoroughly and utterly *ticked off.* If Christ could incarnate as a human and mutter His own doubts in the garden at night, surely ordinary mortals had a bit of leeway to snarl at fate.

"It's the only thing I agree with the liberation theologists about," Myrrh had said under her breath, so the two priests wouldn't hear. "Believing the poor have the privilege of God's grace simply because they are poor, no matter the state of their souls? And they call me a heretic."

Going to have to add that to a long, long list of things to look up, Aidan thought now, watching so Myrrh would actually drink her soda, instead of swipe condensation off a drop at a time. He wasn't going to pester her, she'd been at this more than long enough to know her own limits, but... he worried.

We're all straws in the flood. And Myrrh - she'll throw herself into it, if she has to, to save people. It's what she does.

Maybe he ought to do a little screaming after all. "You rest, okay?" Aidan gave her a sideways glance. "I'm going out to the graveyard."

"Make sure you make noise," Ricci advised. "Father O'Malley's ears aren't as good as they used to be."

Somehow, Aidan wasn't surprised to see O'Malley having a soft-spoken discussion with Phoebe Savonarola's gravestone. He hung back, not wanting to intrude.

The priest must have caught a waft of unseasonal warmth on the wind; he glanced Aidan's way, bowed his head a moment more, then straightened. "Come to pay your respects?"

"Not exactly." Aidan worked his fingers loose; they wanted to curl into fists. And that would be wrong. "You should have told me."

The Father shook his head. "So long as any aspect of the demon remained dormant, there was nothing to tell-"

"I died because I didn't know!"

There. He'd said it. Gotten that ugly truth out, like pulling loose a barbed arrow.

"I died," Aidan felt ice rattle down his spine, "because I had no clue - *no clue* - that demons were out there. That my father *summoned* them. That my own brother... didn't have anything as clean in mind as just a little jealous Cain on Abel murder."

Why, Steven? Why?

"You didn't kill me." Aidan knew that, to the bone. "But you damn well didn't make it easier for me to stay alive. Why... *why* couldn't you have let me talk to Myrrh back then? Before all this happened?"

"Oh yes, I should let the heretical hell-raider enchantress talk to a rapscallion young troublemaker who'd avoided any trace of demonic power," the priest said dryly. "She'd have had you out Hunting before I could say a Hail Mary-"

"Maybe that would have been better!" He was not going to shake, Aidan told himself. He *wasn't*. "If I'd known something about the supernatural, if I'd even known enough to realize a creepy book following me wasn't my imagination, then maybe-" He cut himself off.

"Maybe you wouldn't have been murdered?" O'Malley's eyes were haunted as the twilight. "Aye, lad. I've thought of that."

"No," Aidan got out. "Maybe we would have stopped Steven before he got this far."

O'Malley flinched.

"He's my brother," Aidan said, very quietly. "I loved him. But *he should have been stopped.*"

The priest inhaled, and shook his head. "I have a duty to all of my flock. Even one who later proved to be... straying."

"Yes you do." Aidan stared him down. "And I was in your

flock. And my mother. *And Megan.*"

And if Myrrh can't teach Dorren how to Hunt, I will, Aidan realized. *Nobody should hurt like that. But Dorren is, her sister's dead, and all we can do is help her make sure other people don't suffer like she has.*

Like I did.

...What happened to Myrrh, that started her Hunting?

O'Malley gave him a look askance. "*Let he who is without sin among you, cast the first stone*, young man."

"That was adultery, Father. Not cold-blooded murder. Steven had decades to make up his mind to *go and sin no more*. Guess what? He picked demonic sacrifice." Aidan shoved clenched fists in his coat pockets. "Steven's responsible for what he did. But you, Father? I just want you to think about one thing. If it weren't for the blind, *stupid* luck of Rajas Feniger tossing a skull he didn't ask for where the dawn could hit it, Church would be dead." He had to stop, and wrestle the fires inside down again. "And eaten by a malursine is an ugly way to die. Believe me. *I know.*"

Uncle Jim might say this was just a stupid way to die.

Loitering in the shadows of a juniper bush outside the second level of the computer lab, Dorren wiped her hands on her jeans again. Juniper ought to be safe. Burning juniper was one way to cleanse and bless places, and juniper berries were one of the ingredients in Miss Shafat's non-alcoholic Hunter tonic. Even tree-imitating fairies ought to shy away from pretending to be a juniper bush.

Is she Miss Shafat, or Sister Shafat? Father Ricci said something about her being a kind-of lay sister....

Which was a lot safer than thinking about her father's face when her mom found the little bottle of tonic in her dresser drawer. First off, what were *either* of them doing going through her drawers, she was almost sixteen! And second - there'd been actual *gold* in that bottle, even if it was just a little, and between that and the herbs and the whole complicated recipe - Miss Shafat had given it to her and it *wasn't cheap.*

And her father had just poured it down the drain, and *arrrgh.*

At least I sent Uncle Jim the recipe.

That had gotten back a very short reply. *Hugs,* and *Noted, getting refill, keep new vial in safe; will leave usual. Very useful. Good work.*

The usual meaning the university library; Uncle Jim used the references, too. And this afternoon when she'd shown up for her independent study in library science, Mr. Truhaft had handed over a shopping bag she'd "forgotten". Inside were three hairbrushes... well, they looked like hairbrushes. Were actually pretty good nylon-bristly brushes, and she'd used one right away to snarl it with hairs in case her parents got suspicious *again.*

Poke and pry just the right way? The ends came off, revealing one thin stack of cash and two glittery vials of tonic.

Whew.

Uncle Jim understood. Uncle Jim tried to make sure she could stay safe. Why couldn't her parents do that-?

Sunlight flashed off the lab door. She froze, as Eric Chang walked out of the level below.

He's heading downhill? I thought he'd hit the library.

Dorren waited until Chang had his feet on the rough-pebbled path worn by the broken steps to the parking lot before she moved. Nothing suspicious to see here, just another high school student taking extra credit to up her chances of getting into college....

After all, anime-orange outfits aside, the way to be a ninja was not to be *literally* invisible. It was to *not be seen.*

The best way to be sneaky is not to look sneaky at all.

Skidding a little on rocks and sandy loam, Dorren followed the programming student down through the multi-tiered parking lots perched on the hillside and over the cracked sidewalk. The stoplight on the campus main road and intersecting cut-through road was always tricky, if there'd been cars coming she would have had to stop and risk packing up in the same crowd as her target... but there weren't this time, so she just scurried across, red light or not, same as any other student hot-footing it toward the statistics courses shoved way out here.

Where the heck is he going? Stat courses are up to the right- Oh. Oops.

There he was, heading over the stubborn grass off to the left of the cut-through road. Toward the campus cops' headquarters.

This isn't good....

Chang stopped on the edge of the parking lot, glancing over his shoulder. "You know, being followed is kind of annoying."

...Oh, *why* couldn't the earth open up and swallow her now?

"Are you okay?" Chang gave her an up-and-down look, like her mother checking for scrapes and leaves. "You were with - um, those kind of strange people. And the detective. Church, right?"

Throat tight, Dorren nodded.

"...You don't look okay."

Sneaking wasn't working. Maybe the truth? Part of it, anyway. "There were monsters near my house," Dorren got out. "Near... where a body was. And there used to be a body here, and the same holes - and you did *something*, and I need to know what to do, they can't get away with it!"

"They?" Chang looked even more doubtful. "Look, if I did anything, it was just for hungry ghosts, anybody could have-"

"It's not ghosts!" Dorren jabbed her finger toward the forest creeping up behind the cop station; even with the college expanding here, there, and everywhere, there was still plenty of woods and swamp back on the north side of campus. "It's - things that look like trees, and aren't...."

Something pale moved in the woods.

It can't be.

Small. Blonde hair flashing with just a hint of strawberry red.

Jeans, and a t-shirt with a purple-feathered pegasus.

It can't be. Megan's dead.

Blonde hair ducked and turned, blue eyes widening. The little girl shivered, and ran into the underbrush.

Her heart *hurt*.

It can't be. Dorren bit her lip, tasting blood. *So it isn't. It has to be-*

"What's a kid doing out here?" Swearing, Chang headed for the trees. "You'd better tell the cops, some idiot let their daughter roam loose. What were they thinking, sometimes there's bears-"

Dorren grabbed blindly for Chang's sleeve, surging forward a few quick steps to catch up. "That's not a kid!"

"What? Come on, let go, I saw-"

"That's my sister!" Her voice spiraled up, as if she could shriek away the truth. "And *she's dead!*"

He stopped.

She was not going to cry, Dorren told herself fiercely. She was strong and she'd faced monsters and she was *not* going to cry-

"Wrong time of day for ghosts," Chang said reluctantly. "It could be another kid. In trouble."

"It had," no hiccups, no *tears*, damn it, "it had her t-shirt."

The look he gave her made Dorren want to *bite* something. Because that was grownups all over. *Did you really see that? You couldn't have, you must have been imagining things, it's not real-*

But the crease of dark eyes said he wasn't sure. He wasn't sure, and that kept her stalk towards the woods a measured pace, instead of a run.

"Wait."

Still on the grass, she stopped. Fuming.

"If it's not a ghost and it's not a kid... we could be in big trouble," Chang said in a rush. "Look, this is - please don't laugh - it's supposed to be kind of a general *evil get gone*, okay?"

It was a little like a ninja seal. Only it was more out from the body; right arm bent, hand raised, all fingers together so the palm pushed toward the enemy. Which made sense, most seals in anime focused your energy in, and this was more to shove youki *away*.

Lifting her hand, Dorren folded her fingers like his. It wasn't as easy as it looked. Her fingers kept trembling. When it came to fighting monsters, that wouldn't be good.

"It's the abhayamudra," Chang shrugged, "picked it up from my parents... you're not laughing...."

Throat tight, she shook her head.

Do I tell him about the tonic? I can't tell him about Uncle Jim, and Mom and Dad won't get this at all, but.... "Did you know there are werewolves on campus?"

"Yeah?" Chang glanced between her and the woods. "What makes you say that?"

"Mr. Lindisfarne smelled them."

...It'd sounded so much better in her head. This wasn't an anime. Darn it.

"Anyway, that's not the point!" Dorren hurried on. "There was something *worse* behind my house. They looked like trees, and aren't, and - and they were planted around where they found my sister's body, and-"

She couldn't go on. Not with visions of her little sister in that coffin whirling through her head; only her face showing, because whoever'd taken Megan had - had-

I want to kill them. I want to kill them all.

"Something planted around a body." Chang gulped, pale. "That'd explain a lot of hungry ghosts." His gaze flicked between the police station and the woods.

Fingernails bit into her palms as Dorren stared at a flicker of purple between autumn-leaved trees. Because Uncle Jim had told her not to be stupid, and running after a maybe-monster when she didn't know what it was or how to kill it had to be stupid to the max.

But it looked like Megan. It *dared*. The world flashed red, every breath stabbing like knives.

"It could still be a kid," Chang muttered, punching in a number on his phone. "You head over to the cops, I'll-"

"You want to die? I'm coming with you." One hand fisted around another vial of iron-holy-water, Dorren headed into the woods.

"Oh for the love of- Detective Church? Um, Eric Chang, I think there's something up here on campus...."

Dorren didn't listen to the rest, stalking into the brush under the trees like an angry cat. She'd duck around greenbriar, only a moron tried to put their own eyes out, but anything less-!

Wind rustled past, fallen magnolia leaves rattling against more fragile maple and hickory. She tried to keep an eye on every direction at once, relieved to see Chang's dark hair every time she glanced back. Because that purple at the edge of vision was taunting and terrifying at the same time. It looked like Megan. It looked *real*.

No. You don't get me that way. I saw her buried.

Chang's sneakers crunched the duff behind her, louder than the whoosh of cars on the campus drive. "This is a bad idea, this is such a bad idea... Detective? Can you hear me?"

Dorren didn't hear the answer. She heard the giggle, how the hell did it know Megan's giggle-

"Tap your heels, and say it three times...."

Dorren shivered, shadows chilling her as if the wind had come straight down from Canada. "You're not her! I know you're not her! Come out and fight, you coward!"

"There's no place like home. There's no place like home...."

Just like Megan, teasing her sister the way Mom and Dad still tried to; from ruby slippers to a stuffed Toto under the Christmas tree. The way everybody had before that horrible September day when Megan had vanished - and the worse day in November when they'd finally found-

And her parents had screamed at Uncle Jim at the funeral; they'd blamed *him*, just because he thought he knew what'd happened, and he'd tried to tell them how to keep it from happening again. How to keep the monster that'd taken Megan from taking their other daughter too - and that'd sent her mother right over the edge. *Nothing* would happen, Maeve said, nothing at all; Megan had died because she was sweet and innocent and her other daughter was too much like her damned uncle to ever be either....

And if that was being a normal person Dorren didn't want to be one anymore.

I'm not Dorothy!

Orange and red and fading green, trees rustled against the wind.

"I can't get a signal." Chang shoved his cell phone into his jacket pocket, stepping almost back to back with her. "I don't- which way is the road?"

Silly question, it was right back....

Shadows loomed, jagged as thorns. Dorren swallowed a shriek, yanking her hand up-

Please let us be in time!

Aidan was out the door before Church switched off the ignition, yanking open Myrrh's door to haul her onto solid ground. The hell-raider was white as a sheet, still not over the trainwreck of yesterday at the casino. But damned if she'd have let them leave her behind, not when they might catch more of these things in the act.

Not when something's trying to eat Dorren. Though it sounds like this time the kid went looking for it - there!

The woods behind the campus cops' station were *fuzzy* at the edges, in a way that had Aidan grabbing for the white braid at his throat. It didn't feel like it was pushing on him, not the way Yaldabaoth's illusions tried to slip and slide into his head. More a hanging shadow-mist, dampening every mind that brushed near-

Sunlight flooded back, letting the air carry shaky breaths and whimpers.

Church and Myrrh were both behind him; Aidan aimed at the noise and headed for red and dark hair.

Pushing past a thorny rope of greenbriar, he let out a sigh of relief. Chang, all right, and Dorren; knees shaking, but still standing back to back, one hand up in a shape that-

Yow!

He felt no shame about ducking behind Myrrh. Dorren'd already gotten him good once. What the heck had she found this time?

"They're gone!" Dorren blurted, eyes bouncing from him to Church to Myrrh as if she wasn't sure they were real. "We - we couldn't see anything but trees, and they were moving, and we-" She gestured again, rippling the world.

"Eep!" He couldn't help it. What *was* that twist of fingers?

"The abhayamudra?" Still pale, Myrrh kept herself between him and Dorren's hand.

"The who what?" Church's hand was near her gun, as her gaze searched the trees. "You don't need your hands up, I know you're you."

"Um, actually, we did." Chang slowly lowered his right hand, flexing fingers as if they ached. "It's... well, Buddhist. Wards off evil influences?"

Oh, *ow.* Aidan tried to stand straight in the face of the college student's wary look. His *reasonably* wary look, damn it; the guy'd nearly got eaten by walking trees, he had a right to look sideways at anything that flinched from protective magic.

"It also tends to ward off anyone of demonic heritage, even those pure of heart and converted to the paths of the sages," Myrrh said easily. "The *gesture of fearlessness*. There are reasons the most feared Buddhist demon-slayers have been left-handed."

Dorren's head whipped toward her so quick, Aidan thought he heard something crack. "You mean the anime got the Journey to

the West *right?*"

Myrrh brightened. "You've read the Journey to the West?" A chuckle escaped her. "Oh dear. It isn't wholly accurate...."

Right. Look off-guard, so we can lure these things out if they are still lurking. "Okay, what's the Journey to the West," Aidan slanted a glance from Myrrh to Dorren, "and, there's an anime? I only saw a couple in college before... well, before."

"Yeah," Dorren nodded, "at least the *Japanese* still think monsters are monsters, even if they make some of them cute to get past censors-"

Church made a strangled noise. "Can you fangirl over monster-hunting later? *Away* from the man-eating trees?"

"They are no longer here," Myrrh said firmly. "But yes. Back on human-claimed territory would be wise."

Church sighed as their wayward students headed back toward grass and asphalt. Cast Aidan a wink. "Wards off evil, huh? Think you could teach me that, Mr. Chang? I've got a lawyer breathing down my neck. And I can't *wait* to try it on our dear mayor."

"It doesn't work on human evil," the college student said ruefully. "Trust me. I tried it on the differential equations prof; everybody in class agrees *he's* evil."

"Darn."

"But it did work on our foes," Myrrh mused, sandals shushing on dried grass. "For them to flee two souls otherwise unarmed - you must have found a vulnerability. Fearlessness? The mudra? A balance of ying and yang? Many creatures can only attack where there is an imbalance of energies-"

Church groaned. "Can't it *ever* be simple?"

"Were it truly as simple as a silver bullet to the brain or a wooden stake to the heart, vampires and werewolves would never have dared risk the light of TV cameras," Myrrh said dryly. "And Hunters would be seen as simple officers of enforcement, just as any other cop. But it is not simple, it is not easy, and too many Hunters must live and die by guesswork and tradition. You match prints and take witness accounts; and if all goes well, a jury of a man's peers convict or set free. One facing claws and fangs must sum up all they know in an instant, and pray they are close enough to right."

Like Chang was praying right now, Aidan could tell, watching the computer geek watch him. Though oddly enough, the guy didn't seem scared. Nervous, cautious, but not scared. "Go ahead and ask. I'm getting used to it."

"...Um." Chang stopped on the sand and gravel edging the parking lot, then deliberately stepped back onto asphalt. "You have... legends of a yaoguai in your family?"

Demon. Ghost. Spirit-creature, the word seemed to say. And, well, close enough. "They're not legends," Aidan shrugged. "Long story."

"Direct descent, paternal side," Myrrh stated.

Aidan huffed a laugh; trust Myrrh to put it in a way that didn't hurt. Much. "So, not that long."

"Your father is a... whoa." Chang shook himself. "Okay, don't think I'm complaining about crazy Uncle Shone An's opera ever again."

"Aidan's one of the good guys." Church glanced back where they'd been. "We can see where you were from here, which means you should have been able to see the station from there. If you couldn't...."

"They made us see things that weren't there." Dorren's voice was small and hunted, as she gave the woods a dark look. "One was pretending to be... Megan."

"That's what I thought," Church muttered. She lifted her left hand to rub the back of her neck, tension finally draining as seconds went by with no trace of angry shrubbery. "Those lenses you were talking about? We need them. Right now the three of us are the only ones who can check body dump sites and be sure that we saw what was really *there*."

"Ouch," Aidan agreed.

"I was able to contact with the apprentice of my former source." Myrrh folded her arms, frustration ghosting across her face. "There's only so fast one can rush glassblowing, Detective. Even with friendly elemental help."

"We need them for more than just the cops," Church said soberly. "We need them for the NCBI, too."

"Huh?" Aidan frowned at her.

"Investigation. Ongoing," the detective said with strained patience. "IPD can't get involved, conflict of interest. The NCBI has to do it. How else are they going to check if that video's not really Cushman?"

Chapter Nine

"We have lost some of the saplings." Fingers tapped on polished granite, dark as clouds shadowing the sky.

"It would have been too hopeful to think we would not, Lord Ahi." Stimson kept his head bowed before soul-shriveling power, the sense of *thirst* that had drunk whole rivers dry. "They were only seedlings. A loss, but not as great as the others would be."

"We lost them to *humans*." A rumble like far-off thunder, the aftershock of an earthquake. "Even if one of those is among the *buddhi*."

And how painful that had been, to have his own conclusions confirmed, Stimson reflected. Yes, he'd known his not quite mortal employer had defeated a hell-raider, but... hell-raiders were *legends*. Vanishingly rare, and prone to wiping out supernatural witnesses when they had walked the face of the earth. No one truly knew what a hell-raider could or couldn't do.

No one who would talk, at least.

If a hell-raider counted as one of the Enlightened Awake, then Steven hadn't used *enough* kill. Stimson wouldn't believe Myrrh Shafat counted as a bodhisattva, she was supposedly Christian and no believer in the world-as-illusion, but... well. Old memories of his blood shuddered at what even a nun could do to an unwary rakshasa.

Of course, a nun would have to know she was facing a rakshasa, first. Which was one among many reasons why Steven had secured Stimson's spirit - and his services - to begin with. Father Gray O'Malley was old, but strong in faith, and learned in those enemies the Church of Rome had faced in North America. He would have detected any uncanny creature normally found on Intrepid's streets.

And so Steven found me.

And so later had they made their offer to Lord Ahi. Who was not of these hills, nor any ill that O'Malley had ever had cause to learn of. Even if the old priest by some chance or grace came upon them, his prayers would be turned away like blunted arrows from a shield of diamond.

O'Malley is no longer the strongest believer in Intrepid.

It would be so, so much safer to stop his subtle whispers, and let lawyers and monsters alike bury the hell-raider under a host of legal charges. But... Steven had not bound him to be *safe*.

So long as Shafat walks free under sun and starlight, the creatures of the night fear. The more they fear, the more they hate; the more humans sense that threat, and rouse their own fury against it. Fury, hate, fear - all of these lead to blood, and the Demongate grows ever stronger.

A tongue licked at shadows, as if Ahi would devour the stars in the sky. "I shall stride forth to deal with her."

Ah. And that would do him no good, Stimson reflected, not if he meant to steer his narrow path between following ancient blood and serving the man who still had a lien on his spirit. Steven had been clever, in how he chose and fed his servants. "That might not be the wisest course, my lord. Not with the point of human power so close to ours for claiming. She is one who honors the devas and serves mankind. That is her power... and her weakness."

A cavernous chuckle. "Such is ever the way, with those bound to save their fellow man. Go forth, and use your blood to paint her as an enemy in the eyes of men."

"That we will most certainly do, my lord," Stimson bowed lower. "But I am only a lowly tiger-blood, my hands turned backward. It seems to me in my lesser strength that for now, I would be wiser to put forth shadows and whispers, and turn those of the night who would stand against us into the human's enemies, instead. If she is busy hunting those, she will have no time to prepare for us."

"And you have a plan." Lord Ahi leaned his coils on polished stone, amused. "Of course you do. None of tiger's blood would have survived without one, so far from Mount Meru."

"My lord, I need not even the power of maya." Stimson smiled, and lifted one of many disks in its glimmering case. "Howe has no idea what he handed over to me, as executor of Steven's estate. But I know. I know so very well."

He knew, and he was still stunned at the sheer arrogant *stupidity* of it. Yes, Steven was of Yaldabaoth's blood, and demonic pride could never be underestimated. And yes, long before Stimson had crossed his path the Savonarola heir had been a master sorcerer, well-skilled at hiding how he'd tortured and slain animal sacrifices before moving on to humans. But to keep this footage, even if he'd meant it to break his brother's spirit....

Well. Stimson was rakshasa, he knew what it was to savor a tender kill. And what could be more delicious than a kill you'd dreamt of for decades, cozying up to the prey while it knew nothing, nothing at all? Yes; he could see why Steven had kept this.

And as something to turn mere humans on the less savage beings of Intrepid, much less on each other....

Yes. Stimson spun the disk on his fingertips. *For Halloween, this will do nicely, indeed. But in the meantime... for the soup to reach its full flavor, we need to stir the pot.*

Which would be best done if he could separate the demon-hunters for their next move. So how best to-?

Aha. And he should only need a few phone calls to set it up. After all, Church was too dedicated a cop to sit on her hands. His sources in the department and courthouse personnel claimed Captain Sherman had the detective tracking down off-site copies of paperwork lost in the fire, trying to free up those officers not on leave as the city grew more and more paranoid.

The best bait is the one the hunter cannot resist.

"My lord." Stimson smiled. "My skills at maya are small, and the detective's Sight is keener than I had imagined. Perhaps you would like to... play a bit?"

~*~*~*~*~

Never thought I'd be dropping half a week's pay in a hardware store. Church pushed out of the swinging glass door with a double armful of long things that went clang and bags slung over her arms of smaller bits. Duct tape, bits of pipe, screws, nails; even one foot-long brass hinge, because it was brass and reasonably stiff and pointy when she folded it together.

Dumping stuff into the passenger seat, Church sat down, making sure to lock the doors before she concentrated on her new acquisitions. *Now all I need is some fertilizer, and Homeland Security will land on me like a ton of bricks.*

Heh. For all she knew they might do that anyway. Things had changed since Shafat had last walked the earth, and the IPD hadn't exactly made it a secret Church was working with the hell-raider.

Church shrugged, flicked her pocketknife open to free a roll of duct tape, and went to work on a bit of brass pipe with a useful curve to it. She could swing it as it was, but some tape to roughen the grip seemed like a good idea. The last time she'd seriously tangled with monsters she'd ended up soaking wet, and trying to hang onto slippery metal in the middle of a whirlpool? No thanks.

Don't even know if this will do any good. But... pennies at Enchanted Waters, and no trees.

A long shot. But apparently copper alloys did kill some fay things. So... what the hell.

Church paused, and rapped her knuckles on one of the wooden doorknobs in the mess. Just in case.

Let's see. The detective rummaged through the hodgepodge of knobs, nails, railing pieces, and any stray bits of scrap the store had let her carry off. Some of it fit in her pockets; some would go into the little pockets of her denim messenger bag, with the pipe fit into the main body just a little crossways. And some was just going to have to stay in the trunk with the tire iron. *Ornamental cast iron, steel, copper, brass, aluminum - something's got to be vulnerable to aluminum, right? And a bunch of different exotic woods. None of which are hawthorn, so there, Cruz.*

Church was still waiting for the other shoe to drop when it came to the vampires' coven leader. Nuria Cruz had a lot invested in her scary-but-harmless Mistress of the Night image, and Myrrh had pretty much sliced that to bits and set it on fire. Cruz had to want payback, big-time.

Then again, Nuria's actually afraid *of Myrrh.*

Which in Church's experience made the need for payback even worse. Though it'd make sense that Nuria might try lawyers first, and fangs in the back alleys later. One thing vampires had was *time*.

Church had to stop, and smooth down a bit of silver-gray tape. *Vampires have centuries. So does Myrrh.*

Oh man, no *wonder* the hell-raider scared them. Forget the whole holy power and sword of light mess. Myrrh didn't age, didn't forget, didn't *die*. Myrrh had taken a name and *vampire* and come up with a mention of one she'd heard about *centuries ago*. And made it clear the only reason Cruz was still on this earth was that Myrrh hadn't met her before the laws changed.

Myrrh wasn't scared of Cruz. And Aidan... well. Fire-mage. Who'd already proved vampires made excellent kindling.

Church drew in a breath scented with maple and mahogany, and gingerly touched the truth.

I'm not scared of Cruz.

Wary, sure. Cautious, definitely; like she'd be with any three-hundred-pound junkie on PCP. Slip, let a vampire catch her with eyes or bony fingers, and she'd be one dead cop. But scared?

Cruz doesn't scare me. Aariel - he scares me.

And at least until Halloween was past and done, Aariel was kind of higher on her list of priorities.

Stick to daylight, keep hawthorn bullets, and if all else fails, mark the nearest salad bar, Church told herself. *I've got walking trees to... heh. Well. Maybe that's why Cruz is laying low.*

After all, the next scariest thing to a walking flamethrower had to be walking stakes.

Which means, Church grimaced, *the vampires might be willing to talk to us. If they know anything. Nuria didn't even know what a Demongate was-*

Her phone rang.

The ID lifted Church's brow. *NCBI?* "Hello."

"Detective Church?"

"Speaking."

"Agent Callum," the man on the other end stated. "I'm aware that your department and the FBI have some questions about possible identity theft in regard to Special Agent Cushman."

Okay, whoa, stop there. "I'm on administrative leave, you need to contact Detective Eagleman-"

"Agent Cushman's in my boss' office right now," Callum said in a rush. "He's been in there half an hour."

So why are you calling now? "And?"

"According to one of my sources," Callum swallowed, "Agent Cushman just walked into Suntrust Bank."

I just told a state investigator to shake down the secretary for a compact mirror to check his boss is still his boss. I am so not getting my rep for sanity back.

Church parked at the drugstore across the street from Suntrust, hoping Cushman wouldn't spot her rental. Gillingham wasn't going to be glad to see her again-

There he is!

Strolling out in a dark gray suit, whistling way too cheerfully for someone who'd potentially compromised NCBI's investigation into whoever really held that Suntrust account.

Messenger bag over her shoulder, Church slipped into tourist crowds snapping pictures of spoon buskers, living statues, and fall leaves in every shade from hickory acid-yellow to maple scarlet.

Wonder if the statue-guys ever talk to Coral for how to look like stone tips... either I'm good at following him, or the Bureau doesn't teach their guys to check for tails in store windows-

"Purple!" A man whose floppy hat and cargo pants shouted *tourist* waved a fist at his own digital camera. "All the natural splendor of the Appalachians, and those local idiots had to plant *Japanese maples* down at that park? It's an outrage, Edith, an outrage!"

His gray-haired wife rolled her eyes. "Yes, dear."

"It's that kind of backwoods ignorance of ecology that got the blight started in the first place!" the tourist ranted on. "Who knows what they've brought in with that - that whatever it is, hickories aren't orange-!"

Church so wanted to rattle the guy until his eyeballs spun. Anybody who cared about the Appalachians and getting the chestnuts back in knew the blight had started in the *Bronx*.

Focus. Cushman now. Idiot tourists later.

Besides. It looked like the angry eco-tourist had just ranted a bit too close to a gang of black-clad college artists enjoying their Dragonslayer and Black Unicorn ice cream, and he was about to get a lesson in local history as delivered by the Mildly Annoyed Goth crowd.

Mwah-ha-hah.... No laughing, sneak. Keep watching the shop windows, if you can see him he might see you... eh?

She hadn't gotten close enough to see it before. Cushman's reflection in passing glass... wavered. Like air over summer asphalt, instead of the warm but definite autumn they had now.

The guy who *wasn't Cushman* cast a glance back, and smirked.

Wind stung her eyes, a rush of autumn-orange leaves.

Where is he, what's he trying, grab something-!

Church blinked tearing eyes, searching the street for any sign of that dark-gray suit. Or anyone else she hadn't seen a second ago.

Gone.

Fifteen seconds. Half a minute without anything jumping out, eating her, or animating the local vegetation like a grade-B horror movie. A minute.

Church gulped air, hoping her pulse would drop back to jackhammer levels sometime soon. *Okay, so what the heck was the point of that? Show me Cushman's not always Cushman, and - then what?*

Her phone rang.

Swearing under her breath, Church eyed the ID. Blanched, and flipped it open. "Carlisle? Tell me my two troublemakers haven't barbecued a reporter-"

"Get to Wolfe's Park," her fellow detective cut her off. "911's ringing off the hook, and whatever it is has leaves!"

I don't trust this guy, Aidan thought darkly, clutching his mug like a warm blackjack, just waiting to bash the blond over the head. Matt Dayson might have good taste in coffee, and good sense in inviting them to a bookstore to talk; quiet, no one should bother them, but public enough to keep him out of lethal trouble. But good judgment in who was and wasn't out to eat him? Aidan didn't trust that. At all. Witness the fact that Dayson hadn't wanted Church here to talk.

...Then again, maybe that was good judgment, because Church wanted Dayson on a plate, with a little BBQ sauce on top. Just as well she'd decided to avoid temptation, and go chase down paperwork for the poor beleaguered court clerks trying to sift order out of the burned wreckage.

Well. Good for Dayson, anyway.

The reporter tapped his pen, never quite touching the notepad unless he stroked a letter down. "You really intend to ask other supernaturals to help."

"I do," Myrrh inclined her head. "Those who live here

peacefully. And perhaps some of those who do not. They have nothing to gain by letting competitors move in to take their prey."

Dayson reached up with his pen, cap scratching just behind his ear. "I'm surprised you think any of them would come near you, after the *Nightsong* vid."

Patient, Myrrh waited.

Aidan pressed the back of his fist to his lips, stifling a giggle as Dayson tried to stare her down. And tried. And started fidgeting.

Heh. Think if you wait long enough, she'll talk? Guy, one thing we know is patience.

"How did you do... that?" Dayson said at last.

"Faith, light, and a great deal of practice," Myrrh answered. "We did many things. Be more specific."

"Vampires touched you and exploded," Dayson shot back. "You killed people. And you're walking around scot free. How can the Intrepid Police Department justify working with a documented Hunter?"

Aidan twitched. *No. Bad fire mage. No setting the idiot's hair on fire. Even if he deserves it.*

"A Hunter," Myrrh mused. "I see. I offer vampires a warning, and the truth, and defend myself when they choose to attack me, and I am a Hunter. Yet Aidan defended me as well, and you do not attack him." Gray eyes were deep as a cold sea. "I wonder. Is that because I am a Christian, and so must be the enemy? Or because you think Aidan is not human, and so cannot be held to the standards of human law?"

Oh boy. Aidan tried not to swallow too obviously. *Knives out right to start.*

"Mr. Lindisfarne's legal status is a bit blurry at the moment," Dayson said easily. "You, on the other hand, have a solid background and a legal identity that can stand a bit of poking. Even if it is a bit... dusty."

Touché, Aidan thought dryly. *So you've got enough self-control to keep from rising to the bait. Still don't like you.*

"You've admitted you are a Hunter, and you call vampires demons," Dayson went on. "You played the starring role in what's being hailed by Humans-First whacko groups on the 'Net as the best monster snuff film *ever*, and the IPD knows it. You call yourself a Christian? Get over yourself. You're just another monster."

Okay, he dies. No offense-

Myrrh's hand on his arm stopped him. *It's not worth it*, gray eyes said.

The hell it wasn't. But frying annoying people was generally considered evil. Darn it.

"If I were just another monster, Mr. Dayson, I suspect you would think better of me," Myrrh said levelly. "I am not merely a Hunter. I am the one they call when Hunters die."

The reporter held his pen above the page a long moment, eyes flicking back and forth between them.

"And if you wish to know why those who assaulted me died, it is simple," Myrrh stated. "I invoke celestial magic. The blade I call *is sunlight*."

It's a lot more than that, Aidan knew. But there was no way he was going to let on to this guy that Myrrh was literally *made out of dawn*.

Need to know. He doesn't.

"It is well-known among older master vampires what a hell-raider is, and that I am one," Myrrh went on. "If you saw the video, you know Nuria knew *exactly* what she had crossed."

"That doesn't give you a reason to kill people," Dayson shot back. "And they are *people*. Just like you."

Aidan blinked, and relaxed a little from imminent fire-setting. *If he believes that, he's more nuts than I thought.*

"The revived dead with an alternative lifestyle," Myrrh said dryly. "Or so they claim." She smiled slightly. "If you truly believe that, Mr. Dayson, then you must consider that jaguars and tigers have an *alternative lifestyle*. Yet I doubt you would argue they should wander our streets unhindered."

Dayson gave her a sidelong glance. "Jaguars and tigers aren't people."

"I suggest you try that line of reasoning on the next tiger youkai you meet." Myrrh leaned back in her chair, amused. "Although you might not survive the experience. If they allow themselves to be seen, it's usually because they are hungry. And I suspect you well know, cats of any sort are hardly vegetarians. "

The reporter snorted. "Of course not. They're obligate carnivores."

Myrrh inclined her head. "And vampires, if you will forgive the pun, are obligate humanitarians."

Dayson squinted at her. "Everyone knows they don't need human blood to survive."

"Then *everyone* is wrong." Myrrh's gaze never left his. "A vampire feeding on animal blood is a cat forced to feed on rice. It will keep them alive, for a time. But they are starving, they are *stupid*, and they are furious. Sooner or later they must break, and feed. And then people die."

The reporter took a breath, and sighed it out in a *hmph*. "That's why they drink blood bank discards, *Miss* Shafat."

Aidan clapped a hand to his forehead, and tried not to laugh. It kind of hurt. "Oh, man. *Wow*. They actually pulled that one? And people bought it?"

"It would seem so." Myrrh gave Dayson a speculative look up and down. "I see why they have been reluctant to allow people proper knowledge of how magic works."

The reporter started. "What does magic have to do with-"

"Demons eat *life energy*, you idiot," Aidan said bluntly. *Even I do. Just because I can get it from fire, doesn't make me different.* "That doesn't stick around in blood. Not more than a few minutes away from a beating heart. A vampire can suck more energy out of a *bean sprout* than cold blood."

Dayson's pen stopped twitching.

Well, what do you know. I think we got his attention.

"There are reasons," Myrrh said, very quietly, "why one way to find sleeping vampires by day has ever been to look where crops are dying."

"You actually believe that." Gold brows drew down. "I know back in the Middle Ages they blamed any kind of crop failure on witchcraft and demons, but-"

Myrrh dropped her gaze to the table, and slowly shook her head. "Young man."

Don't laugh, Aidan warned himself. *Don't laugh, he is pretty young compared to most of the things he's tried to interview, he probably had no clue how in over his head he was.*

"Young man," Myrrh sighed, lifting her head to regard the reporter with determined civility. "Has it occurred to you that back in those centuries you think of as dark, they yet knew that vampires and werewolves - and, yes, witches and demons - existed? When you enlightened modern men did not? And if they knew such creatures were real, and feared them, and lived with the fact that any stray shadow might conceal supernatural death... has it ever occurred to you those who recounted such legends of horror might know what they were talking about?"

"Miss Shafat." The reporter was almost as civil back. "If vampires were actually creatures of unspeakable evil, why would any of us still be alive?"

Like pounding on a brick wall, Aidan sighed, and dropped a hand on top of white hair. "I present exhibit A." *Moron.*

Dayson frowned. "There's no place in civilized society for any kind of vigilante justice-"

"Why do you think I am currently teaching classes for the IPD? And anyone else who wills to listen?" Myrrh leaned forward, intent. "Do you think any sane person wishes to protect the innocent only from the shadows? But for centuries there was no other choice. The proclamation of those in power was that monsters could not exist, and any who begged help against the creatures of the night were insane, or worse. Those attacked by a werewolf, those losing a child to her addiction to vampire bites - who could they turn to? Who would listen? Who would help them, when they swore they'd never meant to harm another, but their minds had not been their own?"

Calculated risk. Aidan's fingers tightened on the polished edge of the table. *If Dayson hasn't done his research, if he thinks all the night-folk are as pure and virtuous as we know they've tried to look-*

Dayson's gaze flicked sideways, and Aidan could taste the waft of uncertainty.

Or maybe not a risk at all, Aidan reflected. *Demons. Pride. Humiliating and mutilating innocent people. Kind of a given.*

"But now the supernatural is recognized by law, and so its remedies must follow," Myrrh went on. "I do not wish to act outside the law, Mr. Dayson. I would be most pleased if I could teach the average person, the ordinary law enforcement officer, how to defend themselves. For if all justice for supernatural harm must come in the shadows... too many people die."

"Easy for you to say." Dayson leaned forward, eyes intent. "Prove it."

Shadow where there shouldn't be.

Aidan was up and over the table before he thought twice, missing the warmth of Dayson's coffee by a hair. Something distorted through the glass of the coffeeshop window, large and hairy and fluxing in shape and size-

Glass shattered, spraying away from four legs and a spread of gilded antlers.

Why's the glass scattering that *way?*

Myrrh was at his shoulder, studying the spray of razor shards as the screams started. "So Joshua overwhelmed Amalek and his people...."

Right, Aidan thought, as sunlight blazed in his senses. The giant stag with fangs froze. Turned its head toward them, red eyes gleaming. *Get its attention on us. Not the innocent.*

"Deer?" Dayson picked himself up from a fallen chair, eyes darting past slavering fangs. "What are they doing in here?"

"They?" Aidan blinked, glancing where bits of glass crunched under nothing-

Not nothing. Shadows of shadows. A translucence, and another on the other side, like one deer made three; only there was no sense of soul in those glass-clear shapes.

"Glamour," Myrrh declared, sword at the ready. "Ill met, forest-child. There is no prey for you here."

"That's a *deer*," Dayson started to protest.

The long muzzle gaped open, full of dragon's teeth.

I should have gone to the coffeeshop.

Church stabbed the brass tube into leafy bark to a shriek that scratched at the insides of her ears. Served the rooted bastard right.

So the captain wanted the reporter clear of the department. Let Myrrh sink or swim on her own, where the press is concerned. She's got Aidan with her; she'll survive. Sure. Right.

At least so far her hunch was on target. Though she doubted the panicked calls from Wolfe's Park had expected officers to respond with repurposed plumbing. Apparently the local shuffle-board enthusiasts had found something twiggy trying to shuffle *them*. And it wasn't taking whacks with a cue-stick as a clue to get gone.

Which was a cop's trained snark coming to the fore, protecting her mind from looking too closed at slick, clotted red. Streaks led from the points on plastic mats back to drying pools where the most unlucky players had lain. Some had already been yanked out behind the rolling metal screen of squad car, as patrol officers with the guts to keep shooting at something that *shape-shifted* moved in.

At least one victim wasn't ever moving again.

Bark fingers tried to yank the pipe from Church's hand. She

snarled back at it, gripping the duct tape of her makeshift handle grip and *pulling*.

Sklorch.

The monster flopped as it tried to leap away, starting a jump with two tree-trunk legs and coming down on four-

Whitetail deer?

It looked like one, as much as it looked like anything; though the fur was fine leaflets, and antlers forked like tree branches reaching for the sun.

And the blood was wrong. Too dark. Almost purple. *Wrong.*

At least bullets worked. When the cops shooting them could *see what they were aiming at.*

"Hanson, track left!" Church barked, as yet another leafy mass surged toward the squad car. "Left, left - there!"

Gunfire was a hail of beanbags against her own body, sound shaking her where she stood with the pipe still dripping ichor. Air in front of her *twisted-*

Church slammed brass through the translucence before it solidified, all too aware that while the damn not-there illusion monsters couldn't hurt *her*, they could kill anyone else who'd stumbled into this mess.

What you don't know will *hurt you. Good night.*

And she just couldn't manage that odd twist of fingers Chang used to ward off monsters. Obviously, she hadn't spent enough time practicing her ninja chakra seals. Or whatever Dorren was into that let her fold her fingers that way without half trying.

Two of them at least, I'm the only one who can see them half the time, what are we going to do? Oh god, there's the ambulance, good-

Tires screeched, as the panicked paramedic driving slammed his brakes in front of empty air.

"God*damn*it!" Church swore, as bumper and engine crumpled against *nothing.*

In that breath, she got *exactly* why vampires had tried to

portray Hunters as the KKK with black sheets and torches. Right now, she wanted to burn everything not human to blackened wood.

Wood. Trees that didn't look right. *Wrong leaves.*

Illusions have a source. Kill the source....

Aidan yanked the reporter from the jaws of death. Thankfully. Myrrh wasn't certain she wanted to rescue the man.

Believe a vampire when it tells you it does no harm....

She moved through the two creations first; light shattering illusions into rainbow shards, coruscating into sunlit air. Skidded in spilled coffee, caught her balance, and headed for the true creature in a snowdrift of shredded napkins.

Gold eyes blinked and bolted, near-deer flowing into something with claws and tentacles instead of hooves, catching the top of a low booth to fling it farther than even a deer could leap.

Oh no you don't.

So far it hadn't killed anyone. Which meant she needed to use something a bit less lethal than Dayson expected.

"For he is thrown into the net by his own feet," Myrrh breathed, reaching out with mind and voice and spirit to the very dust of the air. "And he steps on the webbing!"

Gossamer-fine, sunlit dust snared shifting legs, and brought it crashing down.

Myrrh dodged tentacles flailing at her and what was left of the front window; moved in front of the creature's head. "Who are you? Why do you come here?"

The snarl of Sanskrit threatened to singe hairs off the back of her neck. Granted, it wasn't the first time she'd been accused of doing that with a crested porcupine and a peach. Still, if Aidan understood any of that-

"Disgorge her honor from your worthless mouth, you unclean offspring of a lamia and a basilisk's dead egg!"

...And now she was hoping Dayson didn't speak Syraic. She'd known Aidan couldn't *read* hieroglyphs, but given those were divine symbols that was only to be expected. He'd need to learn them, the same as any human lettering. Still, she had wondered if Aariel had taught him the tongues of his inhuman enemies.

Question answered. Oh dear-

Oh no. Mother Mary, no!

Sanskrit. Copper and turmeric had harried them; a sutra driven them from a kill site. Not glamour, not fay-

"Maya," Myrrh declared, switching sword from hand to hand, fingers folding into the abhayamudra. "Ill met, rakshasa. There is no prey for you here."

What on earth are rakshasas doing in Intrepid?

This one was frozen in the net; apparently realizing exactly what it'd attacked. Deer-eyes rolled white in panic, equally terrified of edged light and the promise of demonic fire.

As well it should be, Myrrh snarled, despite the fear shivering her nerves. *Aidan has no idea how terrifying he can be... Oh Lord, Church's people have no idea what they're dealing with! We need to warn them!* "I'll ask once more. Who are you, and what do you seek here?"

"What *is* that thing?"

Ah. Dayson was definitely a reporter, to run toward thrashing tentacled monsters instead of away. "This is a rakshasa," Myrrh said calmly, holding down the net with will and a bit of tetchiness. "One of many, many creatures in the shadows your vampire and werewolf sources have not told you of. Deer has ever been one of their favored forms for ensnaring the attention of human prey. But as you can see, they are capable of many shapes."

"You think it speaks English?" There was no fire around Aidan's hands, but she caught the barest glimmer of sparks.

"I know it understands English." Myrrh watched calculating black eyes. "Whether it will deign to speak anything but Sanskrit, who can say?" She glanced at the reporter, currently scribbling notes like a madman. Part was a quick sketch of what he'd seen; wise man, to make a record thus, untampered-with by digital fakery. "So, Mr. Dayson. Exactly how do you propose I take this creature in for questioning?"

Dayson lifted wide eyes from his notes, darting between her and the netted rakshasa. "...What?"

"Here is a monster, bent at least on mayhem if not on devouring humans whole," Myrrh said patiently. "How does the law treat him? Bear in mind, this is a shape-shifter, who might burst his bonds by growing to an elephant's height, or slip through holes the size of a mongoose. My net holds him, because it is magic; but without objects I can link that magic to, and a source of power, it will only hold so long as I can concentrate."

Never mind that she could hold that concentration for days, *if* nothing else interfered. There was far more than one more rakshasa out there, and a waiting Demongate. Something surely would.

"You claim there should be no Hunters, no vigilante justice against those with more than human powers," Myrrh went on. "Very well. *What do you expect the cops to do?* They have neither the training nor the tools to keep a rakshasa captive. I do know what will keep a rakshasa held, but you are likely to balk; for while a human captive may be shackled with steel, and take no harm, a rakshasa can *only* be shackled with metals that will pain it, so it will not shred them asunder." She took a breath. "That, or by spell-work and oaths that would shiver your very soul. Spells, I will remind you, that most humans *do not* have the strength to work on their own. I hold this creature not with my own strength, but with faith."

A faith you and yours have worked so long to destroy....

"I don't- no one said anything about-" Dayson cut himself off, as his pocket beeped; snatched out his phone with the look of a man rescued from drowning.

And then his face fell, as if a drowning man's plank had crumbled to dust.

Aidan raised an eyebrow, and flicked a spark at a tentacle that tried to creep through the net. "Don't do that."

"Scanner app," Dayson said, dazed. "There's- all over town, crazy things happening, things that aren't there, things that look like...." He trailed off, staring at the almost-deer under a net of sunlit dust.

"Church," Aidan breathed.

Not just Church. Every cop in this city.

Sword blazing, Myrrh advanced on the net. "One way or another, root-foe, you will *talk-*"

Aidan yanked her back.

Leaves heaved, like the roiling of swamp muck before a noisome burst of stench. Dark eyes jittered as the rakshasa convulsed, again and again-

"Something's ripping the soul out of it!" Aidan was quite sensibly still pulling; all too aware that as magic-embodied souls they might be just as vulnerable to whatever foul snare this might be....

Black eyes filmed with white, and a rattle of wood collapsed.

Myrrh stared at violet-black slime dripping from dead leaves and twig-bones, and shuddered.

Gripping her shoulder, Aidan swallowed hard. "What could do *that* to a rakshasa?"

"What could do that, without either of us sensing a spell cast from elsewhere?" Myrrh breathed. Though something about it tickled memory; something of seeds, and rakshasa legend-

A glint of sun caught her eye; Dayson's phone, as the white-faced reporter moved from dead slime to taking photos of growing screams outside.

"Oh no you don't," Aidan snarled; releasing her to grab Dayson by both shoulders and pluck him bodily from the ground, before striding out the door into bloody chaos. "You want to write about how no one needs Hunters? You just come and *find out!*"

~*~*~*~*~

Brass pipe through an inhuman set of ribs, Church finally let herself collapse.

I hurt. Everywhere.

It was distantly interesting to watch the monster that'd been aping a purple-leaved maple dissolve into slime and wooden bones. Ebony-black, she thought. With that purplish ichor for blood she couldn't be sure.

"...Detective? Ma'am, can you hear me?"

Church blinked, rushing in her ears fading as she focused on a bloodstained paramedic checking her pulse. "Any more of those things?"

"We... don't think so?" *Smith*, flashed his nametag; Church found herself absently wondering if there was enough copper in it to make whatever-it-was impersonating a paramedic a Very Bad Idea.

"But-" Smith swallowed, hands lifting off her wrist as if she were a bomb he didn't want to set off. "I think you're the only one who can see them. Really see them. Ma'am."

He doesn't think I'm normal, Church realized, as the sweat of fear shone along hair and sideburns. *He doesn't even think I'm human.*

Oh hell. Aidan and Myrrh must feel this way all the time.

"It's a knack." Church got to her feet, wobbly or not. "You know, like having twenty-ten vision. Nothing special. Miss Shafat's going to get lenses for those of us who need 'em."

It wasn't a lie. Exactly. She didn't know *why* she could tell what was a tree-thing and what was just illusion. Might as well call it a knack. Sure, Father O'Malley had stories about people born with the Sight, and the bad and good luck they attracted from all the Things they bumped into. But what good would that be to the regular cop on the street?

Those lenses damn well better work, Myrrh. Church glanced over the wreckage, trying not to look too hard where one ravaged body was still lying, waiting for cops to document the scene, while

the ambulance crew focused on the living. "I think they're gone."
Or dead.

Not one purple-leaved maple left standing. Though she hadn't found the loud tourist's orange hickory-

"Detective!" Officer Hale, head cocked over the radio on his shoulder. "This wasn't the only spot they hit."

Church's blood ran cold. *If regular cops can't see these things... oh god!*

Chapter Ten

Nobody was laughing at the chalkboard today.

Church watched too-distant gray eyes stare at white chalk, and rubbed her fingers over a curve of brass pipe. She wasn't the only one.

The funerals are going to start tomorrow. We killed some of the bastards, but... we couldn't even hold the spooks we caught. They just dissolved into dead leaves and blood. And some of those things got away.

How many more people are going to die?

Maybe a few less now. Myrrh's lens-crafting contact had finally come through. Some were set in old wire frames, a few were in magnifying glasses, one was a very British Indian pince-nez. Ironically fitting, given what they knew now.

"One of the most deadly factors in dealing with the super-natural is determining what you are dealing with in the first place." Myrrh's voice was quiet, but deliberately clear. "Across the world, there are powers alien to man who hold reign over deadly woods. One of those groups, not usually found in the Americas... includes rakshasas."

Church winced. *You can't find what you're not looking for. Not unless you get really lucky.*

It was all well and good to realize what sutras and copper pennies and root-holes meant *now*. After they had a body count that had Intrepid on the national news, and too many people howling for blood. Church didn't know about Myrrh, but she was finding it hard to sleep; nerves convinced every time the sun went down....

Aariel's face rose up in memory, a lion of flames.

Not yet. The Demongate's not open yet. Please, let us find a way to stop it.

"Unfortunately, *rakshasa* is a very broad term." Myrrh's eyes were suspiciously shiny. "Similar to the use of *youkai* in Japanese lore, or fairy in the tales of Europe. Some of them are demon-tainted, some are actual demons, and some just truly cranky."

Church gripped brass, and stared at distant gray. "So if they're fay or demons, does iron work on them, too?"

"Sometimes." Myrrh's shrug was painfully casual, shadow-shift not even pretending to be normal clothes. "They are more vulnerable to panchaloha and brass because of those alloys' associations with divine idols. But like werewolves, do enough damage in any fashion, and you will kill them." She frowned. "Given the traces remaining on the bones, we are likely dealing with *pishachas*, haunters of the graveyards, and *yakshas*, who guard that which is hidden in forests and under the earth." One white brow lifted. "Though some regions use yaksha to refer to those born of mixed human and rakshasa heritage. Folklore is oft our best source for banes and precautions, but it can be annoyingly imprecise."

"Ouch," Aidan muttered; keeping an eye on Myrrh, without making it look like he was keeping an eye on her. Church would have applauded, if she wasn't so damn *angry*. "There are halfling rakshasas?"

"Some, yes. I have not met one in some time." Myrrh blew out a slow breath. "We are definitely dealing with yaksha rakshasas in crime scenes around Intrepid. I will cover the highlights, given some have already proven themselves of lethal intent."

Which pretty much boiled down to, walking tree-spirits India-spook style; sometimes trees, sometimes almost human, males like less-bearded dwarves and the ladies something Rubin might approve of painting, rounded and happy. Though malevolent ones tended to have white clothing and sometimes their feet on backward. Which, what.

"Those are their normal forms," Myrrh observed. "Like all rakshasas, though, they are shapeshifters."

Flicks of Myrrh's fingers painted the chalkboard; a bark-skinned creature with *teeth*. Church recognized the green leafy that had grabbed Dorren, and tried not to swear.

Then came other kinds of rakshasas, each depicted in flowing color. The rat-faced pisacha, haunting graveyards, or anywhere bodies might be left unguarded. The whispering, gaunt pani, taunting and manipulating; that one Myrrh illustrated with a short, grim tale of an Indian peace-guardian driven to madness and near dying at the hands of an outraged mob, before a very cranky priest dragged the creature out of its possessed victim by the ear. The brahmarakshasas; horned, shaved-headed ghostly creatures with one long tuft of hair, who might grant boons or eat people as they pleased, might *command* lesser rakshasas, and were usually found hanging upside-down on tree trunks like a gigantic bat.

Note to self: tell the acrobats and parkour-geeks in town to pull their tricks anywhere but in the trees.

"And last, are the asuras," Myrrh summed up, eyes still distant. "Like other rakshasas, they can fly, vanish in a blink, and create solid illusions that take many human minds to break. Unlike them, they are far less vulnerable to brass; less vulnerable to almost anything save a sage or a hero's weapon. To other rakshasas they are as demigods, and often revered leaders. In ages past they led armies in the thousands, and heroes and devas alike were forced to combine their strength to stop one asura. In this day and age...." Her voice hitched. "I would suggest triangulating its location and applying high explosives." Myrrh blinked at the board, as if trying to make it clearer. "I devoutly hope we do not have an asura in town."

Church eyed the graceful, godlike creature sketched in chalk, handsome except for the skull-cup filled with blood, and hoped right along with her.

"I would... I would that I could have given this lecture days ago." Myrrh's voice was ragged, knuckles clenched and pale. "This is Intrepid, a place of Celts, Cherokee, and later folk from Europe. When I knew we were dealing with homicidal greenery, I expected strangling willows. Wodewoses. Moss-folk, hamadryads, woken pines. Other such creatures, from lore those raised here would have been familiar with. I... I had no reason to look for rakshasas."

Oh no, the detective thought, as Myrrh brushed the first drops of salt water off her cheek. *No, this is not good....*

"Forgive me." Myrrh's voice was thick, as tears kept falling. "I believe we shall have to cut this lecture short."

"Hey." Aidan offered a tissue as Eagleman turned the camera off and Church chased anybody who looked vaguely reporter-like out. "You going to be okay?"

"Tired." Myrrh pressed soft paper to the trickle of tears. "So much hate and fear already. So much we cannot say...."

In front of the cameras, Aidan finished. *Oh man. Oh, so not good.* "Get everyone in here and shut the door." He glanced up at Church and Captain Sherman. "We've got problems."

Sherman grimaced. Church... sighed. "Of course we do. Because homicidal trees aren't *enough.*"

Getting a handful of detectives and patrol officers sorted out took another minute. Aidan watched Myrrh use it to dry her eyes, and brace herself.

She doesn't want to do this. And I don't want to ask. But we've got to. Aidan glanced at the gathered detectives, and nodded. "You think there's something worse than rakshasas. Spill."

The hell-raider dabbed at her eyes, as if she couldn't bear the heat of more tears. "Rakshasas are shapeshifters, able to sway even blessed souls into peril with their arrogance and charm. But." She swallowed. "So far as I have known, just as European fay, rakshasas are limited. They can mimic a human form, but not a specific person."

"But those were yakshas out there," Church protested.

Which Aidan sympathized with. Totally. But.... "Yakshas

shouldn't *dissolve* like that." He shuddered. "If they died, yeah, maybe. Just getting caught? No way. Something tore the *soul* out of the one we trapped. Something with a hook it couldn't fight." And what that might be, he really didn't want to know.

But I have to. We all do.

"A brahmarakshasa might have been able to weave such a horrible work of magic." Myrrh flinched. "The lesser rakshasas are more mundane, mortal breeds. Brahmarakshasas are closer to the asuras who are their blood and kin. Yet, if you did see Agent Cushman's double, Church, a creature that could mimic not only his form but his *aura* well enough for one with Sight to doubt they were different entities...."

"You think we've got an *asura* loose in Intrepid," Aidan breathed. "Oh, hell."

Myrrh scrunched in on herself, white and shadowed misery. "A moment. Just-"

"Breathe," Aidan advised. "And listen, so you can fill in the gaps. I got this." He took a step away, turning to face the dozen-odd detectives and cops still standing here-

Eeep.

He had to take a breath himself. These were cops, these were the good guys; even Glover, who might have a beef with Myrrh on a lot of things, but was willing to listen when it came to monsters eating people.

These are the good guys. Heh. No wonder I'm scared.

Breathe. Did this with Church already, right? Though that was Fay Lords, and they're kind of less scary and... eep?

So he'd better warn them the way Aariel had warned him. They'd seen yakshas. Asuras were whole new levels of terrifying.

"Somebody warned me about these guys." Aidan touched braided white, feeling the subtle heat of silver-steel knives under cloth. "Someone who was *not* a nice guy, so when he leaves a list around saying a demon's best option is strategic retreat...."

Church's hands clenched. "You telling me asuras are demon

lords?"

"They're heavenly creatures who got thrown out and decided to go to war with the devas," Aidan said practically. "I think that's close enough."

"An incarnation as an asura is one of the four unhappy births of Buddhism," Myrrh managed. "Along with being reborn into one of the Narakas." She shifted slightly; not quite a shrug. "If they are not precisely the Christian Hell, they are, shall we say, close enough for government work."

"And the Narakas are how the asuras drop in on Demon Lords for tea and blood wine," Aidan informed the crowd. "But like she said, they're not *exactly* Hell. So *asuras* can get up onto Earth if they feel like it." He glanced at the board again, amazed how well Myrrh had caught that elegant menace. "Lucky for everybody, most of the time they can only open gates at the base of someplace called Mount Meru. Which is in India, kind of. Devas know that, and they keep an eye on the place to bring down smitation. Or a horde of sages," he reflected. "Pretty much the same thing."

"I might equal a sage," Myrrh got out. "I cannot equal a deva."

"You can't?" Church raised an interested eyebrow. "So, any way we can call one in as backup?"

Myrrh blinked, then cleared her throat. "Ah. You likely have not read the Ramayana. Devas fighting asuras tend to inflict a certain amount of collateral damage. Fortresses. Kingdoms. Mountain ranges...."

Church winced. "They're Godzilla, we're Tokyo?"

"Pretty much," Aidan agreed. "If we have to get help that's out of this world... seriously, it'd be way better if we can track this thing down. Though that'll be hard if the werewolves ate the corpses. Maybe we can look for *missing* werewolves. Asuras that eat bodies would definitely be annoyed enough to eat the werewolves, too. Poor bastards."

That earned him Glover's skeptical look. "Like you care about the furries."

"Do you care about junkies hopped up on crack?" Aidan shot back. "That's what the curse *is*. Makes people think they're on top of the world. Makes them think everyone else is just... something to feed the need." He grimaced. "But even when a crackhead's got a gun, you try and talk him down first. I *hate* werewolves. Doesn't mean I'm going to stand by and let something eat them piece by screaming piece."

Sherman raised a hand, cutting Glover off before he could start. "An asura can do that?" Her voice was loud and clear: *listen and think about this*. "We need silver to cut a werewolf apart, and an asura can...?"

"Tear them apart bare-handed," Aidan said bluntly, remembering a storm-lashed stretch of time when skirting close to demon-eating monsters had been the best of a lost soul's bad options. "I've seen them do it with lesser demons. Like pulling apart a roasted chicken. Only a lot more blood."

Okay. He definitely had their attention.

"Asura auras taste a little like nectar and stone... right, not going to help." *Argh. Think.* "They gorge, and they drink. A lot. What they really want is *soma*, but you're not going to have much of that on Earth, so look for the guy drinking the whole bar under the table and still complaining nothing's strong enough. They like gold so much, they jingle when they walk...."

"They will probably look of India, in human form," Myrrh murmured.

"Outside of the ten heads and fangs, yeah," Aidan agreed. "Not that all of them have those... a lot of asuras are water-based powers, so if one goes under, stay out of the wet. It doesn't need to do anything so puny and *mortal* as breathe. Get the picture?"

"Scuba gear still out?" Church muttered.

"Assume they've got wind powers," Aidan agreed. "You'll live longer."

"Dammit."

"The big problem, you've seen already with the yakshas. They

can fool your senses. Here on Earth. Asuras can do that *in Hell*."
And that still made Aidan shudder. "That is... I'd say end of the
world bad, but we've already in for a Demongate on our doorstep.
So - usually only a Demon Lord can pull that off. Even a
guardsman can't weave mind-tricks that good."

"Just as Fay Lords, asuras are masters of glamour; though the
term used in India is *Maya*." Myrrh uncurled a bit, eyes reddened.
"Consult Church's notes on glamour, and you will see it describes
exactly what happened with the ambulance. Had that been an
ordinary illusion, the paramedics would have passed through it,
terrified but unharmed. But it was not, and they struck it; and the
damage was *real*."

Church flinched. She wasn't the only one.

"I can see through fay glamours," Myrrh observed, "though
that will blast me as rude. But I am as a sage, not a deva; and even
the devas have been fooled by asura maya."

"But we've still got a chance. You have to be close for them to
mess with you," Aidan said firmly. "Get *away* from them. Don't
let them touch you. They can layer whatever maya they like on
themselves, but they can't trap you in your own head." He paused,
making himself think. "If you can't run, *swarm*. Mob the damn
thing. Maya takes concentration, just like spellcasting. The more
eyes you have on it, the harder they have to work to keep it up."

"That's what happened." Church stood straighter, gaze gathering her fellow cops with the promise of an answer. "They got
easier to hit when there were a lot of us looking their way. The
illusions - the maya - it got *sloppy*."

"Bingo," Aidan agreed, relieved. "Myrrh, you still think ten or
so people?"

Myrrh blinked at him, and smiled ruefully. "The problem is not
that they are more powerful than Fay Lords. The problem is that
their powers are different, and my weapons are not so honed
against them. So yes. Ten or so demons, or sages, should still
suffice." Gray eyes half-closed, seeking memory. "And yes,

distance, if at all possible. Ramachandra wounded his asura foe with arrows first, before closing for the final blow."

"Too bad bowhunting season's not for a month yet." Church glanced at both of them. "Lead work? It did on the yakshas...."

"I should like to find out," Myrrh mused. "Hopefully, yes. While yakshas are lesser asura-kin, they are still kin. Lead is in panchaloha, after all."

"Fire still works if you can get it in the cracks," Aidan added.

"The cracks?" Church echoed, obviously not happy.

Which, well, point. Cops didn't usually carry flamethrowers. "Um... sometimes, to fight, asuras like to take stone forms. Like living statues. Snakes are a big one," Aidan shrugged. "Stone's tough, but it's not alive. It has to have cracks to move. Fire plus cracks in stone equals a whole lot of crumbling."

"So we're back to flamethrowers and mass destruction." Church shifted her shoulders as if her holster was binding, definitely not happy. "I knew we should have called the National Guard."

"Chief Lyter's still considering it. If he can convince the mayor," Sherman sighed. "Problem is, we have no proof. And no *location*. The biggest bomb in the arsenal's no good without somewhere to aim it." She crossed her arms, gaze raking them all; detectives, officers, fire mage, hell-raider. "We need an informant."

Aidan blinked, eyes wide. "Um. Did you miss how trying to catch these guys ended up with a lot of dead leaves and blood?"

"Word on the street says you caught one for a few minutes, Shafat." Glover smirked, eyes challenging. "Think you can do better?"

Myrrh knuckled her chin, looking into the distance. Took a breath, and looked up. "I need help. I have the power, but not specific knowledge of these creatures. Not as they may be in America, instead of ancient India. I cannot identify if we are dealing with common rakshasas run mad, yakshas under a brahmarakshasa's leadership, or a true asura. I need an expert."

"An expert on American rakshasas," Aidan said, stunned. "Where do we even start?"

"Vajra Hall," Church stated. Shrugged, at the center of odd looks. "What? Buddhist monsters, Buddhist temple. If O'Malley knows how to slam a teenage werewolf with Bible study so the kid has a chance at reforming, I bet Priest Sakai knows something. Or knows somebody who knows something."

"It seems the best course of action," Myrrh nodded. "But convincing a master of Hunting lore to make contact may take time." Her fingers curled, white-knuckled fists, before she loosened them. "In the meantime... Captain. If it would not offend, I would attend the funerals, and take measures to ensure no seeds will be planted to feed on the honored dead. Let me ensure that our fallen truly rest in peace."

Chapter Eleven

Saturday, October 25th

"Ghouls," Church snarled under her breath, uniform hat snug over dark hair as her glance cut to camera-flashes in the crowd attending yet another funeral. "Say I'm hard-hearted and call me pharaoh. At least Moses never called down a plague of *reporters*."

Aidan grimaced, all too aware most people wouldn't have heard that, standing where he was behind the rows of uniforms. He didn't want to draw attention; he *hoped* he wasn't drawing attention, hence the thick dark wool hat covering his dratted fire-copper hair. But even if Myrrh hadn't been taking anti-evil-seed measures, there was no way either of them planned to let Church face this grief alone.

"It's possible some of them are ghouls," Myrrh mused, white wisps straying from under her hood. "Some Arabian *ghuls* appear quite human, unless they are feeding."

"Not helping," Aidan muttered. There was no way Church or her fellow officers would have heard that, but the two of them at a police funeral were more than distraction enough. The reporters would probably wait until the bodies were in the ground. Probably. Then they'd be on the survivors like a pack of starving hellhounds.

"I know." Myrrh sighed, heart-worn. "I know. Sometimes the only way I can look the dead in the eye, is to remind myself what we can yet teach the living, so none of us join them too soon."

Aidan shivered, despite his trenchcoat. "Amen to that."

Part of his chill came from knowing they weren't just here for the seeds. The formal funeral salute was usually enough to warn off malign spirits from wounded hearts, Myrrh said, but given the massive shock all of Intrepid had had, the amount of maya and maleficent magic that'd been thrown around during those deaths-

Well. Better safe than sorry.

"Ashes to ashes, dust to dust...."

Father Ricci was handling the funeral. Aidan would have felt worse about Father O'Malley being back at church, alone, but the good Father was currently preparing holy water for a bunch of nervous cops, various parishioners, and one very aggravated hell-raider.

Not that Myrrh couldn't make her own holy water. But she'd been up to her ears in other requests. Including blending salt, cinnamon, cane, cassia, and the myrrh that was her namesake with enough olive oil to set a car on fire.

It made him want to smile, despite the grim day. Myrrh hated olives, but she wasn't at all averse to a little holy fire-starting.

With more yakshas out there, we're going to need it.

How many more was the worrisome question. How many seeds had been planted in unmarked graves, fed by murdered bodies? How many people had gone missing, that the IPD had never found?

How many went missing just these past few days? Aidan ducked his head into the collar of his coat, all too aware his glare would frighten any innocent it landed on. *We don't know. We just don't know how many people are missing 'cause they're missing, missing 'cause they're* dead, *or missing 'cause they saw which way the wind's blowing and they're getting the hell out of town before their neighbors figure out they're not as human as everybody used to think.*

Xanthippe Coral's memorial business had already been egged once, and there'd been a flaming bottle by the road where someone had been too spooked by her security lights to throw it. The Nightsong was still standing, but patrol officers working nearby said the club was only doing half the business, and given that meant hungry vampires, Aidan expected an explosion from that quarter any night now. And reports of New Age alternative medicine practitioners and other people who'd been living as quietly as Coral had, now suffering everything from keyed cars to getting thrown out of jobs and apartments, kept trickling into the IPD and the church like a muddy flood.

Thank God Father O'Malley sent Raphael out of town.

On the one hand, it was kind of a necessity; the kid was fighting the curse hard, but keeping it under control at this stage apparently involved silver-chased steel manacles and a lot of plain fare to get the taste of humans out of his mouth. O'Malley was past eighty, and didn't have that kind of restraints on hand.

Or, well, maybe he did. Aidan wasn't about to ask. But what the good Father *didn't* have was space to keep the kid voluntarily confined without locking him into a tiny cell that would drive him crazy. Er.

With our luck, some roving reporter would stumble down there, break the kid out, and get bit in the process. Or eaten, Aidan thought darkly. *Which would be too damn bad for Raphael.*

Um. And bad for the reporter, too. Right.

It was not a good sign that he had to keep *reminding* himself of that. Reporters were people too. Annoying, foolhardy, and way too many of them as bamboozled as Dayson had been about the whole *vampires are harmless* facade, but people.

Heh. Poor Dayson.

Somehow, he just could not be sorry that they'd dragged the hapless reporter into the bloodbath that had been Intrepid's Festival of Flavor. Otherwise known as enough beer and cheese to choke every mouse in the city, then float the corpses downriver.

...Damn, he was morbid today.

Dorren's alive. We won that much. She *won that much, smart kid.*

Smart enough not to leave her threshold no matter what illusions rakshasas had wiggled past her, of Megan and her uncle and who knew what else. Dorren had taken up a slingshot and brass ball bearings, sniping anything that so much as twitched near her house no matter how her mother screamed at her. Aidan was so proud he could have *hugged* the little brat.

Though he wanted to leave that for Switch. Who was still in FBI custody half the time for "assistance with inquiries", driving the hitman into a seething cold fury Aidan totally understood. It was like the FBI *wanted* Switch to do something they could charge him on, whether or not that'd leave his family twisting in the wind.

Agent Cushman probably does, Aidan thought uncharitably. *After all, if he can get Switch put away for* something, *he looks better.*

A human reaction, if a darned less than useful one. Argh.

"I believe we are clear." Myrrh tugged the hood of her shift up, judging reporters' lines of sight. "I did not think our enemies would send tormenting spirits here, but there was always the chance something else might have taken advantage."

"I'd ask 'what something else', but I can think of at least four things without trying hard," Aidan sighed. "Including an unhoused vampire demon. We did zap the ones in the Nightsong, right?"

"Oh yes." Myrrh smiled, darkly satisfied. "That is one advantage of using sun and fire. A wooden stake may simply drive them from the possessed body; fire and purification sear away their hold on this realm, driving them down into Hell."

"Might want to not mention that to the roving reporters," Aidan observed. "They really don't want to hear the *going to Hell* thing."

A *hmph*. "Actions have consequences."

"You, need more sleep," Aidan said bluntly. "Trust me on this. Tired people make mistakes. If we're up against what I think we are, we can't risk that."

Myrrh sighed, and rubbed under one eye. "Rakshasas tend to hunt on their own, unless compelled by one of greater strength. There is no reason there should be so many attacks, so publicly-"

"Unless someone's trying to pick a fight," Aidan finished. "And if it's something that thinks it can stir up a whole city and get out in one piece...."

"A brahmarakshasa, at the very least," Myrrh agreed. "But it is not simply stirring up this city, is it?"

"No." Damn it. Granted, he was no talking head expert in national politics, and bits he could snag off the TV news and Father Ricci's favorite websites didn't tell him anything he could swear in his gut was true. But what was happening in Intrepid was getting attention, *lots* of attention. And not of the good kind.

"I had not grasped how much the world had truly changed," Myrrh reflected. "In its opinions voiced in the light of day, at least. We are here, facing those who would destroy us; those who have slain the innocent and their protectors alike. Why on earth do people in *Belgium* think they have the right to declare our tactics violent and barbaric?"

"Got me," Aidan shrugged. "I just hope the idiots don't...."

A rattle of drums from the direction of the cemetery gates. Still out on the road, if his ears were right.

Please tell me that's not what I think it is.

Myrrh was already moving; an angry, shadowed ghost. He took off after her, though he *knew* he'd draw too many eyes. Myrrh was the closest thing to a saint he'd ever met. She was also angry, hurting, and *incredibly ticked off.* Given he could hear the protest chants drifting into earshot, meaning another minute and the cops would hear them too-

Myrrh was already on top of the rugged stone wall encircling the cemetery. Perched like a white-haired raven, feathers ruffled in the wind of self-righteousness coming off the crowd.

"No maiming." Aidan rested a hand on her shoulder, chilled even in the sunlight. "And usually you're the one telling me that, so I *know* this is not good."

Myrrh drew a deep breath, eyes raking the placards of *Dark Lives Matter* before she let it hiss out in frustration. "I do not *understand* people."

"These guys in specific, or your Joe Average human in general?" Aidan wondered. Because frankly, Myrrh had been around a *very long time*, and that had to play tricks with anyone's view on the world.

"Ha. Both, I must admit." But some of the tension eased out of shadowed shoulders, and the way she reached out her hand didn't worry him....

Much.

"They have prepared a net for my steps," Myrrh murmured, low and haunted. "My soul is bowed down." An indrawn breath of quiet triumph. "They dug a pit before me; they themselves have fallen into the midst of it. *Selah.*"

Aidan arched a brow. He couldn't see anything happening, though he felt that whisper of world-reshaping, persuading....

Ask, and it shall be given unto you, Aidan reflected. *Myrrh just takes that literally.*

He blinked at the flock of reporters fluttering out the gates, setting up to catch footage of cops filing out from filled graves. "What did you just do?"

"Gave them what they truly want," Myrrh said dryly. "Attention."

Which was a far cry from the *avoid if possible* reaction she'd had at the demolition site days back. Then again, back then they hadn't had a bunch of dead cops.

And the voices in the crowd chanting *"Pigs in a blanket, fry 'em like bacon!"* had none of Aidan's sympathy, even if they were about to collide with reporters hot for a story. "You know they're not from around here, right?"

"I've dealt with enemies stirring up enmity with outside agitators before. They have no shame. Funerals are for the living, not the dead; and the living deserve time with their grief." Myrrh dropped back inside the wall. "Someone intends that they do not have that time. Someone plans to rub every wound raw, until blood flows in the streets."

"Steven," Aidan growled, thumping back to cold earth beside her.

"Or those he was in league with. Or someone else with

demonic influence, who senses the Demongate and seeks to keep our men of faith far too busy to purify its foundations." Myrrh's lips tightened.

"You can't do it all yourself," Aidan stated. "You *can't*," he repeated, when gray eyes sought his with weary indignation. "You need rest. I need rest. Hell, even Church needs rest, if I have to hit her over the head with a blackjack to get her to close her eyes. We pour her into bed, we hit Our Lady's, and we pull the covers up over our heads for at least eight hours. Intrepid's going to have to take care of itself."

She sighed, and rubbed knuckles between creased brows. "I simply do not understand it. I have *never* understood. Those who have never met monsters, who have never been preyed upon - they always think someone must be evil to fall to talons and slavering fangs. That they must have *deserved* it." Myrrh grimaced. "As if there were ever any walking this earth who had not sinned, save two. Monsters do not attack because you are evil, they attack because you are *there*."

"Yeah, but you got that pounded in early," Aidan pointed out, as cameras met marchers in a low-pitched roar. "Magic means target. Right?" He had to shake his head. "And me... well, Mom had her hands full with everything I did. And everything I didn't do, but everyone else tried to pin on me 'cause trouble just *followed* me."

"Most humans never knowingly touch magic," Myrrh nodded, walking close enough that her shadow lapped his. "Still, the stories were always there."

"Only these days, people thought they weren't real," Aidan shrugged. "Then they found out they are, but don't worry, the things that go bump in the night don't *really* want to hurt you. Now we're all trying to tell them sorry, some of those things really do want to eat you after all. Way to shatter their nice safe lives." He straightened. "Come on. We should at least warn Father Ricci before we sneak out the back."

Chapter Twelve

Sunday, October 26th

Captain Sherman's footsteps stopped by Church's desk. "You should go home."

"What, and stare at the walls?" Church shuffled through yet another pile of paperwork Agent Cushman was using to keep Switch O'Connor pinned down. "Why is he even bothering with this? People saw the rakshasas all over town; he could tell his superiors right now that was never him at the bank, and they ought to buy it."

"He could," the captain allowed. "In fact, he should. Between the hate crimes, the possible kidnappings, and the *riots*, he ought to be way too busy to worry about his own neck. Right?"

The sardonic lilt finally got Church's attention. "You mean, he's still worried about the world going on as usual after Halloween."

"Most people are," Captain Sherman allowed. "Hell on earth? Demons? The end of the world? Everybody knows that's crazy talk."

Church looked up at her captain. "Except it's not."

"Church." Sherman dug fingers into her hair. "I've seen almost everything you have, and I *wish* it was crazy talk. And I've got a lot less vested in the status quo than Mayor Green and his buddies."

Yeah. If she ever found a direct link between Mayor Green and the professional agitators making Intrepid's night streets even scarier than usual, Church was tempted to feed it straight to the press.

If they'd listen. So far Dayson's the only one even half willing to take our side without trying to paint us all as slavering Humans

First loonies.

Not that Matt Dayson was *nice*. His columns on Myrrh as a self-avowed Hunter didn't bother to mention that someone Hunting things that didn't legally exist couldn't exactly go to the cops. Nope; he was up one side of the webpage and down the other about Myrrh handing out info on monster-banes like an anarchist gleefully putting bomb-making instructions out on the Net. Only in his mind Myrrh was worse, because what average human would think twice about throwing a few rowan berries at someone they didn't like? Never mind how much harm it'd do to someone who wasn't human.

Frankly Church hoped Aidan was sitting on Myrrh, because she'd never seen one human being go to sputtering incoherence so fast without staring cross-eyed at a pistol up their nose. They'd just barely kept Myrrh from typing up half the banes she knew and dumping them on social media without even *trying* to sort them out by category, because the enchantress was utterly furious people could blatantly ignore information crucial to *saving lives*.

"Next they'll be banning hand-washing," Church had heard her snarl. "And alcohol for cleansing. What is *wrong* with these people?"

Church had wondered that so many times, she'd lost count. Right now she was specifically wondering what the heck was wrong with Cushman. It didn't make *sense*.

Wait. Wait just one minute....

"Church?"

"Was going back through our stuff on Switch," Church said absently, rifling through papers. "Just so I had it all straight when we do talk to him. Maybe I'd trust him to keep Dorren safe, but that doesn't mean he's going to tell us the truth about Savonarola." Where was it, she knew she'd seen something-

Got you!

"Hel-lo," she sing-songed. "Well, Captain. Would you look at that?"

One brow quirked up, Sherman took that particular bit of the file. It was old, just a little over two years-

Sherman tensed like she'd been hit with a taser, and Church knew she'd seen the date. "Megan went missing-"

"Right when Special Agent *In Charge* Dwyer had Switch in for questioning about a few of his acquaintances, live and dead," Church finished. "Then let him walk."

"Just to see if his mob buddies thought Switch ratted them out, so they could take care of the problem for the Bureau," Sherman agreed. "Cushman's covering for his boss."

"If by covering you mean trying to make Switch mad enough with him to not go after Dwyer," Church reflected. "I wouldn't bet my life on that. Which means... ah, hell." She dropped her notes. "Captain? I've got no way to prove this, but...."

Sherman grimaced. "You think it really was Cushman at the bank after all."

"No, I think it *wasn't*," Church sighed. "But if we dug into the good agent's finances, we might find something... well. Like Tom's."

Captain Sherman stared, then pressed her fingers right on the crease between troubled eyebrows. "...You think Steven framed the guy for a crime he actually *did* commit."

Church grinned ruefully. "Yep."

"...I need to go *hit something....*"

"Well, I have some kind of good news?" Church shrugged. She felt like punching things herself. "Though it's probably better not to spread it around."

Never let it be said Captain Sherman was slow on the uptake. "Myrrh said she'd find a rakshasa expert."

"And ask locals for help," Church agreed. "She and Aidan are still plotting on that; they asked me to come along to Vajra Hall this afternoon. Said somebody just flew in from California last night, and they're going to make sure none of her sutras crash into a stray little-folk while she's figuring out jet lag." And she wanted to apply head to desk over the fact that crashing into little people was actually a *possibility*.

Given the nifty book by Mooney she'd snagged out of the casino gift shop, it definitely was. *Yunwi Tsundi*, the Cherokee called them; sometimes bearded, sometimes horned, associated with rivers, sandy hills and *copper tools*. No wonder no seedlings had been planted at Enchanted Waters.

"But I'm talking about - other kinds of help." Church met her captain's gaze, straight on. "People Father O'Malley's run into a few times. He said he sent some letters."

Sherman winced. "I really don't want to know, do I?"

"If it helps," Church said neutrally, "I've been told they work undercover for the U.S. Marshals. And... other agencies."

Captain Sherman opened her mouth; closed it again, ears red with suppressed fury. "You're telling me our friendly local Feds have Hunters on the unofficial payroll."

"I don't think anybody said that, exactly," Church said judiciously.

"No, of course not," the captain fumed. "Let me guess. The usual DEA setup?"

As in, we caught you doing something illegal, work for us or go to prison; if you get caught, we never knew anything about it, Church reflected. "I didn't ask, and Father O'Malley didn't say. But there were a lot of specific things he said he couldn't say."

Captain Sherman took one deep breath. Another.

No fool, Church kept her mouth shut.

"They're letting our department twist in the wind," Sherman growled, "saying we're racists and speciesists and who knows what the hell else, when they know damn well what we're up against?"

"I don't know that," Church stated. *Not for sure, anyway.* "But if Myrrh's had this arrangement with the Secret Service to leave them alone if they leave her alone... she's said she'd rather work with the law when she can. If she thinks she can't- I have to wonder."

"Feds." Sherman straightened her shoulders. "So what's going on over at Vajra Hall?"

Okay, Aidan thought, watching tension seep out of Myrrh's shoulders as she exchanged polite greetings with the shaven-headed young Californian nun in scarlet and saffron. Usagi, he thought he'd heard her called. At least he thought it was Usagi, he'd also heard *Rabbit* and *Moon-dweller* and his ears were obviously not trustworthy on this. Maybe because it was an ordination name, spirit-stuff rang louder in his head than actual words. *Okay, good. Maybe we should ask to crash here some nights.*

Which depressed him, that Myrrh felt safer here than in the PD or at Our Lady's. Then again... the police were gearing up for active self-defense, and Father O'Malley's church was full of a whole bunch of people who'd never wanted anything to do with the supernatural besides praying hard and trying to live decent lives. Ordinary, average, decent people, who looked at him and Myrrh like they'd escaped from a zoo. Or maybe an insane asylum. Ouch.

Aidan sighed, and shrugged, admitting the obvious. *If you're a Buddhist in North Carolina, you've already decided to be weird.*

It wasn't all roses and kittens here, either. Priest Sakai, a middle-aged guy with his own shaved head and thick glasses, was looking at the two women of faith like he wasn't sure when he'd fallen into the Twilight Zone. Aidan didn't know if that was because Myrrh was a hell-raider or because she knew polite Sanskrit greetings with a very old accent.

He glanced at the lovingly carved wooden Buddha on the low altar, enshrined in front of a wildly-knotted wood bole that spread up and out like chestnut-red flames. Careful not to approach the offerings or votive candles too closely; the power here wasn't old, not like Our Lady's, but it felt solid. Definitely dangerous enough to give a rakshasa a headache.

How do I know that?

"I'm still not certain I understand the situation." Priest Sakai's gaze flicked between Aidan, Myrrh still trading low words with Usagi, and the various trying too hard to look ordinary people filtering in through the glass front door. As if they'd just come for the bookshop next door, really, stealing a few temple chairs to sit down and chat with stray fellow citizens was just an afterthought. "You say those creatures in the news are rakshasas? Actual rakshasas?"

"They fit the description," Aidan nodded. "I believe Myrrh when she ID's something. She's been around."

Sakai's gaze slid to Myrrh again. Warily.

Aidan raised an eyebrow. "What?"

The priest shrugged. "It's nothing, I must have misheard...."

"Then we'd better clear it up, whatever it was," Aidan said practically. "One wrong word, and spells go south in a hurry."

The priest mouthed *spells* like he couldn't believe the word had come out of Aidan's mouth. "It's just... she said something about traveling through India during the Tang Dynasty."

"Okay?" Aidan said, uncertain what the problem was.

"The Tang Dynasty was over a *thousand years* ago."

"O...kay?" Aidan shrugged. "The way she complains about people changing the calendars she might be off a year or two. What's that have to do with fighting rakshasas?"

Sakai took off his glasses. Polished them on his robe sleeve. Put them back on, looking up to meet Aidan's gaze with incredulous disbelief. "She can't possibly be a vampire, she walked into this temple without an invitation. And I've never seen a were-creature so calm. What kind of supernatural is she?"

"Um. Not?" Aidan tried. "She's an enchantress. And a hell-raider. But she's human." He was going to leave out the whole *magical construct* bit. Sure, Myrrh was magic, but so far as he knew spells alone didn't bring dead bones back to life. And if it was magic... he didn't feel like helping someone else get a clue to unraveling it.

Sakai's mouth dropped open. He started to say something; shook his head, as if he wanted to shiver all over. "You cannot expect me to believe a bodhisattva just walked through my door."

"Nope," Aidan grinned, relaxing. "Myrrh likes followers of the Way okay, but she's a Christian. She's no bodhisattva. Just a saint."

Oops. There was the glare he'd earned back in Sunday school for *utter cheek*, as the church ladies deemed it. He'd better do something to soothe down ruffled priestly feathers, so Sakai would be willing to work with them. Or at least not get in the way. "You might want to bless your threshold a little harder." Aidan nodded toward the door. "After all, I got through it. I grant you I'm maybe not the lightest weight out there; don't know how it translates into your faith. Myrrh said something about not as strong as Lord Mara, but probably up there with Hārītī?" He had to scratch his head. "I really need her to tell me the details. I don't even know if I'm pronouncing that right."

"You believe you have demonic heritage." Sakai pushed his glasses up, as if now he'd heard it all. "Young man, demons are but another manifestation of the world's maya, its illusions. They aren't *real*."

"Ah, but by your own teachings, nothing in the world is real save for the quest to pierce through illusions to reach enlightenment," Myrrh put in, as Usagi stifled a giggle. "In that vein, demons are as real as an eighteen-wheeler driving downtown. And should be given at least as much caution, so that one avoids doing violence to the body, in the true path of the Way."

"Not sure you want to get her started on reality and faith," Aidan advised the priest. "The last time she and Father O'Malley went at it, they hauled out *dictionaries*."

"Seeker Shafat is legendary for providing opportunities for

enlightenment through questioning what we think we know."
Usagi's green eyes danced. "Even if she finds a cross in the lotus,
not a jewel."

"Compassion without meditation is blind; meditation without
compassion is cruel," Myrrh smiled. "One who follows Christ
without attention to the lessons of Buddha in mercy and right
action, even if they come from another teacher, walks half-blind on
the road to Heaven."

"Oh." Priest Sakai sighed, as if this explained everything.
"Ecumenicists."

"Hardly; that would be far too narrow." Myrrh paused. "Ah.
You refer to the inhabited world as a whole, not the Roman
Empire. Words do change over time." She nodded at Usagi. "Sister
Usagi tells me she was requested to travel here by her monastery,
as she has experience in exorcising chants and your temple has
contact with many who use nonstandard religious practice to cover
some of their less human habits."

Behind glass lenses, Sakai's eyes were a bit too wide, as he
looked over the no longer innocuous crowd. "We do?"

Aidan thumped a hand down on an orange-robed shoulder, and
never mind that it prickled a bit. "Just listen. And don't scream.
Unless somebody's trying to eat somebody else."

"No one here should be," Usagi said easily. "I bet the greater
creatures wouldn't want to live in town. Or at least, they wouldn't
show up inside a temple without reservations." She bowed to Priest
Sakai. "With your permission, Elder Brother?"

"Go right ahead," Sakai said faintly. "Creatures?"

"You'll get used to it," Aidan muttered. "You should have
coffee with Father Ricci sometime. He takes the whole *demons*
thing hard, too."

Wind-chimes at the door clinked, and Church walked back in
with a disgruntled look. "Idiot teenagers."

Sakai straightened, back on more familiar ground. "A little
paint won't hurt the windows, Detective. We can always clean

them later."

"It's not the tagging, Priest Sakai." Church scowled. "It's that they're willing to pull that in broad daylight. To Buddhists. It's not like you're a Santeria shop or something."

Some of the late arrivals obviously hadn't realized one of Intrepid's finest was going to be here. One or two scraped chairs back, ready to bolt-

"This isn't official." Church projected her voice to fill the whole hall. "In fact, it'd damn well better not be official, I'm still on administrative leave. A little matter of trying not to get eaten by some of the local werewolf gang-bangers." Blue eyes swept everyone there, from a nervous thin woman in gray and a leaf-patterned jacket to a scowling thick-set man who wouldn't have looked out of place in a football lineup. "I'm just another citizen right now, asking - *asking* - for help, from anyone who's willing to give it. Our city's in big trouble, as big as it gets, and we can't turn anyone down."

"The *city's* in trouble?" The woman in gray shuddered. "Do you know what's going on out there? Our neighbors, people we trusted-!"

"People tell me I have the Second Sight." Church stuffed her hands in her coat pockets. "So yes, ma'am. I'm beginning to get the idea."

"You have the Sight?" The not-linebacker scowled harder. "And you're...."

"Admitting it out loud?" Church shrugged. "Like I said. Our city's in trouble. If we go down, it could be the whole world in trouble. I think that outweighs me getting to live a quiet, normal life. But I chose to be a cop. I volunteered to put my life on the line. None of you asked for that. None of you *have* to do anything. You want to run for the hills? Believe me, I get that. I met a demon lord's guardsman a week ago. Every time I think about it my knees turn to water. But this is my city. I'm *not* letting it go down without a fight." She looked over them all, blue eyes tired. "Captain

Sherman asked me to do this because I *am* on leave. This isn't the city asking. Not even the cops. I'm just another citizen, asking if someone wants to come load sandbags with me. Because there's a dark river breaking the banks, and I'll take any extra hands I can get."

Sounds like my cue. "Like me, and Myrrh, and Sister Usagi over there," Aidan put in. "Though I have to admit for me and Myrrh, it's kind of personal. If the Demongate opens up, there are people who are going to be looking for us, and not for a friendly hello." He had to stop and think about that. "Well, I call them people. Most of you would probably call them things not meant to set foot on this world. I haven't been back long enough to get everything in my head straight, yet."

"Back?" The gray lady shuddered, eyes falling on him as if he'd stepped out of thin air. Glanced at Myrrh, and stiffened. "You! You're the one from the Nightsong, you're a *Hunter!*"

"And if you'd notice, she's also *not* between you and the door," Church jumped in before the crowd could snap. "I know she's scary. Shafat scares *me*. Just hear me out, okay?"

"I am saddened that such as the vampires have shaped your opinions of Hunters so thoroughly," Myrrh stated. "They attacked me. Would any of you do less, did a vampire thirst for your blood?"

From the looks on a half-dozen faces, none of them wanted to think about that. Aidan sighed.

"Try to ignore the prickly demon-slayer," Church advised. "If I could, I'd ship her down to Bermuda to soak up the sun and not think about anything more lethal than the next mai-tai. But until and unless we get through Halloween alive, that's not an option. Just take it as given that she's not going after people just for existing, okay? She's here to help."

Sakai cleared his throat, leaning one hand on the back of a chair. "You can't seriously think the world is going to come to an end on Halloween."

"No," Aidan agreed. "But it is going to be seriously in trouble. Lethal trouble." *Oh boy, how do we get this through, these people may be a little supernatural but they sure aren't Hunters....*

Well, neither was I.

"Look, when it comes to the Demongate, Myrrh and Church and a whole bunch of faithful types," he nodded at Usagi, "we'll be doing what we can. The main thing we need is to cut down the homicide rate. Every death, every riot, every bar brawl funnels that much more power into opening the damn Gate. So one of the first things we need from you is for you to *stay alive*." He spread his hands. "You're here because you know things aren't looking good. How can we help?"

"Your phone call said brahmarakshasa, or asura." Usagi snared a chair after cranky locals departed, leaning on it as she studied the three of them. "Most of the time I'd say asura? No way. Even with your reputation, Seeker. But you know what a brahmarakshasa is, when most people have never heard of 'em, so...." She shrugged, almost hiding a shiver. "Lay it on me."

Myrrh nodded, all too sympathetic. She didn't want to think of the consequences of an asura on a Demongate herself. It was terrifying. "First, there is the simple fact that a substantial number of yakshas have planted themselves here, without being torn limb from leafy limb."

"There's a lot of other things - other *people* - who should have pulverized 'em," Aidan stated. "Water-cougars, nunnehi, wakened pines - all kinds of things should have made their lives hell."

Church leaned on a chair of her own. "Do I want to know what a water-cougar is?"

"Somewhat akin to a water dragon. Though more catlike than most European dragons," Myrrh informed her. "If one was near Intrepid, I suspect it's relocated, or gone into slumber. Because..."

Sister Usagi, do you know the legend of the asura Raktabīja?"

Usagi whistled. "Wow. That is... give me a sec... the blood-seed guy?"

Myrrh nodded.

"Oooo boy." Usagi glanced at the other two. "Legend says Raktabīja had a special boon. Don't ask me why devas hand out boons like that, there's reasons you don't have to believe in gods to be a Buddhist.... Anyway. From every drop of his blood that got spilled, another Raktabīja would spring forth to fight. That's how he got his name; *he for whom every drop of blood, is a seed.*"

"And thus, when he was among the forces that drove the devas from the heavens, was born Kali by Durga's will," Myrrh agreed, "that she might swallow every drop of blood Raktabīja and his duplicates shed, and so devour them all."

"Um." Aidan gulped. "Is that the same Kali-?"

"Whom the Thuggees claimed to honor?" Myrrh finished. "Yes."

"Hey, don't knock Kali," Usagi spread a hand. "Sure, she's a destroyer. She's supposed to be a destroyer of *evil*, not life. Kind of... the ultimate Hunter, you know?"

"Think I'm starting to find out," Church muttered. "So. Dangerous, but not evil?"

"She is death, and wrath, and fury; but so is a hurricane, or the thunderbolts of Heaven," Myrrh agreed. "The Thuggees justified their crimes and plunder in her name. They are not the first to do evil and claim it was in the service of good; nor, unfortunately, will they be the last."

Aidan winced. "Amen to that."

"Ditto," Usagi agreed. "Okay, legend says Kali devoured Raktabīja to the last drop of blood. There's no way we'd be facing *him.*"

Myrrh breathed a sigh of relief along with Aidan. Neither of them felt up to murderous god level violence.

"But... asuras are related to rakshasas," Church put in. "And if all of a sudden we've got a bunch of rakshasas where it's really weird to have *any* rakshasas...."

"Yeaaaaah." Usagi scratched at cropped hair. "We... could have an asura. At least, I've never heard of a brahmarakshasa who could do anything close to this."

"You believe an asura might be able to cast forth seeds of their lesser kin?" Myrrh asked.

"Maybe," Usagi nodded. "Or maybe just one very powerful brahmarakshasa with demonic help. You did say sorcerer, and human sacrifice?"

"Sacrifices." Church watched Aidan try not to flinch. "Plural. We're estimating over fifty at this point. Maybe over a hundred. Maybe more."

"...Oh." The nun swallowed.

The detective gripped her chair, obviously weighing the atmosphere. "Okay, I get this is bad. Maybe I don't know how bad. But neither do you. We need information. Specifics, right? You're an enchantress, Myrrh. You can shift the whole world if you get specific enough."

"Not the whole world," Myrrh demurred. "But with enough knowledge of what and who we target - yes. I could at least shape a working that might tie it down long enough for mass gunfire." She glanced at her fire-gifted friend. "And you are not a weak power. Many asuras *do not like* fire."

"See? Specifics," Church grinned. "So... we need info. And the best way to do that, is get somebody to talk." She raised a brow at Usagi. "So how do we catch a rakshasa?"

Chapter Thirteen

Tuesday, October 29th

"Thanks, Mrs. Harvey," Church said politely, holding her new pots of catnip and rainbow-colored hot peppers gingerly with one hand, as Sally Harvey gave her back a few cents change. Turned out the lady in gray ran a greenhouse and nursery, perfect fit for someone who had rumors of actual tree-spirits hanging out in her family tree. It also meant Sally had been one of the first to realize years back that someone had dumped a murdered body on her land to taint the earth; and while she hadn't been able to tell that to the cops, she had dragged the IPD out to the first of several grisly discoveries.

And she's been terrified ever since, Church thought darkly. *Scary enough to find a body on your land. To find it by the feel of someone twisting everything you've grown and worked for? Brrr.*

"Thank you, very much," Sister Usagi echoed, picking up her ring-topped staff - Myrrh called it a *khakkara* - from the nursery's front door after she settled her own bag of plants in one arm. "You're right about spreading the pepper spray on your boundary lines. It should keep out the weaker rakshasas."

The gardener finally smiled. "Hard to believe that will work, when chilies aren't native to... wherever these things came from."

"They used pepper and ginger in India before they had chilies," Usagi offered. "Humans are pretty unique in being able to handle the hot stuff!"

That won them a laugh, even if it was strained. Church couldn't blame Harvey. When the rakshasas had hit last week... well, in the short run, all Sally's customers had been glad the vines planted around the place *just happened* to trip one dragon-fanged deer before a screaming toddler could be torn to pieces. But after people had had a few days to think....

Church touched her hat to the gardener, trying not to let frustration leak onto her face. She was a cop, sworn to protect the law and the citizens, up to and including laying down her life for her fellow man. But sometimes she didn't like her fellow man much.

Be honest. Right now, you don't like yourself too much.

Administrative leave. Right now she was the only cop in the city not working back to back shifts trying to keep a lid on... everything. There hadn't been another mass rakshasa attack; the lenses *worked*, and after one pair of patrol officers shot down a rakshasa pretending to be an ice-cream truck guy before it could eat any of the kids it'd grabbed, the rest of the yakshas had stuck to ambushing lone unlucky citizens and tourists who hadn't gotten the word to stay out of dark alleys.

Right now, we don't know how many missing people we've got. Has to be a lot. Father O'Malley says all the churches praying to weaken the Demongate are... stalled. Not getting anywhere.

And instead of sneaking back into work, Church had spent the last few days on the scavenger hunt from hell. Chasing bits of this and that across the countryside, including such bizarre treasures as wild native polyphemus silk, a haunch of fresh fatty bison, and the shop that served the best mocha latte in town. All to prep a wild plan spun out of her book on Cherokee lore, Usagi's know-how on rakshasas and what fought them, and Myrrh's age-old knowledge of exactly which of the world's monsters were more or less the same creatures under different names.

Aidan had sat back and kibitzed. At least until they'd gone up on Cullasaja Bald, to find....

Eep. Church still didn't want to think about it. Or the little wooly-bear caterpillar that wasn't, currently curled up and snoozing in a silk hatband, deep in a bag of fedoras on the back seat.

Please let it keep sleeping. I really *don't want to wake it up.*

Did no good to know that the Caterpillar of Doom was her own damn fault. Or that Aidan's fire backing them had been the main reason what they'd found up there on Cullasaja had *listened*, instead of eating them or slithering off out of mortal sight.

"Don't worry," Myrrh had said dryly, before they'd headed up to near-certain doom. "If we're right, it won't care if any of us are virgins. Though it may shake us down for coffee and library cards."

"And if we're wrong?" Church had asked, morbidly fascinated.

"Then we are likely to survive." Gray eyes had been shadowed. "Without a backup plan against an asura... Intrepid will not."

Which turned what Church thought she knew about Hunters on its head. If the past week was any clue, Hunters weren't the tabloids' crazy masked vigilantes swooping in on supernatural crimes in progress. Hunters *planned*. And made backup plans. And backups for the backups, scavenging tiny bits of power here, there, and everywhere; pitting whispers of magic from rock and tree and water against creatures that could squash a SWAT team flat.

And part of those backups was figuring out *what you could talk to*, so that if all else failed....

Like telling the Mob that MS-13's in town, the detective thought now, heading out the nursery's front door. *The bullets are going to fly. You just hope they fly at the bad guys.*

Usagi followed her out, the four brass rings topping her staff chiming. Church had thought the noise would get on her nerves, but so far, no. "You're worried about Sally's business, right?"

"Damn right I am," Church grumbled. Such a tiny worry, compared to the plan the four of them had set up parading around Intrepid together the past few days; here were the two mortals of the team, with no visible backup, in the middle of a nearly empty parking lot. "Hypocrites. Act normal, look normal, you get by. Blow the lid of not being normal to save a kid, you get *this*." She gestured at way too many empty parking spaces.

And if that gesture happened to encompass a few shadows that were just a bit too large and dark, well, accidents happened.

"People are pretty attached to their illusions," the freckled nun said cheerfully. "Reality's a *bitch*."

Church choked with laughter, even as a shadow twitched in the corner of her eye. "You sure you don't want to try out for the academy sometime?"

Usagi smiled, a little wistful. "Couldn't make the physical."

That was a shock. "But you look...."

"Fine? Yeah, I am. Most of the time. Long story." Usagi shrugged, a Californian shimmer of crimson and gold cloth. "Let's just say, life is short, and no one knows what'll happen tomorrow. This is my path. I'm pretty happy with it."

So if I drop dead on you in the middle of fighting monsters, not your fault, Church translated. *Ow.*

...I'm dealing with a rakshasa-expert nun who might drop dead on me right in the middle of a sting. It would have been nice to know that before we set this up, damn it!

Though Church suspected if it had come up, she'd have gotten the same reaction from Usagi as she got from Myrrh. Back off? People were *dying*.

We're all the help they've got. And we're running out of time.

Hence why they were going to try something... risky. Eep.

"Honestly, I'm surprised we had as many people show up at Vajra as we did," the nun went on. "Anyone who got too curious about our leafy pals probably got eaten. And anybody who laid low enough to get missed... well. Those are the ones smart enough to know what happens if you go public with things normal people can't do. Eggs. Molotov cocktails. Mobs."

Church frowned. "Myrrh and Aidan...."

"I should show you stuff written down about Shafat a few centuries back. It'll curl your hair." Usagi's grip shifted on her khakkara, serious counterpoint to her teasing tone. "And Aidan - that poor guy's in shock and you know it. Who wouldn't be? He got *murdered*. And then things got worse."

Things are about to get much, much worse right here. If we didn't get this just right. Church breathed out, juggling pots in her grip before she set them on the trunk. Just above where Usagi had pasted a whole bunch of sutras on the inside, topped off with Eagleman's gift of a preserved Venus flytrap leaf. All meant to contain, bind - and lure. *Shadows shifting any more? Nope, not yet....*

"Guess I am surprised so many people decided to help." Which was honest, Church thought, and maybe distracting enough to explain why they were still standing here chatting instead of driving off. "I mean, I was there when Myrrh cut loose. Anyone who's seen the vid- it's got to be like standing between the devil and the deep blue sea."

Usagi grinned, green eyes not giving the game away. "Well, kind of. Good thing Aidan's around to prove she's not just see monster, slay monster."

"Yeah? He was in that video, too." Church arched an eyebrow at the too-cheerful nun as she unlocked her rental. Peppers to warn off the bad guys as humans being too hot to handle, okay. Catnip? What good would that do?

Then again, some rakshasas were tiger-based, according to Myrrh. And Aariel definitely had elements of a lion.

So we might have a goofy snoozy demon instead of an angry one. Meep.

"But he admitted he has demon blood," Usagi said soberly. "Not a weak demon's, either. Not a tainted rakshasa, or a hungry ghost. If Seeker Shafat thinks his line is a match for the rakshasi Hārītī... she led the Ten Demon Maidens in years of slaughter before she was enlightened by the Buddha. Now she's a protective goddess of the faith, but legends say she remembers all that murdering magic when some idiot ticks her off by attacking innocents."

Wait, Church thought, back of her neck crawling as she leaned into the car to put bagged pots in the back seat. *Wait just one minute.* "Did you say *goddess*?"

"Yep. Though like I said, Buddhism actually doesn't require

you to believe in any divine entities," Usagi shrugged. "Gods have to seek enlightenment just like any other mortal. Or demon."

"Goddess," Church insisted, straightening up. "You're telling me Myrrh says the scary, scary guy who's Aidan's dad is like... a demon turned *goddess?*"

"Well, to quote C.S. Lewis, *he's not a tame lion,*" the nun said wryly. "Yeah, she did. From what the head of my monastery said before they sent me out here, she ought to know...." Usagi trailed off. "Wait one. You mean you didn't know?"

Church blinked, and ducked back into the car to snug her innocent plants a bit closer to the back of the seat. "Sister, right now I don't even know what I don't know. Are you seriously saying Aidan comes from the kind of power that can take down *gods?*"

"God, the all-powerful, as Christians think of him? Not a chance," Usagi shrugged. "Lesser powers like devas? Oh yeah. Haven't you sensed it? He... shivers the world, when he walks. Just a tickle, to a mountain, but I am so glad he's not out West on one of the faults."

I can match a sage, Myrrh had said. *I cannot match a deva.*

Church shuddered as she backed out of the car again, remembering sheer terror as she'd faced burning eyes. Aariel had the power to attack - what, lesser gods?

I can believe it. I so can.

"He has no idea." Church swallowed hard, as Usagi set her own plants inside, ringed staff never far from her hand. "Heads up," she added, quieter. Not that she'd seen anything, but there was something in the silken feel of the wind....

"I know. Isn't it cute?" Green eyes twinkled, wide with fearful anticipation where Myrrh's would be storm-gray calm. But there was still that sense of centering, *the world will be so-*

Usagi snatched up her khakkara, the thin tip of the finial lashing out across glistening black.

Tiger-deer, leafy fur-

It flinched from razor brass, just enough for the nun to shift a

half-step aside. The rakshasa crashed into the doorframe like an
oak falling, hard enough to raise the rental car an inch off the
ground.

I'm never getting my deposit back.

Church shook out her baton, pale brass bound to the tip flicking
back light as she swatted another leaf-tiger mid-spring. Panchaloha
was as good as Myrrh said; the alloy of Indian idols crackled as it
struck, blackening leaves and shedding purple blood.

And staff-girl knew her rakshasa-stuff, the detective thought.
Leave a drool-worthy opening, wait for a strike-

Rustling like a forest in a hurricane, a horde descended.

-Slam them first!

Church tried to keep her back to the rental car, swings short
and brutal to smash rakshasas off Usagi's blind side. The nun herself was a whirl of blunt and sharp ends of her staff, rings jingling
a merry counterpoint to the blows that socked into chests, claws,
the hollows of green-furred throats. One hit wasn't enough to put
any rakshasa down, but it made them fall back, as long as they
could keep this up....

Church jabbed one bastard right under the ear, switched her
attention to the next as it reeled away. Her heart was pounding, her
blood racing, but she was just too busy to be scared. *Leave off the
leaves and fangs, it's like getting jumped by a crazy biker gang.*

Because *this* time she wasn't eyes for a swarm of frightened
cops and paramedics. Usagi could see these things just as well as
she did. Every glassy swirl of maya was hit by a brassy jingle,
dissolving like salt in water.

But even in green and leaf-tan tiger stripes worked *so damn
well*, all Church saw was a blur leaping over the roof of the car.

Panchaloha hit, jarring through her wrists and shoulder in one
bright bolt of pain.

The rakshasa slid down the back windshield, smoking; but
there were still more, hurt and fangs out and angry-

"I have laid a snare for thee!" rang out, clear as church bells.

"And thou art also taken, o Babylon, and thou wast not aware: thou art found, and also caught, because thou has striven against Jehovah!"

God, I hope that's the net!

Flames roared, and suddenly Church could breathe.

Remember the plan.

She'd hang her head and grumpily apologize to Myrrh later for laying out how this was going to happen, complete with toy truck and action figures. Because if Shafat hadn't gone over and over and *over* how they were going to do this-

Baton still in hand, Church covered Usagi. Because the nun was very, very busy; slapping strips of inked paper onto the magic-netted rakshasa before her hands flashed through a series of complicated signs. All the while chanting without a pause for breath, as the light of Myrrh's sword cut away any rakshasa close to the flames and Aidan's crackling bursts of gold and blue showed the rest of their unwelcome guests the door.

Wriggling weakly, the rakshasa flexed from tiger to deer to something like a leggy rosebush, but couldn't shed fluttering paper. A knot gaped open into wooden fangs, snarling something Church couldn't identify. Though from the tone, she'd bet it was a crack about a certain nun's mother.

"Sorry," Usagi half-sang back. "My Sanskrit's pure California. I kind of don't get the accent of *tree*."

Light flickered out, though Myrrh kept watch as flames slowly lowered. "He said he means to eat you to gain a life of his own, and that his seed-brethren shall keep coming until you are consumed, woman of the Bodhisattvas." She cleared her throat. "It is a common threat, from rakshasas."

"Hah! Straight out of the *Journey to the West*." Usagi grinned. "I knew they'd go for it!"

"Wait, you were the bait?"

"Eep!" Church jumped in place, raising her alloy-wrapped baton before she realized that shadowy patch was copper-bright hair. Damn crazy half-demon. Sure, the way shadows seemed to creep around him when Aidan didn't want to be seen had been useful, hiding their pair of magical heavy-hitters until the rakshasas had made their move. But right now.... "Make some noise when you walk!"

Aidan blinked at her. "I did?"

"Argh." Church breathed out. "You two couldn't have jumped in just a *little* sooner?"

"Sorry," Aidan shrugged sheepishly. "You looked like you were having fun."

"And we had to be certain no more were lying in wait." Myrrh was still sweeping her gaze across the parking lot, lingering by the nursery's front doors. "They seem well and truly gone. And our prisoner is still alive."

He was at that. Though now he'd twisted into a white-robed dwarf with leaves in his hair, and glared at them all with the cold, predatory interest Church had seen on a pack of briarweasels trying to shred her into bite-sized pieces. "Mortals. You cannot hold me!"

Looking anywhere but at Aidan, Church realized. *Interesting.*

"Holding a soul prisoner when it would flee this life for the Wheel is a chain on your own karma," Usagi said plainly. "The detective probably wants to toss you in jail and throw away the key, but I'm the one with the ofuda. I won't keep you bound to this body longer than it takes for us to get the information we need." She paused, as if the thought had just occurred to her. "Or maybe you don't *want* to die."

Black eyes narrowed.

"It is possible," Myrrh said plainly. "The Sister's prayers hold what passes for your essence, while mine hold your physical body. It should not be difficult to bind the two together in willing life, shedding the curse that would drive you into death." She paused. "Now that we have some time to examine it, it is a very sloppy curse. Much as I would expect from a mere brahmarakshasa condemned to that existence for-"

Her next words weren't English. Church was honestly glad. The way Usagi jumped at the phrase, them was fightin' words.

Aidan blinked, and leaned next to her ear as the rakshasa started snarling back in tones that wanted to rip out a spine and crunch it like potato chips. "Myrrh just accused the guy in charge of killing his mother with a bone ripped out of his father and a couple of other things I'd rather not mention. Go to Naraka, go straight to Naraka, do not pass Go, do not collect two hundred...."

"I get the idea," Church murmured back as the rakshasa's spittle-laced tirade went on. "Touchy guy, huh?" Which were some of the best for getting info from, if you just knew which button to push.

From the growing horror on Usagi's face and the way Aidan stiffened, they'd found the right one.

A bad one. "Talk to me," Church muttered.

Aidan swallowed hard, eyeing the rakshasa like he wanted to swat it *right now*. "Church? We're going to have to use plan B."

Plan A was find, fix, and pin down or kill the brahmarakshasa running this mess with a combo of magical might and heavy gunfire. Plan B meant - oh, hell. "Isn't that the one that's mostly not dying?"

"And fedoras," Aidan agreed numbly. "Can't leave out the fedoras."

Church was not going to giggle. Nope. Crazy fire-mage, crazier hell-raider, who knew how crazy the nun was....

At least those bottles in the trunk aren't going to waste.

"So we have an agreement," Usagi said firmly. "We seal your soul to your body, so you don't dissolve just because your high and mighty lord decides you failed. And you take us to him, so we can... properly regard his majesty."

"He will suck the marrow from your bones, and use your skulls to drink the pure soma," the rakshasa snarled.

"I am certain he will try," Myrrh mused. "But one's word is one's word. If you hold to your word, this will heal you." She held out her hand over the shimmering net. "She is a tree of life to them that lay hold upon her: and happy is every one that retaineth her."

Paper shriveled as if in flames. The net fell apart, black eyes blinked-

Deer-swift, he bolted.

Aidan touched Church's shoulder before she could reach her gun. Shook his head.

The rakshasa spasmed at the edge of the parking lot, collapsing in a rattle of leaves. Shuddered, coughing.

"If you hold to your word." Myrrh's voice rang across asphalt. "You *will* take us to your lord, or the healing will unravel, and you will be left at your master's mercy. If he has any."

Church tensed. "This is *wrong*."

"What are we supposed to do, put him in handcuffs and offer Witness Protection?" From the way Aidan's shoulders hunched, he wasn't any happier about it than she was. "Without Myrrh's spell, the guy's own boss is going to kill him. And we need to find that guy."

"That doesn't make it right."

"It's not." Amber eyes were haunted. "It's just less wrong than letting these bastards open the Demongate."

And the rakshasa had probably killed people. And eaten them. Church knew that.

But I'm still a cop. This is wrong. We just don't have any better options.

We get out of this in one piece, I'm going to find *some.*

"Tell me when we get an address." Church took out her phone. "I want to be sure the whole department knows where we're going."

"The marrow from your bones-!"

Church didn't bother trying to chase their leafy guide as the rakshasa fled, focused on the gaping maw of unfriendly earth. "Oh, *hell* no."

Myrrh studied the low limestone entrance of Marion Cave, a rough trapezoid of darkness in gray stone, overgrown with mosses and fall-bare saplings, and was inclined to agree. "That, is a trap."

"Could it be more obvious?" Aidan wondered, shading his eyes to peer at suspicious shadows under leaf-littered flat plates of rock jutting out of the hillside below.

"It could say *evil bad guy lair here*." Usagi held her khakkara's polished length sideways, comparing it to the opening. "This is not going to go well."

"Of course not," Myrrh said wryly. "When one is a shape-shifter, why pick a lair that suits your enemies' shapes?"

"At least we're not going to need scuba gear?" Aidan offered.

"I don't know about that." Church had a handful of skimpy pamphlets for this private spelunking site, shuffling pages to find out just what they were up against. "There's water under there. Maybe not enough of a river to worry about most of the time...."

"But with the powers of an asura, even a trickle might drown us," Myrrh agreed, feeling the darkness of limestone shadows beyond. Thick as deep velvet; willing to swallow them whole as the most fathomless abyss. The strength of sunless seas was beyond that stone, and that... that was no mere rakshasa waiting below.

"An asura? You're sure?" The nun's eyes went wide, and she glanced at Aidan. "Oh... boy."

Myrrh inclined her head, able to guess what ran through Usagi's mind. After all, she'd been the one to point out the obvious when they'd laid their plan: if they truly did have an asura in Intrepid, did they have any weapon that could kill it?

"Anything besides our resident sage's bones, that is." Usagi's lips had twitched in a wry smile, days past, as she winked at Myrrh. "That'd be messy."

"And impractical, given my spine is long gone to dust, these many centuries past," Myrrh had chuckled. "No fear, Sister Usagi. You've no need to choose between me and a weapon to slay our enemies." She'd let her teeth flash in a smile. "Not to mention, if we ended up fighting this being for most of a year, the governor would most likely call in a bombing run long before we'd defeated our foe."

"But we don't have to." Aidan had looked at her with calculation, and no little wonder. "Asuras get hit by in-between things, right? So... if *you* get close enough...."

"It is possible," Myrrh had allowed. Her form was between flesh and spirit; her blood, the light of dawn. She could hurt an asura, if she could get close enough.

If.

And now they were at that *if*, stymied by a hole in rocks.

It's far from the first time Powers have used the land in their own defense, Myrrh thought now. *But this is not Lord Ahi's land. If we can encourage the local creatures to make his presence below uncomfortable....*

But that would take time. And Halloween was far too close. Hence the current contents of Church's trunk, glass wrapped in muffling plastic so it would not clink - until they meant it to.

"I hate to sound all practical and killjoy, here," Church mused, "but couldn't we just dump a concrete truck down the hole now, and worry about the EPA fine later?"

"Tempting," Aidan agreed, staring down the darkness. "Very tempting. Might take too long to get hard, though. It could turn into a snake and wiggle out."

"Well, if we don't want to go down there, and I really don't want to go down there...." Church looked between hell-raider and nun. "How do we get it to come to us?"

Myrrh smiled.

"Oh no," Aidan breathed. "We're really going to do this?"

"On the advice of our expert? Yes. I took advantage of one of the Festival cards we picked up," Myrrh said virtuously. "Did you know we now have a meadery in Intrepid?"

Of course she knew. They all knew. The question was whether the *asura* knew. Given the meadery had yet to report a massive theft in the middle of the night, Myrrh rather thought not.

And legend said, when it came to their vices, asuras had such *good* ears.

"A what?" Church asked, sweating just a little as she played along. "Wait - you mean that stuff made with honey?" She glanced at Aidan. "And you said they like to drink."

Myrrh grinned, and pulled two stoppered bottles from her shift; one pale green-amber, one red so dark it was near black. "They make a very tolerable rhodomel. Blended with sea-salt and rain-water, and a bit of Zhong Ma Huang from the local Chinese apothecaries...."

"Not true soma, but it just might do." Usagi winked at them all. "We have more in the car-"

"Fortunately. Mortals are so tedious."

The voice rolled like a thunderstorm; an earthquake, plucking up and dropping bits of mountainside as it willed. Myrrh ignored the rumble behind her, and kept her gaze on the cavern opening, even as frightened bats fled into daylight. "Ah, son and blood of Danu," she called into dark stone. "We four mortals have come to look upon your magnificence, and bring offerings for a proper welcome to our city!"

"Hmph. Lying mortals." Another rumble; Myrrh felt sweat start between her shoulders, as casual power crumbled limestone to powder. *"A nun, a guardswoman, a sage, and one who bears the blood of the foul beings of Naraka. Did you truly think to challenge such as I, Lord Ahi?"*

"Alas, I fear we did." Myrrh stood fast, determined not to back down and flee. "To a drinking contest."

"What?"

"What he said," Church muttered, face dead white. Sister Usagi wasn't looking much better, and Aidan had a fine tremor in his hands he likely thought he'd hidden. "We're going to *what?*"

"It's traditional," Usagi got out. "I swear. Legends and everything."

"And it is only polite," Myrrh stated, knowing full well how close to the edges of hospitality this would skate. If they lived. "After all, Lord Ahi has come as a guest to Intrepid, setting his bloodline upon us to eat up our charity. And no few of our citizens," she added dryly. "We mortals are, of course, slow and stupid, so it did take us some time to realize what a noble being had chosen to take his ease among us, and arrange a proper welcome to negotiate the terms of his departure." She took another breath. "From Intrepid, or from the dust of this earth, Lord Ahi, is up to you."

"You dare to threaten such as I, weaklings?"

"Is it too late to say no?" Church murmured.

Usagi gulped. "Way, way too late."

Aidan was silent. Eyeing the bottles, and her, and the cave, knuckles white as he clenched fists to keep them from trembling.

I would I could spare you this, Myrrh thought. *I would I could spare us all. We risk too much, for folk who refuse to realize there is even a danger.* "Indeed, I fear we insult your power even by the offer, Lord Ahi. For we are only four, with pitiful mortal frames. Surely, one of the lordly asuras can consume more of even the strongest soma than we."

Aidan's eyes widened at *consume*. He huffed a breath, almost a chuckle, and nodded to her.

Oh, thank you, Mother Mary. Myrrh tried not to let the world spin from sheer relief. Strip the sense of jungle from it, and an asura's power felt so *much* like a Demon Lord's. If she wanted to run from that breath of Hell on her neck, how much more so must Aidan?

He's with us. He remembers the plan. He will not falter, even in the face of Naraka's power.

"You are weak fools." Limestone split open in a dark rumble,

as a figure of crimson silks and far too many heads strode through a cave too small for it. *"I shall take your offerings, and then swallow you up; as my children shall swallow all your mewling kind."*

"I am certain you will try, Lord Ahi." Myrrh looked up and up at the figure towering beyond the stone-dwarfed cove of trees. "But first you must win." She raised a finger, as if a thought had just occurred to her. "Although...."

"We couldn't fit nearly enough booze in my car," Church said, dazed.

"Precisely!" Myrrh beamed. "It would hardly be enough of a challenge, or an offering, with the meager amounts we weak mortals can carry. Would you do us the grace and kindness of following us to the Rose Meadery, that we might provide spirits in suitable quantity for your magnificence?"

Twenty eyes stared down at her; ten long tongues licked triple rows of sharp fangs. *"If you seek to trap me, Sage, your torments will not end with your death."*

As if they ever had. "I swear on my name and faith, the Rose Meadery is not a trap," Myrrh said with great dignity. "It is a humble font of spirits, made by mere mortal hands, no more. We shall pass through Intrepid unharmed, and unmolested, so you may show your might to disbelieving eyes and have them fall to their knees in fear. And you shall sit with us, and accept our challenge, so all shall see an asura's true power."

"...We are so making the evening news," Church breathed.

From a distance, Stimson felt earth tremble, as Lord Ahi followed a fleeing car back into Intrepid's downtown. He was tempted to turn on the news to see if there were breaking reports... but the local news helicopters flying overhead were more than enough.

As I thought. Even such an enchantress as that woman cannot face a lord of my people alone. She must be clever, she must seek help... and she cannot hide the fate that awaits Intrepid, if they lose. Sooner or later, the word of how helpless mortals are before magic will ooze out like an infection. And like any sick and wounded beast, humans will lash out to defend themselves. Whether they win or lose....

Sensing the surge of human rage, the rakshasa smiled. "Check."

Chapter Fourteen

"Plan B." Captain Sherman thumped a fist on a squad car. "Shafat said we wouldn't like plan B...."

Behind her the steadiest patrol officers she could grab were clearing the Rose Meadery of innocent bystanders. Which was not going fast *or* well; tourists didn't believe there was any real danger, and locals were mad as hell that the cops didn't *do something* about the giant multi-headed *thing* striding their way.

We should do something? About a monster the size of King Kong? We'd be gnats biting a train.

She could hear the soundbites on the evening news already. Didn't help that just looking at the thing striding their way froze people's brains. Myrrh's lenses broke most of the panic - but there weren't nearly enough of those to go around.

And it *really* didn't help that her unholy trio-turned-quartet of monster-hunters apparently Had A Plan if even *this* went wrong. Because the bit Church had laid out of plan C was even crazier than four mostly-humans trying to out-drink a monster out of *Hindu mythology*.

Sherman just knew Church had skimmed over a heck of a lot of details. Probably for the sake of her captain's sanity. After all, given Aidan had advised that anybody of a Catholic bent might want to carry a St. George's medal, just in case....

She'd had to look up St. George. Roman soldier saint; no wonder Myrrh approved. As for what else he was famous for-

The captain resisted the temptation to bury her head in her hands. Because *of course* Shafat's crew would find something that crazy.

Now Shafat putting a several thousand dollar deposit down with the meadery made sense. As did Aidan's grumbling about money none of them were going to get back, and he knew cops were always short of cash but if the mayor wanted his city in one piece and demanded they try everything else before killing the monsters, he could at least chip in on the damages. With that wide-eyed shaven nun nodding all the time, throwing in quotes about charity, good works, and not poking sleeping monsters with a stick.

Sherman had to admit, she'd stuck Church with them hoping for sanity. Or at least an early warning of mass chaos. But the detective had just sighed, muttering about no wonder Switch was a hitman, being a Hunter was *damn expensive*.

Being a captain of detectives, Sherman had had to give the hell-raider a look askance at that. Money didn't come out of nowhere. Especially if you'd been... out of touch, for over twenty-five years.

Myrrh had only smiled. *"There was a time I had to slay a dragon."*

"Don't want to know," Sherman reminded herself now, as Church's battered rental took a hard left into the Rose Meadery's parking lot. "Don't have to know. Keep the good citizens alive first, worry about the crazy later."

Though if they lived, she was going to make sure the department filed a bill with the mayor's office so Myrrh got reimbursed. Because if the evidence her detectives had pulled together so far was painting the right picture, this Lord Ahi critter wouldn't even be here without the Demongate messing up local magic. Given what a staunch friend Mayor Green had been of Steven Savonarola....

Yeah. He really *should* pay for it.

Seeing ten hands reach out to seize up mugs of reddened brew from the table on the meadery patio, Church almost wilted in her chair. "We're going to die."

Aidan patted her shoulder. "Just keep calm," he said quietly. "Try to keep it to sips, and," he grinned, dragging dark cloth out of a shoulderbag to plant a fedora on her head, "don't panic."

Church sputtered, batting away his hand when he offered sunglasses. For shame.

At least I got the hats before we went out to Cullasaja Bald, Aidan thought. *Thank goodness for secondhand stores on Main Street. As long as Ahi stays that tall, even a little brim will make it hard for him to see our faces. Or anything near our faces....*

Like, say, a little carry-on passenger sleeping nestled in Church's hat ribbon. The silk ought to conceal the tiny not-a-woolly-bear from even an asura's aural sensing. Not to mention, Ahi knew Church was a plain, ordinary mortal. The odds of him wasting magic on an active probe of the detective were small. Hopefully.

Lord, please don't make us have to wake the little guy up. He is definitely *Plan C.*

"Very, very small sips," Usagi muttered, pulling her fedora over short-cropped red hair with a bemused look. "Why did I ever think this was a good idea?"

"An optimism that the illusions of this world can be defeated?" Myrrh didn't so much as twitch as Aidan planted a black hat on her head, coiled in her chair as if the bottles and glass before her were deadly as any sword.

Against an asura? Probably more deadly, Aidan thought, pulling down his own brim to shade his eyes. And tried to remember exactly what they'd discussed for Plan B. It wasn't easy; Ahi's presence was a pressure on all his senses, like trying to breathe under deep water.

Which is why Myrrh said, keep it simple. Being around things with a lot of power makes it hard to think. So make sure you don't have to.

Speaking of which. They'd set up a deposit for potential damages, but there was one other *tiny* detail they might've forgotten to cover. "Hey!" Aidan pitched up for twenty listening ears. "Who's paying for this, anyway?"

Lord Ahi stared down, smoldering eyes a mix of surprise and amusement at mortal bravado. *"The price will be your lives, little Naraka-blood. If you happen to survive."*

Aidan spread empty hands. "Just trying to clear things up before we all get sloshed," he said easily. "So! We set?"

"I believe we are," Myrrh murmured. Tilted her head at Usagi, gray eyes alight with mischief. "You've earned the honor."

The nun clapped her hands together before her, and bowed her head. "To break an oath in the service of dharma and the quest to lead all to nirvana is, sometimes, the only right action." She straightened, and waved to white-faced meadery employees. "Bartender, set us up!"

Keep calm, Aidan willed himself, as the asura raised full mugs and they raised shot glasses. *Keep it contained, controlled - now!*

A swift breath across his drink, and four glasses lit with flames. *We really didn't want to have to do this.*

Although planning it in the abstract had been kind of fun, if only for the look on Priest Sakai's *face*. Buddhist monks and nuns weren't supposed to drink. No, not even to save the world. And if one more person brought up a certain anime - or two, or three - he was going to pray at them until they went away.

I have got to see those anime.

Of course monks and nuns weren't supposed to resort to *violence*, either. The various suggestions Usagi had on how to flatten a brahmarakshasa had curled Sakai's shaved hair. And that was before they'd considered the possibility of an asura.

Legends. Demigods. Only slain by devas and heroes. Spend their time drinking, warring, and hunting down dragons or even weirder monsters.

Legends that were all too graphic about the casual damage to the landscape when devas and asuras got going. Innocent bystanders arrowed, whole cities aflame, mountains uprooted and dropped....

Nope. Even Usagi didn't want to try and call up a deva. Not that she was sure what other options they had, you couldn't exactly put a call out over the internet for a legendary hero.

"So we don't be heroic," Church had said bluntly, gathered with the rest of them in the small church annex Myrrh had commandeered to make holy oil and other interesting preparations. Half the folding table was covered with scraps of waterproof paper, packets of ground galena and lapis lazuli; herbs and salts dissolved in oil, vinegar, and odder liquids. A few flint strikers and alcohol lamps were just the crowning touch on the mad scientist vibe.

"I'm a *cop*," Church had gone on, keeping a wary distance from the gold-dusted bottle of hunting tonic. "Not an Old West marshal out of Dodge. We're supposed to arrest the bad guys, not challenge them to single combat. How can we blindside this guy?"

"Outside of run away?" Aidan muttered, staring down at Myrrh's scratch paper of what they had, what they could get, and how little of any of it would make an asura even twitch. That was all he'd ever been able to do with Yaldabaoth. Run. Survive. Winning wasn't an option.

"Church has found an option, if all else fails. But first... we need to challenge him," Myrrh reflected. "To something that is not combat, but that he thinks he can win." She raised a pale brow at Usagi.

The nun looked at her askance. "We can't out-wrestle him, we probably can't out-shoot him, and if you think we can out-eat somebody who might give Kumbhakarna a run for his money-"

Myrrh grinned. "Have you heard the story of Thor, Utgarda-Loki, and Loki's eating contest?"

Which earned her three blank looks. "No?" Church admitted.

Myrrh tore off a scrap of paper, and offered it to him.

Aidan sighed, and took it, lighting the white fibers for a tiny rush of energy. Wasn't much, compared to a good candle, or one of Myrrh's spirit-lamps for compounding potions....

Spirits. Alcohol.

He'd looked up, into Myrrh's quiet smile.

"Loki's opponent," the hell-raider had said plainly, "was nothing less than fire itself."

After all, she said consume, Aidan thought now, smoke wafting hot honey and herbs through the cedar-raftered meadery bar. *So long as I burn out the alcohol - we can* drink *the rest.*

Not that it was easy. Mead wasn't exactly high proof. Dragging everything burnable out of it to his flames was already an ache of concentration.

But it's our best chance. Have to try.

Flames sputtered, and Aidan downed his shot. Hot, but not a tingle of alcohol left on the tongue.

Myrrh drank hers in the same moment. Usagi gave her own glass a speculative look, shrugged, and slugged it down.

"Administrative leave," Church muttered, and gulped her own. "Captain's still never going to let me live this down... next!"

A pale-faced server in an Old West bartender's white shirt and embroidered red silk vest poured the next round. Eyed what was left in her bottle, and dragged out a dozen more.

Myrrh was focused on the asura, a low whisper under her breath that Aidan felt seek out any stray swirl of maya and swat it flat. Usagi was just praying, aura dim and shimmering with fear, hanging on in the face of a power that could tear mountains down. Church-

The detective's gaze strayed to doors and wide glass windows, where even with Captain Sherman and a half-dozen patrolmen at work, a crowd was starting to gather.

Oh, hell.

Church caught his look, and grimaced. "Any way we can get this over with quick?"

Ten sets of fangs gleamed, slick with saliva. *"Only if you wish to forfeit, little morsel."*

"Slow's good." Church raised her second glass, fedora tipped to shield tiny flames. "Just didn't want your magnificence annoyed by the tourist crowd. *Leaf season.* What are you going to do?"

The swirl of dark water in Stimson's scrying bowl was a surprise. He eyed the tentacle-shape suspiciously, one hand reaching for the iron knife hidden at his back. There was showing proper respect to his lord and master, and then there was not having his face eaten off.

Gurgles formed the mockery of a human voice. *"You let the asura walk Intrepid's streets?"*

As if *let* was even close to reality. "It will be to your advantage, sir," Stimson inclined his head. "The mortals will see their champions fall, and lose heart-"

"Are you insane? Do you truly think a hell-raider would start a fight she cannot win?"

Stimson started to reply to that... and paused to think it over.

"Do something!" The gurgle slowed, more controlled. *"Something that does not involve the rakshasas."*

Stimson eyed a certain website, and tapped out two texts on his cell phone. "Already done, sir."

After all, the first mortals he'd just contacted would be glued to the news reports already. Quite willing to believe the IPD was blowing everything out of proportion, and a *harmless* creature was about to have its civil rights trampled.

As for the second group, nursing their grief and their fears in the wake of the yakshas' bloodshed....

From his courthouse sources, at least three on that list had concealed carry permits.

All it will take is one.

Round three. Church downed the still-warm glass. *And we're still alive.*

How long that might last, she had no idea. Ahi had swallowed enough mead to float a battleship, but he was starting to look suspicious. Worse, the crowd outside was getting bigger. And louder. And cameras were starting to flash-

A blond head slipped through to the front of the horde. Church had to stifle a groan. Of *course* Dayson would find his way to the scene.

"Here comes four," Aidan murmured, jarring her attention back to the fresh mead filling her glass. "Wow. You see those swirls? Our honored guest is very... persistent."

Church saw them, all right. Like patches of mist under morning sun, or wavers over summer-hot asphalt. All of them trying to spin her head like she'd downed three shots of tequila; if it weren't for a firm grip on her chair and the fact she *knew* Aidan was burning the alcohol out, she'd already have gone facedown on the table.

But she hadn't. Not yet. Because each disorienting swirl of air and magic was swatted by a grimly muttered Ave Maria or prayer to St. Michael on one side of her, and Usagi's patient Sanskrit on the other.

Can't be helping Aidan at all, Church realized, seeing the fire-mage twitch and grip braided white as he lit their latest glasses on fire. *They've got to fight the maya, or we're all screwed - but it's hard to target a near-demon without hitting a* half-demon *with the backsplash. Lousy cheating asura....*

It's an endurance contest. Which of us breaks first?

"Did you know," Myrrh murmured, as they tipped brims down to hide flames, "in times of old, most folk watered their wine?"

Sure, fine, they were drinking *mead,* not wine, what did that have to do with-

Church blinked, and snuck a careful glance at their ten-headed opponent. Were those wild eyes... just a little glazed?

Great googly-moogly. We might be able to do this!

Endurance, will, and pure bluff. Poker never had been her game. And this *was* poker, Old West style, everyone at the table cheating and doing their best not to get caught.

All I can do is keep a clear head while Ahi the Jackass keeps trying to snare us in illusions that aren't working-

Wait. The maya wasn't working *on them.* But the crowd outside....

There's a lot of them. That means any maya he uses has to work harder. Good, right?

Only Church couldn't shake the feeling she was missing something.

The news helicopter droned overhead, and her blood ran cold.

Sherman gave up trying to look strong and professional, and just hugged herself, shivering. How Church could sit at a table and drink with that - that-!

It was like trying to stand in the face of a tornado, or walk through a raging flood. The creature in there was power, was *fear*, and everyone in the crowd trembled as if they'd grabbed a live wire.

They'd run if they could. I'd run if I could.

It ripped at her like barbed wire. She was Intrepid's captain of detectives. She was supposed to face murdering criminals. Not run from them. She was braver than that.

At least, she'd thought she was. Only the heart inside her was shaken and wailing, screaming at her that all the horror of night lurked inside with dripping fangs; to stay was to *die.*

And right behind the fear, lurked the hate. Hate for the monster, making her face her own cowardice. Hate for herself. Even hate for Church inside, cool as a cucumber, drinking on the job.

Though she could imagine just what Church would say if someone lobbed that accusation. *"Right now, drinking* is *my job,*

Captain."

A bit of Sherman's mind not swamped with fear almost felt sorry for the Dark Lives Matter crowd that'd shown up. They'd come out with placards for nice fluffy werewolves, or lonely persecuted vampires who just wanted to tap a friendly vein. Not... *that*.

Gold and polished muscles and fangs, all wrapped in a silken kilt....

It didn't look like a yaksha. But even if she'd never heard Myrrh's lecture, Sherman knew she'd never have mistaken Lord Ahi for anything but a rakshasa king. There was just the same... power. And hunger.

And Myrrh thinks they can beat it with a drinking contest, and make it go away, her fear gibbered. *No. It can't be. We have to destroy it, we have to hit first, but it'll kill us if we even try-!*

Trembling, Sherman drew a breath. She was the captain. She was the one who'd let a hell-raider and her half-crazy murder survivor of a fire-mage try to find some way to save her city. And she was going to sit on her damn terror and *let them work.*

Forget the crowd. Forget the chopper. Just get through the next few seconds. And the next....

Blinking sweat out of her eyes, Sherman caught a glimpse of familiar blond heading for the door.

I don't believe it. What is he, nuts?

Dayson was just as white-faced as the rest of them, but the reporter was *moving*. Pen and notepad in hand, jaw set, totally ignoring her and the crowd. Even ignoring the middle-aged guy slowly stomping up behind him, heading in toward the bar like he didn't see anything else in the world.

Know that guy from somewhere, where-?

Usagi downed her fourth shot of burned honey-water. *If I live,*

I'm going to have one heck of a story for the monastery.

If. That might be iffy, indeed. Granted, Aidan had managed to burn off most of the herbs in the first two bottles, and the rest of the mead hadn't been dosed to be soma-like, but... Zhong Ma Huang was better known as ephedra. A stimulant. She hadn't thought it would be a problem, after all she *lived* for that first cup of coffee in the morning....

Caffeine's not a straight shot of adrenaline. Usagi kept praying, even as she felt that warning flutter under her breastbone that meant things were about to go drastically wrong. *I could be in trouble, here.*

Still whispering sutras, she braced fingers against her carotids, and pushed. Firm and gentle. In and out.

Hopefully the fedoras would mask that along with the flames. If Ahi realized he'd stumbled on her weak spot....

The squirmy flutter pushed more insistently through her heartbeat. She knew where this was headed.

We can't help the bodies we were born with. Breathe. Hold. Breathe out.

And pray.

We are so screwed.

Aidan didn't know what was up with Usagi, but the way her aura fluttered against the bounds of her skin couldn't mean anything good. He did know the look on Dayson's face; stormy intent, with a high chance of lightning-strike questions. He had to admire the guy's sheer nerve, walking in here had to be like deliberately strolling into a forest fire, but this was definitely not the time.

Who's that guy behind him?

Middle-aged, salt-and-pepper hair; heavyset, with the weathered look of a guy who spent a lot of time roaming the outdoors. A steel to his jaw that said he'd made a decision, and neither hell nor high water was going to stop him.

Church swore under her breath. "Peter Bannatyne," she muttered. "Watt Bannatyne's son."

Bannatyne? Who's - oh hell.

The chill racing down Aidan's spine had nothing to do with room temperature. He knew that name, reading over Church's shoulder as she reviewed all the rakshasa murders and cursed herself for not being fast enough. Watt Bannatyne had died on a painted shuffleboard ground, eviscerated by yakshas that called Ahi their lord.

Church was a cop, but the way she'd stiffened, she knew better than anyone how thin the veneer of law was over clan ties in the Smokies. Ahi owed the Bannatynes a debt of lives. Peter Bannatyne had come to collect.

Aidan braced himself. "Go get him."

The detective glanced at the glasses, at Myrrh still focused and grim; at Usagi, still chanting even as her face went paper-white. "But-"

He grinned at her, and jabbed a thumb at his chest. "Big shiny distraction. Go."

Wasn't just Ahi he had to distract, after all. If Church saw that quiver along Usagi's neck, she'd call an ambulance - and getting outside aid would break the contest, sure as attacking Ahi. Meaning the asura would be free to attack them. Given Usagi was the Buddhist nun-

He'd flatten her first. Just to be sure. Her chances are better if we don't call. Damn it.

Aidan deliberately flopped back in his chair, taking a swig of not-yet-seared mead and blowing out a plume of smoke.

Ahi snarled, focused on him as Church shoved up to her feet and headed for Bannatyne. *"What deception is this? Worthless half-breed - you dare to cheat a lord of the rakshasa?"*

Says the guy who's been slamming maya at us to throw the contest from the start. "Who's cheating? I'm going all the way by the rules." Another sip, another thread of smoke.

"By what twist of word or tongue do you-"

"The terms," Myrrh cut in, mild as milk and honey, "were to *consume* it, oh great and glorious lord of slaughter."

"Aaaand I'm consuming it." Aidan slurped flames off the top of his drink, carefully not glancing at Usagi, or Church holding a low, near-violent argument with both reporter and angry armed relative. He could smell gun oil, and a bitter trace of recently-fired gunpowder. Oh boy. "Mmm. Now, *that's* a proper burn."

From the detective's set feet and Bannatyne's grimace, she had the would-be gunman listening to reason. Or at least listening to the sanity of waiting until Ahi was even more sloshed to take a shot. Good.

Which was the only thing good about the situation. Ahi loomed like a thundercloud, twenty eyes gleaming with frustrated fury.

He knows we've got him cold. All the tales of asura say their pride's as big as the rest of them, Aidan thought. *Lose to mortals? He's got to be looking for a way out-*

"Is it true you're associated with the yakshas that allegedly murdered citizens of Intrepid?"

Aidan stared at the blond reporter holding up a videocam, and wondered if Myrrh would stop him if he set the idiot on fire.

Then again, from that steel in gray eyes, countering Ahi's maya was the only thing keeping Dayson from getting the whole Old Testament in his teeth.

The longer he talks, the longer it takes to get Usagi help. "Hey! Anyone tell you it's rude to butt in to a challenge?" Aidan nodded toward the asura. "We've got an agreement. If he loses, he takes all the yakshas out of here-"

"How do your fellow rakshasas feel about your attending this occasion with known Hunters?" Dayson drove on. "Can you offer any insight into what provoked the attack?"

"Provoked?"

Suddenly tree-long, an arm swept Dayson up in a giant's

clawed grip.

"Your existence provokes me, little mayfly mortal." Fangs gaped, dripping slime. *"How long shall I let you suffer the pain of this world, before returning to the Wheel to reap your karma and return in a more fitting form? A rock? A slug?"*

Aidan hung onto the edge of the table, strangling the instinct to stop all the pussyfooting around and just set Ahi on fire. They had a truce, it might cover other humans around the contest as long as they didn't directly attack the asura-

He was on the floor before he could think twice, the twinge of *fire-explosion-near* that meant *gunfire* jangling down his nerves before the sound cracked across his ears.

What gun? Cops outside wouldn't shoot in here and Church knows better... oh, hell.

Dayson fell with a bone-jarring thump.

Clawed fingers held a steaming bullet. Ahi.... smiled.

Silk and gold *shifted.*

"...Why did it have to be snakes?"

Myrrh laughed, despite their desperate situation. If Church could keep her head enough to quote that movie, with all Ahi's crushing weight of fear, they stood a chance. "I am a brother to dragons, and a companion to owls!"

Church tossed off her fedora as the silk ribbon rippled; the brown and orange fur of a wooly-bear caterpillar spilled out, shimmering into brilliant scales that towered up, and up....

The Great Lizard of Cullasaja Bald.

So the Cherokee called the basking creature they warily steered clear of. Myrrh had needed only to hear the tale of its glistening throat to guess what it actually *was.*

A dragon's fangs bit into Ahi's scaly coils, drawing blood that thundered like ice water.

"Out!" Aidan swept Usagi up in his arms, rationally deciding that a nun still chanting while her heart thundered wouldn't do anything as sane as retreat. "Everybody out!"

Church tucked a bit of twisted brown into her cheek, and drew her panchaloha-tipped baton. "Damn root better work, tastes awful...."

Myrrh dodged a flailing tail, tackling one of the meadery's slower employees out of the line of fire. The Lizard's raging breath shoved aside even shadows, crinkling tips of white hair.

A true dragon, and no lindworm, this.

She'd hoped as much, venturing out to the treeless bald; and hoped further, when the Great Lizard deigned to shift his shape so they might carry him. Japanese dragons shrunk down into silk-worms for their own amusement. With a bit of bribery, flattery, and Usagi's wide-eyed stories of kin across the wide oceans, Cullasaja's inhabitant had been willing enough to try his own version.

Now drunken asura coils thrashed, shedding icy blood with each rake of diamond claws. The Lizard's fangs lunged for a stone-scaled throat.

Myrrh ducked, dragging the terrified young bartender toward the door, as Ahi's whip-crack of head smashed chandeliers and ceiling alike. *Move, keep moving, before-*

The Lizard *growled*, low and bone-shaking as an earthquake.

Snake or no, Ahi roared back.

Myrrh planted a hand on the floor just in time to keep her face from hitting broken glass. Sound and magic rang through her bones; and if she could barely keep moving, then....

Above, the drone of helicopter blades suddenly beat louder, and louder.

Shards or no, Myrrh dropped. "He shall cover thee with his feathers, and under his wings shalt thou trust-!"

~*~*~*~*~

First the car, now this. Church covered her head with her arms as steel and wood and the stink of gasoline crashed down like the wrath of God. *No one's ever going to take a deposit from me again.*

Not that it looked like any angry creditor would get the chance... to....

The wreckage was *above* them. Barely. Trembling against a golden feathery glow, like a car teetering on the edge of a cliff. Shuddering with every blow of scales, as dragon and asura kept tearing the meadery - and each other - apart.

Bracing the end of her baton against the floor and fear, Church stood.

There she is.

Swaying on hands and knees by a petrified barmaid, white hair flying about her like storm winds. Gray eyes glazed as if she were drunk, will and magic keeping them unsquished. For the moment.

"Everybody out!" Church scrambled over to Myrrh, bracing the trembling enchantress. "We can't hold this long!"

"No kidding we can't." Aidan coughed at fumes, not letting go of Usagi even when she batted at his face. "I'm trying to sit on the sparks, but we've got *diamonds scratching stone* out there...."

Fwhump.

Church screamed. Grabbed the frozen barmaid, and *pulled.* Everything was billowing orange and heat and shrieking steel, sparks stinging the backs of her hands-

Rolling, over and over again, on the grass and now-smashed green clumps of daylilies outside the meadery windows. Breathing in clear, blessedly cool air.

We're not on fire.

If they got out of this in one piece she had to *kiss* that idiot fire-mage. Right after she gave Myrrh a good shake for using herself as a magical reversed Samson-in-the-temple.

...And the fact she knew that story was all Myrrh's fault. And Aidan's. And O'Malley's. And anyone else she could blame for a world gone to the edge of insanity. Damn right.

Helicopter. The crew, where-?

Church looked up at bloodstained metal, crumpled like tinfoil into what was left of the roof, and had to look away.

Aidan thumped down beside her; Usagi over one shoulder, hands fisted in the scorched collars of an unconscious reporter and a barely-conscious gunman. "Take these idiots, I need to go in!"

After a body, Church shivered. *Or a skull.*

And she was a horrible, horrible person, because all she could think was if Myrrh was dead they didn't have much time to get her back, and if Halloween hit without their best demon-slayer....

"Ugh."

All shadows and white hair, Myrrh collapsed out of the smoke.

Oh... good. Church closed her eyes in relief, despite the ongoing roaring, crunching, and crackling of stray flames. She'd feel like a horrible person later. Right now someone had to call 911, assuming the screaming crowd hadn't done that already.

Of course, if the fire and ambulance guys had any sense, they'd tell Dispatch to go to hell. Go in where a dragon and a giant stone serpent tried to tear each other to pieces, yeah right....

Shadows loomed over them.

Oh, not good!

Church opened her eyes to the steaming stone maw of a Godzilla-sized serpent. Shadows swirled about Ahi like thunderclouds, full of all the terrifying strength of flash floods. The Lizard was half the wrecked building away, shaking off steaming blood from a chunk taken out of his gleaming throat, dazed as a prizefighter. The root tucked between her teeth and cheek was *hot*, like ginger set ablaze.

Ahi hasn't eaten us yet. Is the campion root working? Like a little bit of "rattlesnake master" can keep an asura from going anywhere he wants....

Usagi coughed; voice thin, but defiant. "All things in this fleeting world-"

Granite fangs gaped wide, descending. Aidan made it flinch with a lash of fire, but the maw bore in, regardless.

"-are a dream, an illusion, a bubble, a shadow," Usagi forged on. "Like dew or a flash of lightning. *Thus we shall perceive them!*"

Thunder rolled. Church blinked against an unbearable flash of lightning-

Ahi was gone.

Myrrh eyed smoke rising from embers Aidan hadn't had time to quench, and hoped the fire department would reach them before the meadery went up again. "That could have gone better."

Church spat out a smoking bit of campion root, shaking like an angry leaf. "Oh, you *think?*"

"'M okay," Usagi insisted, white-faced, as Aidan hefted her easy as a fainting bride. "Been a couple months... was pretty much time for an attack anyway...."

"And you!" Church shook a fist almost in Usagi's face. "Couldn't pass the physical, sure - you didn't say anything about a heart attack!"

"'S not a heart attack," the nun insisted, breathing deliberately regular. "Just... miswired nerves. A whole bunch of 'em. Short circuit. In the heart. Once in a while - goes off."

"More like a short circuit in your *brain,*" the detective snarled. "Do you want to die?"

"Everybody dies, Detective." Another measured breath. "Hey, I almost bagged an asura. How cool is that?"

"You-!" Church flung up her hands.

"Might as well let it go," Aidan advised the detective. "She's old enough to know better. And *you* got to bring the dragon."

"A dragon." Sherman was still holding onto the side of a police cruiser, face almost as white as her knuckles. "I looked up St. George- but then I said not a chance, there's no way even my craziest detective would bring in an *actual dragon.*"

"If you can't find a dragon-slayer, why not a dragon?" Church leaned against the cruiser beside her captain, still light-headed. *We're alive. For now.*

Even Usagi, the idiot. The nun was still arguing as they shoved her into the ambulance; something about, *just a little tachycardia, no big deal, let me get some electrolytes and I'll be gold....*

The paramedics hadn't bought it. Church hadn't either; but Myrrh was headed in with the nun, Usagi couldn't get better help. And Sherman did need a report.

"You brought a *dragon* to a *drinking contest.*"

"Bribed him with a university library card and one heck of a paid gift certificate on Amazon," Church observed. "Not to mention wild silk, a haunch of bison, and the best mocha latte in town. He was really happy with the bison. Says the woods around here just haven't been the same since they were hunted out."

The noise Sherman made might have been a whimper. Maybe. *"Dragon."*

"One-shot deal. We want him again, we'll have to bribe him again. If we can track him down. Though he's probably headed back to the Bald right now, unless he saw a bookstore he wants to hit-"

"Why a dragon?"

"Asuras are the big guns of the rakshasa world." Church patted glass and steel, glad for something solid and real and *human.* "You heard Myrrh and Aidan. Usagi's got the stuff right out of Buddhist myth, and it'll curl your hair even worse. Pretty much the only thing that does in an asura is a legendary hero, usually an incarnated minor *god.* And even they have to cheat. So... we cheated." She took a deep breath, enjoying the simple feeling of being able to breathe, without choking on the certainty of lurking death. "Be glad you didn't go up to Cullasaja Bald. Trying to walk into a dragon's lair when it's not playing harmless little caterpillar is like strolling into a tornado." She whistled. "All those fantasy games get that right about dragons, alright. That fear aura is something else."

"Fear aura."

"Same kind of thing Ahi was using on us," Church obliged. "I don't know how you guys managed to hold the line out here, Captain, I swear. You must have dragged in everybody with nerves of steel. I knew who I had ready to back me up at the table, and *I* wanted to run."

Her captain looked up at that, a little less wild around the eyes. "You didn't look it."

"Yeah, well, Usagi didn't look like she was half-dying, either," Church griped. "Looks like a lot of Hunters are really good at bluffing." She grimaced. "I guess that's easier when you expect to die."

"...What?"

Church nodded, wanting to hit something. "It's a problem, Captain. Every Hunter I've met - it's not that they *want* to die. They just know the odds. And the odds *suck*." Her fingernails bit her palms. "Dorren's headed right that way, and those two plan to help her-"

"Endangering a minor," Sherman said flatly.

Church shook it off. "She's already *in* danger. What are they going to do, pat her on the head and tell her everything's fine when there are rakshasas out there trying to eat her? Her. Specifically. Not just any random human snack. She can see them. They want her *dead*." She rubbed at the back of her neck, wondering if Aidan had let some alcohol slip through after all. Though she felt more like the hangover than the drunk. "We've got to do something about that, Captain. We're cops. Protect and serve. We're supposed to bring in the bad guys. A teenage girl shouldn't have to turn vigilante just to stay alive."

"No," Sherman affirmed. "No, she shouldn't. So what do we do? We don't know half the things that are out there. Much less how to bring them in for questioning."

"Don't know yet. Though I guess that explains... O'Malley." And Chang; though Church wasn't going to bring up Chang unless she had to. The risk if she was right was too much to slap on a poor, mostly-innocent college kid.

"Explains *what* about Father O'Malley?" Sherman pounced.

"He's a priest," Church said simply. "Parish priest. Helping sinners, keeping half-demon kids on the straight and narrow, the whole shebang. Flying under the radar of most of the things that go bump, giving us the little protections he can. He does a lot of good. Why should he give that up to go toe to toe with monsters that plan to grind his bones to make their bread?"

"...You're mad at him."

"Captain, I am flat-out *ticked* at him," Church gritted out. "He's a *good* man. He's been helping. I owe him a lot. We all do. And yes, I am mad as hell because there's so much *he didn't tell us.*"

The captain's eyes narrowed, thoughtful. "Lindisfarne, or Shafat?"

Right. Margaret Sherman knew her well enough to know Church wouldn't get this mad just for herself. Captain of detectives, after all. "Both," Church admitted. "Not so much for Myrrh, maybe; she picked Hunting way before O'Malley was a gleam in his grandpa's eyes. But Aidan? He was *born* into trouble. And nobody warned him."

"Might not have made a difference," Sherman shrugged. "We both know, if somebody really wants you dead...."

"Then they'll probably get you, unless you get damn lucky," Church agreed. "I know. Steven was a subtle, homicidal genius. Telling his brother what was up might not have made any difference. It might have made things *worse*." She loosened her fists, and thought of fear, and fire. "But if I'd been born with that kind of sword over my head - *I would have wanted to know*."

"Because you were," the captain said quietly. "You've got the Sight."

"...Yeah." Church stared into the distance, where smoke still rose from dragon footprints. "And I can't look away when the monsters come calling. I can't."

"Wouldn't ask you to," Sherman smirked. "But I think we need a Plan D."

Do we ever. Church huffed a sigh, and flipped open her cell to check one particular tracking number-

Yes!

Grinning, she displayed the site to Sherman's skeptical brow. "We just might have one."

Sherman looked at the entry. Glanced at her. "Oh no. Now what?"

"Don't worry." Church kept grinning. "This is no caterpillar."

Leaning back in her hospital bed, one thin IV line dripping into her arm, Usagi blinked at the hunk of steel Church had dropped in her lap. "You want a blessing on this? What, are you expecting a possessed squad car?"

"Hey, you never know," Church shrugged. "It's iron. Myrrh says that's good for carrying a celestial charge. I already had Father O'Malley say a few prayers over it. Now... well, given what's out there, I want all my bases covered. Heck, I'll take this out to Old Man Conseen if I have the time." Not that she thought she'd get it. The streets were *tense*.

The nun turned bright steel and worn paint over in her hands, green eyes contemplative. "Any foxhole in a bullet storm?"

"Something like that," Church allowed. "Seriously, I'll take all the help I can get."

Usagi nodded, thoughtful. "Still, sometimes what should help, won't, if it's done for the wrong reasons." She looked up, serious as Church would have expected from someone three times her age. "What do you believe, Detective?"

Damn. The nun would ask the hard ones. "I don't... know," Church said at last.

A red brow arched; *go on.*

"I've been listening to Myrrh when she's helping Aidan keep it together, and - there's a difference between belief and *faith.*"

"There is," Usagi agreed. "A big one."

"Right!" Church waved a fist, oddly relieved. "See, I *know* things like Aariel and that asura are out there. I've seen Aidan shake, and freak out, and set things on fire when he doesn't mean to. Or Myrrh make the world sit up and take notice, with just a few words. Heck, I've seen grade-B plumbing take down a florist's nightmare. So... I can believe there's a heaven, and a hell, and demons. I've *seen* demons."

Usagi nodded. "But?"

"But faith... faith is different," Church said reluctantly, lowering her hand. "I know things are out there. Faith... that's thinking some of what's out there cares about you. Personally."

Usagi grinned. "Nice distinction. I'm going to have to write that one down." She rubbed her fingers over Church's steel, feeling out curves and angles. "So you believe. But you don't feel like you have faith?"

Church rubbed the back of her neck, muscles taut as steel wire. "I've seen too many bodies."

"Makes you feel even more like a fake, right?" Usagi stated. "You know Aidan and Myrrh have seen worse."

The detective bristled. Nun or not, Usagi was a decade younger, and where did a kid get off-

Monsters. Demons. Stick to the truth. "Yeah," Church got out. "They've got faith. Why can't I?" She sighed. "Hell, you have faith, and you...." Church gestured toward the nun's chest, where Usagi's own traitor heart had almost tripped out from asuras, ephedra, and who knew what else.

"Well, that's different," Usagi admitted. "I've known for years I'm on borrowed time. I mean, it's not a given. I could totally get to my creaky nineties or so and keel over from something else. But get stressed wrong, get something out of whack - and spellcasting just does that, no way around it, if you pull any real power - yeah. I could drop dead. It could happen." She shrugged, gown whispering against the pillows. "But I didn't."

Church had to rub her temples; it just didn't click. "And you still have faith."

"It's a gift."

Church snorted.

"I'm not joking." Usagi stared her down. "It's a gift, Church. On my path, in Christian ones, every faith I've shaken my ringed staff at - they all say the same. Belief is what you do. Faith... that's a gift. It comes, or it doesn't. It doesn't make you less if you have it, or more if you don't. It just *is*."

The detective frowned, chewing that over. Felt like the kind of thing she'd want to bounce off Coral, maybe with hot chocolate involved. The gorgon thought all modern religions were equally weird; although given hell-raiders, Coral at least admitted Christ-followers had *guts*.

They'd kind of have to, way back then, right? Church thought. *Because not sacrificing to the gods got the Empire cranky with you, and it was the Empire that kept the monsters off. Roman soldiers knew about werewolves and things, after all that's where St. George got trained to spear dragons....*

I have got to talk to the captain.

"So...." Usagi flipped steel between tired hands. "The real question, I think, is if you're asking me to bless this just because it can't hurt, or because you think it really might help?"

A fine but distinct difference. Church could respect that. "I think it might help?" she offered. "I went and poked around for stuff on asuras. Ahi shapeshifted into a snake, and some guy named Indra was supposed to have gotten a weapon from a divine smith to go after a snake-asura, and it was kind of this shape...."

Usagi blinked, bemused. "It does look a little like a vajra. And we know Ahi doesn't like the Diamond Sutra." A red brow arched again. "You call Indra *some guy?* Boy, I can't wait to introduce you to the head of my monastery. I can see the riots."

"I'm hoping not to see more riots," Church muttered. "Would you mind?"

"I'd be honored." The nun's smile was bright. "But you're going to have to help me sit up."

Chapter Fifteen

Friday, October 31st

I've been waiting for this day.

Stimson regarded the innocuously titled *Snowy Winter Break* video file, and smiled. It was, perhaps, not professional for a proper butler to sigh happily at the prospect of the bloody mayhem about to be evoked. But... just this once, he believed his master would understand.

He stabbed his finger down. Watched the bar creep across the screen. Seventy percent... ninety....

Upload failed. Retry?

Growling, Stimson rattled the keyboard, careful not to break it with the force of his typing. Damned internet. And this was why Steven had not simply left this particular file waiting for a programmed command. He might need a different connection, he might need to load a different copy of the file, he might need to mesmerize a damned cable contractor into letting him at a main server-

File uploaded.

Ah. And sweet, sweet mayhem would soon be his....

"Church! My office. Now."

Margaret Sherman waved her oddest detective inside, wondering if Church was counting down the days she was still on suspension. Her captain sure was. "I have this message on my desk that you still haven't seen our friendly neighborhood counselor."

"If someone wants to mess with my head after Halloween, okay." Church closed the door behind her. "Until then, way too busy to second-guess anything."

Uh-huh. "If you weren't second-guessing something, you'd have gone already," Sherman pointed out. "Let me take a wild guess. You actually like those two, crazy as they are, and you're worried about what's going to happen to them after we all get through Halloween and we can punt them out of the station."

Church stood stiff as if she were in her court-formal suit. "Is that what you think's going to happen?"

"Absolutely." Because she was the captain, and she had to keep her officers focused on the win. Being scared to death wasn't going to save anybody.

Church grimaced. "I'd feel a lot better about that if we could get more help. Help that actually knew what they were doing based on more than just lectures and speed-reading myth books."

Ouch. "Fancy FBI TV shows aside, we can't yank people out of prison just because we think we need them," Sherman stated. "No judge would stand for it. Especially not for Hunters. Everybody in the department knows about Myrrh's thing for handcuffs, so we couldn't even bring them out with shackles, much less just an ankle monitor-"

"Captain."

Sherman raised an eyebrow. Church might be less than subordinate at the best of times, but she knew better than to interrupt a ranking officer. Which meant this was important.

Church took her hands out of her coat pockets, turning them over to look at them; cut up, stained, and nicked by who-knew-what from the monsters she'd hauled off innocent people the past week. "You realize, if we pull this off, *we're* the Hunters now."

What? "That's insane," Sherman said in disbelief. "We're cops. Not vigilantes."

"We're the people who shoot monsters," Church said flatly. "The ones who fight back when something tries to *eat us*. That's what the vampires and all their Dark Lives Matter idiots have been aiming for. Hawthorn's *restricted*. Silver bullets are damn near *illegal.* So Myrrh's telling us the other things that work, and the bleeding-throat mobs are damn well not going to stand for that. Anyone who fights back, anyone even *ready* to fight back, to keep a bag of tricks on hand that can take down one of the night-people and haul them in for questioning when they don't want to go - then we're the bad guys. Because *that's what Hunters do.*"

Sherman wanted to deny it. They were *cops.* Not vigilantes. Serve and protect. Enforce the law. For everybody, human or otherwise.

But she'd heard the marchers at the funerals. Every cop in Intrepid had.

"I knew how to kill a rakshasa." Church turned her hands over once more, stuffed them back in her pockets. "I knew how to stop them, and make them stay stopped. You know what the uniforms call me, after I pulled their nuts out of the fire? Take a wild guess."

"Can you blame them?" Sherman had to ask. "You sat down to a *drinking contest* with that - that whatever Ahi was. Is. And then you dragged out a dragon. Good god, at least tell me that's not coming back...."

"Asura," Church said practically. "What was I supposed to do, shoot him? You saw how much good that did. It just ticked him off." She huffed. "If we were trying to arrest a perp in a burning building, I'd let a fireman take the lead. If I had to go yank him out of a cave, I'd get a spelunker, or a miner and some explosives. If I have to go arrest a *Buddhist near-demon*... I had a nun, a wandering Gnostic who's spent centuries in India off and on, and Aidan, who got told all the ways to run away from asuras before they could kill him. And how to kick them in the shape-shifty balls if they got that close. They said we could get him to swear off having his offspring hunt in Intrepid if we could beat him in a challenge. And damn it, we almost did."

How they'd been beating something the size of a *Tyrannosaurus rex* at a drinking contest was not something Sherman wanted to think about. It involved magic, and twisty hell-raiders stringing even more twisty words together, and it made even Taber Howe's most convoluted legal briefs seem sane, sober, and respectable.

But then, Hunters weren't respectable. Everyone knew that.

Almost everyone, Sherman thought. "Have you talked to Aidan about this? And Myrrh?" There was no point in not recognizing those two were glued at the hip, from mutual trauma if nothing else. Not the mention the evil sense of humor.

"Not much point," Church shrugged. "Those two are going to have things try to eat them the rest of their lives. They know it, I know it, you know it." Blue eyes cut up at Sherman, sad and determined. "Myrrh 'cause she's got a head stuffed full of what kills bad guys, and she can take down vampires single-handed. Aidan... he's *half-demon*, Captain. Anything supernatural he runs into that won't stop to talk, and you know a lot of them *won't*, is going to run screaming or kill the big bad fire-mage before he fries them. Because they *know he can*."

Sherman winced. She'd had a few thoughts that way herself. Sure, Aidan was a homicide victim, he'd saved cops' lives, and he was on their side. *For now*. What happened if he ever decided he wasn't?

Half-demon. Church says it like bringing up your Cherokee great-grandma. When anybody sane, nightsider or not, would *run screaming.*

On the other hand, Aidan had managed to get a werewolf kid to turn evidence, and *had* left the teenager unscratched, even when the rest of that cannibal pack had attacked the three of them.

Meaning Church will be cleared for that mess as justifiable homicide, Sherman admitted to herself, relieved. *So far, he's one of the good guys. But does he have to bring up... come on. Demon for a dad? Maybe that's what something scary told him, but - it's like something out of King Arthur. The horror-movie versions. Myrrh's a Hunter, sure. Everybody knows what to do with vigilantes; get them into the neighborhood watch or arrest them. Saying you're half-demon makes you look* crazy.

Worse, it made the poor guy a target. The past two weeks had seen things plastered across TV *nobody* had known were out there, and if the mood in Intrepid was tense where people could *see* monsters being beaten-

I don't want to think what's it's like in the rest of the world.

Church had been just a teenager. Sherman had been in the Academy on the Dark Day. Called out fast and without all her training, like all the other recruits that year, because the average citizen had lost their minds. If something like that hit the streets again....

Myrrh - if she's really a thousand years old, she's seen mobs before. She's probably got a plan, a fallback plan, and enough magical oomph to flatten a whole block if the first two don't work. But Aidan's a target. Hell, he'd be a target even if nobody knew about the demon; that hair's a giant coppery "weirdness here!"

And when someone hits him, he hits back.

Which was a good thing. Something she'd want in any of her officers. Trap Aidan in a howling mob, and Sherman was sure the man would survive it. Physically.

Which might be worse than not surviving at all, Sherman sighed. *Lindisfarne's had enough human evil to break a cop in half. If he had to kill people to stay alive... God, I wish I could tell him to get on a bus and get out of town!*

Only he wouldn't go, and they all knew it. Even if Myrrh left - and who was Sherman kidding, they'd need a kaiju-sized crowbar to pry Shafat away from the Demongate before she'd purified the damned thing out of existence....

Even if Shafat left - this is his hometown. And Aidan cares about people. Church. Father O'Malley. Dorren O'Connor. Even the local Buddhists, and I never would have seen that coming. He cares. *He knows what might happen tonight. We'd have to shoot him to get him out of here.*

Her desk phone buzzed. "Captain Sherman."

"Captain?" Retired officer Gamble, currently running visitor intake downstairs. "I tried to call first, the mayor wouldn't go for it-"

Church tensed; Sherman didn't have to look to know who her detective had spotted through the door. "Got it, Gamble, thanks." She clicked the phone off. "Not one word about nicknames."

Church tried to look innocent, miming a zipper across her lips.

Better head Herr Mayor off before he spots the plotting demon-slayers in the back corner. Sherman shoved her office door open. "Mayor Green. What brings you down here, right before this really busy night for our finest?"

The man looked proper and sympathetic, she had to give him that. From polished dress shoes to graying brown hair and mustache to the high-class but not *too* expensive gray suit, Mayor Sorley Green was the picture of the educated statesman concerned for his city. He was civilized, boisterously concerned with only nosing the city government of Intrepid into matters when its citizens demanded it, and along with his wife a keen supporter of half the charitable organizations in town. And having him and Church in the same room was just asking for trouble, because usually the detective was calm and professional as a priest, but everyone was tired and Church *hated his guts.*

Given what they knew about Steven Savonarola, the mayor's bestest buddy of all time, Sherman couldn't blame her.

He could have been fooled. Savonarola fooled a lot of people.

Sherman had had a few conversations with Savonarola before his untimely demise, and hadn't noticed anything demonic besides a tendency to manipulate. There'd always been *something* that didn't quite sit right, looking back; but she couldn't arrest a guy on eerie feelings. Politicians were used to people trying to nudge them one way or another. It was part of their job. Which didn't make Sherman feel any better.

"Oh come on now, Captain Sherman," the mayor sighed. "You and I both know this will be a Halloween like any other. Eggs thrown, hysterics from the church ladies and ministers about pagan festivals and corrupting the youngsters, parents convinced someone slipped a razor into the candy and they need an X-ray machine. Nothing else."

Church stifled a snort.

Sherman tried not to blink. "Sir. We have trouble out there, just waiting for nightfall. Man-eating monsters. Some kind of very, very nasty sorcery our local churches have only unraveled half of. Halloween has power, because people *believe* it has power. We have to be ready for it."

"You mean two Hunters you won't get out of this department believe it." Mayor Green glanced toward that corner of the squad-room, annoyance creasing his genial face. "Captain, we all know things are a bit... tense. But if you put the SWAT teams out on the streets there will be riots."

As if the SWAT teams were her call, and not Chief Alexander Lyter's decision. Granted, her boss had had several leafy and fanged reasons to take her requests under serious consideration. Why was the mayor coming at *her?*

Good question. Ought to ask the Chief, later. For now - come at him sideways. "Mayor, the IPD does not cooperate with vigilantes," Sherman stated, plain as if she were quoting the department regs. "Rakshasas are native to Southeast Asia. They aren't something our local paranatural experts know a lot about. We even emailed Ms. Cruz's coven." Which had made her feel as slimy and in need of a shower as digging in a dumpster after evidence of a homicide. But you did what you had to do. "They didn't have any helpful information, so Ms. Shafat and Mr. Lindisfarne are volunteering their time and expertise on our behalf."

"Oh of course, Captain. We've all seen the news reports on how they *volunteered* to deal with that... whatever it was." Green wrinkled his nose. "Considering the results, why are you even allowing them in the building?"

He glanced at Church, and Sherman could almost smell the ozone-snap of her detective's temper in the air.

But Church was quiet. Watching the man.

Right. Because maybe Savonarola didn't *fool him, and who knows what he might have up his sleeve? Even something he doesn't know about?*

Sherman shook her head. That way lay paranoia, and a lot of sleepless nights. She'd trust Church to watch the guy, and tell her if she saw anything wrong. Assuming Church took the time to say anything, instead of taking the guy down first and asking questions later. "They're here," Sherman said plainly, "because I want them here. Where I can keep an eye on them. Aidan's a possible witness to a cold case we want solved, and Chief Lyter knows we don't have enough officers to put him in protective custody-"

The glance Mayor Green threw Aidan's direction was more than a little white around the eyes. "You've seen that video, and you think *he* needs protection? What about the rest of us?"

"Why would we need protecting? We're the cops." Church's hands fisted in her pockets; Sherman couldn't help but wonder what banes the detective had slipped in there for emergencies. "I was there when those vampires tried to eat him, Mayor. Aidan hasn't done anything except defend himself."

Green raised thick brows, utterly unconvinced. "Slander like that, Detective-"

"No," Church cut him off. "Not happening. You can't imply Lindisfarne might burn people, and not say vampires might eat people. We *know* vampires feed on humans. Nobody's proved Aidan's burned anyone who didn't come after him first."

"We'll wait on a court of law for that, Detective," the mayor said sternly. "We've seen what he can do. We don't let citizens walk around with a rocket launcher!"

"We let *vampires and werewolves* walk the streets." Church glared. "If they can do it, Shafat and Lindisfarne can. Either the law applies to everybody or it applies to *nobody*."

"The law?" Mayor Green said, aghast. "You can't think allowing dangerous spellcasters to roam free could possibly be covered by the law!"

Sherman saw Church bristle, and had to raise a skeptical eyebrow herself. "Mayor. We have SWAT teams for a reason. We have detectives licensed to carry hawthorn and silver-"

The mayor shifted his shoulders, obviously not comfortable with this line of reasoning.

"-For a reason," Sherman forged on. "Because even if the vast majority of lycanthropes and vampires are good, peaceful, law-abiding citizens... some of them aren't." She paused. "Now we know there are things hawthorn and silver won't handle. So we need to talk to the experts. That doesn't mean any of us likes it. But we have to have the tools to do our job. How can we protect the citizens of Intrepid from man-eaters, if we don't know what ammunition loads we need? Let us get the information and the training. I'm sure Ms. Shafat would rather get out of our way herself, as soon as possible."

"This isn't about our city, Captain. It's about what's right," the mayor shot back. "You are *officers of the law*. You *can't* go in to a - a *situation*, intending to commit murder!"

"Damn right we don't, *sir*." Blue was bright and dangerous as sparks. "Didn't you get what Myrrh was doing with that asura? *She was trying to negotiate*. How is that different from what we do? Please. Tell me how."

Aspirin, Sherman decided. *Lots and lots of aspirin.*

"We don't negotiate with something the size of King Kong. We call in the National Guard!" Green said sternly. "Every victim that creature takes is on Shafat's head. She will be arrested, Detective. And charged with a considerable amount of crimes. It's just a matter of time. Captain Sherman describes you as a good detective. Don't let her drag you down with her-"

"Well of course she'll be charged," Church growled. "Nuria's going to see to that, self-defense or not. Don't you know what Myrrh is? She's living proof faith *matters*. That some ordinary Joe's *belief* is as deadly to vampires as that great big ball of fusion we call the sun. Of *course* the vampires want her locked up. Or dead. She's a Hunter. Like herding the cows in to slaughter, only the first one in's a longhorn. No nice, tame, tasty meat. Just horns, hooves, and a bad attitude."

Sherman desperately wanted to laugh. She didn't know whether to get out the duct tape or sell tickets, but the look on Mayor Green's face was *priceless*.

He rallied quickly. "Of course, you've been through some trauma these past weeks, Detective. I hope you're speedily cleared to return to duty. But as for Shafat, and *Aidan Lindisfarne....*" His lip curled. "I've heard that story he's spreading about Steven Savonarola. How *convenient* he accuses a good man of horrific crimes after he's no longer around to defend himself!"

I hope Aidan's ears aren't as good as I think. Sherman kept her face professional by an act of sheer aggravated will. Mayor Green hadn't felt his mind crushed by a fog of demonic power. She'd been grateful when Xanthippe Coral's burning eyes stiffened the world into quiet stone. At least as a statue, she couldn't be used against her own people. "Mayor. I don't know what gossip you've heard, but Aidan's never accused Steven Savonarola of anything." Not by name, at least. Aidan knew as well as anyone what kind of awful legal mess this was. How did you prove you'd been murdered when you weren't even in the same body anymore? "I have my orders from the Chief, and none of them said anything about the National Guard-"

"Of course they wouldn't," the mayor harrumphed. "That was the governor's decision. They'll deploy in the next hour. And you will keep your officers out of their way."

Sherman's jaw dropped. The chief hadn't said word one about this. Sure, she and Church had both thought about the National Guard... when they'd been after one, singular, mind-bending supernatural target. Myrrh could take one bad guy. Or at least keep it tied down long enough for mass gunfire. Scattering Guardsmen through Intrepid with Halloween about to hit? Having her officers on the streets against rakshasas would have been bad enough. This was going to be a disaster.

"Wait a minute," Church broke in, looking as incredulous as Sherman felt. "You're going to put armed Guardsmen on the streets, full of people, when they can't see through rakshasa illusions? We don't have enough Sight-lenses to equip the cops, much less a bunch of nervous guys in uniform!"

"Lenses of- do you have any idea how ridiculous you sound?" the mayor said scornfully. "Everyone in Intrepid is having hysterics. Seeing things that aren't there. Vampires snatching babies from cribs. Werewolves eating Chihuahuas. All of which impulsive, malicious morons are using to excuse everything from obscene graffiti on temple walls to throwing a torch into the Nightsong's front doors. If it weren't for Steven Savonarola's example, showing that crimes against those of paranormal origin *will* be investigated and solved, *especially* against Hunters, we'd have our nightside citizens panicking in self-defense!"

Oh boy. Sherman narrowed her eyes at Church, who looked all too ready to punch the mayor about the blatant hypocrisy of allowing campaign-donating vampires like Nuria Cruz to defend themselves, while a penniless fire-mage was considered a danger to life, limb, and property.

Matter of fact, she felt inclined to punch Green herself. It just wouldn't solve anything.

Would make me feel better.

"With the Guard on the streets instead of a bunch of jumpy, *stressed* officers, these illusory incidents will vanish into the mass hysteria from which they came," Mayor Green declared. "And that will be the end to it. Calm the city down, and the country will follow. Innocent people are dying out there, Captain. I intend to stop it."

Green's intentions were good. Probably. But there was one sorcerous elephant in the room the mayor was all too obviously overlooking. "Sir," Sherman said quietly, "there's a Demongate primed to open in downtown, as soon as it gets enough blood. I need my people on the streets to stop that, or we're going to have innocent people dying *everywhere*."

The mayor drew in an aggravated breath-

Eagleman thumped a fist on the door; yanked it open. "Captain! Up on the web - you'd better see this, it's-" He shook his head, as if he could shake away reality. "I think your cold case just went red-hot."

Say what?

Church almost beat her through the door. Church *did* beat her to Aidan and Myrrh; the fire-mage was chalk white, Myrrh yanking him around and away from Rinaldi's computer screen with a low litany of *don't look, don't listen, focus on me-*

Then Sherman saw the blood, dripping dark off obsidian knives. And the *smile*.

Myrrh felt fire tremble under her hands, and hoped Steven's darkened spirit had ended up somewhere soul-wracking *cold*. "Look at me," she repeated, low and quiet, voice calm as a moonlit ocean. "Look at me, you know it's not here, you know it's not now. Look at me, come away...."

Voice and hand, and not a trace of magic in either. She didn't know how aware of reality Aidan was, but she knew Sword Aariel. Aidan had dealt with illusions; he'd been trained to *react* when his perception of the world was foggy. And sort out the bodies later.

But I am here, and I am real. So long as I keep others from touching him.... "Mother Mary, will someone *turn that down?*"

Pale as a ghost, Rinaldi muted the video.

Good enough. She had amber eyes turned toward her; and if they were glazed with horror, at least Aidan was *trying* to see her.

"It's over," Myrrh declared, as heat shimmered above a half-dozen wastebaskets. "Captain Sherman has her plans, she will call when we are needed. For now... Detective Eagleman, will your cousin mind?"

From the way the Cherokee detective glanced around the room, he saw that threatening heat clear as anyone. "I'll give him a call *right now*."

"My thanks." Myrrh inclined her head, relieved. "Church-"

Church tore narrowed eyes from the sputtering mayor. "You need a ride out of here?"

"Walk," Aidan croaked. "Walk would be... better."

"Got it," the detective said firmly. Reached across, and gripped his shoulder. "We got him. Remember? And if the damn bastard tears open the Demongate and comes back - we'll get him *again*. As many times as it takes."

Church kept an ear peeled toward the door until feet started down the stairwell. Trying to keep an eye on her fellow furious detectives, and not the grainy old digitized home videotape of a gasping man being carved apart, skin and muscles deliberately peeled back before Savonarola started on less-important organs-

Some cop still within reaching distance of sane grabbed the mouse out of Rinaldi's slack hand. One click, and the web browser blinked out.

Thank goodness. Shuddering, Church turned her attention to the mayor's stammering protests. It was hard to *care*, but - damn it, someone had to hit the man between the eyes with reality.

"...Has to be faked," Mayor Green blustered. "Someone trying to ruin Savonarola's good name - god, if this gets out, do you know what's going to happen?"

"Yeah, I do," Church said, before she could think better of it. Because damn it, she'd recognized both faces; the smirking teenager and the dying young man surrounded by ritual tools. The same smirk Savonarola had had trying to drown them all, and the lurch of her stomach told her that last desperate fight hadn't gone nearly as much their way as she'd hoped.

He planned it. He planned it all. Oh, he probably didn't plan to die - but he planned exactly *what he wanted to happen if he did.*

And he started planning it all the way back before he murdered his brother.

"Blood in the streets," Church stated, ice down her spine. "Supernaturals afraid of humans, or just pissed off that some of us decided to fight back. Humans who know the vampires and were-wolves have been lying to them, that there's worse monsters out there, and who just found out the champion of the nightside was a murdering, lying scum all along, who killed his own brother in a *demonic sacrifice.*"

"We're going to have riots," Captain Sherman breathed, as officers traded grim looks and angry glances at the mayor. "Oh god, people are going to *die.* He's in the grave and he's still going to kill everyone-"

"Of course he is." Church had to laugh, harsh and bitter. "He set this up, Captain. For *twenty-six years*, he set this up."

"Church?" Kirsten said, uneasy.

Church held up a finger at a time, relieved to get it all out. "First he killed Myrrh. Got her wiped out by the train, locked her down in Hell so she couldn't stop this. Then... then he killed Christophe, to start building his powerbase-"

Mayor Green shuddered. "You have no proof-"

"God damn it, *shut up*," Church snarled. "He killed his *own brother* so that when the supernatural came out in the open, he could look like the sweet little martyr. The good guy. The one both sides could *trust*. And now-" She slashed a hand toward the blank screen. "Now everybody knows that was a *lie*. Right when he's got a Demongate *just waiting for murder.*"

"Everyone knows? We can't have everyone know!" The mayor jabbed a finger at the screen. "You have to shut that down before we have a riot-"

"Shut it down how?" Captain Sherman stared him down, resigned and weary. "It's on the web. Magic, murder, and names on the vid. No matter how many people report it, it's going to be viral by now."

"My god." The mayor was paper pale. "What do we *do?*"

"Do? I'm going to go get every priest and person of faith I can grab, down to the altar boys, and see if there's anything we can do to weaken the Gate before sunset." Church stepped over to her desk; hefted blessed steel wrapped in her messenger bag, with little pockets for plastic vials of holy water and some of Coral's just-in-case stones. "And then I'm going to make sure the two people who might be able to close it stay alive."

Chapter Sixteen

"Is he okay?"

Lee Eagleman's voice. A friendly voice, in the crackle of flames. Even if it was worried.

"He is definitely *not* okay." Myrrh's voice was wind to the flames, fanning and feeding. But a light wind, a soothing breeze; not the gale to drive fire to devouring fury. "Someone very cruel struck him in the face with violence from his past. And I would wager much that they did so deliberately, to harm one who can stand against them, at the worst possible time." Her tone softened. "But Aidan knows that as well, and I know he is strong enough to master himself. If your kindness will give us some time."

"Just keep everything clear of the welding tanks...."

Aidan breathed in, and out; concentrating on the precise heat and hunger of flames to devour cleanly, so only ash remained. A regular fire would allow vapors to escape, making burning debris very unhealthy for anyone nearby....

But this fire is mine. And I don't want it to hurt anyone. Either by what it does - or what it fails to do.

Concentration. Precision. The flick of will or finger to urge flames hotter here, quicker there. It took everything he had....

And fire was clean. Not good; not evil. Just fire, tamed to his hand like a patient tiger.

Can't ever turn my back on it. But... it's not demonic. Even if I am.

He could kill with flame, he *had-*

But I don't have to torture someone to death. Ever.

Steven... Steven chose to do that. No one made him.

I'm his older brother. I was supposed to protect him. Why... why did he choose that? Why couldn't any of us see it, before it was too late?

Why couldn't I save him?
Aidan closed his eyes, and let flames lick his tears.

"I thank you for your patience." Myrrh planted her hands to shift her seat on the pile of salvaged lumber, hardhat properly on her head. Lee's demolition crew had kept well clear of Aidan as he burned out his rage and sorrow; and if there were more than a few low whistles, or too many excuses to stop and stare, she could hardly fault them for that. "I was worried I'd need to find a forge, or a bit of blighted wasteland no one cared to see remain."

"From what we heard about those leafy deer rakshasa things, you guys earned it." Lee folded his arms, watching flames. "Whoo-ooof. How much of that can he do?"

"That's part of our problem," Myrrh admitted. "At the moment, neither of us is entirely sure. I can estimate, based on fire-mages I have known in the past. But what Aidan is used to burning is... much, much harder to burn than anything here."

As well it should be. Aidan had trained the strength of his magic to burn creations of pure spirit. Mere physical matter? That was far more easily lit.

Which reminds me.... "It may look impressive, but it's less helpful in facing foes than you might think," Myrrh said practically. "Some do flinch. Werewolves have fur, so are wary of being singed; and vampires are as flammable as any other dried-out corpse."

A few of the men *stared* at that. Good. Vampires had had two decades to paint themselves as harmless night-dwellers. Tell anyone who'd believed that he was wrong, a man would argue to defend himself. Make him curious enough to question... he might just find out the truth.

"But humans are not easily burned by elemental fire," Myrrh went on. "It responds to emotions; and most mages would no more raise fire against their fellow man than they would draw a gun."

"Or go after him with a welding torch?" Lee said, almost casually.

A good foreman, who considers his men's worries. "Very much so, Mr. Eagleman," Myrrh agreed. "It is good to be around people who understand hazardous work." She coughed into her hand. "Though you might do me a further kindness, and not repeat that around Father O'Malley. He'd walk me into the ground to prove I've been taking it too easy these past years."

He might be right, at that. Oh, not physically so; even the good Father would ruefully agree expecting a spirit to keep a nonexistent body in running condition was a lost cause. But missing the past quarter-century of technology had left her woefully unprepared for the *scope* of evil's spread.

Steven didn't just shame Aidan in front of a town, or even a kingdom. This... a whole world can drink the pain of an innocent man, and save it to savor over and over again.

She'd blast something into oblivion, if she could only decide *what*.

Steven would be the preferable option.

Rendered down into twitching components, yes. Just as she would a vampire who kept killing, or a werewolf who would not restrain the curse. *Destroy that which is evil, that that which is good may flourish.*

But Yaldabaoth's born son was most likely in Hell. Quite possibly, in his own father's demonic court. Drat.

Then again, he might have ended up in some other layer of the abyss, in which case he was surely suffering all the torments Hell reserved for those so steeped in sin. She had no right to interfere for mere human vengeance.

If we are fortunate, he slipped sideways toward the Field of Reeds, Myrrh mused. *Whereupon he would meet with Ammit by the Lake of Fire, and find his black heart devoured.*

She might be a Christian but she was still a child of

Alexandria. Surely God would not be so wasteful as to discard a perfectly good lake of fire and soul-devouring creature guarding the right order of the world simply because *modern* Christians found them too daunting.

You'd think someone told them following Christ was supposed to be easy.

For now, Steven was out of her reach. She should set thought of him aside, and focus on the real problem.

Whoever set that video to load to the internet. And why.

If Steven hadn't set it to go off himself. Apparently computer programs these days could be that complicated, and set up in advance. Drat, again.

The video itself would have been impossible last I walked this earth, Myrrh thought grimly. *Oh, to film was easy enough, but to broadcast video without access to a TV station? It's no wonder people swarm to even the darkest creations posted on the internet. That they exist at all seems as wondrous as a new oasis created by years of patient ritual-*

Years. The Demongate should have taken... years.

Chill tiptoed down her spine, as Myrrh turned that frightening thought over in her head.

The rituals and sacrifices to build a Demongate have to be done over years, because they take time. *One man, or devoted followers blind enough not to care they mean to loose Hell on earth - it does not matter. Human flesh and voices have their limitations. We can only work so fast.*

Most magic was similar. It took steps. Time. Specific preparations, to convince the world it should be other than it was. Her enchantment and Aidan's fire were terrifying *because* they were swift, called upon with a thought.

Because we've cut most of those steps out of the equation, Myrrh knew. *Aidan was born with the essence of flame. He is Aariel's son, his true-born and loved child, and that fact is written into the very fabric of the universe. When he wishes fire, the world itself bows and burns.*

Her own case was a bit more complicated. She was mortal.

...Well, mostly.

Myrrh grimaced, pushing past fury's exhaustion to *think*. It wasn't her physical body that mattered for magic, but habits of mind. As an enchantress she delved into the truths of the universe; science, lore, the little quirks and foibles of everything from her fellow man to the internal combustion engine to the tiny animalcules Romans had believed in and van Leeuwenhoek had drawn so wonderfully centuries later. She knew *how the world worked.*

That knowledge created shortcuts in her magic. It made what she wished to do much, much faster, because she knew precisely what levers magic must apply to the universe. Her enchantments served as shorthand, the truths of the universe through the Word gripping magic fast; while her knowledge, her *gnosis*, did the heavy lifting other enchanters could only perform through long, complicated rites.

Much as this cell phone does. Myrrh took out the little device Father O'Malley had given her and Church had gone over, making sure the enchantress knew which buttons to push. *I can use it as an ordinary phone, and dial the numbers one by one. Or I can hit the preset - and it dials a specific number* for *me.*

That in itself wasn't enough, or computer programmers would have been summoning Hell for decades. The computers she'd known *couldn't* work magic.

They couldn't snatch images and voices of life and death out of the ether at one's convenience, either. Myrrh scowled at the cell phone. *Chants are never the whole of a spell, but they are often a key part. What if computers allow - not spellcasting, but* shortcuts?

It would fit. It would fit everything. How the Demongate had been raised in less than a year; the blink of an eye, in Hellish time. How Steven had managed to master no less than three forms of magic enough to be dangerous. How he'd wielded the power to keep herself and Aidan at bay, and even trap Sword Aariel... for a time. Thank goodness for Church, and a detective's sheer stubbornness.

So if computers could allow shortcuts... how does that affect the Demongate?

First and foremost, it meant a continued search for elaborate measures within the Demongate's reach - an organized cult, or a ritual working center - was a waste of time. Steven could have scattered pieces of magic across all of Intrepid, just as he'd scattered bodies, all to be invoked at the moment the stars were right.

Halloween, Myrrh thought, *or later, in one of the dark turns of the year. But given the rakshasa attacks, the blatant disregard for life and sanity, pushing the city farther and farther - Halloween.*

Because the second factor computers implied was *timing*. Once conditions were met, programs fired, sure as a bolt from an arbalest. Delays could be built in, but that would add extra complexity; and the more complex a spell, the more that could easily go wrong.

Which implied the third likely factor; someone, human or other, spellcaster or not, was out there, making certain Steven's spells went off as intended. Because a sorcerer of Savonarola's thoroughness and malice would never have left his grand plan to the chance of a mere *power outage*.

If we could find that one soul, we might stop it all.

If. Eighty thousand people in Intrepid itself; near half a million in the greater metropolitan area. And Halloween was hours away.

We have to try. It's possible Halloween will not be the night. I need to make notes, talk to modern magic-workers. Church saw more of Steven's workshop than I did fighting the water-summons, she might recall details I missed-

The tiny instrument of doom buzzed.

Aidan let fires flicker and die, feeling anger flame out with them. *I don't know why Steven did what he did*, he thought wearily. *And I really don't know why he did it to me-*

He flinched, and tried not to think about cold, and pain, and bloody death.

As well not think of thorns in my feet; a nail in my side. Cold and drowning water....

It shouldn't cripple him like this. Twenty-five *years*. He'd seen so much worse.

But Aariel taught me to fight. And Myrrh... Myrrh taught me there was still hope. Still something I could do. *Even if it was just help watch each other's backs.*

Hell, for him, had been so much saner than Earth. That scared him. A lot.

What'd that one doctor say? Aidan drew a breath. *"In Hell, there are no innocent bystanders."*

Now he was back where there *were* innocent bystanders. Where people got hurt for no more reason than they were in the wrong place at the wrong time when some massive jerk decided they wanted pain-

He flinched again. What'd happened to him... hadn't been anything like just *bad luck*.

I can't. I can't deal with it now. Not with Halloween coming with sunset, and riots simmering in the streets. I can't get lost in my own head. I just - can't.

He felt darkness push at the edges of the world, strengthening as the shadows grew longer. Myrrh, Father O'Malley, Priest Sakai and everyone else they could grab - they'd done all they could to weaken the Demongate. Which was probably why it hadn't busted open in the last round of rakskasa-caused slaughter. They just couldn't *break* the damned thing.

I wish I knew why-

Ash and heat-haze rippled, like a curious blink.

Aidan tensed, ready to move... then, reluctantly, relaxed. That wasn't an illusion. It wasn't even an entity, exactly. Just heat, ash, and the aftermath of his fire, tied to a part of Intrepid being rendered down to its foundations.

...I'm an idiot.

Crouching, he placed his hand on ashes. Trying to *feel* at it, just as he'd felt at quarried stone.

You're something built, and so is the Demongate, and I've used fire on you both. Talk to me....

It wasn't words. Not even images. Just an impression.

Cut too deep. Bled too long. Sickness. This wound needs burning.

"Aidan?"

Aidan blinked, and rose, shaking ashes off his fingers. Black still stained his fingertips, but he knew Myrrh wouldn't mind. "I don't think we can close the Gate from this side."

Gray eyes narrowed. "Tell me."

He had to swallow, first. "...You're not arguing with me."

"I have dealt with Demongates in the past. That does not mean I can *feel* them. Not as I suspect you can," Myrrh said practically. "I do know that even an inactive Gate is like a puncture wound in reality. It can sicken with demonic energies, very easily."

Deep puncture wound. That made a scary amount of sense. That horror of lightless light on the Wailing Plains, swallowing up lost souls and predatory demons like Intrepid's tales of whirlpool-catfish.... "You mean, if we want it to heal up, we need to - clean it out from the inside?"

"We've been treating the outer layer, so to speak," Myrrh nodded. "With more time, that might well suffice; as applying hot compresses to an inflamed wound can kill the sickness within. But."

But. Halloween. Riots hanging in the very air.

"We will have to face what comes, when it comes." Myrrh straightened. "I'd thought to track down whoever must be directing this chaos. But if the pressure is that great, then spells or no, it may no longer matter."

Like an abscess busting loose from sheer concentrated infection. Aidan wanted to wince, and yet....

I know that face. It buoyed him, even against the gathering darkness. *That's "I've got a plan" face.*

"I have another idea; though I must speak to Sister Usagi, first," Myrrh stated. "*Thokcha* is more in her line of faith than the Church's. But if the Emerald Earth Science Museum is still open, we can find what we need. For now - I know you need more time to calm yourself, before nightfall. But I could well use your aid to take with me."

Aidan eyed the cranberry-glass vial she held out with wary curiosity. It wasn't the soul-jar Myrrh used to snatch spirits from Hell; that had gone with her when she'd last died, while he distinctly remembered this particular vial falling through his fingers onto mortal earth. The hieroglyphs annealed to the surface were particularly interesting. He recognized the wavy line which meant water, yet rendered in scarlet enamel, it meant *lake of fire*. Then there was the Syraic engraved on the other side, which he could actually read. *"Every thing that may abide the fire, ye shall make it go through the fire, and it shall be clean."*

Myrrh inclined her head. "Elemental fire is a powerful component in many spells; works of cleansing not least among them." She touched the pocket in her shift that held O'Malley's phone. "That was a call from Sacred Heart. They've a case in their emergency room of a woman badly mauled. They believe she is stable... but they've seen enough werewolf attacks to know the signs. One of the nurses called, to ask if there was anything that could be done."

Werewolf, Aidan shivered. *Cursed forever to hunt humans; to* want *to, even if you beat down the urge like the rat bastard addiction it is.* "Is there? She hasn't had any tonic."

"There may be, if this is indeed a fresh bite, and she has never changed by the moon's pull," Myrrh said soberly. "But it is not lightly done. It will not take long; it *cannot* take long, or the curse will outfox me even in my unraveling of it. I will need to invoke all the cleansing I can, in one moment; by blood, and water, and fire." She paused. "One of the most effective enchantments I have found against the wolf's curse... also invokes lions."

Aidan froze. For a moment, he wasn't sure his heart was beating.

Lions. Aariel is a lion.

He wanted to shiver. He wanted to wail, and tear something apart. And he wasn't even sure *why*. "You think demonic fire can help - help fix a *curse?*"

"Elemental fire. Demon or angel, fire is ever a deadly danger; and I need that danger, to burn out this curse. It would help. If you can bear it," Myrrh said gently. "I know your feelings toward Aariel are complicated. Mine are less so; I know him as my honorable enemy. And the father of my friend. Your fire will not harm this woman. It may, indeed, save her life."

It hurt. "You want Aariel's fire."

"I want *your* fire, freely given." Myrrh took a step closer, looking up into his eyes. "For as you stand between worlds, so does she, as the curse works in her blood. You have died and fought your way back from Hell. I cannot grant you a human life, no matter how much I might wish it." She turned her palm up, red glass catching sunlight like rubies. "But you can grant *her* life."

Chapter Seventeen

Centuries didn't matter; Myrrh had never gotten used to the slap of her sandals on a hospital's tiled floor. Most of her work was done before a paramedic yanked a victim off the scene... or after doctors' best efforts had failed. To be in a hospital meant something was drastically wrong.

Something is. Myrrh approached the bright blaze of crimson of Usagi's robe by the nurses' desk. *At least they called. And believed they could try.* "I'm glad you could come."

The nun twitched, ringed staff jingling as green eyes sought her face. "Whoof, you are *sneaky.*"

"Old habits," Myrrh winked. "You've no trouble leaving the temple for a time? I know Priest Sakai is more than busy-"

"Leaving the temple? You shouldn't even be out of bed, Sister Usagi." Behind the desk, Nurse Meikle glared impartially at them both, brown hair caught neatly back from her face to be covered for surgery. "Miss Shafat, I called you, not somebody who's walking wounded."

"I'm fine," Usagi said firmly. "As fine as I'm going to get, anyway. If someone needs help - that's my job."

The nurse glared harder.

"...At least if I keel over, I'm already in a hospital?" The nun shrugged. "Bitten person. I want to help."

"In truth, her effort should not be great," Myrrh said practically. "I merely need someone present who can defend herself from a curse, to distract it while I strike."

Some of the strain eased around the nurse's eyes, leaving weary hope behind. "Can you help?"

"There is a chance," Myrrh allowed. "But I cannot guarantee it; not without examining her myself."

Meikle's shoulders fell. "There'll be a problem with that...."

A problem. Myrrh took in the nurse's rumpled scrubs, the furtive quiet around the desk, the sweating faces of security down by the doors. "A... pelted problem, Nurse Meikle?"

"Cousin." The nurse's knuckles paled on a clipboard. "Glen Patterson. Says he'll take care of her. The law says nearest next of kin who's lycanthropic can take in a victim-"

Myrrh held up a hand. "Perhaps it would be better if you claim I didn't know," she said mildly. "And of course you cannot remove him without violence, when he has not threatened anyone... yet."

"You have a look," Usagi mused behind her. "It kind of reminds me of paintings of Sun Wukong after peaches."

"Hopefully I won't end up with a punishing gold band on my head," Myrrh mused. "Nurse Meikle. I know you would not wish violence inflicted upon next of kin visiting a wounded patient."

"It would be against hospital policy," Meikle said wistfully.

"Of course it would," Myrrh agreed. "Might I see your clipboard?"

Eyebrow raised, Meikle handed it over. Myrrh hefted it, gave it an experimental swing, and nodded. "A large rubber band, if you would. Two or three would be better."

"What are you doing?" Usagi asked curiously, as Myrrh used blue and green rubber to strap a heavy iron nail to the back of the board, point sticking out just above the clip. "Is that a *kunai?*"

"The term you wish is *shuriken*; kunai are larger, and oft improvised from trowels, not nails." Myrrh wiggled iron to make sure there was not too much give. "This alone would suffice for me, but for a layperson, some reinforcement is wise." She drew a breath, and laid her finger along the length of metal. *"Behold, I send you out as sheep in the midst of wolves; so be shrewd as serpents, and innocent as doves."*

Taking her board back, Meikle's eyes were very wide.

"It's not widely known these days, but to strike a werecreature on the head with an iron knife or nail will force them out of animal form," Myrrh announced to every listening ear hanging around corners. "If they are already in human form, while the wound bleeds, they usually cannot shift out of it." She drew a breath. "It may be condemned these days, but there was reason for those who held witches or shape-shifters to cut the skin below the nose. As you know, it bleeds easily."

Meikle swallowed, shoulders shifting uncomfortably.

"But I doubt we must aim for so sensitive a target," Myrrh said gently. "All we need is a scratch... and preferably, some hand-cuffs."

From the interested looks on the guards' faces, that wouldn't be a problem.

"Let's be swift." Myrrh stepped forward. "I have a friend in trouble."

"A friend-" Usagi stiffened, ringed staff almost striking the floor before she caught it, a quiet jingle. "Where's Aidan?"

"In no shape to come here, where innocents are flammable," Myrrh answered plainly. "Which I believe someone was counting on. And that... makes me *very angry*."

"Oh boy," Usagi said faintly. "Incoming mage-splosion in five, four...."

Halfway down the corridor, Nurse Meikle braced herself. "So, I just-?"

"I will knock," Myrrh smiled. "You may do as you think fit, for the good of your patient."

Knuckles firm, she rapped the door.

A low growl inside; a burly dark-haired man yanked it open, looking across, then down. "I thought I said we shouldn't be disturbed- *you!*"

"Ah," Myrrh said, heart speeding just a little faster. "You were at the club."

Whack!

Usagi followed through on Meikle's lovely blow with staff-leverage against the werewolf's neck, pushing him down dazed and bleeding, so Security could cuff him. "You really work the short thing, don't you?"

"I've had to for a very long time." Taking out a vial of orange rust, Myrrh dashed it across the bleeding scratch.

"Yeooow!"

"Tch. Stop mewling, Mr. Patterson," Myrrh *hmph*ed. "That will merely ensure you remain marked a few hours. You're a werewolf; you'll heal."

"You can't go in there," Patterson coughed, straining against steel; his jaw dropped, as if he couldn't believe the cuffs still held. "She's infected, she's not safe yet-"

"Do you know, I think you believe that," Myrrh mused. "Do not worry for me, Mr. Patterson. I am quite immune to the wolf's curse. I was called to render emergency medical assistance." She paused. "But then, your packleader already knew I would be, did he not? Which is *why* he bit your cousin."

A guess, based on what she knew of angry wolves and angry men, and too many werewolf packs to count. But from his wide-eyed start, likely accurate.

Meikle flushed angry red. "You - you-!"

"You can't prove anything," Patterson said defiantly. "You're a *Hunter.*"

"My, my. How confident you are in human law. How very sure it will protect you here, where you have so carefully arranged that the cops will not be called... in time." Myrrh smiled, and saw him pale. "After all, if you truly think I am a Hunter, bent on slaying every supernatural creature I see without cause or pity," she let her voice drop, "then *why are you in my way?*"

"Patient," Usagi reminded her, halfway through the doorway.

Myrrh drew a breath. "Thank you, Sister." Gave Patterson one more quelling glance, and raised a brow at Nurse Meikle. "We'll leave him to you. We should only need a few minutes."

"To do what?" Patterson managed. "What are you going to do to Erica?"

"Treat her," Myrrh said shortly. "If we can."

In. Shut the door. And *breathe.*

"Need a minute?"

Myrrh shook her head. "Meditation is wise for many spells, but for this...." Another breathe. "This is deliberate malice. The passing on of a curse no soul should have to bear. To fight this, I must rouse an equal passion. But mine... mine must be *righteous rage.*"

From the bed, someone whimpered.

"Miss Erica?" Usagi lifted her staff in a friendly jingle. "*Namaste.* I'm Sister Usagi, currently working with Vajra Hall downtown. And this is-"

"The Hunter. I heard about you." Stitches ran the length of Erica's tear-streaked face, and white bandages shrouded her shoulder and neck under blue hospital gown. "Are you here to kill me?"

"No!" God, what did people think of Hunters in these days? "I am called Myrrh Shafat, and I have some skill at healing supernatural wounds. Even those thought impossible to mend." Myrrh smiled; gently, this time. "We are here to save you."

They probably think they're being quiet.

Aidan stretched his shoulders, hands empty of fire, waiting for scrapes of sneakers on concrete and scuffs against dirt to change their pattern. The rest of the demolition crew were packing up gear a good fifty feet away by the pickups and heavy trailer, doing the sensible thing and clearing off-site well before the sun could fall over the edge of the world. They hadn't noticed a thing. Compared to most humans who weren't Myrrh, whoever was coming *was* quiet.

Next to a pack of briarweasels, they might as well have hired a brass band.

Moving for an ambush.

Or at least they had been. Some footsteps of those meant to

close the ring tight had stuttered. Not stopped, but definitely slowed down.

The ones who're downwind. Aidan drew a breath, catching what he could from lazy currents of air stirred by drowsy heat. *No leaf-scent, no graveyard... fur. Almost-human.*

A familiar scent. Too familiar, in his few days back on solid earth.

Werewolves.

That narrowed his options. If it were just him, slipping off would be fine; a pack of man-eating idiots wasn't nearly as high on his list of priorities as making sure the Demongate didn't crack open. But with Eagleman's crew on the site-

No. I won't let them be hostages. I can handle this. Aidan's lip curled, baring teeth. *It's just like dodging the Hunt.*

It was dangerous to think that way. Part of these people were still human. Cursed, corrupted humans - but *not demons.*

Right now? Hard to care. "Why don't you all come out where I can see you?" Aidan turned toward the point of the pincer, where the biggest, baddest wolf had to be. "Unless you're scared."

Get them mad. Get them in plain view. Do not *let them get behind you.*

"You're the one who should be scared." A burly guy in motorcycle gang black leather stepped out from behind concrete rubble. Others followed, filtering in from the sides; most in leather, a few in torn sweats they obviously meant to shuck off for furry work. "We're looking for a rat. Loser by the name of Raphael-"

"No idea," Aidan cut him off. Shrugged, deliberately unimpressed at their numbers. *About a dozen. Wow. They must really think they can kick my ass... or maybe they're too used to people folding when they think about being bitten.* "Not that I'd tell you if I did. Kid wants to kick the werewolf habit, I'm all for it. I've got enough of my own bad habits. Gnawing on human corpses? Eww." He let his gaze settle on the slighter guy who looked like Burly's chief henchman; dark hair, shaved face, leather jacket and pulling off the bad-boy look something fierce. "I don't suppose *you* know a Derek."

And we have a flinch, Aidan saw, tasting hate in the air as gray fear washed over that wolf-shadowed aura. *Bingo.*

A white-hot flare of rage sparked, remembering Hell's darkness, and a lost ghost pleading with her lover not to eat her alive.

Don't move. Don't start this. You don't know *it's him. You can't kill him just for a twitch. That would be wrong.*

Scary, that he had to remind himself that was wrong.

Damn wolf scent. Damn instincts.

Instinct and reflex. Instinct - a wolf pack that didn't retreat from a lion meant business, and a smart lion got on with *killing them all* before one of the pack could get lucky. Reflex-

I am Sword Aariel's student. You're just accursed. If you don't have the smarts to start running now....

Huh. Aariel - was my teacher. That doesn't hurt. Weird.

"What do you care who we know?" Burly almost didn't glance at his second. "You're not paying attention. If you don't know, you know who does. Tell us, and you walk out of here without fang marks."

Now that... that was *funny.* "Oh man, are *you* ever barking up the wrong tree," Aidan grinned, anticipation running through his veins like fire. "You think I'm worried about you biting me? You have *no idea* what you're dealing with."

Hah. That had them stopped.

Maybe they'll be confused enough not to fight?

...Naah.

"There's no vaccine for a bite." Derek's eyes slid back and forth, checking everyone was in position to jump one lone fire-mage.

"There wasn't," Aidan agreed. "With you guys slinking out of the shadows - I wouldn't count on that lasting. Congratulations. You managed to do something most Demon Lords can't pull off." He bared his teeth. "You got my partner *mad.*"

Burly snorted. "So let the Hunter be pissed. She's not here."
Teeth, not a smile. "We are."

And you set it up that way. You bit someone, and dumped them at the hospital, knowing a Hunter would have to do something. You bastards.

Aidan stared into wolf-yellowed eyes, and slowly shook his head. "You guys don't listen so good. Myrrh's not just a Hunter. She's a *hell-raider*. She's been at this longer than Nuria Cruz has slurped blood. You think she doesn't know a trap when some idiot tries to set one off in her face?" He turned one hand upward, thumb ghosting across fingertips to feel the promise of fire's warmth. "You think she'd have left me on my own on *Halloween* if I couldn't handle assholes like you with one hand tied behind my back?"

Low growls; Derek looked pleased, but Burly held up a hand. Like he was about to do the civilized thing, and call the whole thing off. "We're not vampires, carrot-top. We're *wolves*. By the time you get one knife out, the rest of us will have your throat."

"You're cursed." An odd calm settled in Aidan's blood. "And you're not listening to the wolf. If you were, you'd know it was telling you to *back off*. You're werewolves, sure, and you're a pack... but I am *so much worse*."

Aariel taught me what I was. Not who I was; that was Mom, and Father O'Malley, and Myrrh reminding me that even in Hell, you can still hold onto something good.

But Aariel didn't lie to me about what I am.

"My name is Aidan Lindisfarne." Aidan swept his gaze over the pack. "And I'm giving you one last chance to let me take you in alive."

Take the option, you bastards. Be smart. Be human.

Burly's hand dropped.
Skin twisted into fur.
Aidan *moved*.

~*~*~*~*~

"In the past, it was often hard to tell if one had been bitten by a cursed werewolf or simply a rabid, ordinary wolf." Myrrh laid out three vials on the patient tray so Erica could see exactly what she was doing; blue-tinted, light-blocking brown, and cranberry glass, each topped with a string-laced stopper. "The safest treatment in many areas was St. Hubert's Key. A hot iron, dedicated to the saint, that both invoked heavenly protection and cauterized the wound. Applied soon enough, well enough, it stopped both virus and curse in their tracks."

The brunette sitting up in bed went even paler. "Cauterize... you mean burning?"

"Lycanthropy is not a light curse." Myrrh inclined her head. "The measures to cleanse it from a wound are not gentle."

"Kind of like chemo?" Sister Usagi offered from the side. "Only you'll get to keep your hair."

"But," Erica swallowed, "being a werewolf doesn't kill you...."

"Not directly," Myrrh agreed, studying the size of the tray to determine the most efficient layout of her components. "But it makes it so very easy to kill others. Even when you do not mean to. For the wolf carried by the curse is no normal beast, but one touched by darkness. Think. You have seen film of wolves in the wild, yes? Does a sane wolf attack a human? No. They run. But a werewolf... a werewolf struggles *not* to attack a human."

Erica's hand lifted, not quite touching her bandages.

"I have known a few werewolves, a very few, who could beat the curse. For a time. But most-" Myrrh had to shut her eyes, blotting out dark memories. "Most only survived by locking them-selves within iron cages every full moon. And always - always - they carried a silver knife." She paused. "Suicide is a deadly sin. But to take your own life so another may live... that can be forgiven."

"Suicide?" The woman whispered. "But my cousin-!"

"Attacked you. Or allowed his pack to attack you." Myrrh stared her down. "That is what the curse drives you to. Murder. Chaos. Sowing the seeds of that darkness wider and wider, until at last those around you must defend themselves, to your death. Is that the path you wish to take? Or will you accept the pain, accept that *you were attacked*, and take your life back?"

"Me, I'd go with the *screw you, furry assholes*," Usagi winked, fingers stroking polished wood. "But my faith has opinions on the various illusions that make up the world. And being a werewolf just violates the Path so many ways, it's not funny. Right action, right effort, right mindfulness - you can't *be* a good Buddhist when you're a werewolf. And right livelihood? Goes right out the window. How can you avoid being a source of suffering to other beings when you always want to eat them?"

Erica's mouth opened and closed, searching for words.

"I would I had more time to explain." Myrrh felt the grains of seconds seep away. "In brief - what I mean to do will *hurt*. Yet it will not harm you, or change you. You will have your own mind; your own choices for the future. All I mean to do, *all*, is slay the curse in your veins." She held out a hand. "Will you let us treat you?"

"...What are you going to do?"

"Well, I'm going to be bait," Usagi shrugged, ringed staff jingling. "Not exactly thrilled about it... you've done this before, right?"

"More times than I wish to remember," Myrrh said soberly. "This time, I have help." She touched warm cranberry glass, remembering Aidan's determined face as he'd poured in flames, freely given. Because no one should suffer evil when there was something they could *do*.

"Bait?" Erica got out.

Myrrh lifted a brow. "Lycanthropy is a curse, not a virus. It will not lie down and die simply because the proper medicine is applied. It must be fought."

"And that's what we do, right?" Usagi smiled.

You know your life may be short, so you choose to spend it slaying evil, Myrrh thought. *I shall have to see if there is any way to aid you. When we're not about to have a Demongate open on top of us all.* "If you are willing, let us begin."

Three cleansings. Fire, and water, and blood.

Here was where centuries of experience came in handy. She'd noted which cures of lycanthropy worked, which did not, and finally narrowed down most of *why.*

Time. And strength.

Invoking enough celestial magic to cleanse a demonic curse simply took too many prayers. Too much *time.* The shortcut of fire and celestial power from St. Hubert's searing iron made cures more sure, more effective - but that was not always enough.

It'd taken time and trials on lesser dark magics, but Myrrh had worked out ways to invoke enough power, swiftly. She'd given them to the Church, to any of faith she could find; even daring to meet Muslim scholars, when she found those willing to look past a woman to the dire fate of those cursed by the wolf. She'd seen too many lives ruined to leave any soul unguarded.

I created ways to treat the bite. What has happened to them, that werewolves maim so freely?

She meant to pin O'Malley into a corner and find out. *After Halloween.* "There's a notebook I should give you a copy of," Myrrh informed Usagi. "Church thinks it unwise to loose upon the Internet, but I want it in more hands than just mine."

There. Vials properly set on the tray, cord-bound tops loosened to fall with the touch of a finger. A triangle for the Trinity; holy water for the Father, blood of an honest man for the Son, and fire for the Holy Spirit.

"I just stand here and jingle, right?"

"A prayer would not hurt," Myrrh allowed. "Be a visible nun." She matched Usagi's grin. "Make it cranky."

"Cranky demon-wolf aye." Usagi raised her staff, slammed it

down. *"Oṃ maṇi padme hūṃ...."*

Power swelled like moonlight shimmering on a lotus, as Usagi's throat thrummed with the silent *hrīḥ* that was the heart of the mantra.

And the moon will call it forth....

Erica cried out, hand slapping at bandages suddenly red with blood.

Myrrh's finger found the first twined cord, and yanked. "Therefore they have forgotten me!"

Darkness surged, met by a white rush of water. Shadows snarled.

One heartbeat, Myrrh thought grimly, *let it think it's found its way around the triangle's point-*

A second yank; gold shimmered, rising from blood. "Therefore will I be unto them as a lion: as a leopard by the way will I observe them!"

Darkness snarled, as Erica screamed; Usagi's staff jangled, the glint of hoops flinging darkness back into the triangle as it tried to squirm free.

Myrrh's left thumb flicked cranberry glass, loosing flame. "I will meet them as a bear that is bereaved of her whelps, and will rend the caul of their heart, and there will I devour them like a lion: the wild beast will tear them!"

Fire roared; no longer mere flames, but a shape of fangs and proud mane, pouncing on trapped darkness to devour it whole.

Not done, not yet, her wounds are still open to the curse....

With a lift of her left hand, Myrrh summoned lion's fire.

Erica was limp and panting, eyes wide as she tried to scramble away.

"O Israel, thou hast destroyed thyself," Myrrh gritted out. Aidan's fire was spirit, not just heat; flames fed on her own flesh. "But in me is thine help!"

She planted her burning hand on the bandages, and refused to let go.

Fire, smoke, *screaming*-

Silence. Sobs, but silence.

"Ow," Myrrh breathed, letting Usagi pry her off the no longer accursed woman. "For the record, I truly hate that spell."

"No freakin' - how the hells did you - you are some crazy woman, you know that, right?" Usagi held her arm by the wrist, below the burn.

"So I've been told." Myrrh lifted her gaze to meet Meikle's worried eyes, as the nurse hustled orderlies into the room. "She'll need...." *Breathe. Ow.* "Treatment for a surface burn. But the wound is clean."

"I'm cured?" Tears flowed from Erica's eyes as she blinked at them both. "But... your hand-!"

"Lucky we're in a hospital," Usagi quipped. "*This is going to hurt*, my foot. Next time, you tell me everything!"

~*~*~*~*~

Take down the leader first.

Wolf, gang-banger, demon - some things stayed the same. Hit the biggest, baddest one first, and the rest might break.

Aidan snatched a handful of pure air, and flung out fire.

Not the heart. Don't hit the heart.

Vital organs, fine; the werewolf paled as shock crumpled his knees. A strong wolf would survive. If not-

Aidan lashed out a rope of fire, binding Derek's legs; yanked him off his feet as muscles burned.

Can't just kill them, not unless they try to kill me.

Killing them would be *so* much easier.

Fur and fangs surged toward him, wolf eyes rolling in terror even as they snapped and snarled. Aidan dodged teeth, yanked a furred ear hard enough to knock one wolf into three more like a pelted pratfall; reached out, snatched a tail, and threw that luckless wolf into girders with a crack of shattered bones.

Barbweasels are nastier. Aariel is faster.

And the werewolves were all focused on *him*, not vulnerable humans who had to fear a bite. This was no worse than a spar back at Court.

Of course, the demons had been trying to kill him then, too. Hadn't exactly worked out for them.

Those were demons. This pack - how many of them really *want to kill me? How many of them are just scared? Or... lost, to the demon inside.*

Too many to take down gentle. Don't want to be here-

The world - wavered.

Floaty...?

Aidan breathed without breathing, consuming air as werewolves fell through where he'd been, fur along their spines catching fire. Some rolled to put it out; others lunged at where he seemed to be, the darkness in them impacting like wolf-shoulders against his legs.

No body. Just fire. I thought I'd lost this.

He laughed; wolf ears twitched and flattened. "I warned you."

His view of the world was oddly off, shaded in heat as much as light; the spike in attention from Lee's crew, the blur of running heat as bodies rushed his way.

Better finish this quick.

Aidan dropped from fireball to flesh on the edge of the snarling wolf pack. Planted burning hands on two furred shoulders, and *blazed.*

Shift and move and burn....

A dozen wolves. Six shifts. A dozen werewolves on the ground, scorched and bleeding, the strongest barely able to crawl.

"I warned you." Aidan tried not to let his voice shake. Burned fur, burned flesh; his stomach roiled.

But I didn't kill them. I didn't.

"This fight is finished." Aidan stepped close enough to look down at the pink lobes of lungs growing back in Burly's chest. "I want you, and your pack, out of my town. Permanently."

"What the-" breath whistled in Burly's throat, face white as he healed from wounds he'd never suffered before, "-hell are you?"

Aidan narrowed his eyes, hairs bristling on the back of his neck. "I'm the guy who beat you. *Git.*"

Burly blinked at him. Glanced side to side, where there wasn't a wolf with a prayer of limping out of here, much less springing a surprise attack.

Didn't look behind me, Aidan realized, hearing that near-silent scuff. *Damn stupid suicidal-*

Metal *shikk*ed out, whistling. A wolf yelped.

"Hey, would you look at that." Church waved her police baton, a thick nail duct-taped to the business end. "You don't have to actually be *holding* the nail for that to work. What say we try nail-guns, next?"

Aidan glanced down where Derek rolled in the dirt, blood tracking a crimson path down his forehead. Glanced back up at Burly. *Snarled.*

Scrabbling through debris, Burly grabbed a burnt wolf, and headed for the street.

"Thanks," Aidan breathed. "I'm a little tired...."

The scatter of claps made him jump.

Startled, Aidan glanced at the work crew gathered by pickups and heavy haulers. Hard, burly men watching with dropped jaws, eyes wide with-

"Easy, now," Church murmured, strutting up right next to him. "Look at those grins. They're not scared of you."

He wouldn't go that far. But... if the glow of their souls shaded gray with fear, it also had silvery *respect.*

Aidan straightened his shoulders. Nodded at Lee. "Sorry that went down here."

"Are you kidding? Best show we've seen all week." The construction worker eyed Church's baton with unholy glee. "He was a wolf, and you hit him with a *nail*, and - sweet Jesus, that *works?"*

"You might want to get the nail blessed, but yeah," Church smirked. "I looked it up. Comes out of Sicily, believe it or not. No *wonder* you never hear about mob werewolves."

Thanks for the distraction, Aidan thought. *But I don't think it's enough.* "Lee. If you want to know, ask. I'll tell you."

Eagleman whistled, glancing at his crew. "Kind of don't want to. But... seriously, man. What are you?"

"One of the old names is *cambion*," Aidan said simply. "My father wasn't human. I didn't know, until I ended up in a very bad place. Myrrh got me out." He glanced at the retreating wave of seared fur. "Now I find out *werewolves* are munching down on people in my hometown. This is going to *stop*. If I have to kick every furry ass from here to the state lines to do it."

"I'm going to pretend I didn't hear that," Church said dryly. "Look, if you've kicked enough butt here to get your head straight, we need to get back... what?"

What, indeed. It wasn't a sound. Wasn't a touch. More like a whisper in the wind, of a thousand thousand voices rising in anger....

"Church." Aidan had to move closer to the crew; warm, glorious, *sane* souls, compared to what wailed on the wind out there. "We're in trouble."

Chapter Eighteen

Stimson tapped chased aluminum with a polished claw, setting the dark liquid in the wide bowl rippling. Concentric rings bent and warped at odd angles, twisted by magic into points of light and darkness, flashing up images of *elsewhere*.

White angles, slashed with black; a placard waving through the streets, brandished by one of dozens of half-gloved hands.

"Stop the lies! Stop the hate! Dark Lives Matter!"

Ah, the video had brought the bleeding-heart troublemakers out of the woodwork, just as his master had planned. Stimson had to admit, he hadn't thought it would work nearly this well.

Especially when a few dropped hints online and by way of concerned citizens calling support groups had told anyone with an interest that the DLM *would* be marching. With signs... and pepper spray, and possibly Molotovs. Without a permit. Without a care in the world for those who'd *lost* kith and kin to Halloween... and other nights.

Another ripple, and the scene shifted to streets east.

"Does everyone know what we're going to do? We don't start anything, but if they do, we finish it...."

Stimson smiled slowly. How naive. As if they'd have a choice about starting anything. Steven Savonarola had been very, very thorough in his charity work to those affected by the nightside. Why, there were at least half a dozen souls in that counter-march alone wearing donated coats, or shoes, or carrying blackthorn clubs. All of which had subtle, stubborn enchantments to breathe on flickering embers of hate, and drive them to burning life. And those were the least of magics woven into donated work, and repairs, and monuments; a simmering web of rage that now snared all Intrepid in its net.

Decades of work, all for this night.

More flashes in dark water. The tramp of booted and sneakered feet. The muttering roar as signs met bleeding grief. The first thrown rock.

Stimson's eyes slitted in pleasure as the mob's frenzy reached through water, frothing up splashes of malice that would pour into the waiting Demongate.

Though even that may not be enough. Not yet.

No, that would take more deaths. Some of which should be coming-

Dark waves hit a trough, showing a sweep of brown hair red with blood, caught by a mineral and herb shop; a college-age girl, on her knees and bleeding.

Stimson bared his fangs, wishing he could sink them through scrying water. Not enough to see humans turn on their own, not enough-!

Dark water flashed uniform-blue, flicked with the light of something Sighted.

How dare you!

One of Intrepid's cops was in the fray, putting himself between the mob and their victim. His partner dragged her to her feet, taking the blows, as both used batons to fight their way sideways to the shelter of flashing lights.

Stimson gnashed his fangs, claws almost biting into metal. The mob's fury foamed from the water, as one of its victims got away....

Be calm. There are only so many cops.

Though the IPD weren't the only fools still struggling against the darkness. Little lights rose from churches, temples, and synagogues; one dark splash brought the drone of a Tibetan singing bowl from somewhere on university grounds.

That damned hell-raider. How did she rally them all?

It didn't matter. It wouldn't be enough. People of true faith had always been few and scattered; and they were more so now, in a realm that valued wealth and supposed tolerance over the battle for men's souls.

No, not nearly enough. Not with the sun setting, the wheel of the year turning toward darkness, the mob howling in renewed rage before surging forward to overturn police cars like so many tin cans.

Everything is going according to plan.

Stimson drew in a breath, and pulled maya about himself to don his current disguise. It wouldn't be enough to fool anyone who knew the man... but one advantage of Mayor Green's arrogance was he didn't truly *know* most of those who worked for him. Certainly not enough to see past what mortal eyes told him.

Picking up the other two bottles on the scrying table, Stimson dumped their contents into dark liquid. Lemon flavor, sugar water - and quite a bit of vodka.

Smiling, he hefted the bowl in human hands, and walked out of the kitchen to greet the mayor's teenaged guests. Before the mayor's *other* guests arrived.

"Who wants punch?"

Leaning on a table of supplies the priests had set up for those facing Halloween night, Myrrh glared down at the map of Intrepid and surrounding forestlands, a scatter of red sticky-notes marking the latest reports of mob damage to the east. It'd been some time since she'd last wished to tear her own hair out. Though in preference, she'd tear other people's hair out. Which was a sin of wrath, yes, but infinitely preferable to the consequences of letting this insanity go further. "What part of *potentially active Demongate* do people *not understand?*"

"All of it, I fear, lass." Sealing a vial of holy oil, Father O'Malley sighed, and wiped his fingers. "Mother Church, God bless her, has been less than assertive in telling her children demons do, in fact, exist. We don't have nearly the level of PR people the vampires have managed to snare. And if they can pass for innocent, misunderstood souls with an allergy to sunlight and a grievously restricted diet, well...."

Myrrh pressed the heels of her hands against closed eyes. Above she heard the surviving local news helicopter circling, and wondered how long it'd take for the South Carolina station chopper to join it. "I have a headache."

"Well," Usagi's ringed staff clinked as she leaned over the map, "Good news is, we know where the 'Gate will open, right?"

"Ah," O'Malley said ruefully. "Would it were that simple, Sister."

Myrrh lifted her hands away. "He's right. If Steven has an accomplice on this side of reality, we cannot know where the Demongate will open. The damned things are... heh. I believe the modern phrase is *resilient and redundant*." She waved at the map. "Yes, the bloodshed and chaos make it likely the Demongate will open in downtown. I can see Steven finding that very, very attractive. But."

"Not enough of a screw-you?" Usagi supplied. Shrugged at their look. "Hey, I'm from *California*. When someone says *have a nice day*, you're in *deep* trouble."

"Neatly put," Father O'Malley approved. "Also, loath as I am to acknowledge it, the man was a member of my flock. As was his mother; and while he never knew how much Phoebe told me, he knew *she* knew enough to warn me. Steven saw too much of the evils I've cast out of Intrepid to believe this land would ever be unguarded from demonic influence. He must have known someone would try to derail his dastardly deeds."

"...Can I adopt you as a grandpa?" Usagi said wistfully. "Nobody uses *dastardly* anymore."

The old priest smiled, and patted her shoulder. "Well, and why not? What's one more at the kitchen table to debate how many angels on the head of a pin? Though that'd likely be devas, for you."

"It depends on if the Monkey King has gotten hold of the pin."
Myrrh planted a finger on the map. The concentration of riots was
wrong. Granted, she was no expert. Her preferred reaction to a riot
was to be promptly elsewhere; mobs were not fussy in their choice
of prey, and enchantress or not, a thrown rock at the wrong
moment would take her down as easily as any mortal. Also
granted, downtown was where many vampires held business
interests, and who knew how riots gathered when people had more
than phone calls to connect them, but-

The warmth of restrained flames touched her senses, and
Myrrh breathed a sigh of relief.

"If there's a Monkey King out there, he'd better be a flying
monkey," Church growled, pushing through church doors with an
ash-stained fire mage in her wake. "'Cause nothing else short of a
tank is getting through that mess. Though I hear our good Mayor's
limos work. He's heading over the river with his innocent,
flammable constituents. Because there's no way vampires could be
responsible for all the deaths rakshasas have piled on Intrepid,
right?"

"Don't hold back," Aidan quipped. "Tell us how you really
feel."

"How I really-" Church glanced between them, and grimaced.
"Right. You saw it, Myrrh, but you were kind of busy.... Aidan.
Steven's - video. *Homicide cops* were that close to throwing up.
Green's just stammering about no way, this is faked to ruin the
Savonarola name?" Her jaw worked, mad enough to spit.
"Nobody's that together when they see someone being *tortured to
death*. He's seen blood before. *Somewhere*." She pointed across the
blue-inked wriggle of the river. "Makes me wonder if the Royal
Resort's got places we ought to take the cadaver dogs."

"Vampires are going across a river? On purpose?" Usagi
shifted her shoulders, as if ill intent itched down her spine. "How
bad do they think the riots are going to get?"

"The west bank has ever been the realm of the dead," Myrrh

reflected.

"Ah, lass, that was a *long* time ago," O'Malley said dryly. "Folk here don't believe the west is where the sun sinks into a realm of demons."

Aidan sucked in a breath, fingers clenched. "Demons do."

"Aidan, lad...."

"Aariel taught me to read ancient Syraic," Aidan said tightly. "And a whole bunch of other things that aren't around anymore. Had to, to work on- don't ask, I might tell you. But I learned to read... a lot of stuff that's not hieroglyphs. If Yaldabaoth wanted Steven to pull this off-"

"Then Aariel would have to leave you clues in what he did *not* teach you," Myrrh nodded.

Church blinked, then nodded. Usagi looked between them all, skeptical. "Wait. Are you saying the Demon Lord's main Dragon is trying to undermine him? Because seriously, demons, betrayal happens, but... what else is going on here?"

"What is going on is that Sword Aariel is a demon, who believes his proper place is punishing sinners in Hell," Myrrh said plainly. "If the Demongate opens and Yaldabaoth unleashes Hell on Earth, Aariel will fight at his lord's command, for he *is* loyal. But he believes in having multiple plans. If those of this realm happen to deduce Steven's plots and unravel them... surely, how could that be his fault? After all, he told us nothing that would help."

Church thought that over a long moment, and nodded. "That? Definitely your dad."

"What?" Aidan sputtered. "Wait, how the, you-?"

"Okay, this might be a stupid question." Usagi pointed to riot-markers, then the Royal Resort and Golf Course. "Someone's trying to blast the Demongate open with deaths and blood. We know that. So... what happens when somebody sacrifices vampires?"

Sacrifices vampires? Myrrh shook her head at the very idea. Certainly, a few daring magic-workers had managed to sacrifice one vampire, unleashing bloody chaos with demonic power. Yet no one she'd ever heard of had managed more than that. Vampires, like any vicious predators, tended not to bunch up where clever humans could riddle them with oversized splinters. Not to mention, even the most persuasive human couldn't get so many vampires in one place without being eaten....

Aidan's hand caught her shoulder as she swayed. "How bad is it?"

"I don't know," Myrrh whispered, trying not to shiver. She was an enchantress. Her magic, her *life*, depended on how well she grasped the truths that created the fabric of the universe.

"...I don't know."

Chapter Nineteen

Worst. Halloween. Ever.

Dorren hid behind the gray-skirted table with her uncle, trying not to shiver. She wished Eric Chang was here, but even Uncle Jim would've looked at her askance if she'd asked for a *college guy* to come to a high school party. And what her parents would say about a guy who wasn't just older, but Buddhist - eep.

The Royal Resort was supposed to be safe. That's why grown-ups in her high school had brought kids to the party here in the first place; a "safe alternative" to trick-or-treat, the resort claimed, given the "current political discussion" going on in the area.

Which Uncle Jim said was idiot rich shorthand for "there's going to be riots, we just don't want to admit it". He'd agreed with her parents: a party indoors, smug rich donors or not, was a way better idea than walking the neighborhood in costume. Candy or no candy.

Which had left her mom chewing nails and spitting tacks. Her husband's no-good brother wasn't supposed to be *reasonable*.

Though maybe Uncle Jim wasn't all reasonable. Given Dorren kind of thought he wasn't supposed to be out on the town without the FBI on top of him, or at least an ankle bracelet.

Not that she would tell. Not when Uncle Jim had given her bits of advice on her eggshell-bombs and ninja-costume, and how to snug her brass and silver pointy things into leather bracers under loose black sleeves. Uncle Jim was awesome that way. She'd already learned all kinds of interesting words tonight.

Maybe a bit too interesting. Dorren glanced at a shadow; huffed, realizing it was just a programmed flicker of the LED-lit lanterns decking the cedar pillars supporting the resort's outer wall. Or maybe one of the actual red candles gracing the tables, firelight glinting off a glass abandoned by a guest. Maybe punch, maybe a little more; there'd been an open bar Switch had scowled at, adults or not. She'd rolled her eyes; after all, she was a *ninja*, and a kunoichi didn't get drunk on the job, right? That'd be stupid, even if you were just dealing with regular twitchy samurai. And they both knew she wasn't.

She peeked up just enough to look down the grand sweep of the drive where limos were hauling up to the valet, trying to ignore the growing clamor filtering through the windows behind them. "You're sure those are Nuria-coven cars?"

"Very. Sure."

Dorren shivered. Uncle Jim *was* her uncle, but right now he sounded scary.

But these were *vampires*. Uncle Jim had good reasons to be scary.

This was supposed to be safe! Why are they coming here?

Behind them, a wide glass door opened. "We're sorry for the change of plans, everyone-"

"Brett Hart," Uncle Jim breathed in her ear, hand on her shoulder to shift them both out of the line of sight.

Which was enough, she'd been paying attention when her uncle dropped hints. Hart was Mayor Green's chief *fixer*. A guy who dealt with vampires and werewolves and people with dirty money so Green didn't have to.

"-But due to the current... unrest... it's probably better for everyone to go home," Hart went on, gesturing people out the doors.

Uncle Jim shook his head, one twitch left and right. "Mobs go for the streets," he breathed in her ear. "We'd be safer here, if...."

If the vampires weren't coming, Dorren finished. Tried not to gulp too loudly.

"Some of our citizens will stay the night here rather than add to *baseless suspicions* by defending themselves and their properties," Hart went on. "Sad, but you know how deep prejudices can run...."

Uncle Jim's eyes were cold and narrow. Not - not fighting-family cold, Dorren knew that look by now. This was *family in danger* cold.

So she took a deep breath, and pushed fear back into a corner so she could think. "I'm okay," she whispered, as parents and kids started hustling out. "You do what you have to, Uncle Jim. I'll be okay."

His look askance should have burned, it made her face flame so hot. But she wasn't going to look away. She'd studied vampires. And other things. She'd had to; no one would tell her the truth about Megan dying, not even Uncle Jim, until she'd cornered him with enough facts for him to realize lying was worse.

Uncle Jim's not just a hitman. He's a Hunter.

He'd told her to trust Shafat, because Shafat could be trusted; the enchantress had helped rescue her father from something that drowned kids, back when they were both young and dumb. Trust, but *pay attention*. Because when he'd met her Shafat had been horribly busy just keeping people alive, and things weren't better now, and she'd probably forgotten more about monsters than most Hunters learned *ever*.

Uncle Jim sighed. Tugged her along, leading her in a crouched scamper from table to skirted table until they were around the corner out of sight.

I'm coming with him? Oh boy....

"I should take you home," her uncle said darkly, barely above a whisper. "I'd send you back with the other kids if I thought even one of their parents had half your guts."

Oh. That was... kind of cool. But scary. Because if Uncle Jim wasn't taking her home-

"I've heard Hart talk people down," Switch O'Connor stated. *"That's not Hart."*

~*~*~*~*~

Stimson smiled Hart's annoying smile as he waved the last of the children's cars off while vampires filled up the dining room. A pity to lose the tender bits. But the point wasn't to have fun. It was to crush human - and inhuman - creatures like the buzzing mosquitoes they were. Letting children escape under Mayor Green's auspices would make his *tragic* death at vampiric hands cut all the deeper. *That didn't take nearly as long as I expected.*

Cloaked under his maya, the TV news feed scrawling across one screen already dropped ominous questions of where was the mayor, the first responders in general, the *good citizens* of Intrepid ready to stand against hate and violence.

Most of those good citizens are currently out adding to the mayhem. Stimson kept smiling, and made sure his teeth weren't too sharp. *After all, even for good, concerned, middle-class men and women, that video was one human sacrifice too far.*

Just as Steven had planned. Though Stimson doubted even his master realized how deep the hate had gone. The people of the mountains were a tough, independent lot; from Scots-Irish who'd gotten the hell out of Ulster to tourists who'd felt the Blue Ridges' call to Cherokees who'd managed to outfox, outlast, and outlive the Removal. People didn't live in Intrepid if they wanted to be coddled.

Yet for two decades, they've been prevented from rooting out evil from their midst. And they know it.

If there was a vampire-held property still standing by dawn, he'd eat Hart's hat.

It might taste better than Hart. Some of the man's habits... well. For once, he'd been glad to cook his food first.

Sometimes, one can't be picky. Stimson inclined his head politely to Nuria Cruz as she followed in Mayor Green's helpful wake. *Vegetables first, and then dessert.*

Not that he intended to eat any of the vampires. Oh no. Tasteless, mummified flesh tainted with demonic corruption? Ugh.

But there was more than one way to see a creature consumed.

The phone in his pocket beeped. Stimson didn't have to look to know what the text would read. *"Now?"*

By touch alone, he sent back the preset reply to his fellow rakshasas. All of whom thought they served Lord Ahi's will in this. *"Five minutes."*

That would give him time to clear stragglers out of the vehicles, and gather them in the dining room. Where he'd suggest to Mayor Green that they take a walk on the course, it would be so restful and peaceful....

It was amazing how well turfgrass could be encouraged to soak up blood.

My master may have been too impulsive in facing his brother, but his plan still holds, Stimson thought. *Bargain with Ahi for his seeds' assistance to slay the blood-drinkers and open the Demon-gate. Ahi gets what he thinks he wants: a confrontation with a true Lord of Hell, to vanquish and add to the luster of his pride. A fire demon trapped by a river; how could it go any way but in Ahi's favor?*

Or so lesser rakshasas thought. And sneered at him, for serving a mere mortal - even if Steven would no longer be mortal, by now.

Steven's power is water. Stimson's fangs sharpened. *And I will be on the winning side*

Never thought I'd have to keep our demon-slayer from having a panic attack. Church kept a hand on Usagi's shoulder, making sure Aidan wasn't crowded while he gave Myrrh a thorough *I'm right here* hug.

I didn't even know Myrrh could panic. Thought she'd had her adrenaline surgically removed.

Evidently not. Myrrh was white as a landscape contractor facing an IRS audit, with INS waiting in the wings. Only she wasn't worried about anything so simple as under the table employees filing improper returns.

"Whoa." Usagi leaned on her staff; and if maybe she was leaning a little more heavily than usual, Church wasn't going to say anything. They'd hit the ER later. If they lived. "Seriously? Nobody's *ever* sacrificed vampires before?"

"One vampire, I'd buy." Church kept it down, watching Aidan let Myrrh reach up and grip flaming copper hair like a lifeline. "Vampires, plural? How many humans could handle *one?* Heck with that; how often did the world ever get this many vampires breeding in one city, before the Dark Day? Hard to mass up packs of evil man-eating possessing demons when there's Hunters out there looking for them."

"You're saying this was a plan." Under her California tan, the nun was almost as pale as Myrrh. "A two-decades-old plan."

"Over twenty-six years, counting where Steven set up to dump Myrrh in Hell," Church agreed. "I guess Aidan comes by the stubborn honestly."

"On both sides," Father O'Malley put in dryly. "Phoebe, Lord bless her, had all the willful tenacity of an Alapaha bulldog, or Ruth following Naomi through the alien corn. She had to, to keep up with both those rascals."

Church's phone buzzed. She tried not to swear, eyed the number-

Flipped it open, heart in her throat. "Dorren?"

"Detective!" A low whisper, washed out by wind through dead leaves. "We've got really bad trouble!"

This doesn't look good, Switch O'Connor thought coldly, watching walking trees and emaciated, red-skinned corpses drag one vampire at a time out of the wooden net, stake them down on thirsty green turf with hawthorn and banyan wood, and start carving.

Part of him wanted to clap his hands over Dorren's eyes. But he needed those free for his weapons, his niece would be in more danger blindfolded, and....

It wasn't fair. God damn it all, it wasn't fair what Maeve and his idiot little brother had done, pretending the world was all puppies and rainbows when Dorren *knew* something awful had happened to her sister.

He'd saved Dennis. Dorren had never had that chance for Megan. If his idiot kid brother didn't want that to eat his surviving little girl alive, Dennis had damn well better give her the skills she needed to kill monsters.

Or stay out of my way. Or Shafat's. Church's, even. She's a cop but she's not stupid.

Dorren was an O'Connor, after all. Stubborn as any of them. No way could she sleep easy with the monsters out there. If someone didn't teach her, she'd end up dead.

Not that Switch gave the pair of them good odds now. They were hidden in a screening bit of woods around the ninth green, they were wearing brass knuckles, and vampires and rakshasas both were pretty well *distracted*. But supernatural senses were just better. One wrong gust of Halloween wind, and the two of them would be snacks.

"Th-there's some kind of red glow where the blood's soaking in." Dorren shivered. "It kind of looks like runes- oh. Okay." Not looking toward the monsters and their serrated wood blades, Dorren thrust her phone blindly at his face, almost creasing his nose.

Switch took it. "Yeah."

"I would tell you to run, old friend." Shafat's voice was shaken, in a way he'd never heard even when she'd plunged into a river after him. "But it would do little good."

"Seriously?" Church, with background noises of sirens and shattering glass that said there was no longer a *potential* riot. "I mean, if they could get across the river-"

"This is not a landslide, Church. If the Demongate opens, if it remains open-" Myrrh sucked in a breath. "This is Mount Krakatoa. Or worse."

"Oh."

Which was followed by a spate of swearing that told Switch for all her morals, the detective paid attention when she arrested the scum of the earth.

"I call shotgun!"

Switch blinked. If that was the Sister Usagi Dorren said was working with Shafat, who'd offered his niece tips on that weird mudra gesture she'd used walking out here, they were going to have *words.* No one should be that happy in the middle of a riot.

"The hell you do," Church grumbled. "Aidan's ashes are bad enough. I'm not having a demon-slayer sick in my backseat...."

"So." Switch let out a slow breath, remembering what Shafat had told him decades ago, by the banks of this same river, as they prepared to hunt the dread spirit that'd stolen his brother.

"When you fight monsters, when you are forced to fight, believe that you are already dead. Anything you do, by definition, is an improvement."

"So," Switch repeated. "How can we spike this thing?"

"Do not let them kill you." Myrrh's voice calmed, dangerous as deep waters. "The sacrifice of those who fight monsters is powerful. Do not let them have more power."

Switch's lips tightened. "You know who's with me."

"And I know you are her uncle," Myrrh said gravely. "You will fight for her, with all your strength and all your heart." One quiet breath, as metal thumped. "Remember. Despair is a mortal sin."

"An outnumbered Hunter must accept he may not survive. But for his own soul's sake, he must never despair."

And from what he'd just heard, Myrrh had voluntarily gotten into a *car.*

She's coming to us.

His hand tightened on plastic. "You know this is a trap."

"Of course it is." Lindisfarne, now, irritated and sad. "If we come, we might not make it, and it might blow. If we don't come, it's definitely going to blow. What would you do? There's nowhere in the world to run from Hell."

You can't run from Hell, but I wish I could try.

Aidan flicked a glance to blue and red lights flashing behind them, as what few cops could break loose from the riots kept on Church's tail like grim death. Not many. Not many at all. Which on the one hand made him cringe, because there was something building in the air that he didn't want to face with less than an army behind him-

Numbers aren't going to stop this thing from breaking loose. We have to get there in time. Aidan twisted forward to study the arch of the steel-girder bridge leading across the Little Avon Burn. *We can keep the Demongate from opening if we just-*

Church slammed on the brakes, flinging them against seatbelts hard enough to leave marks. Brakes screeched.

Luck or Sight was on their side. Eagleman's car tapped them, but it wasn't more than a shuddery bump.

"Church!" Eagleman's snarl came over her radio. "What the hell are you... Oh."

Steel and concrete *twisted.*

Aidan hung his head out the window to gape at the massive form snaking up the river, tearing the bridge asunder in its wake. River water was a dank slap on the cold night breeze, gleaming gray-green as serpentine as it dripped from stone scales scraping off what was left of the asphalt hanging over the edge.

That is no snake.

He felt the power rolling off it, the same that had swamped them at the drinking contest. The rolling, crushing strength of rivers; the choking, lingering death of drought. Ahi was deep water, threatening to smother him with just a *look*, and if it weren't for braided hair between his fingers he might already be drowning.

"Sonofa...." A lighter, ragged voice from the speakers; had to be Detective Carlisle. "Oh hell, that's just not *fair*."

"Geh." Church's knuckles were white on the wheel. Her gaze bounced between the tractor-trailer length stone serpent and the stunned cop cars behind her, as she carefully backed away and sideways from crumbling pavement. "Ahi?"

"Yeah." Peering from the seat beside Aidan, Usagi clutched her staff as best she could without poking him in the eye.

"...Think he was easier to handle at the drinking contest." Church blinked, obviously recalling how badly that had gone for their nun. "Um. Sorry."

"No, no, drinking contest was definitely better," Usagi agreed. "Whoa. I mean, I've heard all the stories about asuras shape-shifting into giant stone snakes and... other things, but... wow."

"You think that's... *he's* going to help?" Carlisle said warily.

"I think it unlikely." Myrrh sighed, face a little less pale now that Church had the car stopped. "Were he of a benevolent nature, he would have withdrawn when we challenged him. Instead, he's sent his seeds to hunt - and so shed more blood on our streets. Which he considers *his* territory."

"So." Church turned to eye them all, settling on Aidan. "This is a water-snake versus fire-lion thing? Who gets to eat us first?"

That... felt right. Terrifying, but right.

Church winced at his nod. "Oh, we are so screwed."

"Huh? How?" Eagleman broke in. "Fire versus water? I've seen that movie. They'll be so busy we can do the mop-up-"

Aidan shook his head. "Steven's element is water."

"...Savonarola's dead."

Aidan had to laugh, and pray not to cry. "So was I."

~*~*~*~*~

"Huh." Standing on the dock by his runabout, Hacker knocked ash off his cigarette, watching black water ripple around the biggest flood-churning milk-curdling boat-cracking water-serpent since the Morrigan had turned into the eel that tripped Cú Chulainn. "Busy night on the water."

With a scrape like a scaling knife down a stubborn bass, the stone serpent snaked up into the mists wreathing the far shore. Possibly off to give any late-night golfers the worst surprise of their lives.

Although the flashing lights and thumps of car doors in the parking lot was a close second.

Eyebrow raised to the brim of his hook-decked hat, Hacker waited for grimy, exhausted cops and their odd trio of not-cops to reach him. "Evening."

"Eve-" Church snaked a quick glance over her shoulder, where the white-haired hell-raider was trying to stifle a giggle. Trying. "What?"

Another giggle; the hell-raider leaned against the rippling heat of the redheaded half-demon. "I would not dare presume to make an assumption."

The red-robed girl with short-cropped hair and an annoying jingling staff looked between the three of them, then at Hacker. "...Huh."

The half-demon blinked, and blinked again, and finally shook his head. "It's okay, Church. Just... go ahead and ask him."

The detective aimed a dangerous finger his way. "You're going to tell me what's up."

"When we're not in such a hurry? Sure," the redhead allowed. "After we're back on dry land."

Ah. A smart one, Hacker thought. Heh.

Church glared at them all. Shook her shoulders like a ruffled hen, and looked him in the eye. "We need to get across the river. The bridge is out."

"Happens, time to time," Hacker allowed. "You sure you want

to do that?" He blew his cigarette to glowing life, gesturing toward faint red lightnings dancing inland on the far shore. "That's some bad stuff going down. Like to get a man killed. Or a woman." He slanted a glance at the halfling. "Or even a demon."

"We know," the redhead said quietly. "But we've got to try."

"Hmm." Hacker looked back at Church. "Well, if our city's finest are going to go stop Hell breaking loose... least I can do is take you across." He waved a gnarled hand. "Welcome aboard."

Something is so up with Myrrh. Church growled, leading her motley crew of Hunters and cops onboard. Just as well only Eagle-man and Carlisle had made it this far; Hacker's runabout wasn't meant to hold more than eight, max, and there were not enough life vests. Weren't *any* vests, for that matter, and if she weren't worried about impending demonic destruction she'd have serious words with the guy.

Well. That, and the weird flickers in the corner of her eye as Hacker started the engine to take them out. Like someone had set little windows of glass into the hull; every once in a while Church caught a glimpse of water, fish, and the odd floating bit of algae-strewn branches.

And instead of keeping her staff upright and out of the way, Usagi had one end out over the water, so she could grab her four brass rings and keep them utterly quiet. Which made no *sense*. Yeah, sneaking up on the bad guys was good, but they weren't just sneaking up on vampires, they were sneaking up on rakshasas. Depending on the wind the bad guys would probably smell them coming. And part of the nun's jingle-jangle was supposed to be dispelling illusions and *maya*; glamour, as O'Connor's family tales called it when they talked about fairies and....

Church swallowed hard. Looked at the bottom of the boat again, concentrating on flickers of dark water.

Under the rusted and torn hull, fish glimmered in the starlight. *We're on a ghost boat.*

...I'm going to kill them later- oh hell!

The hole was gaping and her feet were slipping and the water was so *cold-*

Aidan's hand caught her shoulder, yanking her back. "You don't want to look at that. Really."

Warmth, spreading from his hand down her shoulder, chasing off water. Church couldn't help but take one more look at the torn hull, before resolutely focusing on the far shore. "You looked."

"Yeah. But reality's kind of... got more layers, for me," Aidan shrugged. "Spirits can touch me, and I can touch them. I'm fine."

And Myrrh looked almost relieved. Like being on a boat that wasn't - well, *alive* wasn't the word - being on a boat that *wasn't a boat* somehow wiped out all the usual green heaving from not having her feet on the ground.

Why not? Church reflected. *She's got her feet on a ghost. That's kind of like ground. Maybe?*

"You okay?" Carlisle raised one of her own feet, shook off some water. "Hey Hacker, I think your bait-well leaked."

"Might have, might have," their not-quite-solid boatman chuckled. "You doing okay, little Miss Nun?"

"Eh, can't complain," Usagi said shakily, shifting her grip on brass. "Or, well, I *could*, but it wouldn't do me any good... so what's your favorite meal, anyway? I'm so bringing it to your dock slip tomorrow. If we're still alive."

So her three oddballs all knew what kind of a ride they'd hitched, and her fellow cops were clueless. Church was going to *strangle* someone later.

Although that'd have to wait, given Eagleman had stiffened like someone had tasered him. "Is that another boat?"

"Oh, no," Hacker smirked, as blazing light shimmered over the water, trailing sparks that glowed into scales bright as fire. "That's no boat."

Church stared, and decided she'd already had way too much of the supernatural side of the night messing with her. She wasn't going to ooh and ah over a spotted snake thick as a longleaf pine, horned like the father of all deer, with a blazing crest diamond-bright set between the antlers. She was just going to look for killshots.

"I'm never teasing you about the Green Corn Dance again," Carlisle's voice shook. "Is that-?"

"I think so." Eagleman sounded just as dazed. "If it comes near, don't breathe. Poison."

"Uktena." Carlisle gulped. "Isn't just seeing one of those supposed to be bad luck?"

"It is," Hacker grumbled from the wheel. "Saw that snake years ago. Bad luck. The worst. Wreck your boat. Get you killed." He scowled at the great beast swimming upriver, eyeing the bank as if it wanted to avoid asura tracks. "Leave you catching nothing but lousy catfish in a river that ought to swarm with trout...."

Which earned the fisherman odd looks from both her detective coworkers. Then they turned that look on Church, which was... okay, not *totally* unfair, but it wasn't like she'd known stepping onto the boat.

"Let's get to land before we worry about luck." Church yanked her thumb toward Aidan and Myrrh. "I met these two in a *grave-yard*. When it comes to bad karma, I think I've got us all covered."

"That's not how karma works," Usagi started, and cut herself off. "Never mind. Land good."

Hacker nosed them right up to the bank, where a stone serpent's scales had gouged out mud and cattails. "You be careful over there. Things are going to get wild."

Myrrh was already off, helping Usagi get down since the nun had a hand full muffling her staff. Church got out of the way of the others, determined to be off last.

I got us into this. My job to get us out.

Everybody was off but her and Carlisle, when Hacker made his move.

Carlisle yelped at the chill touch, giving the boatman a knee to the groin that should have put down anything male and alive. Didn't faze him. She tried to struggle, but it was as if she were fighting under icy water....

Khakkhara's supposed to scare things off, live and dead, Church thought fast. *Usagi kept it muffled - ghost boat, she had to, it'd dissolve right out from under us! If she shakes it now Carlisle might go with the boat, what can I-*

Fingers diving into her bag, Church hurled a papery packet of iron filings.

Tissue paper burst on impact, scattering gray glints over the living and the dead. Carlisle coughed, spewing up water.

Church saw fingers whiten from flesh to bone, and drew her weapon.

"Sorry, Church." Hacker's voice wasn't just the phlegmatic fisherman. It was thicker, darker; water choked with weeds and bones. "We've had some nice chats. But this night, of all nights, I've got to take a fee."

Church aimed, dead center. "The hell you are. Or as my friends here might say, *let the dead bury the dead*."

The boat shivered.

"A fee," Myrrh's voice said lightly, "is quite fair enough."

Something thin, hard, and knuckles-wide thwacked Hacker right between skull-set eyes, sending the ghost reeling. Carlisle twisted, enough for Church to grab her and yank-

Hacker snarled, seizing her shoulder like a glacier's vice. Church scrabbled for the edge, but both of them were teetering back-

Hot hands seized her arm and Carlisle's. *Pulled*, like popping the cork from a bottle.

They landed on top of Aidan in grassy mud, as Usagi's staff jangled keep-away. "Ow," Aidan coughed. "You two are heavy."

Said the guy who'd yanked out two grown women like pillows.

Church rolled off, gun still somehow in a chilled grip, aiming at-

A very sour looking ghost, gripping a roll of dimes like he wanted to strangle it, and Myrrh too. "This? You want me to take *this?*"

"Two coins of silver for each of us, and more." Myrrh inclined her head. "As you said. On this night, of all nights - in this time, of all times - the ferryman *must* have his fee."

"Huh." But there was a smirk on the skull under the hook-set hat. "Won't even buy my lousy gas...."

A curl of mist, and he was gone.

"W-what the fuck?" Carlisle managed through chattering teeth, spitting up more dark water as Eagleman helped her stagger upright. "I mean, what the-?"

Not saying the Hell word, Church thought, trying to smear some of the mud off. *Can't blame her.* "Sorry, guys. I had no idea he was a ghost."

"That's not the point!"

"Shh," Usagi tried.

"Vampires and werewolves and sorcerers, okay, okay - but now we've got man-eating deer and giant snakes and *ghost fishermen* and-" Carlisle coughed, and shivered. "Just - why? Why now? It's been *twenty years* since the Dark Day!"

"I have my suspicions." Church glared at a certain half-demon, and demon-slayer.

Myrrh cleared her throat. "In our defense, anyone with a measure of Sight will tend to draw the more unusual aspects of creation. Some things *want* to be seen. Poor Hacker." She glanced across the river. "Steven's measures to obscure the Demongate likely kept more cautious supernaturals at bay. But with the walls between the worlds weak, many things are moving."

"No," Church said firmly, glancing about to make sure they wouldn't be jumped before Carlisle calmed down. Putting two and two together - that things like the Uktena were out there, but no one'd heard about it because Hacker hadn't survived seeing it -

they didn't need to think about that now. "There's no way you're pinning any of this on me."

"No?" Myrrh blinked, innocent as a white kitten. "You were targeted by the malursine before we escaped Hell."

"They were trading your skull around," Church shot back. "Still your fault." She stretched up onto the balls of her feet to take a look through the gathering darkness. Lightning still going. With any luck, that meant nobody'd noticed them. "Okay. Here we are. How do we shut down this whole sacrifice-Demongate mess without getting ourselves made demonic street pizza?"

Myrrh closed her eyes, turning her head slowly from side to side as if she were trying to track a noise right at the edge of hearing. Opened them again, gray determined as an oncoming storm. "We can't."

Given how pale Eagleman and Carlisle went, that was *not* what they needed to hear. "Seventeen centuries and you're *still* lousy at dealing with people," Church grumbled. "Why."

"More like a couple decades out of practice," Aidan shrugged. "What?" he added at Church's angry squint. "When something in Hell went boom, sugar-coating it didn't help."

Church heaved a sigh, and eyed Usagi.

I'm looking at a Californian Buddhist nun for normal. I want milkshakes after this, damn it.

"Okay," Usagi breathed, "so we can't close it up... right now. What do we do?"

Aidan cleared his throat. "You know, I might be wrong about the whole can't close it from this side...."

Myrrh shook her head. "With vampiric power sacrificed along with human lives, the wound in reality is too deep. We need to burn it clean." Shadow-wrapped shoulders shrugged. "Which will be difficult, with an angry uktena and an asura in water-serpent form in the way."

Church felt her heart give notice, just before dropping to chilly wet socks. "Oh no."

Aidan's grin had a manic edge that belonged on someone fingering razor-edged steel. "Oh, yes."

Usagi's fingers clenched and unclenched on her staff, as the other two detectives unconsciously clumped a bit closer to the one sane person on the bank. "Speaking for all of us, eep?"

Church dragged fingers through sweat-knotted hair, and absently wished for a comb. Though right now she suspected her hair might eat it. *I wonder what Coral uses for combs... focus.* "You're planning to let the Demongate open, so the big nasty fire-demon can come through and make sure the water-guys are... distracted."

"*Let* would imply I had some manner of choice in the matter. Yaldabaoth is coming through. Ahi *intends* to fight him," Myrrh said flatly. "We need to use that to our advantage."

"Eep?" Usagi managed, as all eyes fell on her. "Hey, Buddhist, sure, but I've never fought an asura!"

"Nor have I," Myrrh said practically. "Nor have any of us. Lore is all we have, and yours is more fresh than mine."

"Um. O...kay," Usagi said faintly. Swallowed hard, and took a few deliberate, meditative breaths. "Okay. From the lore... we got him into the drinking contest, go us, so the lore has to be partly right.... Asuras are all about the glory. Formal challenges, even if the people they're out to beat aren't the ones they make the challenge to. If he really wants to trash a Demon Lord - he's got to make a show of it. People have to see it, or it won't count."

"Yaldabaoth likes glory." Amber eyes reflected lightning in a way that chilled Church's bones. "Challenges, not so much." Shoulders shifted, like Aidan had gotten nettle leaves stuck under his coat when no one was looking. "Steven only likes a challenge when he can break all the rules. Guarantee you, if he comes out that 'Gate, that's exactly what he'll do." A shrug. "'Course, if Aariel gets the chance, he'll just take Ahi out from behind. He's the Demon Lord's *guard*. He doesn't mess around."

Which, oddly enough, fit exactly what Church had seen, those horrifying minutes Savonarola's house burned. Aariel hadn't wanted to kill them, so he hadn't. If he had - well. Church was no idiot. They'd have been toast.

That time. This time... well, what I've got might work. Maybe.

"Glad you take after him," Church muttered. "Because that sounds like our best shot. Sneak into the middle of the mayhem, and do... what *are* we going to do?"

Myrrh rubbed her whole hand over the bandaged one, warming chilled fingers. "Ordinarily? I'm not certain there would be something I could do. I am one enchantress. What has been sacrificed here, what is being sacrificed, is a weight of blood such that-" She cut herself off, shaking her head.

"I don't want to die here," Carlisle whispered.

Church tried not to snarl. *Like any of us want to die anywhere?*

"Detective Carlisle, I assure you *I* most certainly do not want to die here." Myrrh flexed her fingers, ready to grasp pure light. "For if I perish in this attempt, I will end up in Yaldabaoth's realm of Hell, and he will be very. *Ticked. Off.*"

Church shuddered. That, with Aidan's declaration that in Hell you couldn't even die? No wonder their hell-raider was terrified.

"Yet there is one advantage humanity has in dealing with Hell that even angels cannot seize." Myrrh straightened, and brushed a pocket of her shift that clinked like stone on stone. "We know how to cheat."

Usagi was grinning. Carlisle... didn't look convinced, but at least she seemed a little less petrified. And Eagleman-

Eagleman'd tuned out, staring up and across the river at the smoke-hazed night sky. "You said the asura's looking for a show?"

"Yes, if the stories are- oh." Usagi stared up, following Eagleman's pointing finger. "Oh, *man.*"

Church glared up at the white-and-orange helicopter of WWBM, TV-13's local mountain news, and muttered a few words she'd picked up from Coral on a three-drink tear. "Right. Of course we make the evening news."

Chapter Twenty

"I can't even describe this, Will!"

"Then I wish you'd quit trying," Captain Sherman muttered, glued to the screen like anyone else not out on the streets breaking heads or hauling yet another rioter into a police van. Because... well... damn.

We can't handle this. Even if it were just riots. We need the National Guard. The Army. Something!

And it wasn't just street riots flashing across the TV. The yakshas were out there, killing and feeding; some as leaf-deer, some as who-knew-what. Other rakshasas had showed up to add to the carnage; everything from a mini-gale to tiger-deer to something with way too many hands hitting a pizzeria.

...Which had actually turned out to be bad news for that one, given lead *did* hurt rakshasas if you hit with enough of it, and that particular pizza parlor had held an NRA Halloween bash.

So chalk one pizzeria up as safe territory. Some officers and paramedics over that way were using it as a makeshift triage spot, sending people to the hospital or just away from the riots and teeth. Ditto most spots of consecrated ground were holding against the crazy, although she was getting reports of assault with intent to disco from a nightclub-turned-prayer meeting hall, and one Baptist church had caught fire. Heck, even some of the prayer areas on university campuses were okay, from the very nervous campus cops using them as sanctuary.

It's not enough. Just a few safe places, against a night set on fire.

Who knew when the Guard would get here. For now Sherman had to do what she could, with gorgons and mosswife-bloods and choirboys backing up the cops with prayers, sleepy herb darts, and one or two stony gazes when all else failed.

My city's dying. And I can't stop it.

Sherman shook herself, gripping one of the lenses so the brass edge dug into her fingers. The hell she couldn't. Serve and protect. She'd keep people alive, one flattened tree-monster at a time-

"Will, are you getting... that can't be what it looks like...."

Sherman blinked. Rubbed her eyes, blinked again, and looked through the lens at the TV. The smoky darkness pouring down the street didn't change.

That's not smoke. That's... branches.

Crackling and black, curving like endless talons as stalking roots shattered asphalt. Chunks of street were shredded and cast away, as the camera backed up faster and faster-

Splinters shot out like spears.

Static.

"Walking trees," Sherman said in disbelief, as *technical difficulties* flashed on the screen. "Myrrh said they could control forests...." And Intrepid was *filled* with greenery. All those tourists, out to see leaves turn and fall; yellow, orange, purple-red.

Red as blood.

"Never thought I'd feel sympathy for anyone trapped in Isengard," Father O'Malley muttered. "I do wonder if Ents were a kinder gloss on tree-spirits."

"We'll... try to get back to Mike on the ground- what? This just in! Our helicopter crew has spotted...."

The reporter's voice died. Sherman felt hope die with it.

This is how the world ends....

She tried not to look too hard at scattered bodies in a rough semi-circle on mowed course grass, though the part of her that was pure cop noted that Myrrh was right again: dead vampires looked like very long-dead bodies, all the way to bog-mummy and desert-desiccated things that crumbled at a touch. Quite the contrast to the bloody mess that had been some of the resort employees. Or the wide eyes of a not-dead-yet Mayor Green.

Not dead *yet*. Sherman had no illusions that Green would last

out the night. The closest bridge across the Little Avon was out, every cop in the city was kind of *busy* right now, and outside of the news crews, she didn't think there was a helicopter pilot in a thousand miles crazy enough to fly into that mess. Not after what Ahi had done to the last one. That pilot was still hanging on in a burn ward, drugged to the teeth; scaring the doctors, babbling about the world flipping upside-down until it seemed like the sanest thing in the world to fly into the meadery instead of open air.

Nope. No sane pilot would risk that. Not even reporters.

Besides. A distance shot of black blood in lightning-flashes was so much easier to look at than reality... *twisting*, like a whirlpool rampaging around and down through the bottom of the world.

Only something's coming back up.

Wave-blue and lava-black, swirling in mists that hissed and laughed like lost ghosts. Mists that hit some invisible limit and-

Sherman squinted, and swallowed against her unruly stomach, as *form* twisted out of vapors and crackling lightning to stride onto mortal ground. Tentacles made of mud and rotting flesh, squirming thorn-beasts, giant flayed hounds with insect eyes, walking pillars of fire....

Myrrh came out of that. Aidan *came out of that.*

Gritting her teeth, Sherman clamped down on the screaming in her head to *think*. "Okay. Okay, people, it's... across the river. That's going to hold them back. Or at least slow them down." For eastern Intrepid, at least. The western side, oh god. "Father! Ms. Coral! Can we bless a whole river?"

"...Now and at the hour of our deaths, amen." O'Malley straightened, old back giving an audible *crack*, and picked up a phone. "We've at least three churches, a temple, and two covens cooperating. We can give it a damn good try!"

"Get them to follow us down to the river." Xanthippe Coral's fingers clenched and unclenched, knuckles white. "My people are going now."

"We've got riots and tiger-deer and who knows what else out

there tearing people apart," Sherman pointed out. "If we don't stick together, we'll be dead before we can stop them."

"I've seen riots. Though the Roman Guard was far less restrained in stopping them than your officers... there is no choice. We have to go, now, as soon as we can gather anyone with power." There was a susurrus under the gorgon's veil, as she pointed to wet-jade scales coiling into view, facing off with a fiery shadow-shape that made Sherman's spirit cringe and whimper.

"*That* won't be stopped by holy water."

I wish I could pray.

Church huddled with mortals and not-quite alike, and tried to just... breathe. Keep breathing. Ahi had flattened her with power and arrogance, fear crawling up her spine to choke rational thought. This was *worse*. Usagi was wide-eyed. Myrrh was pale. Aidan-

Aidan had one hand planted on each of her fellow detectives' shoulders, a warm bulwark against that twisting scream in reality. "Hang on. You're going to be okay."

Half-demon, Church remembered. *This - he's* used *to this.*

Which made her want to bury her face in her hands and just cry, because *no one* should be used to this....

I'm an IPD detective. And if these guys aren't disturbing the peace, no one is.

Church shivered, toes to hair. Raised her head, and looked.

Don't... don't try to get it all. Just pieces. Enough to know where to move.

Briarweasels, all coiling thorns and teeth. Walking fire-lions with flaming manes and scorpion tails. Slithering mounds of muck, reaching out with tentacles of dark water whose stench choked Church's throat. Humming creatures that darted through the air like man-sized mosquitoes, one or two descending to suck up bloody ash before flitting off again.

Withered man-mosquitoes. Church stiffened. *Wait, didn't Myrrh say vampires were really-*

With a terrified shriek, Nuria tore loose from wooden chains, leaving pearl-skinned feet burning to ashes. She scrambled away, pounced on Green to suck down life in a desperate red flood, bare bones of her ankles starting to regenerate-

A crowned tentacle of muck waved. Vampire flesh *rippled.*

Something pulled free of withering flesh and bone, twisting and crackling. Behind her, Church heard someone retch.

Wish I could.

But she couldn't look away, as what had seemed to be just a blood-drinking criminal homicide suspect contorted and warped, flaps of leather beating the air like wings, joints and limbs crooked into insectoid angles.

The worst of it was, when she looked... it still had echoes of Nuria's face.

Church gulped, wanting to hide in a deep hole until all of this *went away.* "So that's what you guys meant."

"Yeah." Aidan didn't sound any happier about it than she was. "Like we said. They're pretty weak, for demons. All the Lord of Midges had to do was... yank."

Weak. But there's so many of them... focus. "Your... relatives. You said they were fire." And a lot of what was out there wasn't on fire. The muck-piles, for one, and the squid-women of icy water-

What. The. Hell?

It wasn't big, but most of the demons were giving it a wide berth. It looked... mostly human, though corpse-white skin was shadowed in spots with a see-through like Hacker's ghost boat, and scaled in others, throwing back mother-of-pearl glints.

Why do I think I should know that face?

Beside her, Aidan shivered.

Myrrh huffed. "Some men simply do not have the good taste to stay dead."

That's Steven? Oh hell. Church readied one of her best glares, nobody needed to hear that about their own brother-

Aidan shook himself, and gave them a weak grin. "Should have known. After all, did you see what he did to the house? Lousy styling. Ugly. I could've blended in traps better than that."

Yeah, she'd seen it all right, Church thought, world going faint again in the face of lion-maned fire. Just before Sword Aariel had burned that horrid mansion to the ground.

There he is. Church took in the leonine stride, the lava-black sword the size of Aidan, the seriously ticked-off look on the demonic bodyguard's face. *And he is not happy.*

A swelling inferno poured from the Demongate behind him; a torrent of shadow-flames and ruby fire coalescing into a ten-foot giant, licked with ebony and bright blue flares of heat like a Roman general's armor, blood spattered across him to flow like a crimson cloak.

"....What is *that?*" Usagi croaked, ringed staff pointing at dark flames.

Aidan sighed, matter-of-fact as a weatherman reporting a force-five tornado. "That, would be my uncle."

Hell has not been kind to my master.

Stimson inclined his head regardless; a bit of scales and water-flesh was no bar to any true shapeshifter's sight. "Welcome back."

Eyes like cold wells sought his. "Did you have any doubt I would be?"

"Not the slightest. Intrepid has been richly sown with hate, and now you harvest the blood." Stony scales scraped behind him; Stimson bowed more deeply. "One hopes your dread father is well pleased."

The titan of flames turned toward the stone serpent, flickering eyes impassive as a volcano. A blazing limb tapped against an armored thigh, waiting.

Jade fangs cast back firelight. *"You trespass on my domain, fallen one. Yield your power to me, or-"*

Flames lashed out like throttling hands, searing jade to white heat.

"Oh, this should be short." Steven tapped wet fingers together as jade struggled against fire. "So where is my beloved cousin?"

Cousin? "Your... brother?" Stimson hazarded.

"Mortal blood makes no difference to those who've walked in Hell." Steven's smile was the chill of deep oceans. "Where is he?"

"According to our *valiant* men and women of the airwaves, Lord Ahi's progress demolished the main bridge," Stimson informed him. "I doubt any fire-mage could win his way across the Little Avon easily...."

Wind shifted, bringing an uncanny scent he'd grown too familiar with, the past few years.

"...Especially with *that* on the loose."

Oh, I've got to watch this, a watery specter smirked, balancing on his misty boat. Technically Hacker shouldn't have a clear view of the golf course from the Little Avon... but he hadn't relied on mortal eyes in years.

Scales like sparks cast from a fire. Fangs that dripped venom, choking the air with deadly mist. A body thick as a longleaf that'd stood two centuries and more, weathering ice and hurricanes and fire. Antlers wide as an ancient elk's, a blazing diamond-crest set between them, the light of it dazing demons and rakshasa alike. Dozens of monsters ran toward endless coils of snake, not away, reaching out to stroke spots of bright color before their enemy's breath choked their lungs.

Uktena. Hacker's skull-eyes narrowed. *All the deadly bad luck of the world, in one scaly package.*

Bad luck and magic, Cherokee lore said. Grabbing that diamond-crest gave a man power to work wonders, heal the sick, maybe even chase the raven-mockers off their prey and restore the liver within. Not that Hacker figured any of the not-mortals currently getting constricted to death wanted to heal anyone.

Think I should tell 'em to aim for the seventh spot?

....Nah. Demons.

After all, technically the demons were the bad guys. Hacker certainly wouldn't mind seeing their tentacled butts get kicked back to Hell. On the other hand....

There was something immensely *satisfying* about the crack of bones, as the serpent that'd killed him was swatted by a fist of fire.

"...Meep."

Dorren gripped her phone in nerveless fingers, fighting the insane urge to run into the middle of the swirling fight, because *fire pretty....*

Uncle Jim's hand closed on her shoulder. "Here and now, kid. Monsters. Don't look too close."

"Miss O'Connor? Are you still there?"

Dorren looked away from the snakes and swirling hole in reality, focusing on the drone of a Tibetan singing bowl coming over the phone with Eric Chang's worried voice. "Yeah," she said shakily. "Can you do it?"

"You try hacking one-handed... oh good, their security sucks." Keys clacked over the droning. *"I think I can get into the loud-speakers from here... what'd you want with them?"*

"My niece says your ward-off hits the rakshasa hard." Uncle Jim flicked a glance through the night. "What else hits them? Bear in mind, we've also got demons. Not youkai, not rakshasa. Fallen-from-Heaven *demons.*"

"I don't... demons? Oh boy...."

"Don't freak out on me now!" Dorren demanded. "I've got an idea."

"Eagleman." Aidan shook the shivering detective, trying to figure out how to get through. "Come on, snap out of it, we need you to focus!"

The Cherokee shuddered, and shook his head, looking away.

Improvement, Aidan told himself. *At least he's still in there.* "Look. *You don't have to fight that.* If we're lucky none of us is going to fight that. Your badges should keep the little demons off, St. Michael's awesome that way, and for the big things - we're going to sneak."

That... got him a blink. Still too fast. But aware.

"The demons aren't the problem," Aidan said firmly. "The rakshasas aren't the problem. Even that crazy horned snake - not the problem. The Demongate is what we need to hit."

"And for that, I have a plan." Myrrh patted her shift. "Like calls to like, and the local mineral shops are very well stocked. Between that and Church's prudent acquisition of a modern vajra - it *can* be seared shut."

Slower blinks. Eagleman took a breath. Good.

"Seared?" Carlisle said uneasily.

"We probably want to hang back." Usagi grinned, face paper-pale. "At least, if she's thinking what I *think* she's thinking. Indra would sure do it that way, but last I heard the New Testament didn't go in for that kind of smiting anymore."

"I was born before all of the New was written," Myrrh said wryly, staring at the hole in reality. "And in the Old - it is, shall we say, a classic."

"So we just need to get you close enough without getting fried, drowned, poisoned, eaten, or squished," Church observed. "Easy."

Eagleman blinked again, then gave them an incredulous look.

And, he's back, Aidan thought, relieved. "Hey, knock on wood when you say that."

"A rakshasa heads this way, I'll knock all the wood I can handle." Church hefted her messenger bag. "So, you take-"

"No." Myrrh shook her head. "If we mean to cleanse the Demongate - I am a soul who has been to Hell and returned. I can draw the power to sear the wound, but to close it? I might... resonate too well with the portal itself." Gray eyes sought blue. "You are a mortal born of this earth, Detective, in this body. You fight for this world, though all Hell stands against you. That steel should remain in your hands as long as possible."

"Oh, joy," Church muttered. Glanced at Aidan. "Well, if she's too close to being borderline I'm guessing you- Whoa. You supposed to be that white?"

"Heh." Aidan shuddered, wishing he could laugh it off. "Sorry, Church. Forgot you don't know how those things go up on the other side... it *eats* souls. Like a glowy black hole. Especially anything a little bit demony. I go near that thing, I end up *fried* little fire-spirit."

"But those...." Carlisle didn't even try to describe the creatures tearing at rakshasas and one huge snake. Wise woman. "They came out."

"Because one very big Demon Lord used his own power to make sure it didn't eat them." Aidan felt a shiver start at his skull and work its way down. "My uncle's kind of *ticked* at me."

"Which we can use," Myrrh said firmly. "We will go as far as we can by stealth. But it is likely we will need a distraction."

Static crackled.

"Hear now the wisdom of impermanence...."

Aidan flinched from the diamond-edged words coming over the loudspeakers. But grinned. "How's that for distracting?"

~*~*~*~*~

Simple plan, Usagi told herself, leaning on the broadcast chant of the Diamond Sutra as Aidan led herself and two shaken detectives in a half-arc away from where Church and Myrrh snuck toward twisting light. *It's a really simple plan....*

At least the sore thump of her heart meant she wouldn't have another spell of tachycardia anytime soon. Month or so at least, probably. An eternity, given their chances of living through this night.

I'm so afraid, I just want to cry.

She'd become a Buddhist *because* she had proof the world was impermanent. And then a traveling nun who smote Bad Things, because life was short, hers was going to be shorter than most, and if you had to go out why not do it in *style?* Helping people, even more scared than she was. Because after you'd felt your own heart stop... and then start again? Monsters weren't that scary.

Ahi was scary. Yaldabaoth was *terrifying.*

The wind from blows and thrashing snakes made her robes billow around her. Water rose and spat from the Little Avon, crashing against Yaldabaoth like a melting glacier, sweeping away briarweasels in a scream of scraping thorns. Fire arced through what grass was left, searing it to smoke in an instant, sandy turf turned to molten lava.

Everything is impermanent. Even fear.

Staff in hand, the nun *moved.*

Stalemate. Aidan stabbed fingers of fire through a rakshasa that'd had the bad luck to notice them. It wasn't alone, but that was fine; Carlisle and Eagleman hadn't quite got the hang of where to hit to take a yaksha down, but they were making plenty of distractions for Usagi to play whirling staff-monk of death. That brass tip on her khakkhara was vicious. And going to need one heck of a polish afterward. *Asuras eat demons for breakfast, but*

Yaldabaoth's a Demon Lord. Part of Hell. Not something even one of those near-gods tossed off Mount Meru can wipe out without getting lucky.

On Yaldabaoth's side - he was a *Demon Lord*. Nothing border-line about him. Meaning his chances of actually putting a finishing blow in on Ahi were Slim, son of None.

So the fight boiled down to whose little guys might have the edge. Tricky. Yakshas were weak against fire, but they could charge right into anything with water and suck it dry. Muck was harder, but working with the pisachas, still doable. And when it came to any demon of fire - the pisachas had teamed up with the translucent pani, sucking away air and fuel like mini-tornadoes.

Anyone's guess who's got the edge... though that Uktena seems to be after Yaldabaoth.

It didn't fit. He *knew* his uncle. Yaldabaoth didn't go for a fair fight. Ever.

But here he is. Even Aariel's hanging back-

Looking that way was a *mistake*. Lion-eyes of fire met his across the battlefield; Aariel reached for his blade....

Halted, a wry smile curving one side of a lion's maw.

That chilled Aidan more than the Demongate.

He doesn't think he needs to fight. Which means - Yaldabaoth's already won this.

But how? Between stone-serpent and fiery Uktena, scales had wrapped the fire-titan limb to burning limb. The horned head dove in for a venomous breath, as Ahi *squeezed*, and there was no way Yaldabaoth could strike a blow that spanned two worlds-

No. Not Yaldabaoth, Aidan realized, as yet another rivulet of dark water behind Ahi flexed into a half-familiar form. *Steven!*

"Oh lord God, to whom vengeance belongeth...."

Sneaking along with a murmuring hell-raider, Church gripped

thrice-blessed steel, and thought about a few prayers herself. Myrrh didn't haul out a Psalm unless it was all or nothing. But then, if a Demongate didn't count, what did?

It was weird, but - after fighting through the maya, and Hacker's boat, she could *see* the edges of what Myrrh was up to. Anger and rage laced the air like the Uktena's poisoned breath, so Myrrh was... *blending* them with it. Covering human auras with energy demons and rakshasas expected to be there, nothing to see here, moving on....

And yet. Under the concealing shimmer was a gathering sense of weight. Of *attention*. Of eyes that saw, and ears that heard, and the silence after a whirlwind.

"...For the Lord will not cast off his people, neither will he forsake his inheritance...."

Oh. I'm an idiot.

Steven had built the Demongate on lies and the murder of innocents. Myrrh's Psalm was calling on the *vengeance of God*.

Put that together with the tektites Myrrh had tied onto her little surprise....

I will not faint. I will not run.

She might die here. But Church was a cop in Intrepid. Risking death was part of the job.

...Facing down gut-wrenching holes in reality, not so much. But what the heck. You only died once, right?

Unless you're a hell-raider, or half-demon-

Water rose up in Steven's form, and Church *knew* they'd all been played.

Stimson sighed, feeling the magical compulsion Ahi held over every rakshasa fray and snap. *My master is delightfully efficient, sometimes.*

No chanting, no rituals, no smirking taunts of the asura soon to die. Just a knife of foam and ice, slipped between stone scales to sever Ahi's spine.

The great lord didn't go easily. Stone fangs twisted into a forest of spears, shooting at his ambusher; the limp tail melted away into ice-water that surged up Yaldabaoth's thighs, each drop smoldering with the acrid taint of acid. Ten arms surged forth from a snake's skull, crushing lesser demons swarming in like chalk dust. Lamps of eyes blinked and blurred, dripping blood that sprouted even from smoking earth as screaming twigs of yakshas and leather-skinned pisachas to strike out at Ahi's attackers-

Leaning forward, Yaldabaoth's mouth gaped into a maw of obsidian lava, deep as a plunging volcano's heart.

Sluuuuurrrrrp.

"Um." Dorren looked at her uncle, feeling very very small. One of the bad guys was down, yes, but given he'd been distracting a *demon....* "Oops?"

"Happens," Uncle Jim shrugged. "There's not a Hunter in the world who knows everything. Not even Myrrh. She'll tell you that herself."

"Oops?" yelped over the phone. *"What oops? Oops is not good!"*

"Demon Lord munched snake-rakshasa," Uncle Jim said dryly, peering out at the night. "The little rakshasas are mostly scattering... wait one. Dorren? Earplugs."

She yanked them on. Uncle Jim's rifle *cracked.* One, two, three....

"Some of them decided to scatter this way," her uncle said into the ringing silence. "Think they're reconsidering that. The problem is the demons."

"I'm a Buddhist!"

"That does make things interesting," Uncle Jim smirked. "Not the same kind of demons. I think."

Oh, Dorren *so* wanted to be as cool as Uncle Jim when she grew up.

If she grew up. Right now she'd just be happy to see dawn. Monsters worse than anything that'd lurked outside her window were loose, and it was partly her fault....

If it's your fault, then don't just sit there crying. Fix it!

Sobs hitching her breath, Dorren thumbed through her phone's playlist. *Think. Think. What'd Miss Shafat say? Bells, and singing....*

Blur over them, plea winging its way to the heavens, Myrrh whispered the Ave Maria and tried to husband her strength.

This close to the Demongate, it wasn't easy. She hadn't been lying; as a soul who'd walked on Earth and in Hell, she was too akin to its magic for anyone's comfort. Holding her body together in the wake of its tearing power; a *constructed* body, just as Aidan's or any demon's was on mortal ground....

Too close, and I might flicker out. Like a candle.

Which, if the worst came, was exactly her plan. Like called to like; if the power she sought to call down on the Demongate was to be enough, she needed every scrap of similarity she could muster. Tektites would help. Church's blessed steel - would help.

But if all else failed....

I am born of dawn. And to light I will return.

She's up to something.

Aidan couldn't read Myrrh's intent through flickers of fire, there was just too much flame thrown around the battlefield as Yaldabaoth's minions gobbled their way through any rakshasas that hadn't bolted. But he *knew* she was up to something. Something about the little crease between her brows before she and Church had started off.

...Or, you know, just the sober knowledge that they had a breach *to Hell* here, and Myrrh had stated flat-out it'd taken the mass efforts of dozens of brave men and spell-casters to close the last one.

There aren't even a dozen of us here. We're going to die.

No. That's the despair talking. Remember that? That's Hell. I got dragged down there once. I'm not letting it latch on again!

Hell might be the enemy of anything human, but above all, evil meant it was its own worst enemy. Hate, envy, rage; if he could just figure out a way to peg a rock at the Lord of Midges with Yaldabaoth's aura on it, water and fire ought to start ripping each other apart....

Even half-water and scaly, he knew Steven's smirk. That slight crook of blue lips was the moment before his brother turned on the charm, weaseling his way into taking credit for whatever had just gone right, and shedding the blame for anything wrong onto any hapless fools that didn't run away fast enough.

Evidently Yaldabaoth knew it too. The fiery backhand cracked like a thunderbolt, shuddering down Aidan's nerves like stray lightning.

Oooor I could just let them take care of the shredding-

The flex of shadows screamed.

Venom-knife!

And *damn* magical correspondences. He was Yaldabaoth's nephew, not his son, but he still felt orchil-edged poison skim into fire-

A sizzle, as clawed gauntlets of flame caught the purplish blade. Aidan blinked, vision blurry. *Yaldabaoth* had caught that? When the heart of his pride was that Aariel was his mere Sword and bodyguard?

Aariel's sword was still sheathed.

Why?

~*~*~*~*~

An opening!

Myrrh lunged, Church's longer legs rushing beside her. The Demongate twisted reality like a whirlpool - and like any rushing torrent, there were eddies in the raging fury. Calmer ripples. Places that were not *safe*, but if she could reach one she'd be closer to smiting the wound at its heart.

And any demon will have to get through that torrent to reach us....

Even over the Demongate's roar, she heard the crackling whistle of a flame-lash.

She leapt at Church's waist, and prayed she could bear them both down.

~*~*~*~*~

I knew you were the greater threat, hell-raider.

Fire-lash recoiling, Aariel strode across burning grass, covering mortal earth with patient speed. Behind him the roar of his brother's fire crackled against the Lord of Midges' corrupted swamp... but that was no matter. The swamp-demon had been Steven's ally; *of course* he meant to betray Yaldabaoth the moment he had an opening.

Steven hates his brother because he dare not hate his father. Not to Yaldabaoth's face.

Give him a back to stab, though, and the young soul would not think to pass up the chance. How... innocent.

As if we could not see that coming centuries before you were ever born.

Myrrh rolled back to her feet, a gladius of deadly sunlight in her hand. But her form shimmered and rippled to immortal eyes, as

Hell's eternal power struck out at the fabric of mortal creation. Without the stubborn human cop beside her, clutching one shadow-clad shoulder, his enemy would unravel in half a heartbeat.

Pity. Myrrh of Alexandria. Thief of doomed souls. Lost child of a faith no longer breathing in this world. It would have been an honor to give you one last, true battle.

But he was here not for honor, but to stand at his brother's side, on Earth as he had in Hell. And Yaldabaoth wished this realm conquered, and his own.

As is only right. This world was given into mortal care to ward and watch. They have failed in their guardianship, and they must pay the price-

"Hey."

Silver and steel pierced deep, into the bone of his whip-arm. Aariel growled, whirling on the soul he *knew* had to have thrown it.

Aidan stood white-faced and ready, another silver-steel knife in his right hand, fire limning the fingers of his left. "Didn't your Mom tell you to pick on somebody... closer to your own size?"

The Sword showed his fangs. "Your priest taught you better than that, cub. I was *created*, as all of Heaven were. Mothers are a gift to mortal creatures; I had none."

Which was letting the cub buy the hell-raider time, and he knew it, but....

Aariel huffed, letting the young one hear the first rumblings of the growl that would end his existence. "Do not do this, cub. You cannot hope to stand against me."

"Sure I can." Aidan grinned at him, though fear shot through that young aura like sparks. "Hope's kind of a mortal thing, too."

My half-brother is still a fool.

A living, breathing fool, with a near-mortal frame in this world; and for that, Steven could hate him for all eternity. Just moving a form of will and water cost him more than he ever dared to admit. Especially after *maneuvering* the Lord of Midges into this fight.

It will play out to my advantage. If the Lord defeats my dread father, I will have arranged it, and gain in power in his court. If Yaldabaoth defeats him as he did Ahi - again, there is one less challenger for his power, and I have earned my place.

As Christophe never had. Yet Sword Aariel had taken him in, *cosseted* him, until now the half-breed thought he could face Yaldabaoth's weaker brother and stand even a ghost of a chance.

He doesn't. Steven raised a torrent of an arm, summoning a drowning-circle of water-beasts. The lesser demons flowed even more freely between forms than he; now scaled with claws, now near-women, now the unearthly beauty of undines with a succubus' draining fangs. Eyes liquid blue as the killing deeps regarded him, one languid blink.... then turned toward their prey.

"Go," Steven breathed, suppressing the gurgle by pure will. "Kill him. Strangle him. *Smother his flame.*"

Taloned tentacles lifted-

Halted, at a bright brassy jangle.

"You know, trying to kill off your own brother? *Really* bad karma."

He blinked; he had to. What stood before him bearing that pain-jangling staff was in no way the searing *light* of the hell-raider's presence, and yet....

Ripples. Like a pebble dropped in still water; the haze of a thousand pines, rising above the Blue Ridges.

This is one who echoes of the divine.

With two shaking mortals behind her. He could use that.

A mere slant of a brow, and one of his drowning-circle shifted to unearthly curves of female beauty, swaying as she walked toward the male detective.

Hmm. I'd swear I have his name, but I can't place him.

Dark hair, male, a breath of presence that echoed of these mountains; there was only one soul in the IPD it could be.

...Odd, how Detective Eagleman looked so *different*, with his tender soul showing through the cloak of flesh.

Steven's lips twitched. *So tender, and so very vulnerable to its temptations.*

Another, panicked jangle. "Whoa, whoa, I know what you think you see, but-!"

Eagleman's voice was thick and dreamy, as pale blue loveliness slunk closer, clawed nails brushing a stubbled cheek. "It's okay, Sister...."

It is not. Though how sweet, that you may die never knowing why.

"...I've seen *this* act before." The detective's hand leapt from his coat pocket, scattering diamond-points of blazing white.

Blessed salt!

Caught in the spray, the water-succubus wailed.

~*~*~*~*~

Switch O'Connor stood guard over his niece as Dorren searched her playlist, slitting his eyes against searing glows of demon-fire and unearthly ice.

I'd knock her out and run, if it would do any good.

As it was their sheltering copse of trees was an oasis of terrestrial magic; not much cover against tearing currents of demonic power, but better than nothing. And the surging overflows of magic were *just* close enough to keep most of the rakshasas at bay.

Though he had to snipe the odd demonic mosquito-thing. Thank goodness for special loads. Silver-iron-lead combo rounds were expensive to get right, but oh so worth it.

I don't think they'll even scratch those two... creatures.

Demon Lords; he'd stake his last payout on that. The walking tentacled muck-pile, he didn't know the name of, though it looked a bit like an old description of a demon of malaria, back when that sickness stalked every Pope that dared to come to Rome. The fiery titan-

Yaldabaoth. Fallen angel. The real power behind the Savonarolas.

If he'd had one bit of proof - he could have happily shot Steven in the dead of the night, and avoided this whole mess.

Or maybe not. If Myrrh says the Demongate was primed to go off - that might have just made it worse.

Granted, he didn't know how things could get worse. But he was sure demons would find a way-

The blast threw them both off their feet.

Thank God for trigger discipline!

He hit hard, but rolled, keeping his rifle clear of most of the muck and his trigger finger unbroken. Dorren had managed to ball herself up; she was dazed on the ground, rocking back and forth around the phone still clutched in a grimy hand, but in one piece.

Switch coughed out a breath that felt like pure smoke. *What the hell was that- oh.*

Red-black fire climbed into the sky, a towering inferno of raw power. Yaldabaoth smirked, and waved it forward, languid and flowing as a lion about to break a tiny neck.

Below, so far below, a host of root-streaked tentacles flailed-

Yaldabaoth's laughter shattered the earth. He strode forward with the flames....

Cold breathed over Switch's neck. Not the cold of ice, or the clean heart of winter. River-cold, drowning-cold, the cruelty of stagnant swamps surging through cracked earth from the Little Avon like a hungry geyser.

Fire hit water, collapsing into gray sludge-

Switch scooped up his struggling niece, and scrambled up the tallest tree.

~*~*~*~*~

"Ugly sick incoming!" Church yelled over the lahar's roar.

Sword of light still in hand, Myrrh clapped her palms together hard; the ancient driving-off of evil spirits of infection, before gunpowder and fireworks had become commonplace. "O Lord my God, I cried unto thee, and thou has healed me!"

The ill violet aura lacing the mud sparked, and died, white fire racing outward from where they stood.

Let it be enough, Myrrh prayed. *It doesn't have to be a cure. Just enough that we hold our own minds against whatever's in there, long enough to seal the Demongate.*

She doubted any healing would spread far enough to touch the sickness-curse swarming the lahar's mud as it swallowed Yaldabaoth up. Not with her strength fraying to the bone-

Like the pop of ears at altitude, the Demongate's winds eased. It was still there, still tearing at her; but only sandpaper at her skin, not the rending hooks of Hell.

We've found the eddy. Thanks be unto God!

~*~*~*~*~

Hot lava-mudslide plus illness-spirits plus- Usagi felt mud brush past them, still hot even thinned out to near water, and tried not to panic. *Oh shit I* know *that creepy feeling!*

She'd been swimming in Crater Lake, once. A little matter of a drowned spirit to lay to rest. Getting that soul to come in and pass on, once her lost trinket was found, had been an easy fix. Almost coming down with a case of *brain-eating amoebas* hadn't been.

Note to self: Midges does not play nice, and Myrrh taunts crazy things. "Tayata om, bekandze bekandze, maha bekandze, radza samudgate svaha!"

May the many sentient beings who are sick, quickly be freed from sickness. And may all the sicknesses of beings, never arise again!

Medical researchers could toss statistics on did-or-didn't work all day. But *damn* did the Maitri tradition pack a punch on evil-tainted illness.

Ice hissed. Gripping her staff, Usagi cringed-

There was an odd pattering, like heavy rain off a tin roof.

"Will you look at that?" Carlisle's voice shook, as if the detective stood on the edge of an abyss. "I guess oil and water really don't mix."

The nun blinked. There was a vial clenched in Carlisle's hand, and something oily still dripping off her fingers. Where the drops hit salted ground, it steamed.

That's not the only thing steaming.

Steven was snarling at them, all scales and fangs. Fingers curled into claws, throwing power at them again and again. Ice-water and hail covered the outside of an arc around them, running up into the air, as if an ocean of malice lapped at an invisible seawall.

Usagi glanced down. Honest dirt touched with blessed salt and demon-tainted ash... now streaked in an arc around them with the yellow-green of blessed oil, soaking into thirsty earth. "Finish the circle!"

"Um...." Carlisle tipped the vial. One more drop spilled out. Not nearly enough to seal them in.

Oh great. Just great.

Usagi scrambled to her feet alongside both shaken detectives, trying to figure out how she could keep an eye on three directions at once. Fire and water lashed the world, spilling over from the Demon Lords' fight; half her strength was going to just nudging what came their way, spinning it back into the illusion of reality it ought to be. Thorns and fire-maned lions prowled outside the waves of Steven's deadly waters, just waiting to pounce. The half-demon himself slurped along outside the arc of oil, searching for the unprotected gap.

She had Steven's true name, and he didn't have hers; that gave her an edge when it came to deflecting his magic. But it was like a spoon diverting a flood. If she didn't get her angles exactly right-

Hissing stopped. Steven smiled, scales and fangs smoothing back to something too awful to be human.

Gray-faced, Eagleman raised his gun. Carlisle matched him, wiping her hand down her muddied suit so she had a chance at a solid grip. "I guess now we see about hot lead-"

Usagi flinched back from the crack of gunfire, and wished she had earplugs.

Steven... stood there. Rippling, the hot glow of bullets in water quenched to deadly black, before his flesh spit out lead slugs at their feet.

"Oh, that's just not *fair*," Eagleman breathed.

"Mortals." Steven raised a hand, slow and languid as a rising tide, fingers stretching into fleshless claws. "So very *fragile*-"

Bells chimed with the downstroke of guitar power chords, shaking the world.

Stimson shook his head, trying to drive the ringing from his ears. Not as damaging to his flesh and spirit as any of the sutras... but those incessant, vibrating ancient *bells*, backed by pounding drums, a purely modern frenzy of electric guitar....

Oh how they pound! Raising the sound!

Barbweasels squealed and tangled each other. Vampire-spirits shriveled, as if touched by pure sunlight. Undines shook apart into murky water, unable to hold even a touch of unearthly beauty against the unceasing barrage of mortal music.

O'er hill and dale! Telling the tale!

The rakshasa hissed, shifting to near-tiger form to lessen that world-shaping impact. What insane soul played *Christmas music* on Halloween?

"You've got them on your playlist, too? Awesome!"

"Yeah," Eric Chang breathed, glancing back at the blond reference librarian hovering over his shoulder. Last thing he wanted was to hack in the university library. But thanks to the campus cops freaking out about one measly little sorcerer-wannabe on a body dump site, the computer lab was now closed for Halloween. Damn it. "Though I think I'm dropping anything about Beethoven's Tenth out of my loops. Too close to home now."

"Boss!" Tattered and wind-blown, one of the library aides staggered back inside through the open sliding door; someone had jammed the electronic closing switch, allowing terrified students to flood in and determined librarians to dash out. "Need reinforcement on the northwest runes!"

"Of course we do." Truhaft cracked his knuckles. "Demon gate, it's classic Oriental lore...." He patted Eric on the shoulder. "Keep it up. This library has stood through blizzards, hurricanes, and campus riots. We can handle one bloodthirsty pani."

This is what I get for picking an out-of-state college... focus!

Thank Dìzàng, Guanyin, and any tech bodhisattvas as yet unknown to man for hands-free headsets. Eric could spin his singing bowl and type as needed to keep the golf course sound systems under his control. And he had to type fast. He didn't *think* there was another hacker on the other end of the line, the system's efforts to throw him out were too spastic for that. More like... something rooting around in quarantine files to try and throw nasty fragments at him. Exactly what kind of something, he was trying not to think too hard about. One thing to figure a rakshasa or hungry ghost was hanging around sites with serious bad karma. Those he could do something about. Heck, anyone with a little Buddhism under their belt could do *something* about rakshasas. Even if it was only ward a house so the nasty things tended to ignore it.

Fallen angels? Um, well....

But he couldn't just hang up. There was a kind-of-okay, bright, *determined* kid on the other end of the line, and without help she was going to be toast.

And so was Intrepid. And maybe the world....

Don't pass out. Don't pass out. Breathe, slow and deep.

There were reasons he hid any magic he might have behind a computer monitor. Computers didn't care if you panicked. Rakshasas? *Chomp.*

Like whatever was howling outside would chomp him, if it got past the librarians. And now his damn traitor imagination tossed up images of Dorren, and bloody tiger-teeth, and-

Please let her uncle be a really good shot!

Eric had to put his head down, worn edge of the desk pressing into his forehead. Just for a second.

Okay, panicked. Up and at 'em.

He sat up, checked over his screen for any shifts in the flow of code, and typed a precautionary stomping of the quarantined files again. "Anything else I can do from here?"

Uncle Jim snorted. Another shot rang out. "Pray."

Somehow, he didn't think the guy was joking.

Like a kitten playing with a lion....

Aariel's sword trimmed red hair as Aidan ducked, and he knew *playing* was the last thing on the Sword's mind. The demon was bigger than he was. Longer reach. And so much, much stronger.

But this is my world. Church's world. Myrrh's world.

And Aariel was *slower.*

Aidan rolled back up to his feet, another sliver of silvered steel leaping from his fingers toward Aariel's throat. Snatched flames roaring overhead with his free hand, flaring them from malevolent red to blinding blue.

Aariel batted fire aside with his own flames, but the knife still scored deep across corded muscle and fur, smoke rising in its wake.

He is *slower. Mortal earth, mortal air - they don't catch the way he's used to. Hellfire can be fast as thought; fire on earth has to burn fuel-*

A whirling lash of muck howled through, tornado-strong. Aidan had to slit his eyes against deadly grit, crouching behind whatever seemed solid in hopes Midges' shrapnel wouldn't take his head off. The mud-storm squelched, thundered....

Fire! Pull it in, wall the swamp out-!

Fiery heat. Safety. Air to breathe that was smoky, but clean as burning oak.

Thunder faded, dying back to the hiss and rumble of more attacks clashing, Demon Lord against Demon Lord. Aidan smeared off fire-dried dust, and tried to figure out what he'd put his back against that felt warm and familiar and....

Growling. Uh-oh.

Snuggled up against the broad back of a muddy demon, head almost hidden in Aariel's fiery mane, Aidan considered his options. The Sword was too smart to lash fire or a sword-edge against his own back, but Aariel *did* have a temper. Any second now he'd twist, cat-quick, and muscle against muscle Aidan knew he was *screwed.*

Can't calm him down, so - better make him madder. "Oops?" Aidan grinned.

Snarling, Aariel twisted, claws grabbing for his trenchcoat. Aidan felt the yank at his throat, an odd throbbing tear as obsidian talons sank in and pulled....

Eep!

A flicker of fire, weightlessness-

Aidan dropped out of the fireball yards away, panting. It felt like Aariel's claws had sunk into his own ribs. But he wasn't bleeding. He could still fight.

"Is one mortal soul worth this, cub?" Aariel's knuckles cracked, talons glowing like lava under starlight. "This, and all the pain you will suffer, eternally?"

"Why not?" Aidan quipped, trying to catch his breath. "Runs in the family. Find somebody you care about and stick with them; rest of the world be damned." *Oh boy. Oh, this is going to be bad....* "After all... you wouldn't be in Hell without your brother."

Fur rippling into flames, Aariel roared.

Stalemate. Stimson's clawed hand warded away stray gusts of fiery vapor and noxious gas. *The Lord of Midges and Yaldabaoth strive against each other. The nun and her allies have thwarted my master... for the moment. And Aidan has Sword Aariel well and truly distracted.*

All of which gave the hell-raider and Detective Church more time to do - well, he had no idea what Shafat meant to do. But given she'd enlisted one of Intrepid's finest to carry it out, it just might work.

I can't wait for Yaldabaoth to win his fight.

The Lord of Midges *would* lose. He had no second to guard his back, his vampiric spirits were no match for fire-lions and determined human shots, and Steven certainly wasn't about to risk angering his father by stepping in on a muck-demon's side.

He'll lose. But not fast enough.

After all, this hell-raider had lasted *twenty-six years* unsnared in Hell. No soul managed that without being quick, clever, and more stealthy than the ninjas of Hollywood lore. Given two weeks for a plan... Stimson might not know what she believed she could do, but he'd be a fool to assume it wouldn't work.

So. Remove her defender.

Not the detective. Though her continued existence *irked* him. His master's schemes were so much simpler without Church constantly hounding crime back into the shadows. But she was alert and on her guard, watching for any assault, knowledgeable as any of the force in how to kill rakshasas... and a very good shot.

No. His target was obvious.

And if his master punished him for it afterward... ah well.

~*~*~*~*~

What do you know, Aariel can get faster.

There was no time for Aidan to keep track of whip and sword and tearing fangs. There was only reading the flow of fire, rolling to dodge stray blasts of swamp water, and always, always trying to get inside his father's range to strike.

Aariel trained me. He knows... everything.

But he *could not* focus on that. This was Earth, not Hell. His world, not Aariel's. He might just have a chance-

Claws, sinking like knives into his kidney. The world wavered, black with pain.

Go to fire, stop the bleeding!

The world flickered - and *screamed*, as Aariel reached out one commanding hand.

"Blood of my blood. Flame of my flame!"

Aidan slammed out of the fireball into seared earth; breath blasted from his lungs, head ringing like all the bells in Christendom.

Have to get up. Have to move....

Oh, hell no!

The riptides of the Demongate hurt - but Church bolted through tearing currents anyway, steel a heavy promise in her hand.

I'm a cop. Someone's about to die in front of me.

No way in Hell.

Winding up, she let blessed metal fly.

~*~*~*~*~

No hesitation. No sign of the bubbling hate, as Steven's rakshasa servant bowed to him with bloody claws. Perhaps a moment's silent regret, looking into his son's eyes, as Aariel brought his sword scything down.

The cub never stood a chance....

Wind whispered.

What-?

Light exploded in his skull, as a pound of tektites and celestial NASA steel hit like a hammer of stars.

Chapter Twenty-One

Still reeling, Aidan scrabbled aside, as Aariel hit seared muck hard enough to shake the earth. *What the heck-?*

Silvery light shone through watery ash, as Church's wrench winked at him from the ground.

...That's one way to throw a spanner in the works.

And a tendency to bad puns *always* meant he was punchy. Too much fire, too many ripping currents of energy spinning off the Demongate. He had to think. Even if it felt like his head was literally splitting.

Wrench and space rocks. Over here. Not good.

Right. The components Myrrh needed to kick off her Demongate smash. If he could just get to them.

Why'd the world have to pick now to go sideways....

Good news is, big bad fire-sphinx is down, and tiger-guy saw the wrench and ran screaming. Church ducked yet another torrent of flames and shot a pincer off something with spikes that looked like the nightmare offspring of a *T. rex* and a burning millipede. *Bad news is, Aidan's down too.*

Midges and Yaldabaoth were still going at it, but she didn't need Sight to see who was going to lose that one. Swamp-demons and water-monsters had poured out of the Demongate neck and neck with fire when it opened, but now? Only fire was coming through. Midges was crumbling, muck falling away from what might have been a face, as Yaldabaoth glowed a dark magma red, laced with purple lightning.

Came through, they were even. But Yaldabaoth ate *Ahi.* Church swallowed hard. *And now he's going to eat Midges, and then what do we do?*

"Can you reach it?"

Myrrh's voice made Church jump, and want to wilt. No condemnation. No fury, that one impulsive detective had tossed away their best weapon. Maybe just a hint of desperate sadness in gray eyes; the hell-raider could see the wrench, but the way her shadow-shift and hair rippled, like under foaming rapids....

She can't leave the eddy. She'd be torn apart.

"Just stay put!" Church ordered her. "I'll get it."

Yeah, right. How?

How else? One monster at a time. Church took a breath, coiling to spring-

"Oh, I think not."

Ropes of water seized her ankles, throwing her into an undignified sprawl on powdery soil. Earth oozed to muck, then swamp-soaked trembling earth, sucking at flesh and clothing.

Quicksand!

Eagleman never would have thought he'd *miss* bolts of fire flying overhead.

At least it kept the watery bastard distracted!

Distracted and at real risk; demon and fire-mage hadn't been shy about splashing innocent bystanders. Usagi had raised chants against the flames, turning them no more dangerous than a hot wind off high deserts. Steven's water-minions hadn't been so lucky. Thorny brambles with fangs and eyes were now so many sodden lumps of ash. Bits of muck-tentacle were scattered here, there, and everywhere. The undines had just evaporated, leaving nothing but a filmy seared veil behind.

But if most of Steven's minions were ash and smoke, enough were left to tear two cops and a tired nun into itty-bitty pieces. And the rising smoke...

Usagi coughed. Cleared her throat. Started chanting again, hoarse and ragged.

"Oh, we are so screwed," Eagleman breathed.

Rippling water and scales that had once been a pillar of the community smirked at the three of them. "Yes. You certainly are."

The worst part was, Eagleman thought numbly, it wasn't a gurgle. More a torrent-roar, like a thousand tons of poisoned water breaking a dam.

And now Steven was all water, falling into one of who knew how many puddles to strike at them from any unhallowed pool-

Eagleman shoved a hand into his pocket, and tossed a scatter of copper.

For luck.

Sparks flew from pool to pool like doll-sized lightning. Eagleman tasted ozone, and shook himself, as Steven's howl threatened to pierce his eardrums.

Shaking her staff in a bright ring of brass, Usagi gave him a thumbs-up.

"He's down, not out." Carlisle's grin had almost as many teeth as a rakshasa. "Good."

"Good?" Eagleman shuddered again, trying to get the last twitches of that howl out of wire-taut nerves.

"Yeah. He owes Church a spine. For Tom." Carlisle slapped his shoulder, and pointed toward where Church was slowly swimming her way out of boggy water.

Eagleman shuddered, but jogged over there, crouching so Church could grab his arm and start dragging her way out. From the mud smeared head to toe, even up onto her cheeks, Steven had come within inches of burying her in a shallow wet grave.

From the furious glitter in blue eyes, Church was flat out of damns to give. She'd pulverize the water-sorcerer. Just as soon as she could grasp more than a puddle.

All the while, Carlisle kept a bead on the pool roiling the most. As if more bullets would do any good. "You said that snake crest's magic?" the redhead said, tense. "What's it do?"

"Besides glow? No idea," Eagleman confessed. Uktena was a legend. No one had held an Ulun'suti for centuries. No one who'd admitted it, anyway.

"Right," Carlisle muttered. "Maybe that's enough."

She put three shots into foaming water, and ran for the light.

Mud clung like lead weights, but Church dragged herself up to wobbly feet anyway. Helped that Eagleman was steady as a rock.

...Maybe a construction-blasted, fractured sandstone-veined rock. But it was the thought that counted. "See where the wrench went?"

Her fellow detective pointed toward Aariel's still-fiery form. "That way?"

"Comedian." But it was a place to start, so long as Aariel stayed down for the count....

Why do we suddenly have shadows?

Gut dropping to her shoes, Church glanced back.

Magma-red flared sulfur-bright, as Yaldabaoth wrapped fiery hands around a muck-stained spine. The Lord of Midges struggled once, twice, tentacles of algae beating at fire-shadows like moth wings....

Fiery muscles bunched. Bone shattered.

Move!

Running was not an option. Leaning on Eagleman, Church hobbled, every muscle strained to the limit by her desperate battle against the quicksand. But they were so close, so damned close, the bells were still playing and even a demon lord flinched from that mortal hope-

Steel screamed.

The music. It's gone.

Gripping crushed metal that had been a loudspeaker,

Yaldabaoth smiled.

Yaldabaoth moved away from the Demongate.

Myrrh clung to that bare fact, even as her heart keened that Aidan was down, down and wounded, and Steven would not be slow to strike when he recovered from his brush with mortal fortune.

Copper or silver, coins are one of the oldest ways to purify water.... Hold your ground! Aidan loves this city, even now. He'd never forgive you if you abandoned all its souls to save his life.

And there was something she could do, even from here.

The currents of energy are strong, but the winds... much less. This will work.

Wetting her finger to test the breeze, Myrrh nodded, and drew out a thick stack of two-inch-long packets of white paper. Picked an eddy, and threw.

Some landed in water, the outer white layer dissolving to reveal tough waterproof paper covered in intricate colored hiero-glyphs. Some on sparks, where they flamed up in bright yellow blazes of blessed salt. Others fell on dry ground around Aidan, a paper minefield for any incautious demon, water or fire.

She'd had *many* long nights in the pews of Our Lady's, con-sidering exactly how vulnerable Aidan would be to his own blood.

Yaldabaoth and Steven both are prey to Wrath, and burning hate. This will buy us time-

With a shake of a fiery mane, Aariel blinked at her. Amber eyes crossed, staring at fragile paper stuck to his nose.

"I would not move, honorable Sword," Myrrh advised. "The results would be... mortifying. To both flesh and spirit."

The demon breathed in gingerly, all too aware hot breath might weaken the paper. "You will not prevent me from stopping you, hell-raider!"

"Do you see me attacking anyone?"

Yaldabaoth's footsteps shook the earth. Aariel growled. "You seek to keep me from defending my brother- "

"I seek to keep you from slaying your son!" Myrrh stood in the eddy, proud and straight, as unnatural forces shoved at her like a whirlwind. Time. They needed more *time*.

Yet there is no more. A tear trickled down Myrrh's cheek, torn away the next instant by ripsaw tides of lava-heat and black-ice cold. *Any magic I may call upon, Yaldabaoth will hear. And he well knows the harm I can do with one verse. Even if Church finds her wrench, and we can cast that beseeching call... it won't be fast enough.*

For herself she could bear it. To strive against evil and die in the doing, was no pitiful fate. She was a hell-raider, she knew what she risked every night of her life. To die and be dragged into Hell, with Yaldabaoth waiting... those were ever the stakes, and she'd known it from the moment they realized the Demongate existed.

But this city. These innocents. Aidan.

She could not falter. She *would* not fail. Not with those she cared for fighting still, hoping beyond hope that they'd see the dawn.

I have nothing left, save the weave of my own body. Even should I release that light - it would only distract them an instant. If only I could chant! Sing, so the universe could hear, without such dread enemies listening....

Trapped in currents of demonic energies, Myrrh leaned on the memory of those electric notes of the Carol, hoping they could weave up the edges of her fraying light just a little longer. *Christmas is here* had pounded home with guitar and bells and bone-rattling bass; and never mind that it was the depths of All Hallow's, on mortal Earth *Christ was born....*

That's it. The way to tie here and now to what we need the world to be.

For there was one soul who *could* hear her, even in the roaring torrents of Hell. Not with mortal ears, but the trust of braided souls, and the light that shaped them both.

And so I will sing.

"I know you, old foe." Myrrh watched Aariel's ears prick, listening for any possible chant. This would take the finest concentration, the total devotion those of her desert faith had first honed sharp against the darkness of Egypt's tombs. To sing, and pray, even in the midst of *acting.* "I know what you have done, and *not* done. You taught him to fight. To survive. And when you could teach him no more without breaking him, when your own brother would have found a way to shatter him into a tool to be used - you drove him out and hunted him, so that he would flee. So that he would live! Will you help Steven strike him down now, and finish the evil he failed at? Or will you... *wait?*"

"O holy night, the stars are brightly shining...."

A shimmer of light from braided white hair, soothing the horrible ache in his head. Aidan would know that soul-touch anywhere.

Myrrh's here. Everything's going to be okay.

Though from the heat and shadows prickling across his skin, the demonic side of the family was also here. Not good.

Slow. Take it slow. If she's singing, they're distracted.

And when it came to magic, he was scraping the bottom of the barrel. He *hurt.* Everywhere. He might get in one free shot, but....

But what can I do? Fire against fire, Aariel's got me, even if I hit him from behind.

Under shaking hands, shadows twitched.

Keep him talking, Church thought, sneaking as stealthy as squelching mud would let her, hunting around where steel had bounced off a thick demonic skull. *Come on, it's got to be here somewhere....*

She tried to concentrate on steel and meteorite-bits, and the reassuring presence of Eagleman watching her back. Not on the groggy fire-mage digging fingers into shadowed earth, trying - and failing - to get up off the ground. Definitely not on why Aariel couldn't possibly hear dripping mud. Which was that the earth was shaking, the whole world was shaking-

In shadows and fire, white paper fluttered away from Aariel's face.

Myrrh hissed something through the moaning wind. It did not sound happy.

"You gambled, hell-raider. And lost." The Sword leapt up like a lion, fiery blade in one clawed hand, and he looked *ticked-*

"Duck."

Church yanked Eagleman down, Usagi's ringed staff sketching a quick sigil over their heads. It glowed white, then spread out into a heat-shimmering dome-

Fire crashed down.

Can't breathe! Church had to close her eyes against searing flames. Held her breath, chest tight, because the heat was *too much,* hot as touching steel left to roast in summer sun....

Heat beside her lessened; shifted, as something body-sized thumped.

Flames eased back. Eagleman was holding a dazed nun, bits of his hair smoking.

Yaldabaoth loomed over them, hands full of fire.

Demon lords shouldn't smile.

Yaldabaoth was. Like a prison thug she'd seen once, who'd goaded a poor idiot college student into trying to defend his girlfriend's honor. The thug had let the kid have one punch to bloody his lip, and then....

Well. After that had been a laundry list of charges, including attempted murder.

We can't stop him.

Didn't stop Church from glancing around the shattered golf course for anything, anything at all. Heck, if Steven surged back out of one of those puddles she'd body-slam him Yaldabaoth's way; all that water ought to at least slow a fire-demon down....

One, maybe. Two?

Aariel stepped in to stand at Yaldabaoth's left hand, faithful guardsman to the last. As if Yaldbaoth needed any help, with fire streaming from him, casting shadows that writhed and twisted-

Darkness *moved*, whipping around the fire-demons with a keening like lava pouring free.

Aidan was on his knees, fingers bunched around fiery shadows, breathing hard. "Hey there, Uncle."

Church tensed, fighting that slump of relief. Her friend might have worked enough of a miracle to snare his demon family, but there was no *way* he could hold out long.

Keep looking! Faster! Look for what's out of place, what's not demon-touched-

Mud had hardened and cracked a yard away from her. Long, the right shape....

Church pounced.

Gray dust crumbled, unveiling dulled steel and one muddy bag of tektites.

Got it! Now if I can just get it back to-

Lightning-quick, water lashed around Aidan's throat.

Swearing, Church shot at the bastard who *would not stay dead*. Steven shed bullets like rain, as Aariel and Yaldabaoth shook off shadows like loose rope-

"Get out of our city!"

Light.

~*~*~*~*~

"For yonder breaks a new and glorious morn!"

Coughing, Aidan dropped to his knees, hand shielding his face from that blinding, watery *light*.

Bright as diamonds - that's the Ulun'suti! Oh boy. Does Carlisle even know how to use that thing?

At the moment it didn't matter; water and light and magic of this world slammed his relatives right in the face. And the shadow he could pick out against the glow had to be Church, *with* the wrench, thank God-!

"Throw it!" Myrrh's voice carried across the battlefield, a clarion call of dawn. "Up!"

"Oh, I hope this doesn't brain all of us!" Church whirled, and threw.

"And it came to pass, as they fled from before Israel," Myrrh cried out, in a voice like thunder, "that the Lord cast down great stones from heaven upon them... they were more which died with hailstones than they whom the children of Israel slew with the sword!"

Thunder rolled, and light flashed into the sky.

~*~*~*~*~

It's away. Now to buy us one moment more!

Myrrh took a deep breath, laced with only the faintest light of power. Her sword cut; her verses seized reality and bid it bow to greater will. But first, last and always, she was an *enchantress*.

"Fall on your knees! O hear, the angel voices!"

~*~*~*~*~

Usagi *really* wasn't surprised when Eagleman dropped her. Poor guy. Hearing devas sing was hard even on those who'd cultivated the divine ear. Getting hit with echoes of that unearthly power when you were a regular everyday mortal, and no believer - well. She sympathized. A lot.

Ground still hurt, though.

Pain's an illusion. Just a really persistent one. Usagi gripped her staff and shook it, doing her best to chime along with that well-known carol. Brass rings threw back sparks of light....

"Oh night, when Christ was born...."

Church squinted against light and sound, watery ripples clashing with fire as Yaldabaoth tried to tear through his own Demon-gate to get at one defiant hell-raider. Between Carlisle's diamond crest and Usagi's reflecting brass, it was hard to see anything. And the way Myrrh's voice echoed with the skies, finding her by ear was going to be hit and miss.

But he's a lion and he has a nose, how do I - hah!

She'd snatched the packets of garlic salt in case Nuria's coven got nasty. Now Church dragged them out of her messenger bag, and threw.

Fiery winds caught them, and the stench of burnt garlic filled the air. The Demon Lord coughed, and roared.

It might have been her imagination, but Aariel looked disgusted as a soaked cat. With the same ear-twitch of wanting to *maim* something.

Eeep.

But damn it, there went Steven trying to strangle Aidan. *Again.*

Where there's Steven, there's- got you!

Church lined up on the tigerish form trying to sneak up on the brothers' deadly struggle, focused on the ghostly image of a familiar evil butler shining through bloody fur.

Rakshasa or not, lead bullets were going to give Stimson a *really bad night.*

~*~*~*~*~

One more verse, Aidan knew, holding back Steven with knives and sheer determination. *Just one more!*

"And when you sing that note," Phoebe Savonarola had told her firstborn, long ago, "Sing it as if you mean to crack the vault of heaven!"

"Oh night," Myrrh breathed in, "*divine-!*"

Light speared down in a blaze of starfire, screaming steel; the shimmering, tattered foil of what Aidan was startled to realize had to have been a battered satellite-

And, maybe, one red-hot steel NASA wrench.

Aidan hit the dirt, shockwave slamming his bones. *Should've ducked sooner-!*

Black.

~*~*~*~*~

"Oh night," Myrrh whispered, body aching from the will that held it standing in the face of destruction. The Demongate was closed, closed and seared clear; Yaldabaoth and all his ilk were fading, roars shaking the world. This was the moment, the breath she had to hold so light bathed every part of the bloody wound. "Oh night divine...."

With the moan of a Leviathan sounding in the deep, the shimmer in reality faded.

Myrrh let her knees fold, pitching her in a sprawl on seared earth. Blinked as auroras flickered across the sky, green and red and the faintest hints of silver, fading into the wheel of stars before dawn.

Our people are safe.

Well. Safe from demons, idiot asuras, and the spawn of Hell. Anything else was on mortal shoulders.

"Shit, he's out." Staring down at fiery hair, Carlisle tucked the glimmering Ulun'suti into her torn and muddy jacket, Eagleman keeping a hand on her shoulder to steady them both. "Um... are half-demons supposed to be that pale?"

"Probably not." Church wobbled across cracked and scorched mud to Aidan's unconscious form, sooty and tattered as if she'd tangled with a snarl of briar-weasels and lit them on fire herself. "Damn it, did you-?"

"Yes, I knew he was at risk." Myrrh could not look away. Oh, if only she were bleeding there, not him. "Yes, I knew I would hurt him. That much celestial power would harm most humans, much less a half-demon. No, I could *not* use anything less."

She'd dealt with half-built Demongates in the past and *lived* through the horror of the last one opening. Plagues, famines, war, whole kingdoms shattered in evil and darkness - no. No, she could not let that sweep the world again.

I trust his strength; his and his father's. Aidan will live.

"You wrecked my wrench."

Wobbling to her feet, Myrrh blinked at the detective. "Well...."

A pale hand waved away smoke, brass rings clinking. "Technically, *we* wrecked your wrench," Usagi pointed out.

"Sure, sure; just try to take the blame." Church eyed the exhausted hell-raider, as if the detective herself weren't half out on her feet. "You wrecked my wrench. My very nice, crazy-Buddhist-nun-blessed, *space traveled* wrench." She looked around at the fading night still lit with fires, and distantly wracked with sirens. "And what you did to the *rest* of town...."

"Not nearly the wreckage that was left at Kahlenberg Mountain," Myrrh mused. "Although in that case I was more disarming explosions than causing them."

Church gave her a look askance. "Kahlenberg Mountain?"

"Near a city Americans find rather quaint these days," Myrrh said mischievously, making her way across cooling lava to lift a coppery mane into her lap. "Called Vienna."

"Quaint, she says," Carlisle muttered to Eagleman. "Explosions, fire, demons... wonder what she calls Intrepid?"

"I don't know." The Cherokee detective gave a happy sigh.

"But with Cruz and her coven gone, and what Lee told me went down at the site - I think night patrols are going to be nice and *quiet* for a while." He swiped some soot off his face, teeth a white grin. "And if they're not, I hear a nail on a baton quiets down weres *real* fast."

"What happened at the-" Carlisle eyed Church. "You were there, weren't you?"

"Who, me?" Church blinked, almost innocent. "I didn't see anything. Except a bunch of half-fried werewolves suddenly deciding they might want to leave town. Now."

Myrrh listened to the cops banter, feeling the life under her hands. *His pulse is strong. Good.*

Church crouched down to prod Aidan herself; creaked up again, mustering what shreds of energy she still had to shoot anything else that dared to turn up. "Will an ambulance help?"

"There is nothing wrong with his body," Myrrh said wearily. Nothing beyond being batted around by Aariel and Steven's minions like a too-brave mouse in the paws of a cat, but a constructed body would heal from that, given time. "It is his soul that I shocked. We can only give him time."

"Tapped out, huh?" Usagi's rings rang. "I guess even an arhat can hit her limits."

Myrrh sighed, sore and empty. "Were I truly an enlightened sage, I would have managed things better."

"Well, if Tang Sanzang could help the demon Monkey King, I think I can pull a thorn out of this lion's paw." Usagi's staff jingled again, as her voice dropped to a low murmur. "Oṃ tare tuttare ture svaha...."

Myrrh closed her eyes to the familiar mantra of the Green Arya Tara, as that faint light of willing-well reached in to soothe a shocked soul. Other priests might have used the Medicine Buddha Mantra, but Aidan's true hurts were *not physical*. A prayer to liberate the soul from the internal dangers of delusion... yes, that might help.

It's more than I can do, right now.

Enchantment might be too much for her weary soul, but there was still one thing she could do. *"Ave Maria, gratia plena; Dominus tecum...."*

Mother of God, who intercedes for us all, look kindly on one of your reckless strays, Myrrh listened to Usagi's mantra, Church's tired pacing, Carlisle and Eagleman leaning on each other, Aidan's quiet breaths. *I wouldn't mind a hand for the rest of us, either. It's been a very long night.*

Church's footsteps stopped.

"Amen," Myrrh murmured. "Trouble?"

"Maybe," Church sighed. "Don't worry, I've got this-"

"Church!"

A delighted teenager slammed into the detective's chest, the Carol of the Bells still playing on headphones dangling from her sweatshirt. Dorren's uncle followed more warily in her wake, wearing an unlabeled bulletproof vest and carrying what appeared to be a very good rifle.

"Did you see that?" Dorren O'Connor hugged Church in pure glee, bouncing up and down in the ashes. "What you said, and Father O'Malley, and I read on the internet that Tibetans use these prayer flags and singing bowls and prayer wheels that are just like saying the prayer if the wind spins them, so I thought why *not* music, and-"

"Breathe." Church poked her in the forehead. "Okay, I'm not seeing your parents here, so I'm going to have to be a responsible adult and say what you did was reckless, dangerous, and you are up *way* past your bedtime."

Dorren froze. Switch O'Connor scowled.

"That said?" Church slipped the teen a wink. "It was *all kinds* of awesome."

Slowly, Dorren grinned.

"O'Connor." Eagleman didn't try to hide the slump of tired shoulders. Beside him, Carlisle was fighting to keep her eyes open.

"I think Miss Shafat scared off the main bad guys, but...."

The hitman smirked. Just a little. "Need a hand breaking the law a little more, Detectives?"

"Wise guy," Church said wryly. "I'm hoping we're all done for the night. I just don't plan on getting eaten by a rakshasa who didn't get the message." She switched her weapon to her off hand, stretching cramped fingers. "We're cops. We don't like what you are. We don't like what you do." She nodded at the wreckage; cooling lava, pools of dark water, a sand trap seared to iron-streaked glass. "But you kept your niece in one piece tonight, and if word gets out she's the one who brought down the music-hammer on some serious bad guys... you might have to do a lot more of that."

Rifle in hand, Switch sobered.

Church rubbed Dorren's head again. Eyed the hitman like the words wanted to choke her. "I don't like you. But you can change what you do, O'Connor. Think about it."

"Hmm." Switch's gaze slid down what was left of the golf course, where various sneaking not-trees and a few bloodied survivors seemed to have realized they were still alive. "You're a good cop, Church. I'd almost hate to take my cases off your desk."

"Your cases are *never* leaving my desk."

On her lap, Myrrh felt the tremor of a chuckle. "Aidan?"

"If Church... is still arguing about cases... world's not ending, right?" Amber eyes blinked at her. "Hey. Did we win?"

"Svaha!" Usagi thumped her khakkara down, grinning. "Damn, you're a tough one!"

"We won," Myrrh said quietly, barely daring to believe it. "The Demongate is no more."

"Nifty." Coppery hair nestled deeper into her lap. "I'm just going to lie here for a bit. You're comfy."

"We are in the middle of the course," Myrrh observed. Not that she felt inclined to move herself, aching burns or not.

"So if they play through, Church can arrest us for jaywalking,"

Aidan murmured, drawing his arms and legs in a little to curl around her. "S'all good."

"Aww." Usagi bent down to run her fingers through Aidan's mane. "He's just a big fiery kitty." Brass rings swept toward each of them in turn. "But we're all going to the vet. That lahar might have had some gnarly amoeboid nasties in it, and demons are *really sore losers.*"

"Unbelievable," Church shook her head, as Aidan cracked one eye open at the nun. "Let's get you two down to the road before I have to see fire mage versus flying ambulance. Hey, Eagleman! Could use a hand here!"

Chapter Twenty-Two

Wednesday, November 12

"Mr. Palmer."

The wildlife officer stood in the middle of the school gymnasium, shifting from foot to foot, uncertain. As well he should, Myrrh thought. She might not have met Judge Edmund MacRory before today, but the narrowed glint in blue eyes said Hang 'Em High might be about to live up to his nickname.

"If I have this clear," Judge MacRory tapped a very, very thick stack of paper, "it is the State's contention that between the dates of October 21st and October 31st of this year, various officers of the Intrepid Police Department, no few officers of the Intrepid Fire Department, and a vast horde of good citizens of Intrepid and other locales, including one... Buddhist nun of the Sunnyvale Adamantine Chariot monastery...."

Seated in the overflowing dock of bleachers and folding chairs with the rest of them, Usagi grinned sheepishly.

"Did violate or cause to be violated, the laws of take, chase, season, and limit for deer in the state of North Carolina," MacRory continued dryly. "In specific, violating the dates of gun season in Western North Carolina. Violating manner of take by the use of dogs. Violating manner of take by hunting between a half-hour after sunset to a half-hour before sunrise with the aid of artificial lights. Violating the season limit in Western North Carolina of two deer of either sex. Intent to poach, demonstrated by no take being registered or validated. And, not least, no one was wearing hunter orange." He looked up. "Although I suppose anyone who used brass arrowheads is covered under the archery season."

Palmer cleared his throat. "With respect, Your Honor, the State believed these cases should be addressed on individual merits-"

"If any of them have individual merits, I imagine you'll bring them back," MacRory *hmph*ed. "You might have noticed our courthouse downtown. Or its charred wreck. This court will not be taking nuisance cases when there is actual crime to be judged." He pointed toward the defense team's set of desks. "Mr. Greene. I believe you have a counterargument?"

The police department's lawyer nodded. "Yes, Your Honor. The defense would like to submit videos taken on the night of October 31st, by Miss Dorothy O'Connor and various other young citizens of Intrepid." He paused. "I would warn the court these videos are explicitly violent."

"That would be the point," MacRory stated. "Put 'em up."

The phone recordings were jumpy, and sometimes washed out, Myrrh noted. But there was no mistaking the blood... or the teeth.

"In the words of Detective Church, Your Honor, we submit that any deer doing that darn well deserves to be shot out of season," Greene said wryly. Cleared his throat. "Please note that these are also clearly not our local whitetail deer, and there are various measures still in legislative committee in regards to the justified take of alien and invasive species."

"In committee is not law yet, Mr. Greene," the judge said sternly. "Still, the court takes the point under advisement." Mac-Rory leaned back in his chair, black robes settling around him with a huff. "Given the evidence in question, Mr. Palmer, does the State truly wish to pursue these citizens for, in essence, committing self-defense?"

Palmer's eyes were wide, but he stood his ground. "If Your Honor would allow me a moment to consult with my colleagues?"

"Granted," MacRory said calmly. "Talk fast."

Mr. Palmer nodded, retreating to the prosecutor's set of desks to whisper with two other lawyers and at least one shocked woman Church had identified as a Wildlife Resources Commission biologist. Myrrh waited. Poked Church, when the detective between her and Aidan wanted to fidget.

"Come on," Church muttered. "How much can they argue this?"

"I don't care how long they argue," Aidan shrugged. "They've lost. Let 'em have a little face to walk off with."

Church rolled her eyes. "You? Are way too nice."

"Nope," Aidan said cheerfully; fingers woven together in his lap, well away from his grin. "I'm not nice at all. You hear what the judge said? *Pursued for committing self-defense.* Against monsters."

"Well, yeah, but...." Church trailed off. Looked at Aidan, and Myrrh, and her own hands.

"One judge. And not a legal opinion," Myrrh noted. "But for establishing that citizens and officers of the law do have the right to take up banes against the supernatural... it is a start."

A final furious set of whispers, and Palmer sighed, turning to regard the judge with rueful courtesy. "Your Honor, in light of the evidence, the State grants that the supposed rakshasas... do not fall within the jurisdiction of the state's wildlife laws." He cleared his throat. "The State reserves the right to investigate if any *actual* deer were illegally taken. By accident, most likely. Given the confusion of the situation."

"So noted. Case dismissed." MacRory slammed his gavel down, and pointed to the defense. "Now. Given that I've got all of you in one place - would someone like to explain what *actually* happened?"

Seated where she'd hoped she'd be inconspicuous, Myrrh felt a host of eyes staring. Church and Aidan, shameless souls that they were, shoved back their chairs and stood. Pointing.

Myrrh sighed. Got up carefully; the bandages sheathing her left arm were lighter now, but still made using it a bit awkward. "Your Honor. I believe I've been volunteered."

"I believe you have, Miss Shafat," MacRory didn't quite smile, but blue eyes were definitely amused. "Well?"

She inclined her head. "I thank you for the opportunity, Your

Honor. First," she cast her gaze across the auditorium, where onlookers and some of those braver souls who'd come to rescue Intrepid were watching. "I would like to point out that our city is still standing because of the efforts of good men and women; human, and otherwise. I intend to work with the Intrepid Police Department, and others, to ensure it stays standing. The Demongate has been sealed; but such scars in reality take time to heal. I plan to see that no one of ill intent irritates the wound."

"Demongate," MacRory stated bluntly.

"Yes," Myrrh nodded. "So far as I can determine, the original sorcerer who graved the Demongate on Intrepid also lured in the asura, Lord Ahi. Asuras being prideful creatures, and a bit inclined toward sensuous measures... all he would have had to do was make it clear how rich and well-fed the vampires had become with their cultivating of humankind, and dangle the chance to overthrow a rival here in this realm, where a Demon Lord is weaker than an asura. And so Lord Ahi sent his rakshasa offspring to do slaughter in the streets, and open the Demongate for the sorcerer." She paused. "I imagine you have seen the videos of how that did *not* work-"

"Miss Shafat."

Myrrh straightened. "Your Honor?"

MacRory's fingers tapped his desk, just once. "I appreciate your desire to brief the court. With the emphasis on *brief*. But indulge the court, and give us some definitions." A gray brow climbed, patience just a little frayed. "Starting with *hell-raider*."

Author's Notes

"In Hell, there are no innocent bystanders." - deliberate misquote of Benjamin Franklin "Hawkeye" Pierce, MASH.

Oṃ maṇi padme hūṃ - Avalokiteśvara Mantra. In some traditions completed by a final unvoiced "hrīḥ".

Oṃ tare tuttare ture svaha, the mantra of Green Arya Tara; Jetsun Dolma or Tara, the Mother of the Buddhas. Meant to liberate from discontent, external and internal dangers, especially delusions.

Kahlenburg Mountain - Myrrh may have been at the Battle of Vienna (1683). Just maybe.

Zhong Ma Huang - *Ephedra intermedia*, native to most of Asia including the western Himalayas. One of the plants proposed by some scholars to be involved in making *soma*.

Cullasaja Bald doesn't exist. Joanna Bald, however, does - and there is indeed a legend of a giant lizard sunning itself there.

Usagi suffers from Wolff-Parkinson-White syndrome, or WPW; where the heart is miswired due to certain fetal circuits in it not dying off when they're supposed to. This creates short circuits that can lead to potentially fatal bouts of tachycardia. It can go off due to stress, electrolyte imbalance, certain drugs.... Some people go their whole lives asymptomatic. Usagi's not that lucky. The phenomenon of a period of extremely rapid heartbeat followed by several seconds of no heartbeat is called *compensatory pause*.

There are treatments for WPW: medication, or getting the extra nerves burned out with a catheter. That last... doesn't always work.

Myrrh's Biblical verses from the KJV.

Deuteronomy 27:19 Cursed be he that perverteth the judgment of the stranger, fatherless, and widow.

2 Kings 6:6 Then the man of God said, "Where did it fall?" And when he showed him the place, he cut off a stick and threw it in there, and made the iron float.

2 Samuel 24:9 ...and there were in Israel eight hundred

thousand valiant men who drew the sword, and the men of Judah were five hundred thousand men.

Habakkuk 2:2 Write the vision; make it plain upon the tables, so he may run that readeth it.

Psalm 3:1. Lord, how they are increased that trouble me! Many are they that rise up against me. Psalm 3:8 ends with "Salvation belongeth unto the Lord; thy blessing is upon thy people. Selah."

Exodus 17:13 So Joshua overwhelmed Amalek and his people with the edge of the sword.

Job 18:8 For he is thrown into the net by his own feet, And he steps on the webbing.

Psalm 57:6 They have prepared a net for my steps; My soul is bowed down; They dug a pit before me; They themselves have fallen into the midst of it. Selah.

Jeremiah 50:24 I have laid a snare for thee, and thou art also taken, o Babylon, and thou wast not aware: thou art found, and also caught, because thou has striven against Jehovah!

Proverbs 3:18 She is a tree of life to them that lay hold upon her: and happy is every one that retaineth her.

Job 30:29 I am a brother to dragons, and a companion to owls.

Psalm 91:4 He shall cover thee with his feathers, and under his wings shalt thou trust.

Numbers 31:23 Every thing that may abide the fire, ye shall make it go through the fire, and it shall be clean: nevertheless it shall be purified with the water of separation: and all that abideth not the fire ye shall make go through the water.

Matthew 10:16 Behold, I send you out as sheep in the midst of wolves; so be shrewd as serpents and innocent as doves.

Hosea 13: 6-9 Therefore they have forgotten me. Therefore will I be unto them as a lion: as a leopard by the way will I observe them. I will meet them as a bear that is bereaved of her whelps, and will rend the caul of their heart, and there will I devour them like a lion: the wild beast will tear them. O Israel, thou hast destroyed thyself, but in me is thine help.

Psalm 94:1 Oh lord God, to whom vengeance belongeth....

Psalm 94:14 For the Lord will not cast off his people, neither will he forsake his inheritance.

Psalm 30:2 O Lord my God, I cried unto thee, and thou has healed me.

Joshua 10:11 And it came to pass, as they fled from before Israel... that the Lord cast down great stones from heaven upon them... they were more which died with hailstones than they whom the children of Israel slew with the sword.

For further research:

The Art and Science of Staff Fighting, by Joe Varady, 2016.

The Complete Idiot's Guide to Buddhism, Third Edition, by Gary Gach, 2009.

The Complete Infidel's Guide to the Koran, by Robert Spencer, 2009.

Dragons, Serpents, & Slayers in the Classical and Early Christian Worlds, by Daniel Ogden, 2013.

James Mooney's History, Myths, and Sacred Formulas of the Cherokees, by James Mooney, 1992.

The Liar, the Cheat, and the Thief: Deception and the Art of Swordplay, by Maija Soderholm, 2014.

Mountain Nature: A Seasonal Natural History of the Southern Appalachians, by Jennifer Frick-Ruppert, 2010.

Not Peace But a Sword: The Great Chasm Between Christianity and Islam, by Robert Spencer, 2013.

The Politically Incorrect Guide to Catholicism, by John Zmirak, 2016.

The Romance of Religion: Fighting for Goodness, Truth, and Beauty, by Dwight Longenecker, 2014.

The Secret Commonwealth of Elves, Fauns, and Fairies, by Robert Kirk, 2008. Written before the author's death in 1692, first published in 1893.

48499196R00219

Made in the USA
Middletown, DE
20 September 2017